REA

Beijing

北

京

Beijing

A novel

Philip Gambone

THE UNIVERSITY OF WISCONSIN PRESS

The University of Wisconsin Press
1930 Monroe Street
Madison, Wisconsin 53711

www.wisc.edu/wisconsinpress/

3 Henrietta Street
London WC2E 8LU, England

1   3   5   4   2

Printed in the United States of America

Library of Congress Cataloging-in-Publication Data
Gambone, Philip.
Beijing / Philip Gambone.
p.   cm.
ISBN 0-299-18490-0 (hardcover: alk. paper)
1. Americans—China—Fiction.   2. Beijing (China)—Fiction.
3. Gay men—Fiction.   I. Title.
PS3557.A455 B45   2003
813'.54—dc21   2002153736

Terrace Books, a division of the University of Wisconsin Press, takes its name from the Memorial
Union Terrace, located at the University of Wisconsin–Madison. Since its inception in 1907,
the Wisconsin Union has provided a venue for students, faculty, staff, and alumni to debate art,
music, politics, and the issues of the day. It is a place where theater, music, drama, dance, outdoor
activities, and major speakers are made available to the campus and the community.
To learn more about the Union, visit www.union.wisc.edu.

Not the pageants of you, not your shifting tableaus, your
      spectacles,
Not the interminable rows of your houses, nor the ships at the
      wharves,
Nor the processions in the streets, nor the bright windows with
      goods in them;
Not those, but as I pass . . . your frequent and swift flash of
      eyes offering me love.

                  Walt Whitman, "City of Orgies"

We long to be birds flying double.

                  Juan Chi (Ruan Ji), "Gay Boys"

Contents

Acknowledgments

I am grateful to the following people for their careful reading and sound advice: Harlyn Aizley, Christopher Bram, Kathleen Kushman, Vicky Frankel, Jim Mezzanotte, George Packer, Pamela Painter, Maxine Rodburg, Adam Schwartz, Christopher Tilghman, Jessica Treadway, and Kate Wheeler.

Thanks to School Year Abroad and its director, Woodruff W. Halsey II, for the extraordinary opportunity to live and teach in Beijing during the autumn of 1996. While we taught together, John and Lynn McLoughlin graciously shared with me their knowledge and love of China. I thank them for their many kindnesses.

Portions of this novel, in earlier versions, were published in various anthologies and literary magazines. I would like to thank the editors of those publications: Robert Drake and Terry Wolverton, Lawrence Schimel, Brian Bouldrey, and Patrick Merla.

During the writing of *Beijing,* the Massachusetts Arts Council awarded me a small stipend, which gave me the confidence to press on.

I also wish to thank Jodie Rhodes, my agent; Joëlle Cabot for her fine translation of the poem by Victor Segalen; and Nan Ye for invaluable help with my Chinese.

I owe a huge debt of gratitude to Raphael Kadushin at the University of Wisconsin Press and Michael Lowenthal for his continued encouragement and support.

Last but certainly not least, I wish to thank the many gay men I met in China who shared their stories with me. Their names still cannot be mentioned here safely, but their openhearted spirit infuses and ennobles this book. It is to them that I dedicate *Beijing.*

Summer

夏

Chapter One

There is a building in my city—the Old Hancock Tower it's called, though in 1947, the year it went up, people probably still said "skyscraper"—one of the first skyscrapers to be built in Boston during those years of soaring confidence that followed the Second World War. It's not a particularly noteworthy piece of architecture. In fact, you might say the Old Hancock is rather Boston dowdy: solid, foursquare, conservatively dressed in beige, with row after row of polite, neat windows lined up like sensible strands of pearls. No, you would never call the Old Hancock a sexy thing. Except for the crown. There the architects finally had some fun. They capped their Brahmin matron with a stepped-up pyramid, all jazzy rhythms and polished aluminum, then topped it off with a sleek modernist spire that rises lighthouse-like several stories more. That spire is the real whimsy of the pile, housing a giant weather beacon whose lights—blue for fair, red for stormy—are still in use today. Long before the glitzy splendor of video games and computerized special effects, that tower, the last hurrah of the Deco Age, thrilled me with its chameleon lantern. A "fairy wand" I used to call it when I was a kid. My father once taught me a rhyme that explained the beacon's color code. After all these years, I still remember it:

> Clear blue, clear view;
> Flashing blue, clouds due;
> Steady red, rain ahead;
> Flashing red, snow instead.

Beijing

My name is David Masiello, and because it was built the year I was born, I've come to think of the Old Hancock as my building: one foot in the first half of the century, one foot in the second. Homely and sensible, like the cold–roast beef Boston I remember from my childhood, but with that funky ziggurat and gay, dichromatic lighthouse on top, a beguiling, if earnest, attempt to be with it.

These were the thoughts I was kicking around when, just after dawn on a certain lovely June morning—a quite specific June morning, in fact, the first after my forty-ninth birthday—I found myself walking home alone after a long night out. The evening before had begun as a birthday celebration, a dinner with my best friend, Owen, at our favorite restaurant, followed by nightcaps at the Eagle. That's the neighborhood watering hole that Owen and I preferred, or had resigned ourselves to, over the more upscale clubs in town, where the men tended to be younger and prettier and not much interested in guys like us. When Owen went home at midnight, I stayed on, moving to the back wall, the Eagle's "I'm available" wall, nursing one more Rusty Nail, breathing in too much secondhand cigarette smoke, watching the digital clock over the bar ticking off the minutes until closing time. At two, still not ready to call it a night, I made my way over to the Fens, a "quick trip," I told myself, just once up and back along the banks of the river, just to see what was going on.

A lot was going on. It was a busy night. The good weather, steady blue beacon weather, with its promise of high summer in the air, had brought out platoons of hungry men—more than I'd seen all evening at the Eagle—too many for just a quick pass through. I made a bargain with myself. *Twenty minutes, no more.* And when twenty minutes were up, another bargain: *If this guy isn't interested, then I'll go home.* And when he rebuffed me, another: *Just ten minutes more, that's it.*

I followed one guy for half an hour—he'd checked me out longer than most, then walked away, but *slowly* (it was the slowly that got me)—followed him all the way to the museum, gave up, circled back, made another bargain with myself: *Just five minutes more.* And another: *Just five minutes more.* And another. "Safaris" I sometimes called these outings. Though on that June morning, in the astringent

4

first light of a clear new day, my expeditions into the Fens were beginning to feel more foreign and inscrutable than anything I'd ever read about in a *National Geographic* magazine.

The route I was taking home, along the Southwest Corridor Park, the landscaped walkway from Massachusetts Avenue into the South End, was deserted. Saturday night had spent itself into a silent, sleepy Sunday morning. I checked my watch. It was 5 A.M.

"Jesus, David."

That morning, the Hancock lantern continued steady blue; the air still and crisp and clean. It brushed against my sticky skin like an indictment. I wanted a hot shower and lots of soap. I wanted a good night's sleep. I wanted to turn back the clock: back to dinner with Owen that night, back to a year when forty-nine seemed very far away, back to the year my father had taught me that rhyme. I wanted to go back to a time when I felt steady blue myself.

"Five o'clock," I muttered. "Very cute."

Against the dawning sky, the blue in that lantern seemed like no color I'd ever seen before. I tried to find a word for it: powder blue, aquamarine, heliotrope? After a night without sleep, this is where your mind goes. Cerulean. Azure. The electric neon blue of nightclubs in the thirties. I am a gay man. I was forty-nine years old that morning. I know these things.

At the end of the park, I crossed Dartmouth Street to the Back Bay Railroad Station and picked up a copy of the Sunday *Globe* from a stack that had been dropped off at the entrance. I left two dollars (in this respect, I am still a good Catholic boy), then walked on down the street toward the South End. At Shawmut Avenue, inside the little community garden at the corner, two old Chinese women were bent over, doing their morning weeding, the first people I'd seen since I'd left the Fens. Their gardens were lush and tidy, green with growing things I didn't recognize: Chinese vegetables.

It occurred to me that, had he been alive, my father might have been up that early, too, helping my mother with weekend chores, cutting the grass, getting ready for nine holes of Sunday golf. In the years before he died, he had enjoyed his suburban retirement, but still kept to his lifelong routine of getting up at the crack of dawn. He was a good man, my father, a modest man, the kind of guy who, had he been an architect and not the bricklayer he was, might have designed a solid, unassuming building like the Hancock. He might even have put that whimsical spire on top—there was that kind of a twinkle in his nature. I doubted, though, that he had ever stayed up all night. Not if he could have helped it. My father had never been that kind of guy. I was sure, too, that he had never let himself obsess about something as ludicrous as the names for the shades of blue.

———

Back in my apartment, everything was just as I'd left it, ready to impress whomever I might have brought home that night. Even the pillows on the living room sofa looked as if they had just been fluffed and propped. I tossed my baseball cap onto the sofa (my cruising cap, Owen called it, the one that covered my thinning hair), put the newspaper down on the coffee table and went into the bathroom to pee. The mirror caught my eye. I didn't like what I saw: pasty skin, wrinkles under my eyes, gray stubble in my day-old beard. Forty-nine written all over my face. (What had my father thought of his face at forty-nine? I would have been sixteen that year, and already too miserable over my raging acne and un-American nose ever to have noticed what Dad might have been feeling about anything.) As I relieved myself, I looked down at my penis. A surprise there, too. It seemed such a pathetic little thing, hardly the studly glory I had counted on the night before. Counted on for what? I finished peeing, flushed the toilet, and went into the bedroom to take a nap.

But sleep wouldn't come. I lay awake, trying to piece together how I could have let myself stay out all night. Trying to piece together what exactly I'd gone out to the Fens for anyway. *Not just for sex,* I reminded myself, though by three in the morning I would have settled for that, *had* settled for that many times in the past. After all, it was a gamble, really, to expect anything more. Especially at my age. Still, there was always the chance, always the possibility. It could happen . . . It was that *could happen* that kept guys like me out until the wee hours of the morning. I closed my eyes.

But I've never been good with naps. Here, I take after my mother. I like keeping busy, getting things done. I like seeing projects to completion. I stick with things. I stuck with Johnny until the end. Even after he told me I should get out. Even after he said, "By the time I die, you'll be an old man. No one will want you anymore." I was forty-seven when he passed away. *Two years ago already.*

I got up and went to the kitchen. Several boxes of cookbooks lay stacked in a corner. I'd hauled them up from storage the previous day. They had been Johnny's cookbooks, packed away after he died, then duly moved here a year later when I bought the condo, not wanting to remain in the house that Johnny and I had rented our seven years together. I had thought I was finally ready to start using his cookbooks again, but there was no shelf space to display them, all hundred-plus volumes, many of them wonderfully stuccoed with evidence of Johnny's extravagant culinary experiments. Perhaps I'd have someone come in to build a bookcase. It seemed a reasonable project to undertake.

I turned to the counter. The little table lamp I keep there— another inheritance from Johnny—was still burning. *All through the night,* I thought, *waiting for me to come home.* I turned it off. In the silence of the apartment, the clicking of the switch sounded like an explosion. That's when I started to cry.

I'd been crying a lot that spring. Anything could trigger it. Sometimes it was music: a Schubert piano sonata, a saxophone riff by Charlie Parker, an aria in a Puccini opera. Other times it was the news: a quiet act of bravery, a mom-and-pop store going out of business, the obituary of someone I didn't even know. When, the week before, I learned that Ella Fitzgerald had died, I had blubbered for an hour. Sometimes nothing more than the angle of the sunlight falling into a room would set me off. Or the photograph of Johnny that I keep on the mantle: blond, tanned, and smiling, on the beach in Provincetown. Or the change of seasons. That morning, it felt as if I were crying for all those reasons.

The tears didn't last long. Maybe I was too exhausted; maybe I'd cried enough that week. Maybe when you're forty-nine you finally learn to buck up and take it. I went back into the living room to read the Sunday paper.

It was full of the usual: trouble and grief abroad, trouble and grief at home. Civil war in Afghanistan, an uncertain fate for Hong Kong, the Dole and Clinton campaigns both taking soft money, oral sex looking dangerous again. There were bright spots, too. The Red Sox were on a winning streak. I started the crossword puzzle, but got stumped on the references to current TV shows and pop celebrities. Johnny would have known all those names.

I turned to the Help Wanted ads. Usually this was the section I threw away without ever glancing at it. I didn't think of myself as a person who wanted another job. I'd been at mine for close to twenty years. It was a good job, something I felt proud to do, managing the operations at one of the big gay health agencies in town. I liked what my job said about me: organized, responsible, committed, caring. Still, I was curious to see if the ad I'd seen the week before was still running. Some Western clinic in Beijing was looking for an office manager for a year.

I scanned the pages. "Careers in High Tech." That's what everyone was looking for. Systems managers, microprocessor technicians, Web designers, network engineers. "Careers for the New Millennium" one ad read. There were a fair number of careers for the old millennium, too: surveyors, tax consultants, receptionists.

I turned to the medical-related listings. A prison was looking for a chief psychologist. A hospital in Boston sought hyperactive boys for a research study about Ritalin. I'd seen a lot of hyperactive boys in the Fens that night, but I doubted they were the kind of boys the researcher was looking for. At the bottom of the page, I spotted it: the Beijing ad. They were still running it. From the qualifications they listed, I knew I'd have a great shot at it if I wanted to apply. I closed the paper. And then, for all the same elusive reasons, I started to cry again.

———

The café where Owen and I always met on Sunday mornings was a little five-table bakery shop on the corner of a block of bow fronts not too far from my building. When I got there, scrubbed clean of the night's business, Owen was already waiting at the curb. He glanced at his watch.

"And did we continue to celebrate after I left you at the Eagle?"

"Sorry," I apologized. "The boy I picked up last night didn't want to leave this morning. I had to serve him breakfast."

"In your *dreams*," Owen said.

Owen Wiszniewski was my coffee buddy, my movie buddy, my best friend. We'd known each other for ten years, ever since the day he moved into the downstairs apartment of the two-family fixer-upper I used to own with my first lover, Erik. That was the year Erik and I finally finished renovating our kitchen and started rebuilding the front porch. It was the year we started doing couples therapy, too. It was the year I met Johnny; the year of Johnny's and my affair; the year Owen, who'd become my friend and confidante, counseled me to go with my heart's desire. It was the year Erik and I broke up, the year Johnny told me he had AIDS.

"Come on," Owen said, turning to the café. "You look like you need some coffee."

We joined the line of people waiting to be served. They were mostly gay men from the neighborhood. The queue extended out the door and onto the sidewalk, but on Sundays the café kept three guys working behind the counter and it moved quickly. Though not so quickly that I didn't have time to study the neck of the guy in front of us. It was long and lovely, and the edge of his fresh haircut was perfectly trimmed.

"Hey, I'm talking to you," Owen whispered in my ear. "How are we supposed to have a meaningful conversation with you lost in dreamy-ville?"

Over the two years we'd been going there, Owen and I had dubbed the place The Cute Boy Café. Young lovelies (we referred to them variously as stud puppies, yum-yum boys, and morselettes) always seemed to be in as plentiful supply as the mounds of hyphenated muffins—raspberry-walnut, orange-coconut, ginger-peach—that filled the display case. But despite the visual distraction that they created for both of us, Owen never let himself get as carried away by these boys as I did. He never cruised them, never flirted, and certainly never went on safaris into the Fens in search of one. Cute gay boys were just a genial part of his environment, to which he seemed to give no more attention than he would to a beautiful cloud in the summer sky or a squirrel gamboling on the grass.

We got to the counter and put in our standard order. The counter boy was one of my favorites: dark eyes, closely cropped black hair, long sideburns, goatee. He handed over our lattes and pastry, flashing us a big, all-American-boy smile.

"Enjoy, guys."

When I beamed back at him, Owen deliberately poked me in the ribs.

"I'll save you a place," he whispered, motioning to the last free table in the shop. "Don't stay away too long. Your coffee'll get cold."

I paid the boy, left a dollar in his tip cup, and followed Owen over to the table.

"Remember when guys who wore goatees were called beatniks?" I asked him, as I sat down.

"Cupcake, you forget, I'm not as old as you."

"You are forty-five. Four years difference does not put you into a different generational bracket."

Owen raised his eyebrows. "Are we being a bit defensive?"

"Go easy, Owen. I'm feeling very old this morning." I took a sip of the latte. Owen watched me, waiting for more of an explanation. "I went out last night. After you left the Eagle. On a safari."

"And did we bag any wild beasts?"

"I didn't *bag* anything."

"That bad, huh?"

I shook my head. "It felt like I was wandering around with the lost souls in purgatory."

I watched Owen take a sip of his coffee. In the months before I met Johnny, when Owen was living downstairs from Erik and me, I had developed a huge crush on him. Owen was slight, skinny almost, with soft blue eyes and thinning hair, balder than I was, though on him I found it adorably boyish. If I hadn't met Johnny, who knows what would have happened. But Owen, who had been in the seminary until he was thirty-two and still worked for the Church, in a Catholic bookstore downtown, had never had a boyfriend. I used to think he was one of those people who preferred being single. Once, when I asked him about sex, he shrugged his shoulders and said, "I guess I just prefer the comforts of a good book to . . . you know, those other comforts."

Owen put down his latte. "So, exactly how long did you stay out there?" I shot him a deliberately sheepish look.

"I got home after five this morning."

"Five!"

"Yeah, I know, I know." I looked down at my coffee. "What can I tell you? I was lonely, Cupcake." I felt his hand touch mine. "At one point, I was even starting to get it on with some guy, but I broke it off. I couldn't abide the idea of just another jerk off session and nothing more. Not on my birthday. I kept holding out for someone who wanted to come home with me." I looked up. Owen was staring into my eyes. "And that, my dear, is how it got to be five in the morning." Owen continued to look at me, not saying a word. I pulled my hand away from his. "You know, Cupcake, you have the most goddamn annoying habit of always waiting for me to say something more."

"Is there something more you want to say?"

I looked out, across the street, over to Union Park. A grassy ellipse flanked by bowfront town houses, it was Victorian Boston's answer to the formal residential squares of Regency London. Though I knew no one who lived in Union Park, I'd been in three of its bedrooms in the past month: phone sex rendezvous. "Tricks" we used to say, back when I was in my twenties.

"Last week, right over there." I nodded in the direction of an apartment on the opposite corner. "I had sex with some twenty-eight year old. We met over the lines." I took a sip of latte. The next part was hard to tell, even to Owen. "He kept wanting me to play some daddy role. Kept feeding me lines he wanted me to say."

"Not what you were looking for, huh?"

"I could have taken even that if I thought there was any hope of something more. But these guys don't seem much interested in hooking up again. They're not faking the sex, Owen, believe me, but repeat performances . . ." I shook my head. "I guess I'm just not the kind of person that they want to see a second time."

"I wonder if they want to see anyone a second time," Owen offered. "It's not you, David. It's the culture. The youth thing."

"The youth thing," I echoed. "So, maybe I should try the middle-aged thing, huh?"

"Is that what you want?"

"Stop sounding like a therapist," I snapped. "Johnny was ten years younger than I."

"Are you looking for another Johnny?"

"I'm looking for another *someone*." I leaned in closer. "And please don't tell me to try the personal ads. I've done that, Owen. I've done the ad thing, I've done the bar thing, I've done the church coffee-hour thing, the gym thing, the hang-out-in-a-coffee-house thing. You know, there's a good reason why they call this neighborhood Boys' Town."

The line in front of the counter still extended all the way to the door. One guy made eye contact with me, then quickly looked away. Owen noticed, too. I let out an exasperated sigh.

"Sometimes I really hate this place." I caught myself and began to chuckle. "And sometimes I love it. I mean, sometimes I fantasize that this corner is a little bit of Europe—maybe a piazza in Tuscany, or a café in some French provincial town—a place where you can just sit and watch for hours, a place with some kind of continuity, where people understand the important things. A place where growing old isn't fraught with so much panic." Owen murmured. "That's what I want, Cupcake. Just to be in a place where I can take it all in stride."

"And why not?"

I snickered. "Maybe I should go to China."

"China?"

"There's been this ad they've run in the paper the last two Sundays. Some medical clinic in Beijing is looking for an office manager." Owen frowned. "I know, but, hey, it might be fun to go for an interview. Just to keep in practice."

"China," Owen said. "Cupcake, in case you haven't heard, they don't have phone sex in China."

I gave him the we-are-not-amused frown. Just then another guy got in line. He was quite the yum-yum boy. Owen caught my eye and grinned.

"Damn it," I said, lowering my head and knocking it against the edge of the table. "Damn it." Our coffee cups jostled.

"Careful, you're going to spill," Owen said.

"Oo, yeah," I murmured, in my deepest porno film voice. "All over me!"

―――

By the time I got back to the apartment, I was feeling the effects of my night without sleep. I stretched out on the bed and clicked on the remote control. The TV sizzled to life. They were running a Marilyn Monroe festival. I'd seen this one before, *Niagara.*

The beginning of the movie unfolded: Joseph Cotten, a shell-shocked Korean War vet, is moping around Niagara Falls at five in the morning, musing on the littleness of man. He's got another reason to be morose, too. His wife, the Technicolor-luscious Marilyn, is cheating on him. Seems that she goes for the big stud muffins, too. An "armful of groceries" is what Jean Peters, the wife in the motel cabin next door, calls the guy that Marilyn's seeing on the sneak.

Owen and I had watched this movie a half a dozen times before. I knew the plot almost too well. There was no surprise in it for me anymore. My eyes began to droop . . .

When the phone rang, I jerked awake. The movie was winding down.

"Daviduccio, I called earlier this morning. Were you still asleep?"

"Ma, I was having coffee with Owen."

"I didn't bother to leave a message," she said. "I didn't want to wake you if you were still sleeping." She paused. "Owen who?"

"Ma, you met him at Johnny's funeral. Owen Wiszniewski."

"The Polack?"

My mother grew up in the Italian section of Brooklyn. She tended to favor the old terms she'd learned in her childhood: Polack, Frenchie, Chinaman.

"So, what's up, Ma?"

"Oo," she began, her voice full of eagerness to fill me in on the latest family news. That morning it was about her recent visit to my brother and sister-in-law's to see her grandchild, my nephew, Stephen.

"You should see how big he's getting," she said. "So tall, just like you when you were two. And when he walks, David, his little *culillo,* it waddles back and forth."

I started flipping the channels.

"Talking a blue streak, too," my mother continued. "Oo, he knows so many words. All his colors, all the animals. He even knows the names for all the different shapes of pasta. Pretty soon, David, you'll be giving him Italian lessons."

I had a double major in college, biology and Italian. Then, after a few years working in a medical lab, I'd gone on to start a Ph.D. in Italian. Halfway through, I quit. Those were the years, the late seventies, when I was distracted by coming out. My future as a gay man had seemed more important than my future as a Dante scholar. I moved into a sunny studio on Beacon Hill, took the job at the gay health agency (back then, syphilis and gonorrhea were the diseases du jour), started going to the clubs, and found myself a boyfriend. Until Erik came along, my mother had known nothing of this.

"Ma, don't you think Stephen's a little young to be learning Italian?" I hoped we were both joking, but with my mother you couldn't always be sure.

"Eh," she sighed, "what's too young? Life goes by so quick, David." And then, in that way my mother has of never dwelling on sad things, she suddenly brightened. "I can already tell that Stephen is going to be just as smart as you. You know, you were talking in complete sentences by the time you were fourteen months. David, you'd probably be ambassador to Italy by now if you hadn't dropped that Ph.D."

"I never wanted to be ambassador to Italy." I picked up the remote and clicked back to the movie.

"Well, a professor, then."

"Ma, I've told you before, I like my job."

"Yeah?" She sounded skeptical.

"Ma, there's nothing any other job could give me that I don't have at the clinic. I like my life just the way it is."

"Well," she said, "maybe, but sometimes I just worry."

"So do me a favor, and don't."

"David, I'm your mother. That's what mothers are supposed to do: we worry."

"And aren't widows supposed to be out finding another husband?" My father had died seven years ago, five years before Johnny. It was beginning to seem okay to tease my mother a little.

"*Eh, figlio mio,* those days are over. Now it's all just farts and burps. That's what old age is: farts and burps."

"Oh, come on, Ma."

"Hey," she said—and in that transition from her mournful, operatic *eh* to her bright, American *hey,* I could tell my mother's optimistic self was returning—"so find me a guy who wants an old bag like me and I'll consider it."

Hey, find me *a guy,* I almost said, but my mother and I do not have that kind of relationship.

After we hung up, I watched the end of the movie. Marilyn was dead, the boyfriend was dead, Joseph Cotten was dead, and Jean Peters, adrift in a motorboat, had just been rescued from certain death over the Falls.

"I bet that was the only time any one ever used 'scuttle' as a prayer," the police chief told Jean Peters's husband.

I clicked off the TV and dialed the phone sex line.

"Can I ask you something?" the fifth guy I spoke to said. "Are you half as cute as your voice?"

"Only one way to find out," I told him.

In the parlance of phone assignations, I preferred to "travel," be the one to venture out to the other guy's apartment. I considered that safer, more anonymous. It meant, too, that I could show up wearing my baseball cap: I looked cute in that cap, maybe even half as cute as my voice. But when he answered the door, "Mike" took a quick look, flashed me a dubious frown, and said, "I really don't see this happening."

"Hey, whatever," I said, using the phrase that has become the scuttling cry of the yum-yum generation. *Whatever.*

Toward evening, Owen called, asking if I wanted to go to the movies.

"I don't know," I said, making sure he could hear plenty of petulance in my voice. The sun was low on the horizon. Rich amber rays of light slanted through the blinds into my bedroom, glazing the top of my bureau. The atmosphere was very film noir.

"O-kaaay," Owen said, drawing out the word with deliberate hesitation. "So is there something I can do to help you decide?"

"I don't know," I said again.

"Darlene, are we being helpless?"

"I don't know."

There was a pause. "If I ask you what's the matter, are you going to say, 'I don't know' again?"

"Maybe."

"Very cute," he said.

I chuckled. "That's what my father used to say to me."

"I don't doubt it," Owen said. "So, cute boy, what's the matter?"

I scooted up, bracing my back against the pillows. The Sunday paper, which I'd taken to bed with me, slid off my lap onto the covers. "I think I need to change my life."

"Oh, is *that* all?" Owen said. "I thought it was something serious."

"Now don't *you* be cute, Owen. I'm telling you straight."

"Sorry," he apologized. "So, what's wrong?"

"Look, let's just go to the movies, okay?" I reached for the newspaper.

"Will that make it all better?"

"Damn it!" I pounded the mattress with my fist. "I don't know what will make it all better! If I did, I'd do it."

My gaze fell on the night table, where a film of dust glimmered in the dying light. A clean path, a fingertip wide, ran through it. A few days before I'd traced my finger there, checking to see if the table had needed dusting.

"Okay, okay," I said. "You want to know what's the matter? Well, for starters, I'm tired of being alone. Big news, huh? I'm tired of keeping my apartment clean for no one but myself. And I'm tired of not cleaning my apartment and worrying that that'll be the day I do bring someone home. I'm tired of chasing after guys who aren't interested in me. I'm tired of feeling foolish, Owen. I'm tired of acting foolish. Okay?"

Owen didn't answer.

"Jesus, Owen, I'm staring down the mouth of fifty, and I'd just like to feel a little bit more competent about my life. A little bit more in control. Is that so much to ask?"

"Is that another way of saying that you don't want to feel human anymore?"

"Cupcake, why do you always have to treat me like an adult?"

"Someone has to. Might as well be ya best sistah. Wait, hold on. I've got another call coming in."

"I hate call waiting."

Owen laughed. "With all your phone activity, I should think you'd love it."

As I waited, I flipped through the newspaper again. When Owen came back on the line, he told me that it was his sister in Oregon.

"I'll call you back in fifteen minutes," he said. "Pick out some possible movies."

I sat up in bed and scanned the film listings. There were three or four that I wanted to see. I could guess which ones Owen had already been to. Maybe all of them. If so, we could always rent a video. I circled the possibilities, then flipped to the Help Wanted ads again. The clinic in Beijing was interviewing in Cambridge all the next week.

When Owen called back, I suggested we go for a walk instead.

"I have something I need to tell you," I said.

"The weirdest thing about this," Owen said, when I'd finished explaining my decision, "is that I don't think you're joking in the least."

"You're right."

It was evening now, dark and clear. You could see stars. We were strolling through the Southwest Corridor Park.

"But, David, *China*? Isn't that a little drastic? I mean, I know you're lonely and all that, but don't you think a couple of dates with some nice, regular guys would do just as well?"

I laughed. "If I tell you I don't know, will you think I'm being cute again?"

"Unfortunately, no," he said.

"Good. Because I don't know. I have no idea what going to interview for that job in Beijing is all about. But I'm going, Owen, and I know I'll get it." I smiled to myself. "I just see it happening."

"All the more reason why you should think things over for a while. Traveling halfway around the world is not going to relieve you of heartache."

"I don't think this is entirely about heartache."

"And it's not going to relieve you of the fact that—how did you put it?—you're staring down the maw of fifty?"

"I said 'mouth,' Owen, not 'maw.' 'Maw' is your kind of word."

"But why can't you deal with becoming an aging homosexual right here in Boston?"

"Owen, you have such a delicate way with words."

"Come on, David, you're intelligent, you're attractive. You're a nice guy. You don't need to run away just because a few of the guys you've"—he hesitated—"you've *seen* lately don't want to marry you. You're just out of practice. You need to give it time. Join a softball league."

"I have a chance to go to China, and you want I should play sports instead?"

"But who am I going to have coffee with on Sunday mornings? You'll come back and be drinking nothing but tea!" He stopped and looked me straight in the eye, all the funny stuff gone from his face. "You *will* come back, won't you?"

"I told you, the ad says it's a one-year position."

"Yeah, but one-year positions have a curious way of turning into permanent positions. We've already established that you're a longevity queen."

"So maybe I'll learn to let go of my need for longevity." Recklessly, I flung out my arms and began to twirl around like a tipsy Marilyn in *Seven Year Itch*. "I don't know, I don't know, I don't know!"

We had reached Massachusetts Avenue. Owen stopped me as if he were stopping a spinning top and aimed our stroll back in the direction of Dartmouth Street.

"Steady blue," I said, nodding up toward the Old Hancock Tower. Owen looked at me, not understanding. "The weather beacon," I told him. "How would you describe that shade of blue?"

He looked. Against the dark, moonless sky, the lantern was an intense, super-saturated hue.

"I don't know. Blue, I guess." He paused. "David, how are you going to explain all this to your mother?"

"My mother, my mother." I weighed the heft of that name. "Do you know how long it took me to come out to her, to *them*? God, I

18

used to be so coy with my parents. I started to tell you today: when I was a kid, my father had this expression. 'Very cute, David,' he'd say, 'very cute.' It was his way of letting me know that he wasn't going to put up with my shenanigans, that he saw right through me. Like when I'd whine at him that I couldn't tie my own shoe or get the kickstand down on my bike—you know, the kind of willfully helpless behavior kids get into sometimes? He used to say that a lot to me when I was young. 'Cute, David.' Then I guess I grew out of it, or he grew out of it, because I don't remember him saying 'cute' to me again for the longest time. Not until he got diagnosed with leukemia. Then all of a sudden, he started up again. 'Very cute, David. Very cute.' He had no more patience for my lame excuses about why I couldn't make it to Sunday dinner, or why I didn't want to attend a family wedding, or why I wasn't bringing Erik around anymore, and who was this guy Johnny anyway?" I looked over at Owen. "For the first time in my life, I'm going to tell my mother something straight out: I'm going to tell her that I want to do this thing, and that I have no idea why, and that it quite probably will do nothing to advance my career, modest as it is." Owen's brow furrowed. I saw him studying my face. "Owen, I don't want to be that cute kid anymore."

We stopped walking. Owen turned and embraced me. For the longest time we stood there, just holding each other. I wanted to give all my attention to nothing but this moment, to this friendship, but in my mind I was already composing the letter I would write asking for a leave of absence from my job. When we resumed our walk, I took Owen's hand.

"That blue," I said. "Remember the scene at the Miami airport in *Written on the Wind,* that scene where Robert Stack convinces Lauren Bacall that he's not a heel? Remember the color of the sky?"

"That's it," Owen said. "Yes. Exactly! God, I love Technicolor. You know, some day we should try writing movie reviews together."

"Cupcake, we'd never get beyond the first paragraph."

Suddenly, Owen let go of my hand.

"But who will I see movies with next year?"

"Jesus, Owen, don't make me feel guilty, not yet. I haven't even applied for the job."

We walked across the street and into the train station. In the lobby, Owen pulled out his subway pass.

"You really are expecting this to change your life, aren't you?"

"Is that bad?" I asked.

He smiled. "No, but you know that I love you just the way you are."

"I know," I said.

"Okay, just checking. I'll call you tomorrow." He pushed through the turnstile.

"Not too early!" I called out to him. "Remember, I haven't had much sleep in the past forty-eight hours."

I walked out of the station into the warm night air. I was exhausted. I knew I'd have no trouble getting to sleep. But excited, too. Tomorrow I had a résumé to put together, and calls to make, maybe even a trip to a bookstore to pick up some travel guides. I jogged across the street and headed home.

Halfway to Tremont, I saw a blond guy coming down the sidewalk in my direction. As we passed, he checked me out. He was older than the yum-yum boys at the coffee shop—in his mid-thirties, I guessed—though still quite scrumptious. I figured he wouldn't give me a second look, but when I turned around, he had turned, too. I stopped. He stopped.

"What's up?" he said, walking back toward me.

"Not much. What's up with you?"

"Hangin' out." He was studying my face. I was glad I'd worn my baseball cap. "Wanna take a walk?"

"Sure," I said. "I live down this way."

"Cool."

"I'm David," I told him after we'd gone a block. I put out my hand.

"Rick." As we shook, I noticed him studying my face again. "You're really hot," he said. There was alcohol on his breath.

"Thanks. So are you."

The rest of the way, we talked, but I can't remember a word of what we said. There was another conversation going on inside my head. *Cute, David, cute,* my father was telling me, all the way back to my place.

Chapter Two

Two weeks later, I landed the job. And once I accepted, everything else fell into place, too. The health agency where I worked gave me a one year leave of absence. I got a visa for China, all the necessary inoculations, a sublettor for my apartment. I even got a blessing from my mother.

"David, I'm so proud of you," she said. "Go, honey, go. You'll never get a chance like this again."

I bought travel books, listened to advice from all my friends, put together a list—a very, very short list—of the gay spots in Beijing. "Exercise extreme caution," was the gist.

By the middle of July, I was taking language lessons with a private tutor. Mrs. Duan was a graying, well-coiffed woman in her mid sixties, whose three children, she proudly told me, were all married with children of their own. At our first Chinese lesson, she gave me a new name.

"David Masiello," she mumbled several times to herself. "Ma-si-el-lo." I could hear her turning the sounds over in her mind, trying to find something Chinese in them.

We were in the Chinatown Community Center. Our classroom, which during the week housed an after-school program, was decorated with colorful posters of smiling Chinese kids flying kites and riding water buffaloes. Flash cards, each boldly painted with a character in standard calligraphy, festooned the doors and windows. Thin cotton sleeping mats were rolled up in one corner.

"Yes," Mrs. Duan said at last, "I think you take last name of *Ma*."

"Ma?"

"In Chinese, family names only one syllable long. So we take first part of your last name"—here she bent over a sheet of paper and wrote it out, first in its romanized form, then with a Chinese character—"Ma." She looked up. "Means horse. Your patients can call you Dr. Ma."

"But I'm not a doctor." Earlier, over the telephone, I'd told her I was going to Beijing to work for a Western health clinic.

"Not a doctor?" she challenged, as if I'd been deceiving her all along. "What, you a nurse?" There was a scowl on her face.

"Office manager. I'm the one who makes sure everything runs smoothly."

"Why you can't be office manager here?" she demanded. "Why go to Beijing?" She frowned at me with disapproval. "Never mind. *Ma*," she pronounced again. "Now you say."

"Ma," I repeated.

"No, third tone. Falling-rising. Listen." She demonstrated, exaggerating the way the syllable dipped down and up, almost like a two-note phrase in music.

It was weird and exciting, getting this new name, one not at all recognizable as mine. All those years in high school and college, when I took Romance languages—French, Spanish, Italian—my teachers would give me a classroom name that was much like the one I'd arrived with, David, but with the *i* pronounced long, in the European manner, and the accent on the second syllable: *Da-víd*. But now, under Mrs. Duan's tutelage, even this bit of linguistic familiarity was gone. I felt as if I were being baptized again.

"Ma," I tried again.

"Better," she said.

The table where we were sitting was low enough for a third grader. Already my knees were beginning to ache. Mrs. Duan interrupted the lesson to ask where my parents were from.

"They were born in this country, but my grandparents all came from Italy," I volunteered.

"Yes, I thought so. Easy to make Italian names into Chinese. Very clean vowel sounds. Not many bunches of consonants. Ma-si-el-lo. Ma."

"My mother's maiden name was Squillaciotti." I gave her an impish grin.

Mrs. Duan sucked in a teacupful of air. "Okay, but not so difficult, I think. Not like English names. I have other students: Quigley, Satterthwaite, Lefkowitz." She made a face. "Names in English one big crazy jumble."

"I don't think Lefkowitz is English."

"Yeah? Sounds English to me."

"How about my first name?" I asked. "David."

"David. David . . ." She retreated into her pondering mode again. "Dexing, I think. Means 'moral integrity.' Very strong name: Ma Dexing."

The moral integrity of a horse seemed like a dubious mantle to carry through life, but I tried it on, copying Mrs. Duan's pronunciation as best I could.

"No, listen to the tones. *Ma Dexing*. In Chinese, grammar is easy. Pronunciation difficult. You must develop your ear. If I can learn English, crazy jumble English, you can learn Chinese. How old you anyway?"

I told her forty-seven, cutting off, as was my mother's custom, two years from my age.

"Forty-seven? Okay, not so old. In Chinese we say that's *zhuangnian shiqi*. Prime of life. Easy for you, so young, to learn Chinese. Now say again."

"Ma Dexing," I said.

Mrs. Duan shook her head. "No, you say it this way: *Ma dei zheng*. That means something else, like, 'The horse must go on long journey.' You want that name? Very queer, I think."

———

That night, I met Owen at the Eagle.

"How was the lesson?" he asked.

I shook my head.

"I don't know what hurts more, my brain or my butt. Trying to hear the differences in the tones is bad enough, but then she's got us seated at these damn little kiddie tables. I don't know, Cupcake. I'm not so sure I can do this. I spent an hour with her and we barely got through my name."

"Of course you can do it. You learned all those other languages."

"*Romance* languages. They were easy: I grew up hearing Italian at home." I paused. "Besides, I was younger then." Owen stared at me without saying anything. "What?" I barked. "What?"

"I'm just wondering what's really the matter?"

I gave him a sour smile.

"Owen, do you know how many times over the years you've asked me that question?" His eyes went to my fingers picking at the label on my bottle of beer. "I guess I'm getting nervous about this so-called adventure I'm about to embark upon."

"Nervous?" he coaxed.

"I don't know. Sometimes I get the feeling that going to China is just a way of postponing things for a year."

"Postponing?" he asked. "Things?"

"Yes," I said, *"things."*

"As in? . . ." he prompted.

"As in 'my life.'" Owen gave me his I'm-not-convinced look. "Okay," I conceded, "as in 'finding a boyfriend.' In case you haven't noticed, I don't do well as a single man."

"Cupcake," he said, "you're forty-nine years old. Most guys your age have fallen asleep already. You're taking off to China for a year. What could be more thrilling than that? The boyfriend can wait another year."

I leaned in toward him. "Is it really necessary to announce my age to the entire bar? Does everyone at the Eagle have to know I'm forty-nine?" Before Owen could come back with one of his quips, I added, "And don't say, 'But ya are, Blanche, ya are.'"

When he wasn't selling books, Owen wrote prize-winning movie reviews for one of the city's alternative papers.

"I would never quote such a hackneyed line," he said.

"But ya have, Blanche, ya have."

We clinked our bottles of beer.

Mutual love of movies was one of the things that had also endeared Owen to Johnny. Johnny had adored two kinds of movies, those that made him laugh and those that made him cry, anything as long as it had a happy ending. Toward the end of his life, when Johnny was too sick to do much else, he and Owen would cozy up on our sofa twice a week and hoot and weep over their seventeenth viewing of *It's a Wonderful Life* or *The Women* or *Harold and Maude*. Those evenings were Owen's gift to me as much as to Johnny, giving me a chance to get out of the house for a few hours' respite.

"It's just that sometimes I feel like I'm working on two different futures simultaneously," I told him. "The one in which I'm going to be single for the rest of my life and the one where I'll have a lover again. It's kind of hard embracing both those possibilities, you know? I worry that if I go to China, I'm really telling myself that I'll just be a middle-aged bachelor traveler the rest of my life."

I looked out over the room. With its pressed tin ceiling and tiled floor, I'd always guessed that the Eagle had once, long ago, been a drugstore. Even the mahogany bar had a turn-of-the-century soda fountain look to it. The century would soon be turning again. Where sarsaparilla and root beer had once been served to beribboned school girls and boys in knickers, now men in baseball caps and tight, chest-hugging tee shirts drank bottles of beer, nursing, as I imagined those long-gone children had once nursed, their diverse crushes, their monumental romantic dreams.

"Cupcake, where do all these guys come from?"

"The same place we do," Owen said.

I took another swig of beer.

"My Uncle Carmine was a bachelor traveler." I caught Owen's eye. He was waiting again. "He was my favorite uncle. I worshipped him. He'd bring me presents, tell me stories about his travels. I still have a pair of maracas he brought me from Mexico. He died of cancer when I was thirteen. In a veteran's hospital."

"David, being a single gay man does not mean you're going to end up dying in a veteran's hospital!" He touched my hand, the one that was ripping the label off my bottle. "China, Cupcake! *China!* It's the right decision. Absolutely. Come on, say something for me in Chinese."

"Like what?"

"Say, 'I love you.'"

"Mrs. Duan and I haven't gotten that far yet."

He gave me the look Mr. Conklin used to give Eve Arden on the
Our Miss Brooks Show.

"Haven't you heard of independent study?"

I put on my brave face.

"Look, I'll be okay."

"But I don't want you to be 'okay.'" Owen set down his bottle
and grabbed my shoulders. "I want you to be ten times better than
okay. I want you to have an extraordinary time out there."

I bent my head toward his and we touched foreheads.

"Thanks."

"You're welcome."

"You give and give, Owen. When do you ever take? Huh? Who
takes care of you?"

"You do, Cupcake. And don't you forget it." Suddenly, he pulled
away. "Now get away from me or people will think we're an old married couple." He mocked slapped me. "You and I are history, sistah!"

I slapped him back. It was a schtick we did. "Well, I'm through
with you, too."

The guy standing next to us looked over. He was not my type:
too much the burly cowboy. I turned away, toward the pool table.
An Asian kid—he looked underage, nineteen or twenty—was playing with an older white guy. Leaning against a stack of beer cases
nearby, another Asian kid was watching them.

"Hello," Owen hooted at me.

I turned around. "Sorry."

Owen looked in the direction of the pool table. "Which one?"

"Those two Chinese guys."

He studied them for a minute.

"How do you know they're Chinese? Maybe they're Korean. Or
Japanese students from BU."

"Owen, gay boys from Japan are not going to come to the Eagle.
They're going to hit some upscale, Eurotrash dance club."

"Ah, excuse me, but are we indulging in a little ethnic stereotyp-
ing here?"

"Come on, Owen, look at them. They *look* Chinese." Owen
stared at me impassively. "Okay, so I *want* them to be Chinese.

Anything wrong with that?" I glanced at the two boys again. "You know, it's so weird. Ever since I accepted the job in Beijing, I've begun to notice how many Asian guys there really are in Boston. I mean, suddenly everywhere I look, it's Asians. My brother tells me that whenever his son learns a new word, he starts pointing out that thing everywhere. Dump truck! Dump truck! Dump truck! That's how I feel. Asian! Asian! Asian!" I looked down at my beer bottle. The label was almost gone. "I'm embarrassed to tell you this."

"What?"

"I've been looking at Asian guys for weeks now: the teller at my bank, the check-out kid at the grocery store, those pool players. And . . ." I paused. "I just don't find them—well, you know—that attractive."

"So is that what all this anxiety is about? You know, Cupcake, it's perfectly possible to go to China for something besides sex. Remarkable as it may seem, people have traveled for other reasons."

"Jesus, Owen, you make me sound like one of those men who go to Bangkok just for the rent boys." He stared at me. "I did *not* take this job in Beijing so that I could get laid."

"Then the fact that they're—what did you say? not *attractive?*—it shouldn't be an issue."

I looked him straight in the eye. "But, it is, Blanche, it is."

At my next lesson, Mrs. Duan taught me some basic conversational patterns: how to introduce myself; how to say "I am an American"; how to ask for a cup of tea.

"How do you say, 'I'd like some chop suey, please'?"

Mrs. Duan frowned. "Chop suey not Chinese."

"Just joking." To reassure her, I patted her arm, but she jerked her head back, looking at the place where I'd touched her as if I'd taken a branding iron to it.

"In Beijing, you ask for chop suey, no one will know what you mean. Okay, now we go on with the lesson."

She taught me two words for "where"—*na* and *nali*—and when to use each.

"Use *na* to ask which country someone from. Use *nali* when you already know country and want to know whereabouts that person from more precisely. She demonstrated.

"Ni shi na guo ren?"

"Which country are you from?" I translated.

"Good," she said. "Now listen. *Ni shi Zhongguo nali ren?*"

"Again, please," I asked. She repeated. Haltingly I translated, word for word. "You are China, um, whereabouts person? Ah! Whereabouts in China are you from?"

She smiled. "Good. Now you ask me where I am from."

I paused to compose the sentence in my head. Romance languages used to trip off my tongue. I could still ask that question, and scores more, in French, Spanish or Italian.

I hazarded a guess: *"Ni shi nali ren?"*

Mrs. Duan laughed for the first time since I'd begun lessons with her. "You joking again?" she asked. "You ask me, 'Are you whereabouts person?' Can't say it that way. People think you very queer." She looked at her watch. "You tired? *Ni lei ma?*" I nodded yes. "Okay, so we work five minutes more, then stop. Do some vocabulary words."

She fired a list at me: happy, airport, country, friend, goodbye. I got them all.

"*Hen hao!* I think you arrive in Beijing speaking good Chinese. You know lots of words. Can make many sentences. Yes?"

I thought about all the things I could say in Chinese: *The airport is not far from the city. I am happy to come to your country. Where is the post office?* But these phrases seemed so thin, so sanitized, the stuff for ten-day tourists, not me. The week before, I had tried looking up "homosexual" and "gay" in my pocket dictionary, but they weren't listed. Now I wondered how, indeed, you might get someone in Beijing to think you were queer—that other, very American kind of queer.

Late in August, on the last Friday night before my departure, Owen and I met at the video store for our weekly movie pick. We'd been making our way through a series of classics about China: *The Last Emperor, Fifty-five Days at Peking, Shanghai Triad.* As we roamed the aisles, searching for a movie, the clerk asked if he could help us.

"Something with a Chinese theme," Owen told him.

The clerk was a new one at the store. He had buzz-cut hair and blue eyes, my favorite. As he ran a search on his computer, I studied his face—the shape of his nose, his lips, the way his sideburns cut across the upper part of his cheek. With my Roman nose and big ears, I'd often been mistaken for a European—a Lebanese, a Frenchman, a Jew. But this kid—I guessed him to be in his mid twenties—I couldn't imagine that there was anywhere in the world he could go and not be pegged immediately as an American.

He typed in a few more words, looked at the screen, waited.

"Chinese, huh?"

"Oh, it doesn't have to be," I told him. Out of the corner of my eye, I saw Owen giving me a puzzled look. I smiled at the clerk. "What would you suggest for a steamy summer night?"

"How about *Chinatown?*" he asked. "Faye Dunaway's really fabulous in that."

"We're looking for movies *set* in China," Owen said dryly.

"I don't know," the clerk mused. "I think you've pretty much covered what we have." He looked over at me. "We've got a few old Charlie Chan movies." He flashed me a sweet, helpless look. It was calculated to seem more fetching than feckless, and it worked.

"Hey, cool," I said. "I haven't seen a Charlie Chan flick a long time." I wondered if "flick" was a word guys of his generation still used.

The clerk punched something into his computer, scanned the screen and read off a few titles. Owen wandered away.

"What about *Charlie Chan in Panama?*" the clerk asked.

"*Charlie Chan in Panama?*" I called out to Owen. He was browsing in the Film Noir section.

Owen turned away from the rack and sauntered over to the counter. "Hey, *cool,*" he said, biting into the word with a total lack of mercy. "Cooool."

We left the shop, Charlie Chan in hand, making our way down Tremont Street. Lots of men were out strolling in the warm, humid evening. I tried picking out which ones were couples, which ones on dates, which ones just friends. The men who were dating always seemed the most self-conscious. Owen broke the silence.

"Sorry for the sarcasm, Cupcake, but you were acting as if he was about to propose marriage."

"He was flirting with me."

"David, everyone they hire in that store flirts."

"Not with me they don't."

We walked the rest of the way in moody silence.

When we got to my place, Owen set up the tape in the VCR while I poured us glasses of wine. I kept the television in the bedroom so that I could watch movies—usually classics, occasionally porno—late into the night. It was on this bed, our heads propped up against the pillows, that Owen and I had conducted our summer-long Chinese movie festival.

I set the glasses down on the night tables—right side for Owen, left side for me—then climbed onto the bed. Owen reached over, took the remote control, and aimed it at the television. We still hadn't spoken a word. I stayed his hand.

"You really are upset that I flirted with him, aren't you?"

Owen sighed. "I don't know what I'm upset about. You leaving me for a year, I guess."

"It's just a year."

"Easy for you to say. You're the one going."

I leaned my head on his shoulder.

"Owen, do you think we could ever have become lovers?"

"What, and ruin a perfectly good friendship?"

"Come on, be serious."

He scooted up more against the backboard.

"I *am* serious," Owen said. "You're way too romantic for me, David. You need a boyfriend who'll be that kind of romantic in return. Like Johnny was."

"Sometimes I think I won't ever find anyone like Johnny again."

"Of course you will," Owen said. "You're the marrying kind. Your kind always finds someone again."

"And what about your kind?" I asked. "Why aren't you ever hot and bothered about all this stuff?"

"If you're asking if I ever wished I were more like you," Owen said, "the answer is yes."

"Because," I continued, "I often wish I were more like you."

"My God," Owen said, "I wouldn't wish that on anyone!"

"Owen, you're very attractive."

"Hush up and watch the movie." He pointed and clicked the remote.

It was a creaky little piece of filmmaking, a cookie-cutter mystery full of creepily suspect characters, among them a German biologist who raised bubonic-infected rats, a sultry Czech cabaret singer, a morose Egyptian tobacconist, and a demure schoolteacher from Chicago, the most innocent-looking of them all, who, of course, turned out to be the culprit. Owen and I shook our heads in disbelief at the obvious red herrings and groaned each time Charlie Chan uttered another Confucian proverb.

Throughout the picture, I kept studying Sen Yung, the actor who played Jimmy, Charlie's "Number Two" son. I tried to see him as a heartthrob, even a nineteen-forties heartthrob. There was a scene where Jimmy takes a bath while he talks over the case with Charlie. I studied his body, the hairless chest, the smooth, white face, the silky black hair. I tried imagining myself touching a body like that, excited by a body like that, desiring a body like that. For the first time all summer, I guessed it could be a possibility.

Chapter Three

A few days later, on a sweltering Tuesday afternoon, Owen drove me to the airport.

"That's for you," he said, motioning to a paper bag on the seat between us.

Inside were a box of condoms, a small bottle of melatonin, and a pocket edition of Daoist sayings.

"Why only a dozen?" I asked, holding up the box of condoms.

Owen kept his eyes on the road. "I debated whether to give you any at all. You be careful, Cupcake."

"I don't think you have anything to worry about," I told him. "More than likely, I'll come back next June with *two* dozen." Owen glanced over at me. I grinned. "I already packed a box."

"Like I said, be careful."

I flipped through the book.

"The *Dao De Jing.* I read this once in college."

"That's for your spiritual health."

The price sticker with the name of the bookstore Owen worked for was still on it.

"Catholic book stores sell this kind of stuff now?"

"It's considered philosophy, not religion. I guess they figure it's not really competition. You know, it was the early Jesuits in China who first translated a lot of these classics. Some of them even went around dressed like Confucians. They thought there was nothing incompatible between Christianity and Chinese philosophy."

"What happened?"

"The pope put a stop to it."

I looked over at Owen.

"You know, I have never understood your loyalty to Holy Mother Church."

"It's one of my most endearing idiosyncrasies, isn't it?"

"Your ability to live with contradictions astounds me."

"That's what that's all about."

"What?"

Owen nodded toward the book.

"Daoism. It's about living in contradictions, you know, the yin and yang of life? The paradoxes that, looked at another way, turn out not to be paradoxes. Don't you remember? I thought you said you'd read it in college."

"That was years ago. You keep forgetting how old I am."

"Darn it, why *do* I always do that?"

I glanced at the book again. "Thanks, Cupcake. I'll read it on the plane."

Owen took his right hand off the wheel, gripped my left, and gave it a good squeeze.

"It's not a homework assignment, David. Read it when you feel like it." He glanced over and smiled at me. "When the spirit moves you."

We rode on for a while in silence, holding each other's hand. I thought about living in contradictions and how, even though I was no longer a practicing Catholic like Owen, there were plenty of contradictions I still lived with all the time. Just having gotten to 1996 as a healthy, HIV-negative gay man seemed like one. Going to China as a gay man seemed to be another. And what about once I got there? What would be the greater contradiction then—trying to continue to live as a gay man, or putting all that on the back burner for a year? Those clever Jesuits had tried both: being Catholic and Chinese. I guessed I could pull off something similar.

Owen let go of my hand and shifted gears. I put the book into the bag and pulled out the bottle of melatonin.

"To help you get some sleep during the flight," he explained.

I shook my head. "Six hours to San Francisco and then something like another thirteen hours across the Pacific. Ay."

"But think of it, Cupcake. Tomorrow you'll be in China."

33

"You know, I still don't get it."

"Don't get what?" Owen kept his eyes on the road. The traffic was bumper-to-bumper.

"I'll be flying *west,* gaining time, right? It'll get earlier and earlier in the day." I looked at my watch. "Like right now. It's two-thirty here, ten-thirty in the morning in San Francisco and . . . what? seven-thirty in Hawaii?" Owen nodded. "Then why do I *lose* a day?"

"It's the international date line, Cupcake."

"I know, but . . ." This time business seemed such a puzzle. "But what if I was to fly *east* instead, across the Atlantic?"

"Then you'd lose hours."

"But I wouldn't cross the international date line."

"Right."

"So, in that case, would it still be Tuesday when I landed?"

"I hate to tell you this," Owen said, "but time marches on, no matter which direction you're traveling in."

We inched into the tunnel to East Boston. The yellow tiles were black with soot, begrimed by that relentless march of time.

"But how about this?" I said. "Two people leave Boston really early on a Tuesday morning—like one minute after midnight—one eastbound, one westbound. They both arrive in Beijing twelve hours later. But for one person it's Tuesday and for the other it's . . ."

"Impossible," Owen said. "You can't do it in twelve hours."

"But what if you did it in a supersonic jet or something?"

Owen looked over at me.

"Hypothetically I suppose, but in reality it doesn't work that way."

"I thought you liked contradictions!" I teased.

"Yeah, but in some things science has the final word, no matter what."

He went on about the sun and the earth's rotation and why the international date line runs down the least populated area in the world. But all I could focus on was the fact that it couldn't be both Tuesday and Wednesday in Beijing, though it seemed, depending on which direction you traveled in, that it might.

The whole family was waiting for us at the airport—my mother, my brother and his wife, my nephew Stephen.

"Oh, thank God," my mother said when she caught sight of me. "We got here a little late and thought maybe you'd already gotten on the plane."

"*You* thought he'd already gotten on the plane," my brother said. He looked at me and raised his eyebrows.

"Ma, the flight doesn't leave for another two hours," I told her.

"I know, honey, but . . ." She brought her hand up to her face, pressing two fingers into her right eyebrow. After so many years, I could read her body language fluently: this was Mom's way of trying to stop from crying. She sniffled, then looked at Owen.

"Do Polish mothers get this emotional?"

"Only the emotional ones," Owen told her.

My mother shook her head in disbelief.

"The other side of the world. I still can't believe it. David, you're going halfway around the world! Think of it!" She took out a tissue and blew her nose. "I can still remember back in the thirties when the family would drive to New Rochelle to visit the New York relatives. It would take us all day and your grandfather would have to stop every few hours to fix a flat tire."

My brother and I shot each other another a glance. We'd heard this saga countless times before. At that moment, though, I was glad to hear my mother's story again. It made me feel young.

"Uncle David," my nephew said, tugging at the straps of my backpack, "can you bring me a present from China?"

I bent down and lifted him up into my arms.

"Of course I will, Stephen. What do you want Uncle David to bring you?"

Stephen looked at his mother. Confusion and indecision were written all over his face.

"What do you want, Stephen?" my sister-in-law coaxed. "Use your words. What do you want Uncle David to bring you?"

Stephen hesitated. Then, suddenly, his mouth stretched into a broad, aren't-I-cute? smile.

"A fire engine!" He stretched his arms out far apart.

Everyone laughed.

"Do they have fire engines in China?" my mother asked. Underneath her smile, I could see the anxiety.

"Sure they do," Owen said. "Red ones!"

And everyone, even my mother, laughed again.

———

In San Francisco, I switched planes. It was a huge cabin, ten seats across in economy class. My seat was on the left aisle, in a row of three. The other two seats were occupied by Americans, businessmen, I guessed. They looked as if they had made this flight many times before. One had already put on eye patches and was settling in for a long nap; the other was busy rummaging through his briefcase. I took a peek inside: reports, lists of figures, a calculator, a day planner, a business magazine. No condoms, no melatonin.

I pulled the flight magazine from its pouch and began flipping through the pages, trying to imitate the casualness of my seatmates. The airline company was based in Hong Kong, and the feature article was on the handover next year. The writer suggested that a wait-and-see stance was best.

I closed my eyes. A babble of conversations in a half dozen languages was going on all around me. Most of the passengers were Chinese and Chinese American, but when I listened closely, the words they were speaking, though they sounded Chinese, didn't match the language I'd learned from Mrs. Duan. They were all speaking Cantonese.

Just then another flight attendant came by and handed me a hot face cloth. Like his colleague, he looked young enough to be a teenager. I glanced at his lapel pin. His name was Desmond Woo.

"Duibuqi," I said.

He smiled. "You speak Chinese?"

"Well, a little." I smiled back. "But I'm not sure it's going to do me much good on this flight." He didn't seem to understand what I was getting at, so I explained that I had been learning Mandarin.

"Oh, we speak Mandarin *and* Cantonese," he said. "We have to. It's our job."

"But it *is* Mandarin they speak in Beijing, right?"

"Oh, yes. Mandarin. In China, we call it *Putonghua.*"

"For a minute there I was worried." I let myself give him a mildly flirtatious smile, then ran the hot towel over my face. "So, how about this?" I asked, and composed myself to say something in Chinese, Mandarin, *Putonghua,* or whatever language it was that Mrs. Duan had taught me. *"Wo shi Ma Dexing."*

"Excuse me?"

I tried again, with textbook precision: *"Wo shi Ma Dexing."*

"Wow, you already have a Chinese name." Desmond's English was practically accentless. He sounded half British, half American.

"Yes, did you understand me?"

"Sure," he said. "Your name is Mr. Ma. Welcome aboard, Mr. Ma."

"And my first name? Did you understand that?" I was determined that he was not going to address me as Mister Ma for the entire flight across the Pacific. "Dexing," I said.

"Dexing," he repeated, but I could tell it meant nothing to him.

"I think it means something like moral integrity."

"Ah, yes." Desmond nodded his head politely. "So who gave you that name?"

"My Chinese teacher."

"Wow, so you have taken lessons?"

The businessman next to me glanced over at us, then resumed his nap.

"Yidian," I said.

Desmond nodded. "A little bit. Yes, I understand. Mr. Ma, I think you speak very well."

"Thanks, but I need lots of practice."

"Of course." He smiled and held out his tray for me to deposit my used face cloth. "Now, if you will excuse me, I must continue with my duties. But maybe we can practice more later. Okay?" He smiled again, then went off down the aisle, proffering more hot towels.

For the next hour I watched Desmond come and go. I studied the way he poured coffee and tea, the way he squatted down when he spoke to someone in a seat, the way he carried himself. Was there anything to be made of his delicate mannerisms and slightly feminine gestures? Twice more he stopped by my row, once to serve drinks and once to serve dinner. (There was a choice between Chinese and Western cuisine. I selected Chinese.) Although he was quite busy, Desmond took the time to chat briefly with me: a sentence or two in Mandarin, a few more sentences in English. He seemed unusually friendly. I wished my seat mates had not been sleeping, because I would have liked to observe how they, these all-American business types with their frequent-flyer experience on Chinese airlines, how *they* might have responded to this lovely, slightly swishy boy from the East.

After dinner, they dimmed the lights and started up the first movie. I put on my headphones and turned to the classical music channel. "Tales from the Vienna Woods" was playing. I closed my eyes, hoping to be lulled to sleep. But the Strauss was too loud and lush. It swooped and swirled around in my ears, accosting me like some heavy, whipped cream-rich dessert, its drunken rhythms and lavish harmonies cloying in their sugary sweetness.

Goodbye, I thought. *Goodbye, Western music. Goodbye, Western harmony. Goodbye, German pastry and French coffee. Goodbye Hancock Tower and Mom's spaghetti sauce.*

I turned down the volume, then reached under the seat for my backpack and the bottle of melatonin. I shook one out onto my hand. A stewardess breezed by, but she was too busy for me to catch her attention to ask for a glass of water. There were no other attendants in sight. I unbuckled my seat belt and made my way down the darkened aisle toward the flight attendants' station. I parted the curtain and peeked in. Desmond was tidying up.

"Excuse me, Desmond. May I have a glass of water?"

"Certainly, Mr. Ma." He poured a glass and handed it to me. Again, the same friendly smile on his face. Gingerly, I reached for the glass, deliberately letting my fingers brush against his.

"Xiexie ni."

"You're welcome," he said. A shock of glossy black hair fell over his forehead. He brushed it back. A little bit theatrically, I thought. I took a sip of water. It was cold and delicious. I realized I was sweating.

"Anything else?" Desmond asked.

I looked into his eyes. They were black, exquisitely shaped

almonds, not at all like the Fu Manchu eyes that some Hollywood makeup artist had once painted on Sidney Toler's Charlie Chan.

"No thanks." I knew this was my cue to leave, but I hesitated, making as if to check my watch. "You know, I'm all screwed up on the time. Where are we anyway?"

"Here, I'll show you." He motioned to a flight chart taped to the wall of the galley. "Here." I moved in closer. Desmond was wearing expensive cologne. "We'll be crossing the international date line in a few hours."

"Oh, wow! The international date line!" I could see the look Owen would be giving me right now. Desmond smiled, pleased to have been of service. "Thanks," I told him.

"No problem," he said. "It's my job."

I waited a beat.

"So, would this be a good time for us to practice some more Chinese?"

Desmond's smile faltered. "Well, I must get back to my duties soon, but . . . sure, let's try for a few minutes. Go ahead, say something."

Random sentences raced through my mind.

"Okay, how about, *Wo hen gaoxing jiandao ni?*" I fired it off too rapidly. Even in the dim light, I could see an uncomprehending look on Desmond's face. "Did you understand?" I asked.

"Mandarin is not my first language," he apologized.

"No, I think maybe my tones are off."

"Please, try again," he encouraged. I repeated my phrase, one I'd practiced a dozen times with Mrs. Duan.

"Ah, *jiandao, jiandao!*" Desmond nodded his head. "Yes, I am happy to meet you, too." When he repeated the phrase in Mandarin, I could hear how my version had differed. "Another?" he invited.

"Um, *Wo yao shi nide pengyou.*"

Desmond giggled. "Yes, I would like to be your friend, too, Mr. Ma."

"I'm getting better, huh?"

We smiled at each other. His face looked as soft as the fingers I'd brushed against earlier.

"One more," he said.

I felt myself squeezing the plastic cup of water. "My repertoire's pretty limited," I told him.

"Anything," he said.

I was aware of how private we were, alone in that galley with the curtain drawn over the entrance. My face felt flushed. Looking him straight in the eye, I said, *"Ni shi nali ren?"*

A puzzled look came over Desmond's face. "I'm sorry, you want to know if I am *what* kind of person?"

"Nali ren?" I tried again.

Desmond shook his head slowly. I could see him trying to puzzle it out. I kept looking at his eyes, trying to see if he was picking up on anything or not.

"Um, 'whereabouts person'?" I suggested.

"Whereabouts?" His brow furrowed, and he glanced around the station. "This is called the galley, Mr. Ma. In Mandarin *chufang*. Excuse me, but is that what you wanted to know?" The plastic cup cracked in my hand. "I think," Desmond continued, "maybe if you ask me in English?"

I shook my head. "I don't want to say it in English."

Desmond laughed politely. He must have thought I was making a joke. Sweat was beading up on my forehead. Water from the cracked cup dribbled over my hand. "I mean, I'm trying not to rely on my native tongue anymore."

"Ah, that's good," Desmond said. "Yes, that's exactly the way you'll learn. You're a good student, Mr. Ma." He beamed at me again. "Very good."

"Thank you."

I popped the melatonin capsule into my mouth and drank down the water that remained in the cup.

"Would you like some more water?" Desmond asked.

I did, but I was mortified that I had cracked the plastic cup.

"No, thanks." I tossed the cup into the trash.

"Okay, so you want to try again?" Desmond invited. *"Nali ren?* What did you mean, 'whereabouts person'?" I could see he had no idea what I'd been getting at.

I brushed away the question with my hand.

"Nothing. I think I just really screwed up. I'll have to check my dictionary and get back to you."

"No problem, Mr. Ma."

"Look, I've taken up way too much of your time already. I should go get some sleep now." He nodded his agreement. "Thanks for the practice, Desmond."

"You're welcome, Mr. Ma. I'll wake you when it's time for breakfast."

Through the darkened cabin, I made my way back to my seat, re-playing the conversation Desmond and I had just had. I felt so fool-ish. *Nali ren!* I winced at the awkwardness of it.

My seatmates were fast asleep. I sat down and closed my eyes. Clueless or gracious: what had Desmond been showing me back there in that galley? He had responded to everything that I'd gushed and sputtered at him with charming cordiality. I could still hear the encouragement in his voice, well mannered and courteous, friendly even. But the undercurrent: what had he been trying to show me all along? Was it personal or corporate, a bit of ancient gay solidarity under that Hong Kong accent or just dutiful Chinese courtesy? No, I still couldn't quite catch it, those subtle, elusive, insidious, deli-cious tones.

Chapter Four

It was night when we landed in Beijing. I say so on the evidence outside the plane window and on the declaration of Desmond Woo, who, in three languages as we were taxiing down the runway, announced that the local time was ten minutes past midnight, Thursday. But this seemed impossible to me. While my seatmates, the two American businessmen who had not spoken a word to me for the entire length of the flight, closed down their laptops and snapped their briefcases shut, I sat back, practiced deep breathing exercises, and tried to fathom how it could already be Thursday when I'd left Boston on a Tuesday. No explanation of the international date line had prepared me for a *two*-day jump in time. Where had Wednesday gone?

Perhaps it was this chronological confusion, or the jet lag, or the labyrinthian shuffle through a warren of gloomy back corridors to the passport control, where an unfriendly official stamped me through; but whatever the reason, I emerged into the commotion and chaos of the baggage claim area without a clue as to how I was going to find the fellow who was supposed to take me into the city. Back in the States, I'd been briefed that a certain Mr. Zhou, Winston Zhou, would pick me up upon my arrival. "He'll be holding a placard with your name on it," I was told. But now as I clutched my bags, trying to feel the charm, the cultural novelty, of being jostled and shoved by people pushing toward the customs stations, I couldn't for all the world pick out anyone who looked like he might be waiting for me.

I stood there, bathed in the artificial daytime of the fluorescent lighting, hoping I looked sufficiently American and lost and ready to be taken care of that someone would notice. Some of the people meeting our flight had been allowed to come into the baggage claim area, but others, I saw, were still being held back on the far side of the customs barriers, craning their necks to catch a glimpse of us coming off the plane. Maybe Winston was one of those whom the officials had not allowed to cross the barriers. But if I went through customs and he wasn't there, then what?

I recognized one of my seatmates. Briefcase in hand, his matching luggage neatly laid on a pushcart, he was being welcomed by someone who looked like a Chinese businessman. For a second I thought about asking them to intervene—maybe they could have Mr. Winston Zhou paged—but my seatmate had been so uncommunicative during the entire flight that I wondered if he held some animosity toward me. Maybe he'd noticed me flirting with Desmond.

Just then, a group of Chinese American tourists, all two dozen of them wearing identical red and white baseball caps emblazoned with the logo of their package tour, shuffled by. They were following their guide, a smartly tailored Chinese woman, who held aloft a silk scarf in the same shade of red. Maybe it was the official types, like tour leaders and business people, who were being let through the customs barriers to meet their parties. It seemed that Winston Zhou should fall into this category, too. He was, my instructions said, the son of one of the staff members at the clinic where I was to take up work.

Relax, I told myself. *You're having an adventure. Worse comes to worst, you can always take a cab into the city and spend the night in a hotel.*

But what was the word for "hotel"? There had seemed no reason to learn this word with Mrs. Duan. I set down my bags and slipped the knapsack off my shoulders. Inside the pouch, I'd stuffed a little Chinese phrase book. Between my crash course with Mrs. Duan and the lists of tourist phrases in the book, I was sure I'd be able to cobble together the necessary sentence or two. *You've done this before,* I reminded myself.

I supposed I had. There was the summer after college, almost thirty years ago now, when I'd backpacked through Europe: a half dozen countries in ten weeks; and, a decade later, another trip abroad—in those days "abroad" still meant Europe—that time with Erik, when we concentrated, rather sophisticatedly, we thought, on only France and Italy. But I'd been in my early thirties then, when "having an adventure," especially in a rental car with the man you loved, was easy.

I opened the phrase book. I wanted "hotel"; I wanted "safe"; I wanted "clean"; I wanted "moderately-priced"; I wanted "central location." I wanted a thousand words that weren't at my command. And where was this Mr. Zhou? I was trying to see his absence as just another part of the fun of it all, the *adventure,* but this only made me feel worse, like a nervous, middle-aged tourist, pitifully attempting to recapture his lost youth.

As I was flipping through the pages, a young man approached me.

"You Mr. Davis?" he asked in heavily accented English.

"No, I'm Mr. Masiello." I smiled at him: someone who spoke English, and good-looking, too. Maybe he'd be able to help.

A puzzled look appeared on the young man's face. He glanced down at his placard, to the back of which a snapshot had been taped. He held it toward me, pointing to the face. It was a color photo of . . . *me!*

"Mr. Davis, yes?" he asked again.

"David, David," I told him, ecstatic at having been found. "David Masiello." I held out my hand and we shook.

"Okay, no problem."

"You're Mr. Zhou? I mean . . ." I paused to compose the sentence in Chinese. *"Ni shi Zhou xiansheng ma?"*

"Hey, okay." He gave me the thumbs up. "You speak very well Chinese."

He was wearing a white nylon windbreaker over a white polo shirt—a hearty, athletic look I hadn't anticipated in someone named Winston. His handsome features, too—full, square face; dark eyes; crew cut—and the prominent collar bone displayed in the open vee of his jersey, further amplified the jock image.

"Wo hen gaoxing . . ."

Winston interrupted me.

"Sure, I'm very glad meet you, too." He smiled and slapped me on the shoulder.

"You know, when I saw your sign"—I nodded to the placard—"I didn't understand . . . because my last name, I mean my family name . . ."

"No problem, no problem." He pointed to his watch. "You suppose to be here three hours ago. I think maybe your flight very late."

There was so much noise and confusion in the baggage claim area that I found it difficult to pay attention. I kept getting distracted by all the sights and sounds—the greetings, announcements, faces, clothing, at once so familiar and yet so altogether foreign—all around me.

Winston picked up one of my suitcases. "Okay, Mr. Davis, I think we will go my car now."

I followed him as he hustled along, pushing and jostling his compatriots, who were pressing toward the customs booths. There, the security guards, wearing uniforms in a sensationally bilious shade of khaki green, were checking forms and baggage. They, too, looked like teenagers, but their faces were frozen in severe, impassive expressions. I couldn't help thinking of all those pictures I'd seen in the news a few years back of PLA soldiers in Tiananmen Square.

"So, do I call you Winston, or Mr. Zhou, or Mr. Winston?" I called out, trying to slow him down. I was dragging the heavier of the two suitcases, which seemed to have lost its tote wheels somewhere between Boston and Beijing.

Winston turned around, grinning and nodding. "Sure, no problem." He motioned for me to follow him through an exit that had been left unguarded. I grabbed at his arm.

"Wait a minute, Winston. I think I'm supposed to have my bags inspected before we leave."

The smile on his face dissolved into a look somewhere between annoyance and alarm, and he shook his head in quick, conspiratorial spasms.

"Not necessary, I think. Please, this way. No problem." He pushed me forward. As we hustled through the unmanned gate, I fully expected to hear an alarm go off or someone screaming "Halt!" but nothing happened and soon we were on the other side. Winston turned around, grinning at me again.

"In China, too much red tape." I began to assure him that we had red tape in America, too, but he interrupted me. "Joke," he said. "Red tape. Red China. Get it?"

I laughed. "Winston, where did you learn your English. It's very good."

"Not good," he said. "I think maybe you can help me to improve." He reached into his shirt pocket, pulled out a pack of Chinese brand cigarettes, and offered me one. I told him I didn't smoke. He lit up and took a heavy drag.

"Winston's Winstons?" I asked. He looked at me uncomprehendingly. "That's a joke, too. In America, Winston is the name of a cigarette."

He shook his head impatiently. "Yes, I know, I know. No problem." He shoved the cigarette between his lips, picked up my bag, and motioned for us to go on.

We had to make our way through another crowd. Every few seconds the racket all around us was punctuated by a new outburst of joy as parents and children, cousins and uncles and aunts were reunited. The fever and pitch of these exchanges seemed as operatic as any of the reunions at Masiello family weddings and funerals back home. It was almost reassuring, how Italian all these Chinese were behaving.

I stuck close to Winston, but he kept pulling ahead of me. I couldn't help noticing how his trousers hugged his ass, showing off a pair of well shaped buns. Winston not only dressed like a jock, he probably was one and, I guessed, a ladies' man, too.

Once outside, we were immediately set upon by another crowd, this time a phalanx of taxi drivers. When they caught sight of me, they pressed in for the kill.

"Hey, mister, you want taxi?"

"Very cheap."

"I got air condition."

Barking back at them in Chinese, Winston cleared a path for us, and we scurried out to the parking lot, where we were suddenly engulfed in a dark, eerie silence. Tall light poles—they must have been three or four stories high—rose into the black night. I could see bats darting back and forth, though the smog in the air was so thick that the light reminded me of the water in an untended goldfish tank. My eyes began to sting and I coughed. Winston turned around.

"Air is very bad in Beijing, I think. Very much pollution." As he spoke, the cigarette bounced between his lips.

I shook my head. "No problem."

"Yes, I think big problem," he insisted. "Big problem."

In another minute, we reached his car, just in time, too, because I was running out of strength. Winston stuck the key in the lock of the trunk. I was still enough of a linguist to recognize the letters on the nameplate as Cyrillic, ВОЛГА. I sounded them out.

"Volga." It was a relief to be dealing with an alphabet again, even one I barely knew.

Winston shook his head.

"Very, very old. Not so good car." I told him that I'd never seen a Russian automobile before. In the United States, I explained, we didn't have them. "Then you very lucky, I think. In America you have very good car." He gave me the thumbs up. "Mercedes. Ferrari. BMW."

He lifted the hood of the trunk—it opened in creaky spasms—and we threw in the bags. Winston had to help me heft mine up.

"Americans travel with too much stuff," I apologized.

He took a final drag on his cigarette and tossed it away.

"No, not too much stuff. I think you need too much stuff for one year in Beijing, but maybe you must go to health club. Lift weight. You know?" He demonstrated, flexing both arms. "And not so many hamburgers, I think." He patted my belly. "You come to my house, Mr. Davis. My mother cook for you. Beijing style. Very good."

As we began the ride into the city, my attention was torn between keeping up a conversation with Winston and looking out the car window. We were on a dark, lonely stretch of highway, but even here the few details caught in the Volga's weak, fluttering headlamps—road signs, billboards, trucks—felt dizzyingly foreign. *Like that first trip to Europe,* I told myself, trying to recall whether anything about Paris or London or Rome had ever seemed so strange.

We barreled along, the Volga shaking and rattling with alarming constancy. Dangling from the rearview mirror were a few cardboard air fresheners in the shape of buxom women. A fat, red-and-gold plastic Buddha sat on the dash.

"Winston, are you a Buddhist?"

"No problem," he said, punctuating his answer with a long blast of the horn. We were practically on top of the truck in front of us.

"You'd do well as a taxi driver in New York," I told him.

Winston turned his head and flashed me another broad grin. "You can get me a job in New York?"

"No, that was another joke, Winston."

"Americans, too much joking." He hit the horn again, then swerved around the truck. I noticed that he'd let the fingernail on his right pinky grow out. It was a grotesque length, maybe two inches, like the fingernails I'd seen in photographs of the old Dowager Empress.

"So, Winston, what do you do?" I asked. He turned to me with a quizzical look. "Work. What is your work?"

"Ah, work." He paused to consider. "Mm, many thing. Export-import. Restaurant. Tour guide."

"You're a tour guide?"

"No problem," he said.

"I hope you'll give me a tour around Beijing one day, okay?"

"Sure, sure," he said eagerly. "I can give tour to you. And because you are my friend, I will make very special price."

He blasted the horn again. I looked at the speedometer. The needle registered zero. "Mr. Davis, how old are you?" He was lighting up another cigarette.

"Forty-nine. And how old are you, Winston?"

Winston swerved around another truck, then turned toward me to give me a good look at his face. "What is your guess?"

"Twenty-four?"

Winston exhaled a lungful of smoke and smiled with a winner's satisfaction. "I am twenty-nine years old," he said in perfect textbook English. Before I could comment, he asked another question: "Are you married, Mr. Davis?"

48

I hesitated. It occurred to me that I could say I had once been divorced, and once a widower, both of which, if you were speaking in Gay American, were true.

"Guess," I told him.

"I am guessing yes."

It pleased me to hear him say that.

"No, Winston, I'm not married."

For a few moments he said nothing. I wondered what he was tallying up in his mind.

"Excuse me, Mr. Davis, but I think if you not married maybe you are not very lucky."

"Oh, not in America, Winston. Being unmarried is not considered unlucky. Many Americans like being single." As I said this, I wondered if it were true.

"I not married, too," he said, "but I am young. You old, Mr. Davis. You should be married." He looked over at me. "You like to be single?" I toggled my head. "So why you then not getting married? Who take care of you when you will be old?"

"Good question, Cupcake." I bit my lip as soon as it came out.

"Excuse me, please, but what is cupcake?"

I pretended to be more interested in what was passing by my window.

"Oh, just an American expression. It's not important."

That seemed to satisfy him. "I think too late for you now to get married," he said. "Too late for have kids."

"Oh, I don't know, Winston."

"Yes, I think so, Cake Cup."

———

The company had arranged for me to take a one-year lease in a small, Western-style apartment on the north side of the city. But a few weeks before I had left Boston, they informed me that I would have to stay temporarily in a hotel until my flat could be readied for occupancy. I asked Winston what hotel he was taking me to.

"Not hotel," he said. "Dormitory."

"Dormitory!"

He explained that the company had found it more convenient to arrange temporary quarters for me at a university on the west side of the city.

"You mean I'll be living with students?"

"Maybe not students."

"Not students? Who then?"

"I think maybe it's difficult for me to explain."

"A dormitory," I said. "A place where students sleep?"

"Yes, but different. Mm, Mr. Davis, I think maybe you prefer hotel? I can find you nice one, very cheap." I assured him that whatever the company had arranged as my transitional housing would be fine. "But I think at hotel you can have massage?" he pursued.

"Massage?"

"Very nice girl, very clean. I think maybe you understand. I can arrange. Not too expensive."

The fat plastic Buddha bobbed and swayed.

"Thanks, Winston, but I'm not interested."

"No?" He seemed disappointed. "So I think maybe then you stay in dormitory." He turned and grinned at me. "Maybe you can find Chinese student for girlfriend."

"Maybe," I agreed. And then, not knowing what else to say, I asked him for a cigarette.

Soon we were in the city, on an elevated flyway that whisked us past one brightly lit high-rise after another. *Beijing, the Imperial City,* I told myself. But except for the Chinese characters on the neon signs, the place seemed dishearteningly Western. It didn't jibe with all the images I'd picked up—but from where? the guidebooks I'd read? my Chinese history class during college? those Chinese-themed movies Owen and I had watched all summer?— images of Beijing as a place of stiff, brocaded elegance, inscrutable mystery, and fiendish, appalling cruelty. I felt a sinking sense of disappointment.

We continued to speed along. At that hour—it must have been close to two in the morning—there wasn't much traffic except for the trucks. Chain-smoking his cigarettes, Winston had fallen silent. Suddenly, he veered off the expressway, whisked us down the exit ramp, around a large rotary, and onto a city street. I pressed my face closer to the window. The neon signs and high rises had disappeared. Instead, all I could see were empty sidewalks and small, darkened shops. My heart quickened. The real Beijing at last, even if dark, closed, and shut down for the night.

The street we were on seemed like a major avenue, wide enough for three lanes in either direction. Metal barriers ran down the middle. But at this hour, we were the only car in sight. There weren't even any people about. The streetlights, what few of them there were, were dim and forlorn. Only the beams of the Volga's headlights seemed able to penetrate the stagnant, murky air. It felt as if we had entered a sleepy, provincial village.

"Soon we coming to university," Winston said. "Look." He pointed off to the right. "There. You see wall?"

"The Wall? The Great Wall!"

"No, wall of university. Look, there."

Along the sidewalk, the shops had given way to a gray-brick wall about eight feet in height. Behind it, I could make out the silhouettes of trees, which, even in the darkness of the night, I could tell weren't the familiar elms, maples, and oaks of college campuses back home. *Goodbye to all that, too,* I thought. Winston pulled over, stopping at what appeared to be a gate house, a shack so run down (there was a large, gaping hole in its tile roof) that I almost mistook it for a coal bin.

A guard emerged from the shadows and, quite formally, approached the car. He was wearing a baggy navy-blue uniform and a cap, several sizes too big. It made him look like a little boy who'd broken into his father's wardrobe. Winston spoke to him, and the kid—it was hard not to think of him that way—extended his hand, like a crossing guard in elementary school, indicating that we could pass.

As we drove along, very slowly now, I rolled down my window and peered out, trying to get a look at the university. We passed a few buildings, but the campus was even darker than the city streets outside. I couldn't see much. Still, the cool night air smelled good, clearing my lungs of Winston's foul cigarette smoke. In another minute, we had reached what I took to be my dormitory. It was more modern than I'd expected: four stories high with a plate-glass entrance flanked by stainless steel columns that supported a concrete portico. The rest of the building was sheathed in glossy white tiles, giving it the look of a laboratory or a second-rate Los Angeles office building.

Winston tossed his cigarette out the window and hopped out of the car. We hauled the luggage from the trunk and approached the thick glass doors of the building. A curtain had been drawn across them. Winston tugged at the handle. The building was locked.

"Fuck," he said, and began pounding on the door.

"Are they expecting me?" I asked rather feebly. Winston kept pounding.

Eventually, a light came on inside and we heard a key being turned in the lock. The door opened to reveal a sleepy young man wearing nothing but plastic sandals and a pair of thin cotton boxer shorts. As Winston spoke to him, explaining who I was, I waited in the shadows, pretending not to stare at the young man. His upper body was hairless and on the scrawny side, like a prepubescent boy's. Shaggy black hair, disheveled from sleep, fell across his forehead. When he scratched his chin, I noticed that, unlike Winston, his nails were cut short.

Winston turned to me.

"I think maybe you can sign registration book tomorrow?"

The boy nodded, though I suspected that he did not understand a word of English.

"Wo hen gaoxing." I was beginning to feel rather foolish that this was the only phrase I had been able to come up with since I'd arrived. The boy looked at me and smiled. I smiled back. He started saying something, but when he caught the look of incomprehension on my face, he turned to Winston and addressed him instead. The two of them laughed.

"What did he say, Winston?"

"I think, no problem," Winston said.

Still smiling, the boy handed me a set of keys and a ticket.

"Ticket for food at cafeteria," Winston explained.

"Well, I guess that's it." I held out my hand to shake goodbye. "Thanks a lot, Winston. I'll say good night now, and—well, what's next?—will I see you in the morning?" I was eager to ditch him and get to bed.

"Please, I will show you to room," Winston said.

I protested, even daring to suggest—and here I turned and smiled again at the desk clerk—that perhaps *he* could show me to my room. But Winston insisted. He gestured to the elevator across the lobby—clearly he knew his way around—picked up my bag, the heavier one this time, and walked me over. As I got inside, I turned to get one more glimpse of the darling night boy, but he had already disappeared.

As we went up in the elevator, I read one of the flyers that had been taped to the walls. It was in English, and welcomed the *visiting foreign scholars and other worthy dignitys* to the university. *Please pay attention to civilization of appearance.*

"This is a dormitory for visitors?" I asked Winston.

"That's what I am telling you at the airport," he said. "I think, Mr. Davis, you very tired."

We got off at the third floor. Clotheslines had been strung across the landing of the nearby staircase, draped with a couple dozen dingy pink towels. I followed Winston as he turned the other way and led me down the corridor. Once again, he seemed to know exactly where to go. I noticed that outside most of the doors a thermos bottle had been set, just as Mrs. Duan had once described to me. She hadn't mentioned that they all would be ruby red in color.

"This your room," Winston said, stopping at one of the doors. He took my set of keys, tried one in the lock, pushed the door open, and gestured for me to enter. I took two steps in, then waited for Winston to find the light switch. The air smelled of cheap, sweet soap, cooking oil, and mildew. When Winston flipped on the lights, my eyes recoiled at the sudden brightness.

The room was surprisingly ample, about thirty feet long and wide enough to accommodate two twin beds along one wall and two desks opposite. But aside from the spaciousness, the overall effect was cheerless and spartan. The desks, in high-gloss enamel, were painted battleship gray. So were the chairs, the beds, the night table, the walls. Even the bedspreads were gray, printed with stripes in three different shades of it: slate, gray-green, and pewter. The only bit of color in the room was the bright red of another thermos bottle, which sat on top of the night table. It was hard to imagine that anything but studying could possibly take place in such austere quarters.

"I think very nice," Winston said. "Has private bathroom. And also nice window." He motioned to the far end of the room, where a long bank of crank-open windows looked out onto another wing of the dormitory across the way.

"I'm sure I'll be quite comfortable here," I told him, then added for good measure, "that is, until my apartment is ready. When did you say that would be, Winston?"

"No problem, Mr. Davis."

He set down the suitcase on one of the beds, then took the one I was holding and set it down next to the other.

"Now, I think maybe we have some tea?"

"Tea? Winston, it's awfully late."

He picked up the thermos on the night table, pulled out the cork and brought his nose to the opening.

"Cold."

I started to tell him that I didn't really care for any tea, but he was already at the bedside phone, dialing the front desk. Brusquely he said something to the person at the other end, then grunted his satisfaction and hung up.

"Will bring hot water."

"Winston, this is not necessary."

"Okay, now we sit."

He plunked himself down on the edge of one of the double beds. Because the suitcases were piled on the other bed, I sat down next to him.

"Beijing! I still can't believe I'm here, Winston. Beijing."

"Yes, very nice city, but I think Shanghai it's better. You should go there for vacation, Mr. Davis. Lots of fun."

I suspected I knew what kind of fun Winston had in mind. I made a feeble pretense of showing some interest, but as I did so his eyes began to search my face, intently studying something there.

"Excuse me, Mr. Davis, but I think maybe you have Buddha arse." His breath smelled of tobacco and garlic.

"Buddha arse?"

Winston reached out and fondled one of my ears.

"In China we say person with big arse have Buddha arse."

"*Ears,* Winston. Ears. Your 'arse' is this." I pointed to my buttocks. "Ears." I pulled at my ear lobe. "Arse." I patted my butt. "Ears, arse. You could get into a lot of trouble if you don't know the difference."

"Arse, arse," he said.

I toggled my head. "We'll have to practice some more later on." I reached over and gently tweaked one of his ears. "And what do the Chinese call small ears? Baby Buddha ears?"

Winston laughed. "Baby Buddha arse! I never hear before. Very good joke, Mr. Davis. You very funny man."

We were interrupted by a knock on the door. Winston answered it. I got up, too, wondering if the night boy would have put on trousers by now. But when Winston opened the door, the person standing there was a young woman with sad, plain features. Dressed in a gray smock and baggy gray trousers, she handed Winston a new red thermos, mumbling a few meek words. Winston grunted something in reply. When she spoke again, her tone was slightly more forceful. At this, Winston exploded, firing off a volley of angry language. Even though I didn't catch a word of what he was saying, I knew it must be hostile and abusive.

"Winston, what is it?"

Ignoring me, he growled a few more things at the sad, drab girl. She answered, submissively now, and backed out of the room. I thought she might be crying. Winston grunted his satisfaction and closed the door on her.

"Winston, what was that all about?"

"Girl say cannot have new thermos until return old thermos."

"So why didn't you give it to her?"

"I tell her you are American dignity. Very can trust. I tell her you give back two bottles in the morning."

"But it would have been so easy, Winston."

"Mr. Davis, you are my friend?"

"David!" I barked at him. "Da-*vid.*" I let out a sigh. "Yes, Winston, of course, I'm your friend."

"So, I help you save face."

"But it was her responsibility to collect the other thermos. I would not have been offended . . ." I stopped and let out a feeble chuckle. "This is a communist country, Winston. Aren't you supposed to treat everyone equally?"

He frowned.

"Mr. Da-*vid*, I think you can't understand my country."

"Well, I'm trying to."

"Maybe," he said.

———

A half hour and three cups of bitter tea later, Winston finally left with promises to call me in the morning. As soon as I closed the door on him, I felt utter exhaustion permeate my body. I started to get out of my clothes (clothes I'd put on two days ago—in Boston!), when suddenly, through the window, I noticed that someone's light was still on in the wing across the courtyard. In fact, there were no curtains on any of the windows. I turned off the lights and continued to strip down to my underwear. My body reeked. I went to the bathroom, turned on the shower and let it run. Nothing but cold water. I decided I'd deal with bathing in the morning.

I moved to the windows and cranked one open. Cool night air poured in, blowing away some of the mustiness in the room. I looked across the courtyard, to the lit window. I could see a Chinese woman sitting in a chair, under a lamp, reading. Except for the occasional movement of her hand as she turned the page, she was motionless. She looked so calm, so unbothered by the hour of the night, the difficulty of her text, the bewildering recent history of her country. How did you get that calm? I wondered. I thought back to my own graduate school days, to how unable I had been to concentrate on my studies because of all the sexual and romantic longing I was trying to cope with. I wondered, too, if there were other guys in the dorm who were also eavesdropping on this focused, dutiful student and, if so, whether a single one of them was thinking what I was thinking now: that he wished she were a guy.

I pulled down the bedspread—the linens smelled faintly of vinegar—got under the covers, and closed my eyes, but even in the dark, as sleep-deprived as I was, my mind wouldn't shut down. I was alert to everything around me: the pungent smell of the sheets; the nasal crooning of a Chinese soprano, somewhere far off, maybe on a radio; a toilet flushing; the light from the girl's window; the memory of the smooth chest and pretty face of the desk clerk downstairs.

Surreptitiously, as if I were in a bunkhouse at summer camp with sleeping cabin mates nearby, I reached under the covers and fondled my penis, trying to sharpen the image of that night boy. But I felt slightly feverish, and for the first time in my life, I could actually hear blood pounding in my head. I tried switching to a different image: the cabin steward on my flight over, Desmond. (What was it with these Chinese that they all took English names?) And when that wouldn't do, I conjured up an image of Winston. I brought into focus his strong, athletic body; his bristly crew cut; his prominent clavicle; that long, Fu Manchu fingernail on his pinky finger. I tried to imagine what it would be like, sex with Winston, and that bizarre, hideous nail digging into my back.

Nothing worked. Knowing how to rouse a boner seemed like one more thing I had left behind in America. I closed my eyes again and breathed in, deeply, slowly, trying to let go of everything. Trying, most of all, to let go of words, any words: Chinese or English.

Just as I was drifting off, I heard the high, shrill hum of a mosquito dive-bombing my head. I pulled my arms out of the sheets and swatted at the air. The mosquito darted away, complaining—it actually surprised me to hear this—in the same angry, provoked language that mosquitoes use back home. For a few seconds, everything went silent. Then the mosquito returned for his revenge.

Malaria, I thought.

Despite my doctor's assurances that I did not need to take precautions against malaria in Beijing, I'd asked her for a prescription anyway and had taken the first tablet a week before I left. It was time for another. I switched on the night table lamp, got up, and went to the bathroom. As I was running the faucet to get the water cold, I rummaged through my toiletries kit and dug out the prescription bottle. That's when I remembered that I wasn't supposed to drink the tap water in China. I turned off the faucet and, clutching the pill in my sweating palm, returned to the bedroom.

There was still a half cup of cold tea sitting on the night table, but I didn't dare drink it for fear that it had already become contaminated. I pulled out the stopper of the thermos. Steam, reassuring steam, rose up. I took the thermos and my teacup back to the bathroom, dumped the tea in the sink, washed out the cup with some of the still scalding water, then poured myself a fresh cup. In the fluorescent light of the bathroom, I looked at the water: clear and steaming, innocent-looking enough to take a chance. I popped the pill into my mouth and took a sip. It was so hot I could only take a little bit, insufficient for the pill to go down. It stuck in my throat. I swallowed hard, which only made it stick worse. I coughed and it came part way back. I took another sip. The pill still wouldn't go down. In desperation, I gulped down the rest of the hot water. My esophagus spasmed in agony. I closed my eyes against the burning pain.

"Work," I whispered to the pill. "Work. Don't let me die here."

I switched off the bathroom light and returned to bed. But as soon as I lay down, I thought about those two thermos bottles, the shame of my keeping them, and so got up again and moved them just outside my door as all the others along the corridor, my obedient, anonymous dormmates, had done. Finally, my guilt allayed, I got back into bed and closed my eyes. The last thing I remember was hearing that mosquito, still buzzing somewhere in the room, and the sound of myself, half-whispering now, *What is this like? God, what is this like?*

Chapter Five

Somewhere a man was shouting. Loud, frightening, unintelligible words. He was ordering people around, marshaling them to obey. Luckily, he hadn't found me yet. I still had time to hide. But his voice was coming closer. It sounded like it was outside now.

Outside?

Somewhere on the campus.

The campus!

I threw open my eyes. I was in my dorm room. On the campus of a university. In China. My God, I was in China.

The man continued to shout. There was a static crackle in his words, as if they were being amplified through a bullhorn. I listened more closely. He was bellowing commands. But how could this be? I had thought that kind of thing was over.

I leaned toward the night table and squinted at my watch. Overnight, one of the hands had disappeared. I picked it up and brought it closer. My eyes refocused. The watch said six-thirty.

Suddenly, my stomach began to rumble, rising and falling as if there were a small trapped animal, a bird, fluttering wildly inside of me. I took a slow, deep breath. And another. *Zhongguo*, I whispered—level tone, rising tone—trying to anchor myself in the reality of my arrival. Outside, the voice on the public address system went dead.

Go back to sleep, I told myself. I took another slow, deep breath, held it, let it out. My stomach clenched up again, this time more sharply, and a sickening taste arose in my mouth, sour and metallic, like drinking from a cheap aluminum cup. I lay perfectly still, ticking off the reasons why I might have a stomachache. Jet lag? Hunger? Food poisoning? A case of the jitters? Malaria after all. Anything was a possibility now.

I got out of bed. In my shorts and tee shirt, I shuffled over to the door, cracked it open, and peaked out. At the far end of the corridor, two young Chinese women in baggy gray smocks and trousers were folding towels. I recognized one of them as the sad-faced girl who had brought me the thermos last night. When they caught sight of me, the two of them started giggling. I pulled my head back inside the room, then, squatting down, eased my hand out the door, felt for the morning thermos, and pulled it in. Down the hall, the two women giggled again.

I flushed last night's tea leaves down the toilet and set about to brew a fresh pot of tea. A jar of tea leaves sat on the small gray-enamel table near my bed. I shook a few teaspoons' worth into the pot, just as Winston had done, and filled it with hot water from the thermos.

As I waited for the tea to brew, I tried to picture myself living in this room for the next few weeks. There were no cooking facilities, no amenities of any kind. Not even a chest of drawers. The word "basic" came to mind. The word "spartan." The word "monastic." I made a mental note to use these words in my first letter home to Owen. I would make sure *not* to use them in my first letter home to my mother.

I poured the tea. A glob of leaves oozed from the spout and plopped into the cup. I watched them settle, then took my first sip. It tasted as stale and bitter as last night's brew. My stomach growled again. *Ignore it,* I told myself. *Keep busy.* That's the advice my mother gave herself whenever she had another one of her "aches and pains."

The suitcases were still sitting on the other twin bed where Winston had left them. I unlocked one and started to unpack. Released from their two-day confinement, my clothes smelled of the fresh, familiar soapiness of America. I buried my nose in a stack of tee shirts and breathed in deeply.

Where *was* I supposed to store my things? Was the absence of a chest of drawers intentional, a hint to us "foreign devils" that too much clothing was a sign of capitalist decadence? If so, I figured that a good bracing dose of the ascetic life, post-Mao style, might not be so bad for a few weeks. There had always been a little of the monastic in me.

A plain, floor-to-ceiling wardrobe stood against the far wall next to the desk. It was really nothing more than a tall, flimsy box fitted with a door and painted in cheap gray enamel, the same color as everything else in the room. I opened it up. An acrid mustiness, vinegary like the sheets, walloped my nostrils.

"Yes, indeed," I said aloud, just to reassure myself that I still had English, "all the comforts of a monastery."

There was a shelf at the top of the wardrobe. I stowed my shirts there, then unzipped my back pack and spilled the contents onto the bedspread. Lying among the chewing gum, breath mints, melatonin, antacid tablets, condoms, and a English-Chinese dictionary, was the little pocket edition of Daoist sayings that Owen had given to me. My stomach gurgled again. I popped two antacid tablets into my mouth, stretched out on the bed and began to flip through the pages:

> *In the pursuit of knowledge,*
> *every day something is added.*
> *In the practice of Tao,*
> *every day something is dropped.*

I lay the book face down on my chest and closed my eyes.

Why *had* I come to China? To add something? To drop something? Why? To finish grieving Johnny's death? To change my life? To indulge in a lark before my fiftieth birthday? All summer, Owen had joked that I was going to Beijing to get laid, but the opposite seemed far more likely: I was in for a year of celibacy. Part of me even thought that wouldn't be so bad. And though I had not been a practicing Catholic for years—I dated my final defection from the Church to the night Johnny told me he had AIDS—now, as I lay on that drab, cheerless single bed, Laozi resting on my heart, I felt moved to say a prayer. But what? Not even during the worst bouts of Johnny's illness had I prayed.

Just then, the shouting man on the public address system took up his harangue again. He sounded almost hysterical. I got up and went to the window. Down below, I could see lots of students leisurely pedaling their bicycles along the streets and paths of the campus. No one seemed the least bit aware of the announcer or his message. In the pit of my stomach, the trapped bird resumed his wild, fluttering gyrations.

"Not now," I told him. "Not now."

For the time being, that seemed as good a prayer as any. Even Saint Augustine had said it once.

The university cafeteria was next to my dormitory. I followed several pairs of students—boys with boys, girls with girls—across a court-yard that was filled with bicycles lined up in neat, perfect rows. Women in long indigo smocks were sweeping the grounds, not only the sidewalks and gutters, but the grass as well. In the humid morning air, the sound of their straw brooms was steady and purposeful. They seemed oblivious to the crowds of students milling about.

Among the students there were a few Westerners—my ears caught snippets of English and German—but the majority were Chinese. Half the guys were wearing jeans; the others baggy pleated trousers. Their waists seemed impossibly small. Many of the coeds wore blouses, sweaters, and skirts. Hair barrettes, clipped into their pageboy cuts, seemed like the only item of jewelry they allowed themselves. I saw two girls—though I knew they must be older, they looked about fourteen—walking along holding hands. The whole scene felt wholesome and innocent, like a scene from a Mickey Rooney movie.

The entrance to the cafeteria was through a foyer lined on both sides with several large, restaurant-grade fish tanks. I recognized eels and catfish swimming about in the green, murky waters. There was also a dry tank full of frogs, their throats sleepily bulging and contracting. I thought of all the things my grandmother Squillaciotti used to say about Chinese food, words I hadn't recalled in years: *"Mi fa schivare!"* she'd declare, shuddering with disgust. *"Guacchia, porcherría!"* Slop, pig mess!

Fighting back another wave of nausea, I followed two female students into the dining hall. It was a large, sunny room, outfitted with rows of cafeteria-style tables and chairs. Against one wall the food counter, against another the beverage rack. The hall reverberated with the homely sounds of students having breakfast: the clatter of dishes, the murmur of conversation. Incongruously, in the midst of this functional, rather high school–like atmosphere, an elaborate crystal chandelier hung over the middle of the room, strewing tiny brilliant sparkles all around.

I got in the food line and watched as the students in front of me made their selections. Behind the counter, women in long white coats were dishing out ladlefuls of food: rice, dumplings, meat, vegetables, soup. The air was sticky with the copious clouds of steam billowing out from the kitchen. On this thick, heavy atmosphere, the smell of garlic, cabbage, and fish wafted toward me. My stomach turned another flip flop. I pointed to the plain white rice and the soup. They seemed like the most benign items on the menu. At the drink stand, I got a Coca Cola. It was what my mother had always prescribed for an upset stomach.

The dining room was crowded. I approached a table occupied by the first Westerner I spotted.

"Do you mind if I join you?" I spoke slowly, in case he didn't speak English.

The guy shook his head—I'd caught him working on a mouthful of food—and pointed to the seat opposite him. I set my tray on the table and sat down. Making a visible effort to swallow, my breakfast companion took a swig from a can of beer.

"I see you opted for the alternate beverage selection." He nodded toward the can of Coke on my tray. "Twelve million people in this city and no one serves a fucking cup of coffee in the morning." He held out his hand. "David Dawson."

I smiled. "I'm David, too. David Masiello."

"Hey, man."

I guessed him to be in his early thirties. He had many of the physical features that I went for in guys back home—sculpted chin, clear complexion, ski-slope nose, small ear lobes. His eyes were a brilliant blue. And though his dark brown hair was receding at the temples, on him it looked very sexy. I was glad I'd worn my baseball cap.

"So, are you a Dave or a David?" I asked.

"Neither." He took another swig of beer. "Most people call me Daws."

"And what about in Chinese?" I pulled the tab on the can of Coke and took a tentative sip.

"Chinese?"

"My Chinese tutor calls me Ma Dexing."

"Nope, just Daws." He chowed into a bowl of noodles and meat sauce. "You have a Chinese tutor here?" he asked.

"No, back home." I belched. "In Boston."

"Hey, Beantown! My sister lives there."

We exchanged brief stories: about who we were, where we came from, and what we were doing in Beijing. Neither of us, it turned out, was a student at the university. Daws was working for an multinational telecommunications company. He was thirty-two.

"I hate to cook," he said, "so I bike over here every morning for breakfast. Try the *baozi*." He speared one of his steamed rolls and dropped it onto my tray. "Not as good as the ones you get on the street, but decent enough."

I bit into the roll. It was doughy and rather bland, good for tummy trouble, I figured.

"Have you gotten a bike yet?" he asked. "Sometimes you can find one right here on campus, a bike some foreign student who's gone back home has left behind, but the semester's about to begin, so most of those bikes have already been taken. Anyway, you can pick up a brand new one for fifty bucks. If you want, I'll take you to Bike Man after breakfast."

"Bike Man?"

"He's the guy to see for a new bike. His prices are great. Just don't ask where he gets them."

"Why?"

Daws's head bobbed and toggled on his neck. Tiny pinpoints of light from the chandelier danced all over his face, making him look as if he were in a disco, grooving to a tune. "Hey, man, this is China, ya know?"

My next bite of steamed roll brought me to the center. It was filled with a sweet, sausage-like concoction. Some of the pork looked undercooked.

"How long have you been here?" I kept chewing, not daring to swallow.

"Since April." Daws explained that he had been downsized at his previous company, had come to China to spend his severance package, and had fallen into the new job a few months ago.

"The money's good and I figure as long as I'm still not tied down, it's a good time to hang here."

I wondered if "not tied down" meant no girlfriend or no boyfriend. Daws was from Denver, a city as foreign to me as Beijing or Bratislava—both in general terms and in its particular gay manifestation. I pulled a few thin paper napkins from the dispenser on the table. The first one immediately dissolved in my sticky fingers.

"I'm actually thinking of staying a while," Daws continued. "Maybe start my own company. A buddy of mine thinks we could do really well with a limousine service. There's some big bucks to be made here, man."

His eyes followed an attractive Western girl who was walking past our table. Before he could turn back to me, I spat out the rest of the pork filling into a wad of paper napkins.

By the time Daws and I had finished breakfast and had left the cafeteria, the campus was alive with students. As we walked toward the main gate, the bellowing voice on the P.A. system broke through the air once more.

"What *is* that?"

"The messages of the day." Daws was adjusting a pair of designer sunglasses tinted a deep metallic turquoise. "A little light propaganda. You get used to it."

"Do you speak Chinese?"

"Enough. I took some lessons when I first got here. But you don't really need Chinese. They all want to speak English."

We had reached the gates of the university. Once again, I was struck by how young the guards were. Toy soldiers was all I could think of. Inside the sooty gloom of the guardhouse, I made out a couple of the boy guards, wearing only undershorts, washing their faces from a plastic basin.

"Hey!" Daws called me back to attention. "This is the East Gate. *Dong menkou*. Learn that. You'll need to tell the taxi driver which gate you want when you come home late at night. The cabbies are supposed to know English, but it's a joke, like a lot of things around here." He pointed through the gate. "And that's Xinjiekouwai. It's kind of a major north-south street in this part of town. Runs down to the Second Ring Road and up to the Third."

This seemed like information I should try to retain, but I was too distracted by all the activity on the street. What had been a deserted, ghostly road the night before was now transformed into a crowded, bustling market. And everyone, *everyone,* was Chinese.

We had to walk slowly, weaving through the hundreds of people jamming the sidewalk. Most of them were pressing up to the rows of display tables piled with merchandise that lined the way. When I could catch a glimpse, I saw stacks of goods—clothing, hardware, appliances, electronics, household items—ready for the picking. A lot of the stuff came in colors that I associated with low-class discount stores back home: hot pink, apple green, margarine yellow.

We continued along. There were cobblers, fruit and vegetable vendors, bicycle repairmen, locksmiths and key makers, and all manner of tinkers squatting on tiny benches, their heads bent over ancient-looking tools. Smoke from countless charcoal braziers clouded the air; the aroma of grilling meat was everywhere.

"I wish I'd remembered to bring my camera."

Daws turned around. The glare off his metallic sunglasses and the scoffing grin that smeared his face made him look like an enemy alien in some sci-fi movie.

"In about two days, the charm wears off. Then it's just a fucking nuisance. The third time you see somebody cough up a looey or blow their snot onto the sidewalk . . . well, it's nasty, man."

We hadn't moved more than a few blocks when we came to a place where the sidewalk was so crowded that we had to stop altogether. Daws turned around again, his face practically in mine.

"They're supposed to have a one-child policy in this country. Think of it." Although it was clear that no one understood a word he was saying, quite a few people turned to stare at us. "And tell me how many dogs and cats you see on the street. Have you seen even one yet? You won't, man. Know why?" The grin on his face was fiendish.

"Let's walk out in the street," I suggested. My stomach was acting up again.

We sidled our way past two shoe repairmen, each seated on a little squat stool. They were carving new heels from tiles of thick, black rubber. As we passed, they stopped and stared at us.

"What do you think would happen if we gawked at them like that back in America?" Daws asked.

At first the street, though less clogged with pedestrians, didn't seem any safer. In the center and far lanes, taxis and buses plied their way slowly down the wide avenue, tooting and honking at every chance. But it was in the near lane, where we were trying to walk, that the congestion was fiercest. Here bicycles and three-wheeled pedicabs piled high with sacks and crates and bales hustled along, a convoy of tottering, wobbly vehicles. Having abandoned hope that Daws knew what he was doing, I started to dodge the bikes as they sped toward me.

"Don't try to anticipate what they're going to do," Daws said. "Just keep walking. Let them dodge you."

I didn't believe him, but when I tried it, feeling a little like a man walking into machine gun fire, it worked. The bikes swerved around us.

At that moment, I noticed two young men coming toward us. Dressed in pea-soup green military uniforms, they were holding hands. Daws glanced over at me.

"Fucking weird, huh? Don't worry. They're not gay. A lot of guys hold hands in China. It's just one more thing you learn to live with. The first time I saw it, I kinda freaked out." He took out a handkerchief and blew his nose. "That's another thing," he added. "Your snot gets really black here. It's the pollution in the air. Really foul."

We moved back onto the sidewalk. In addition to the shops and outdoor stalls, there were also several restaurants along this stretch. In front of one, a large, woolly ram was tethered to a tree. He was placidly eating out of a little tin trough that had been fashioned from an empty cooking oil can. His fleece was beautiful—thick and white—one of the cleanest things I'd seen so far on the street.

"That's a Uighur restaurant," Daws said.

"A wee what?"

"Uighur, Uighur. They're kind of like Turkish people. From somewhere out in the west of China. There's a lot of them in Beijing. Great food, especially if you like lamb."

I thought of shish kebab sizzling on a skewer. I thought of well done meat. I thought of germs seared by fire. Suddenly Turks seemed like such a reassuringly Western people. I made a mental note to come back here for dinner as soon as I felt better.

At the next alley, Daws turned in.

"Bike Man's up this way. Come on."

The alley was nothing more than a narrow corridor running between two rows of grimy, gray brick houses. The ground was littered with corn husks, cabbage leaves, and the rotting rinds of fruit; aromas that were lost among a host of other smells: charcoal, kerosene, urine.

"Act cool," Daws said.

I followed him down the alley. It felt as if a thousand of pairs of eyes were following us. Suddenly, Daws halted.

"Be right back," he said. "I need to take a piss. That breakfast beer goes right through me."

He had stopped in front of one of the brick buildings. Above its two doorways, I recognized the characters for man and woman—*nan* and *nü*—two of the first characters Mrs. Duan had taught me.

Although the stench was revolting, I thought that if I moved my bowels maybe I'd find some relief from the cramps in my stomach. But as soon as I followed Daws into the men's side, I knew I had made a mistake. The room was putrid with the odor of excrement. The only light came from a couple of small windows, air vents really, high up near the cobwebbed beams of the roof. Slowly my eyes adjusted. The whitewashed walls were streaked with yellowish-brown stains.

Daws was already standing at the trough along the streetside wall. Behind him, against the opposite wall, were the squat pits, a row of four or five of them. In the dim light, I could make out a mound of shit in each opening. In the far corner, a man was hunkered down over one of the holes, his arms clasping his knees. At first I thought he had fallen asleep, but he looked up, momentarily took notice of me, then returned to his meditations.

"I'll wait for you outside," I told Daws.

"Hold up," he said. When he turned around to zip up his fly, I caught a fleeting glimpse of his penis. Maybe I was feverish, or sleep-deprived, but the notion hit me that his might be the last cock I'd see, other than my own, for a whole year.

Back in the alley, we walked on. Blessedly, the smell of the public toilet began to dissipate. We passed a few more food stalls. People were tending braziers, husking ears of corn, measuring out spices. They, too, stared at us as we walked by.

"Daws, you sure this is okay?"

"We're here." He nodded up ahead.

A few yards in front of us, a short, stout man stood in front of a doorway smoking a cigarette. He was wearing a knit shirt buttoned to the neck, a tweed-like jacket, and baggy, pleated slacks—by far the best-dressed person in the alley. When he caught sight of Daws, he let out a smile of recognition, took a final drag on his cigarette and tossed it away.

"Dave, meet Bike Man."

I greeted him in Chinese, but my efforts went unnoticed. Bike Man's attention was entirely on Daws, who, still wearing his mirrored turquoise shades, began to negotiate a purchase.

"One speed, three speeds, or ten?" he asked me.

"Geez, I don't know. Three's fine." Despite the pain in my stomach, I forced myself to smile. There were no bikes to be seen.

"*San,*" Daws translated. Bike Man nodded and disappeared into the gray-brick house behind him.

"Is this his shop?" I asked.

Daws shrugged. "It's where he does business. I guess that makes it his shop."

Bike Man returned, wheeling out a brand new bicycle. Daws smiled.

"Yup, a good, reliable Flying Pigeon. Bike Man's specialty. These things are the Chevies of China."

Daws and Bike Man began the negotiations over the price. I

could tell Daws's Chinese was only a little better than mine, but at least he seemed to know the specific lingo for this kind of transaction. After a few minutes, he turned to me. "Eighty dollars sound okay to you?" In a deadpan tone, he quickly added, "Shake your head no. He can go a lot lower."

I complied. Daws turned to Bike Man and again in halting Chinese explained that I would not pay that much. Bike Man said something to Daws.

"He says he can't go any lower, but that's bullshit. Did your tutor teach you the numbers?" I nodded. "Tell him forty."

"*Sishi,*" I said, as forcefully as I could. In addition to my queasy stomach, I was now beginning to feel feverish.

Bike Man scowled and countered with seventy, scissoring his hands in front of me to indicate that this was his absolute cutoff price.

"Don't buy it," Daws mumbled, all the while nodding and smiling at Bike Man.

"*Wushi,*" I said. Fifty. At this Bike Man let out a protest, hurtling what I took to be a barrage of Chinese swears and insults at me.

"I know, I know," Daws agreed, trying to placate him. "Rich Americans trying to screw you out of every *mao* you're worth, you poor bastard."

"Daws, why don't we do this another day?"

Daws ignored me. "He says, sixty-five is tops."

"Good," I said. "I'll take it."

"Not so fast," Daws said, feigning a neutral, chit-chatty tone. "I know he can go lower. Dave, the guy's practically making one hundred percent profit as it is. Just tell him no and walk away. That's the way to force his hand."

By now I was feeling quite sick. All I wanted was to get back to the dormitory. I kept swallowing hard, hoping I wouldn't puke right there in the alley. I looked at Bike Man and shook my head no.

"My friend no pay that much," Daws told him. "He say, '*Tai guile.*'" He threw his hands up—"Nothing I can do, man"—and began to walk away.

Bike Man muttered to himself and began to wheel the bicycle back into his shop. I caught his eye.

"Duibuqi," I apologized, my voice barely above a whisper. I don't know if he understood me or not, but he now directed his angry muttering at me. I raised my hand goodbye and hustled after Daws, who was already halfway down the alley. Every eye seemed to be staring at me with accusatory glares.

"The corruption here sucks," Daws said, when I caught up to him, "but you have the play the game; otherwise you get screwed."

Suddenly, we heard Bike Man hailing us back. Daws stopped and grinned at me.

"What did I tell you? Now turn around slowly. Don't look too eager."

"Wushiwu, wushiwu." Bike Man was nodding his head and holding up both hands, splaying out five fingers on each. He had already wheeled the bike back out to the alley.

Daws slapped me on the back. "Way to go, man. You got it for fifty-five."

We walked back up the alley. Bike Man kept nodding and smiling. *"Haole, haole,"* he called out.

Daws patted the bike. "So, not bad, huh?" He turned to Bike Man and they began negotiating again.

"Now what?" I asked.

"I'm just making sure the deal includes a bell and a basket." Bike Man nodded agreeably. "See how friendly they get when they know the money's coming? Get out your wallet."

"Damn. I haven't changed any dollars yet."

"No sweat, man. He doesn't want *kuai* anyway. He wants American bucks." Daws turned to Bike Man. "Right, my friend? *Meiguo qian.* American dollars?" He rubbed his fingers together.

I pulled out my wallet and counted out the money. Bike Man nodded his pleasure as I handed over the bills. He folded them into his pants pocket, then pulled out a packet of cigarettes and offered me one. I shook my head.

"They all smoke here," Daws said. "It's a fucking lung cancer epidemic waiting to happen." He poked the handle bars with his finger. "Hey, don't forget." Bike Man nodded compliantly.

"How about a lock?" I asked Daws.

"It comes with the bike." He snickered. "Nine million bikes in this city and they still steal them." He patted the little metal platform constructed over the back wheel. "And this is where a passenger can sit. "I've seen two, three, four Chinese riding on one bike. I tell you, they're crazy here, man."

When Bike Man finished attaching the bell, he jingled it twice and proudly handed over the bike to me. We shook hands and said our goodbyes.

"He knows a good thing when he sees it," Daws said as we made our way back down the alley. "He keeps his prices low and I keep bringing him more customers." My stomach clenched up tight, and I grimaced. "Hey, you all right, man?"

"Bad stomachache."

"It's that soup you had this morning. I don't touch that shit. Probably everything from yesterday went into it." He pulled out his wallet and handed me a card. "Look, I gotta get to work, but call me sometime. I'll introduce you to the ladies." Adjusting his sunglasses, he turned toward the Third Ring Road and disappeared into the crowd.

By now I was feeling too woozy to ride. Leaning on it for support, I pushed the bike forward, not caring about anything—the crowds, the staring, the smoky air. I just wanted to get back to my room as quickly as possible. My head was throbbing, my shirt soaked with sweat. I tried not to look at anything that might aggravate my nausea. The cheap plastic goods on the display tables seemed like the safest thing to focus on, but when I thought of the smell of new plastic, my stomach roiled again.

"Christ," I groaned, bending over and squeezing my eyes against the pain.

I pushed on. The cramps in my stomach eased up, enough so that I found I was again taking an interest in the activity all around me. Several yards ahead, I caught sight of some sort of arts and crafts display that had been set up on the sidewalk, something I hadn't noticed when Daws and I had passed by earlier that morning. It looked to be ceramic ware—an artisan's work, not mass manufactured—attractively laid out on a carpet.

Two large pieces in particular caught my attention. One was ovoid in shape, like a huge ostrich egg, and painted with the most lovely opalescent glaze. In shape and color it reminded me of the abstract ceramics I'd seen in galleries back home, pieces by well-known modern potters that went for small fortunes on Newbury Street. The carpet was spattered with the potter's colors, red mostly. The other piece lay nearby. I couldn't quite make out what it was supposed to be: a large cup? a mask?

I moved forward, trying to get a better look. Just then, someone jostled me and my bike nearly tipped over. When I regained my equilibrium, the ceramics had disappeared and in their place were the pearly gray stomach and severed head of a ram, the one I'd seen placidly eating earlier that morning, lying on its own bloody fleece.

My innards heaved. I felt faint. A gagging sensation took hold in my throat. I looked down the street. The university was several blocks away. I didn't think I could make it back to the dorm in time. I remembered the public toilet near Bike Man's shop. I swung around, raced back up the alley, threw my bike against the wall of the WC, and hurled myself inside. My stomach gave a final heave. I wretched and spilled my guts into the trough.

I watched it coming up, wave after wave, studying the contents of my belly with morbid fascination. I recognized food from my multiple meals on the plane, the pork and Coca Cola from breakfast, even the morning's pink antacid tablets. All of it, every bit, I let go. And just when I thought there was nothing left to puke, my stomach lurched once more and I vomited again.

At last, I felt my body relaxing. I pulled out my handkerchief and wiped my mouth. In a corner, I spotted a grimy plastic pail filled with water. I dipped the handkerchief in. The water was surprisingly cool. I dabbed the wet cloth on my forehead. It was then that I noticed a figure squatting in the gloom: the man I'd seen earlier, his arms still resting on his knees. He was looking at me with the same impassive reserve on his face.

We stared at each other, he hunkered down over his foul hole, I standing a few feet away in the dusky light. I felt that I should say something, acknowledge something, but I didn't know what. As we continued to look at each other, I became aware of a tremendous silence in the room. A familiar silence. One I associated with two other times and places in my life: the silence of the pews in church during Saturday afternoon confessions when I was a boy; and, much later, the silence of the sauna at my gym in Boston, especially on those evenings when it suddenly becomes obvious that everyone there is gay but all you do is keep still and wait . . . *for what,* I used to wonder.

I must have still been a bit feverish, because at that moment, in the eerie silence of that public toilet, all I could think to do was to put my hands together, palm to palm, and bow my head towards him, my companion in the WC. At first, he didn't move, didn't even blink, just kept his eyes fixed on me. Then, all of a sudden, he nodded back, a barely perceptible motion, almost shy.

Instinctively, I felt the urge to flash him a smile—the good old American-boy smile that I'd packed along with my gum and condoms and ten starched shirts. But something told me no. A smile seemed superfluous just then, seemed, in fact, like something I could finally drop. I put my hands down, turned, and left.

Outside, in an alley flooded with sunlight, my bicycle was still there, leaning against the wall, right where I had left it.

Autumn

Chapter Six

I spent my first weeks in Beijing concentrating on my job . . . or rather *trying* to concentrate. But even inside that air-conditioned, antiseptic cocoon of the building where I worked, China would not let me go. It was everywhere, distracting me, seducing me, undoing my attention. In every detail of the office: there was China. In the size and feel of the paper we used, in the brand of spring water in the cooler, in the covered cup of tea that arrived at my desk every morning and every afternoon, delivered by "Auntie Chen," the housekeeper. China was in the telephone lines that sometimes didn't work, in the electricity that periodically failed, in the elevator that would be fixed tomorrow, and tomorrow, and tomorrow. It was in the illnesses and complaints we treated, in the pharmaceuticals we dispensed. Most of our patients were from the West, but it was China—in their stomachs, their noses, their throats, their lungs, their blood—China that they brought with them, day after day, into that clinic.

Even more so, outside, every time I left the office, there was China, walloping me. Everything I saw, everything I smelled. Everything I heard, tasted, touched. It was all China. I couldn't get away from it, not for a minute. I was going through rolls of film like crazy, thirty-six exposures in a matter of minutes. China. China. China. I felt like a kid with Attention Deficit Disorder. Everything seemed worth taking in: the imperial grandeur of the Forbidden City, the bleak austerity of the workers' housing complexes. Precincts of crumbling, gray-brick houses in the old *hutong* neighborhoods; ancient temples and stately bell towers; sleepy canals and bustling markets; trash receptacles in the shape of pandas and foo dogs; bird cages hanging in the trees; Swiss cheese–like cakes of charcoal piled high on the sidewalks; pickled snakes in jars; pedi-carts loaded to toppling with sofas, persimmons, bales of waste paper, boxes of appliances, crates of quacking ducks. I saw vegetables I'd never seen before, trees I'd never seen before, combinations of colors I'd never seen before. Even the gleaming international five-star hotels, all cream and pink and chrome—even they seemed exotic, foreign, written in a language I barely comprehended.

After a week, I left the camera at home. There were just too many shots. Too many buildings, too many street scenes, too many people. And still I couldn't get enough. I deliberately chose to ride my bike everywhere I went, letting myself be swept along in the steady, rivery rush that was Beijing traffic. I ate at a different restaurant every night, ordered different foods every night. I shopped for things I didn't need, just to be able to practice my Chinese. And when no one understood me, I altered my tones and tried again.

People were everywhere. It was hard not to think of the streets as infested with people. Tinkers and street food vendors, hawkers and shoppers, students, laborers, policemen, delivery men, shopkeepers, refuse haulers, street sweepers, women who sold you tickets, women who collected your tickets, bands of pensioners doing their morning exercises, others inexplicably banging on cymbals and drums. Everyone moving, crowding, pushing, swarming, hustling, staring at me. There were old people, their features as ancient and beautiful as craggy mountains; young people with broad, trusting smiles and unthinkably slender waists; businessmen, cell phones to their ears, decked out in Chinese knockoffs of Gucci and Armani; soldiers, some not much older than boy scouts, others with looks as menacing as Mongols, guarding who-knew-what in their goose-turd green uniforms; and children, children everywhere: infants, toddlers, youngsters, street urchins. Everywhere. Bicycles everywhere. Scooters everywhere. Dust and pollution everywhere. Bulldozers everywhere. Cigarette smoke everywhere. Exotic aromas, exquisite perfumes, appalling stenches. Everywhere. The *publicness* of everything, everywhere.

"A splendid, atrocious, amazing, horrific, charming, awful, wonderful, bewildering place," I wrote in my first letter to Owen. "Think of the scene in Provincetown during Carnival Week and multiply it by a factor of a million."

Provincetown had been on my mind a lot. I kept remembering the light, how clear and clean and sparkling it was there, especially in September. I thought about the summer vacations Johnny and I used to take and how, after he died, Owen and I had made a trip out to the dunes at Herring Cove to scatter his ashes. I thought, too, about how easy it was to find sex in Provincetown.

I began to explore the university. It was a spacious, walled-in campus, several city-blocks square, crisscrossed by scores of classroom buildings, dormitories, labs, gardens, athletic courts and other facilities. Some of the buildings were new, high-rise structures; others built at the beginning of the century sported tile roofs and quaint, shuttered windows. Telephone poles and rows of trees, their trunks whitewashed to a uniform height, lined the streets and avenues. In effect, the place seemed like a town—a quiet, shady, intellectual town—in the heart of the vast, dusty, buzzing metropolis. I found the university convenience store, the post office, the barbershop, even a restaurant, where the food was better than in the cafeteria. The second time I tried it out, David Dawson was there, presiding over a table of sweet Chinese coeds, giggling and laughing at every word he uttered. I turned and fled.

Evenings, I sometimes went to the library. It was a modern, carpeted building, full of plants and easy chairs and six stories' worth of books I couldn't read. I brought my own book, *Moby Dick,* a copy I had found at an English-language bookstore on the Jianguomen, but after a few pages my eyes would start to wander. Even here, there was too much to look at, especially the boys studying at the nearby tables. I kept hoping for signs of cruising, but the library seemed as chaste and wholesome as a nunnery.

On other evenings, when the weather was mild, I'd set out on my bicycle to explore the farther reaches of the campus. The grounds were poorly lit. There were lots of dark, secluded places that, back in America, would have nicely served as nighttime haunts for gay men.

One spot in particular seemed quite promising. It was a small plaza, the size of a basketball court, nestled between a few academic buildings and a grove of ash trees. Half of the plaza was taken up by a long, vine-covered pergola, under which a few picnic tables and cement benches had been placed. During the day, students would go there to read, write letters, sit and talk with friends. At night, it was deserted: too dark for reading, a little too remote for passing foot traffic. *Ah ha,* I thought. But after my third evening visit, I gave up hope.

Once, though, on a particularly humid night, after a long, sweaty ride through campus, I stopped to rest by a compound of dormitories. This was the "low-end" section of campus, the housing for the poorest students. Their quarters were like barracks. The cement walls were crumbling. There were no shades or blinds on the windows. When I looked inside, I could see rows of cots and bunk beds where young guys in nothing but undershorts were lounging about, studying. Some lay on their backs, their heads propped up on flimsy pillows. Others were on their stomachs, the thin cotton of their shorts hugging their small, firm buttocks. A few lay side by side, sharing a single bunk. Hidden by the shadows, I stood for the longest time, peering in at this bivouac of undergraduate boys. I studied their bodies, their lean arms and legs, their delicate fingers, their pale, smooth skin.

David, you are forty-nine years old, I reminded myself. *This is not why you came to China.* I went back to my room and read another thirty pages of *Moby Dick.*

———

It was about a week later, toward the middle of September, that I finally landed some reliable information about the one aspect of Beijing life that had, up until that point, eluded me. I'd gone down to the university cafeteria for breakfast. (By then, I knew what time Daws showed up and always made sure to have my own breakfast a half hour earlier.) I often ate alone, preferring to start the day quietly reviewing vocabulary flash cards. But as I brought my tray of food into the dining room, I caught sight of a guy eating alone. Something told me to join him.

He was a Westerner. His name was Ross. He was from Baltimore. He was wearing a little gold lambda on a chain around his neck.

"My boyfriend used to wear one of those," I told him.

Ross smiled and fingered his necklace.

"I've been here ten weeks and you're only the second person I've met who even knew what this was."

He was a chubby, jolly, likable guy, the kind who would have made a great buddy that year. Unfortunately, he was, that very day, on his way back to the States after a summer of language study. I asked him where guys met on campus.

"No where." He shook his head gloomily. "Not that I ever discovered."

"Anywhere?" I asked.

"You've checked the gay travel guides, right?" I nodded. "Pretty discouraging, aren't they? They all mention Dong Dan, of course, but stay away from that place. A lot of shady characters lurking about there. Money boys." He laughed. "I only went once. You're supposed to stand around, leaning against a tree with your legs crossed. That's the signal. I felt like I was back in the nineteen-fifties."

As we talked, Ross scribbled down a few other suggestions on a half sheet of notebook paper.

"There's a disco that's supposed to turn gay late at night, and the Ta Ta. You've heard of that?" No, I said, I hadn't. "It's the one gay bar in town. Tucked away. Kind of hard to find. And this one . . ." He pushed the paper toward me. "It's another park, a smaller one. Not very many people know about it. Not so sleazy as Dong Dan. I don't know if you're into meeting guys in parks." I tick-tocked my head back and forth. Ross smiled. "Anyway, it's what works here."

"Is it safe?" I asked.

Ross shrugged his shoulders.

"The police occasionally breeze through and pick up guys for 'hooliganism'—that's the excuse they use here to shake you down and make some extra money—but I think it's pretty safe for Westerners. The authorities don't want to risk an international incident."

I folded up the scrap of paper and tucked it deep inside my wallet.

A week later, on a beautiful, late-September afternoon, during a lull in the day's business, I spread out a map of the city across my desk and located the park Ross had told me about: an easy ride on my bike and, happy coincidence, directly on my usual route back to the university. Through the window across from my desk, I could see the first phalanx of workers peddling home. As they maneuvered their bicycles through the traffic, the expressions on their faces remained still and focused, like Buddhist monks in meditation.

Just then, Auntie Chen came in and set down the afternoon cup of tea.

"*Xiexie,* Auntie. Thank you." I lifted the lid off the cup and took a sip.

"This new tea," she said. "I don't think you know."

"Delicious."

Auntie's name was Chen Lili, but everyone at the clinic called her Auntie. She preferred it herself. She was Winston's mother. Her husband, Zhou Xiaohe, was a professor at the university. The three of them lived on campus in faculty housing. In fact, it had been Auntie who had arranged for my quarters in the dorm when it became clear that my apartment wouldn't be ready until later that fall.

"So, how's Winston, Auntie?"

She shook her head.

"Too much with women. All the time. Go out every night. My husband very angry."

"Well, Winston's still young."

"Not young!" she insisted. "Twenty-nine years old. Time to find wife, make family." She shook her head again, a look that seemed to express as much dismay with me as with her son.

Auntie and I actually got on quite well. All that first month, I'd let her be my mother. She'd brought me moon cakes and almond cookies from home, stitched a broken strap on my backpack, taught me proverbs in Chinese. I had come close to telling her I was gay, but decided to wait until I knew her better. In truth, I was more anxious about Winston's reaction than hers.

"Always running around," Auntie continued. "He love one girl two weeks, love another girl two weeks." She glanced at the map on my desk, then back to me. "I teach you another proverb. Listen. '*Du xing bu kui ying; du qin bu kui qin.*' You understand?"

I shook my head. No.

"'Don't be ashamed, you walk alone with shadow; and don't be ashamed, you go to bed with only your quilt.' Understand?" I hesitated. "Person must have heart with no trouble, no shame, even when he walking alone, even when he sleeping alone. This is not Winston. He never walking alone." She paused. "Maybe he not sleeping alone. I don't know. But too much with girls; not enough thinking to get marry."

"We have an expression in English, too, Auntie: 'Give him time.'"

"Time for what, David? He have enough time already, I think." She looked down at the map again, giving it more of her attention now. "Where you want to go?"

"This? Oh, I was just looking for a new route home on my bicycle."

She frowned at me.

"Only one route. I already show you. Very simple. You go another way, you get lost. Get into trouble. No, you take route I show you." She motioned to my cup. "You want some more tea, David?"

"No, thanks."

"Well, okay, then I going home." She looked at the map one more time. "When I was young, Beijing very safe. Now, not so safe."

"Don't worry, Auntie."

She looked at me. I had the guilty feeling she was not convinced by my assurances to her. "Okay," she said, "then I see you tomorrow. *Zaijian.*"

"*Zaijian,* Auntie. And say hi to Winston for me."

"If I see, I say hello," she called back as she disappeared down the corridor.

I looked out the window again. The sky was bright blue and smog-free, a glorious, late–September afternoon. Since I'd arrived in Beijing, we hadn't had many days like this. I took a last gulp of tea and made a bargain with myself: I would only ride by the park, just to check it out. *And if you do go inside, you will not stand there with your legs crossed.* I grabbed my backpack and went to the staff room to wash up.

Tyson McClennen, one of the doctors, was seated at the lunch table reading a newspaper. He looked up, peering above his half glasses.

"Sounds like Auntie's been giving you an earful, Mate."

"Yes, she's quite the Chinese mama, isn't she?" I went to the sink and turned on the water. "I don't know how these Chinese boys do it, Tyson, living under the eyes of their parents for so long."

"They haven't got a choice, Mate. Combination of two thousand years of Confucian teaching and wretched communist housing allowances."

Tyson was Australian. I'd always thought the "mate" stuff was just a cutesy tourist industry gimmick, but Tyson really talked like that. He was also a student of Chinese philosophy, a fact I'd discovered when we'd first gone out for a beer the week I arrived.

"So, does Auntie really have anything to worry about?" I shut off the water and pulled a paper towel from the dispenser. Like everything else at the clinic, it was completely different from anything we had back home, pink and stiff and scratchy. "I mean, just how naughty could Winston be? As far as I can tell, no one has any privacy around here."

"Never underestimate the ingenuity of the Chinese, Mate. Where there's a will, there's a way."

I chuckled. "Today must be the day for proverbs. Auntie just taught me one about never being ashamed to go to bed alone. I think it lost something in the translation."

"It usually does," Tyson said. He folded the newspaper and pushed it to the center of the table. "Well, now. How about going out for a pint? We haven't had a proper conversation since that time we had drinks—what's it now?—I make it the week you got here."

I hesitated. Tyson's company would be a lot more pleasant than a lonely trip to a park I knew nothing about. But I'd been carrying Ross's scrap of paper around for a week, and I was determined that this would be the afternoon I'd put it to use.

"Thanks, but I can't tonight."

"Got a date?" Tyson asked.

He meant a gay date. I'd come out to him that first time we had gone out for beers. It was easy to feel you could trust Tyson. He had a face that was both handsome and worn. "Criminal Irish stock," he'd told me. "Sent to Australia for Lord knows what offense to the Crown." In his mid-thirties, with deep blue eyes and dirty blond hair, he'd won me over the first day we met. Even his prematurely wrinkled forehead was attractive, the kind that told you he'd been through a lot, some kind of deep pain. Whatever it was, I could see he'd come out of it a sincere, compassionate person. And a fine doctor. Our regular clients loved him.

"A date? No, not really." I tossed the paper towel into the trash. "I'm going to have a wander through a park." I kept my eyes on the wastebasket.

"Mind if I tag along?

"Tyson, I'm not exactly going to look at the lotus blossoms, if you catch my drift." I turned and looked him straight in the eye. "It's one of those outings that Auntie Chen probably wouldn't approve of."

Tyson opened his mouth wide and gave me an exaggeratedly knowing look.

"Ah, a walk on the wild side, the *Oscar* Wilde side, I presume."

"Yeah, I know it sounds a little sleazy."

"Oh, come on, Mate. I haven't been here for three years not to have learned that it can get pretty lonely for you gay boys."

"Hell, Tyson, I've only been here a month and it's getting pretty lonely."

"All right then," he said. "So it's about time you went out and made some friends, isn't it?"

I chuckled. "Tyson, you make it all sound so chummy."

"And why not?"

"Because in my experience, guys you meet in parks aren't usually interested in becoming chums."

"And yet you go to these parks anyway?"

I shrugged my shoulders. "Hey, what can I tell you?"

Tyson considered this for a second, then nodded his head.

"Well, all right, then."

"All right, *what*, then?"

"Chums; not-chums—I wonder if it's just another one of those distinctions we care too much about."

"Is that what the Chinese say about sex? I mean, what exactly *do* the Chinese say about sex?"

Tyson pursed his lips.

"Well, now, the *Chinese.*" He seemed almost stymied by the enormity of the question. "I was actually thinking about the Buddhists. About what they say about clinging to notions of duality. This and not-this."

I laughed out loud. "Tyson dear, never in a million years would I have guessed that telling you I was going cruising in a Beijing park would gave gotten you onto the subject of 'notions of duality'!"

"Yes, I suppose I am—if you'll pardon the expression—a rather queer one, aren't I?"

"So, tell me," I asked him. "The Buddhists: what is their take on sex?"

"I suppose they think about sex the way they think about anything, Mate. With Right Mindfulness."

He threw me a smile that seemed at once facetious and serious and, yes, a little queer.

"What's *that* mean?"

"Mind you, I'm a novice at this, Davey, but the point, as far as I understand it, is not to let anything—sex, food, feelings, desires— overwhelm your consciousness, become attachments."

"But . . ." I felt an objection coming on, though I didn't know how to put it. "I mean, you're not supposed to *care* about anything?"

"You care in a different way."

"How?"

Tyson pondered this a moment.

"One of the early Chinese Zen sages—this was back, oh, in the Tang dynasty, I guess—he wrote a wonderful poem, the *Cantongqi*. Hard to translate, but it means something like 'The Shaking Hands of Sameness and Difference.'"

I chuckled. "Another one of those expressions that loses a lot in translation, huh?"

Tyson ignored me and went on.

"He writes about learning to see the merit in each of the myriad things of the world."

I was tempted to make another quip, about the "merit" of cruising, but Tyson seemed so intent on explicating the poem that I held my tongue. Closing his eyes, he bent his head down, as if to find something deep in his memory.

"'If you don't understand the myriad paths of your everyday life,'" he translated, "'how will you understand the Way?'" He paused, then looked up again. The expression on his face seemed slightly nonplused, as if finding himself still in the office kitchen were a curious thing. "It's all about ceaseless awareness, Davey."

None of this made much sense. I leaned my back against the sink, a myriad of questions seething inside my skull, but Tyson cut me short.

"So, is it a Chinese boy you fancy?"

All month I'd been imagining it, but I'd never posed the question to myself so directly.

"Yeah, I guess."

Tyson laughed. "Steady now. Let's not go overboard with the enthusiasm!"

I felt myself blushing.

"It's just that I never even considered it before. I never paid attention to Asian men before I got this job."

"That's one of the interesting things about foreign travel, isn't it, Mate? How it uncovers all sorts of prejudices you never thought you had."

"Makes me uncomfortable: knowing that about myself."

"So live with that for a while, that discomfort. Pay attention to what's there. Plenty of merit in discomfort, I'd say." He smiled.

I rode my bike down the Liangmahe Road and then, at Dongzhimen Street, kept going west through a district of old gray-brick quadrangle houses. Just before I got to the Drum Tower, I turned north, into Baochao Hutong. In the month that I'd been in Beijing, this area had become one of my favorite neighborhoods, a district of alleys and *hutongs* where Old Beijing charm had yet to be destroyed. To my left, the sway-backed roofs of the Drum and Bell towers rose above the squat houses and shops. Tall, brown grasses grew in the crevices of the gray-tiled roofs. The woodsy aromas of charcoal smoke and roasting sweet potatoes perfumed the air. The street was thick with traffic, but I'd learned how to get around by darting in and out of the back ways. It was easy and I never got lost. Beijing had been planned on a north-south grid. The "imperial axis" my guidebook called it. All you had to do was find the sun, and you knew where you were.

Not so, in Provincetown. The turned-around geography of the place had always confused me. Johnny and I had spent four summer vacations there, and I could never get it into my head that what the locals called the West End was really on the west side of town. There I'd be, every Friday afternoon, driving east along Route 6, all the way from the Cape Cod Canal, and the next thing I knew I was entering Provincetown from the East End, *headed west*. It was as if I'd passed through some bizarre geographical warp. The explanation was simple, of course: the Cape gradually turns in on itself like a conch shell, curlicuing around—east, then north, then west. But that had always remained just information in my head. Somehow my sense of where the sun should be had always refused to cooperate with my understanding of where I stood.

When I got to the Second Ring Road, I stopped and waited for the light. A narrow canal, paralleling the street, ran along the other side.

"Keep going west, following along the canal," Ross had said, "until you come to a foot bridge. Cross over and you're just about there."

When the light changed, I rode on, just as he had instructed, and in another minute I spotted the gate to the park. I got off and walked my bike in. My heart was pounding, the way it used to when I was just starting out in the gay world.

Just a quick look-see, I told myself.

I followed a winding path the led past rocky outcroppings and plantings of evergreens. People were out strolling. It looked like couples and families. The next bend opened onto a large pond, half drained in the dry September weather, choked with lotus pads. At one end three old men were fishing. I watched them for a few minutes, then moved on, stopping again further along to listen to a band of percussionists who had assembled on the embankment to practice. With breathtaking precision, they were keeping up a tricky syncopated rhythm on their cymbals, gongs, and drums—a fantastic racket that had attracted quite a crowd of onlookers.

I had just reached the far side of the pond, when I saw a young man coming toward me on a bicycle. As he passed, he looked at me, but in a way that was different from the stares I usually got from Beijingers. I walked on a few feet, then turned around. The guy had stopped, too, twisting around on his bike to look back in my direction.

Go for it, Doll, I heard Johnny say. It had been his motto for everything.

Casually (but was this how they did it here?) I walked over to a rocky hillock, parked my bicycle, and leaned against a boulder, pretending to listen to the percussionists across the pond. At first, the guy on the bike stayed put, just staring in my direction. Then he started to slowly ride toward me.

As he passed, we made brief eye contact again. A subtle nod from me. Nothing from him. He pedaled on, then stopped once more. He might have been listening to the percussionists, too. Or trying to appear *as if* he were listening. Being able to distinguish the "as if's" of gay cruising from the genuinely innocent behavior was, I'd learned back home, crucial to success if not to walking away with all your teeth intact. But in a country where so much appeared to be innocent, it seemed impossible to tell the pretending from the truly ingenuous. I eased myself away from the boulder and sauntered toward him.

The cyclist looked to be in his late twenties. His black, lusterless hair was cut short, though not as fashionably as Winston's crew cut. We made eye contact again. I wondered if there was a phrase for "cat and mouse game" in Chinese. Cat and mouse seemed like it might be a direct translation of *something* Chinese.

"*Ni hao,*" I said.

He stopped, smiled. From my perch atop the rock, I was looking down at him. He seemed to be waiting for me to make the next move. In silence, we continued staring at each other.

He was wearing a dark blue suit, the same color as an old Mao jacket, but of a slightly more stylish cut, a white shirt buttoned at the neck, and a pair of soft white leather loafers. Except for the loafers, this might have been the Sunday strolling outfit my Italian uncles would have worn back in the forties.

"*Wo,*" I said, pointing to myself, "*Wo shi* David."

He told me his name, but my ear didn't catch all the sounds. I motioned for him to come join me on the rock. He knocked his kickstand down and began to climb up. I extended my hand and he took it. His fingers were thicker than I'd expected. Coarser, too. He squatted down next to me.

"*Ni hao,*" I said again. In fractured Mandarin, I tried to explain that I could only speak a little Chinese, and asked if he knew any English. No, he told me. We fell silent again, but he kept studying my face.

"Slanted" is the way I'd learned, as a child, to describe Chinese eyes. But his were softer and rounder than that, so lovely in the dark, unblinking gaze he fixed on me.

I eased off my backpack and rummaged around inside. There was a pack of gum in the small pouch. As I offered him a stick, I got the uncomfortable feeling that I was mimicking a scene in some cheesy World War II movie: the GI befriending the natives with sticks of gum. He shook his head, no, then said something to me in Chinese. I shook my head. We both laughed.

"*Pengyou?*" he asked.

"Friends? Do I want to be friends? Of course. *Haode!*"

"*Haode,*" he agreed.

I pointed to myself.

"*Meiguo.* American. *Wo shi Meiguoren.*"

"*Meiguo.*" He nodded his head approvingly.

"Okay," I said. "We've established that much. Now what?"

I pulled out my tourist's phrase book and flipped through the pages until I got to the section titled "Introductions and Occupations."

"*Wo,*" I began, pointing to myself again, "*wo shi*"—I scanned the list with my finger, looking for something that came close to "office manager." Why hadn't I prepared all this in advance? "Secretary" was the best I could come up with. He motioned for me to pass him the phrase book and pointed to a word on the list: *gongren,* a factory worker, a manual worker. I nodded.

We continued passing the book back and forth, "talking" in tourist phrases. So much of what it had to offer was useless here: "How much does it cost to send a letter to the United States?" or "What time does the train leave for Shanghai?" I considered showing him the sentence that said, "Do you have a room with a private bath?" but held off. Sometimes, as we held the phrase book between us, I let my fingers brush against his. He seemed not to mind, or maybe he hadn't noticed. I couldn't tell.

When we had exhausted the resources of the book, he motioned for us to walk. Perhaps up there? He pointed to a little red, pagoda-like pavilion at the top of a small hill.

"Sure. *Haode*."

We climbed up. It was a simple structure, an octagonal frame of posts and pillars topped by an elaborate wooden canopy, the whole thing painted Chinese red, though quite faded now. I glanced up. The underside of the canopy was better sheltered from the elements and so had retained its colors—blue, green, red, white—an intricate parquetry of chevrons and zigzags that formed a colorful, geometric heaven over our heads. There were no benches, so we sat on the railing.

"*Nide mingzi?*" I asked. I wanted to get his name again. But when he told me, my ear still couldn't quite pick up all the sounds.

I reached into my backpack and pulled out a pencil and a small notebook. Making scribbling gestures in the air, I motioned for him to write down his name. As he wrote, I leaned toward him, close enough to smell a faint trace of cheap, overly sweet cologne on his face. That and the Sunday suit made me realize that he'd gone to some trouble to spruce himself up for this solo excursion to the park.

When he finished, he showed me what he had written: three neat, square characters. They meant nothing to me.

"*Pinyin?*" I asked, and mimed the scribbling again.

He hesitated, then took up the notebook once more and laboriously began to write a romanized version of his name. I moved closer, my thigh touching his.

"Wang Yonghai," I pronounced.

A smile blossomed on his face and he repeated his name. His tones were different from mine. I tried again. His smile widened.

"*Ni?*" he asked.

I pulled out a business card and handed it to him. "*Wo.*" I pointed to my name. "David Masiello."

He got the "David" close enough, but my last name threw him off entirely. We looked at each other and laughed.

Just then, my attention went to one of the posts that supported the roof of the little pavilion. There on the faded red surface, former visitors had left messages scrawled in pencil or ballpoint pen, the first graffiti I'd seen in China. Were they love notes? pornography? subversive political slogans? I wondered what exactly it meant that Yonghai had chosen this spot for our tryst.

He took my pen again and wrote out a sentence about ten characters long. I recognized a few of them—the characters *Zhongguo*—middle country. That was China or Chinese. And *ni,* the character for you. That one was easy to remember, Mrs. Duan had said. "You see the scale?" she'd asked me, pointing to the pictogram. "Equal balance on both sides? 'You' in Chinese mean people talking to each other are equal: you and you. Understand?" The final character in the sentence was *ma,* the once that looked like "horse," my name, but which meant you were asking a question.

I looked again, trying to make more of what it said. Curiously, in a sentence that ran horizontally across the paper, Yonghai had written one character, the character for "man," above another character, the one for "woman." *Nan* and *nü.* He was asking me something about Chinese men and women. No, Chinese men *or* women. *Which one?* he was asking. Which one did I . . . what? . . . *like?*

"Men," I said. "If that's what you're asking, I like men. *Nan, nan!* God, do I like men!" I was wagging my head like an idiot. "How about you?" I pointed to him. *"Ni?"* Which do you like?"

He nodded just as idiotically and we broke into fits of laughter.

"You are quite adorable," I said.

"Kuai dou bu le," he repeated.

"A-dor-a-ble." I mouthed each syllable precisely.

"Er dou a bu," he said.

"You. *Ni.* Adorable."

I wanted to reach over and touch him, run my fingers along the sleeve of his blue serge suit, clasp his hands. I wanted to use a different language, the one we had both been waiting for all afternoon. But something held me back. Shyness maybe. It was still daylight.

We were on top of that hillock. In a red pavilion that framed us, like a couple of caged lovebirds, for all the world to see. Caution, too. What if I'd gotten it all wrong, that question he'd written down? It seemed unlikely, but you never knew.

Yonghai glanced at my notebook again. I could see he was considering whether to write out another question, but he looked skeptical. He'd already figured out how little I knew of his language. He turned back to me. The expression on his face was full of patience.

"So, what do we do now?" I asked.

Yonghai shook his head: he didn't understand.

I considered the possibility of inviting him back to my room at the university. I tried to picture it. Then what? What would we do next? Back in the States, I'd had encounters with guys where neither of us ever spoke a word. Late nights in the Fens, under the dock in Provincetown, at the baths. Silent sex, quieter than rutting animals. It was something you were supposed to desire if you were a gay man. It was hot, guys told me. It was a scene. I had tried it. I guessed it was a scene, but not much of one, not for me anyway.

By now, the sun had fallen below the tree line and the air was beginning to turn chilly. Yonghai didn't seem to notice. He just kept looking at me, his face full of unruffled calm. At that moment, he reminded me of nothing so much as a peasant farmer patiently waiting . . . well, for what? For flood waters to recede? For a sow to give birth? For his luck to change? *Talk to me! Tell me,* I wanted to say.

He was still holding my business card. I slipped it from his fingers and wrote down my telephone number back at the dorm. He studied it, then looked up at me, smiling and nodding. In what I recognized to be simple Chinese, he said something. I caught enough to know he was telling me he didn't have a telephone number.

"No problem. You call me," I pantomimed.

But as we sat there, looking at each other, I knew that if I didn't make a move now, I'd never see him again. There was no way that we would be able to arrange a second meeting over the telephone.

I reached over and took Yonghai's hand. He watched me caressing his knuckles, studying the way my fingers kneaded his flesh, concentrating intently, as if I were showing him some intricate knot-tying demonstration. *What's next,* I thought. *What comes next?* I looked up into his eyes. He was still waiting.

"You call me, okay?" I pointed from him to me. "*Haode?* Okay?" He nodded.

We scrambled back down the rocky hill. At one point, Yonghai's feet slipped on the gravel, and I grabbed his hand to steady him. When we got to our bikes, I pointed in the direction I was going. He showed me the way he was going. We shook hands. I searched his face for some evidence of disappointment, some last-minute indication that he wished things could be otherwise. But again all I saw was tranquil resignation.

"*Zaijian,*" I told him.

"*Zaijian.*"

By the time I was back on the main road, it was dark. But I knew the way. As I pedaled along the evening streets, I thought again about those summers in Provincetown, and how confusing the lay of the land was out there at the tip of the Cape. West, east—it was never where I expected it. When friends came to visit, I'd point toward the horizon, trying to show them where Boston was: west, home. But I'd always get it wrong. Three summers—that's what it took for me to finally get the hang of that curlicue, to anchor it firmly in my bearings, not to be surprised wherever the sun happened to be.

Chapter Seven

The next evening, Yonghai called me. As I had expected, we got nowhere on the telephone.

"Hold on, hold on," I kept shouting into the receiver as I rifled through my dictionary, trying to piece together enough words to invite him to meet me back at the park the next day.

"*Yuan, yuan!*" It was the word for park, but, like so many other words in Chinese, it was also the word for a dozen other things, depending on the context and the tone you used.

Yonghai interrupted—telling me, I hoped, that he understood what I was getting at—but the poor connection and my lousy command of Chinese made it impossible for me to make out anything he was saying.

"*Yuan,*" I told him again. "*Mingtian. Liu dianzhong.*" Tomorrow, six o'clock. I was suddenly so grateful to Mrs. Duan for teaching me how to tell time in Chinese.

When again Yonghai said something I didn't understand, I realized just how much we had relied on body language to get us through our first conversation back in the park. So on and on we went, babbling past each other like two toddlers in a playpen. After ten minutes, I gave up. I had to trust that he'd gotten the gist of what I was saying. I repeated it one more time: The park. Tomorrow. Six o'clock.

"*Haode?*" I asked. "Okay?"

"*Haode,*" he said. I could only hope that we were agreeing about the same thing.

The following morning, Saturday, it began to rain, a steady shower that didn't let up all day. I stayed home, writing letters and waiting for the storm to abate. When, around five o'clock, it looked like the rain would continue through the night, I figured Yonghai would call and we would work out a new plan. I got out my dictionary and put together a simple monologue, which I practiced for the next half hour: *It's too rainy. I'll meet you tomorrow at the park. Same time. Six o'clock.*

At five minutes to six, I was still waiting for him to call. Could it be that he was going to keep the appointment after all, despite the downpour? I pictured that calm, tranquil expression on his face. Maybe he was the type who followed through no matter what.

I threw on a poncho and went down to the bicycle plaza outside my dorm. The rain felt like a monsoon. I looked at the brakes on my Flying Pigeon: just how safe was this thing? In the two minutes I was out there, I got soaked. I couldn't imagine that Yonghai would venture forth in weather like this. He'd do what I was about to do: wait until tomorrow and show up then at the appointed time. Or he'd call. Maybe later that night. Maybe in the morning. It stood to reason.

All day Sunday, I waited for him to phone me. Instead of going out for meals, I stayed in, not daring to be away from the phone for even twenty minutes. I subsisted on a tin of crackers and a thermos of tea. At six I was at the park, where for the next two hours, I moped around, fighting off the chilly clamminess that lingered in the air while I waited for Yonghai to show. At eight, I rode back to the university. I swallowed three vitamin C tablets, got into bed and read *Moby Dick* late into the night.

———

Every day the next week, I stopped by the park on my way home from work, hoping to see Yonghai again. I retraced the steps I'd taken on that first visit—the paths, the pond, the rocky outcroppings. I even climbed up to the red pavilion and sat there, like a New England sea captain's wife up in her widow's walk, looking out over the landscape, expecting him to appear any moment. There he'd be, I imagined, looking up at me with that sweet, steady smile of his. But he never came back.

Stupid, stupid, I muttered to myself. *Why didn't you act when you had the chance?* It was the following Friday, a week and a day since we'd met, and suddenly, as I sat on the railing of that pavilion, it was so obvious to me that Yonghai had just been bashful, had been waiting all along for me to make the first move, perhaps had even expected me to make the first move. I pounded my fist against one of the faded red posts. Stupid. Why hadn't I seen that?

Maybe he had been as wary of misreading the situation as I had been. Maybe he thought he had to defer to me, the American. Maybe he just wasn't sure what he wanted to get into, had hoped I would show him. Or maybe—this was the hardest one to swallow—maybe he had picked up on how unsure *I* was that afternoon. Maybe my hesitancy turned him off.

Of course I had wanted to sleep with him. It was so clear to me now. I even had the choreography of it all worked out. He could have followed me on his bike back to the university. Getting him up to my room would have been easy. Lots of the foreign students in my dorm had Chinese friends and tutors. It seemed pretty common for visitors to come and go as they pleased. The young desk clerks didn't seem to pay any attention at all. We could have spent the entire night together. We could have . . .

I rubbed my thumb into a graffito on one of the posts.

Well, what? What would we have done . . . the next morning, the next day, the next week? Once we had slept together, what would have come next? What could possibly have come next? Yes, it had been the right thing to do, not sleeping with Yonghai. I would have merely been using him, taking advantage of that lonely, patient hunger he had brought to the park. I started climbing down the rocky hillock to my bicycle. It was time to get back.

But he did choose to come here, another voice whispered inside my head. *It was his decision. He was loitering in the park, the same as you. It was no accident that you met. He wanted something to happen. Come on, didn't he look like a guy who was savvy to the scene? And you're wondering why he hasn't shown up this week? Probably because he knows a half dozen other places where he can cruise. What do you think: that you were the love of his life? Don't flatter yourself, Cute Boy.*

At the bottom of the hill, I got back on my bike and headed for the park gate, but when I got there, I stopped, turned around and headed back toward the pond. *One more spin around,* I told myself.

The spot where the percussionists had been practicing the week before was empty now. Only a couple of old fishermen stood on the bank, as motionless as figures in a landscape painting, silently waiting for a nibble. There was nothing here for me. I pedaled toward the gate again, then turned around once more. *Just another five minutes,* I told myself. *Maybe you've just been missing each other all afternoon.*

His eyes—those beautiful, black, calm, untroubled eyes. I couldn't get them out of my mind. There was something about them. Something that had nothing to do with cruising. Something that said more than just, *I want to sleep with you.* Maybe he had seen more clearly than I what we both had really wanted that afternoon. And what was that? What *had* I been after?

You would think, I scolded myself. . . . After all the work I'd done to turn myself into a "fully expressed" gay man—the relationships, the therapy sessions, the books and newspapers, the summers in Provincetown, the gay pride parades, the move into the South End, the trips to the gym, the learning to like my body, the learning to like *myself*—after all that, you would think I would have understood myself well enough to know what I wanted.

You just wanted to sleep with him, I said, loud enough that one of the fisherman turned and looked at me.

No, you wanted something more, my other self replied.

What?

To get to know him.

Bullshit. You wanted to jump his bones.

Listen to yourself. Do you like that language? Are you proud of that?

On and on they went, those two quarrelsome familiars, the angel and devil on my shoulders, the yin and yang of my mind. Only on one point did they agree: it was time to go home now. David was chilly, David was tired, David was feeling as gray as this gray, dismal Beijing weather.

———

I was getting ready for bed when the telephone rang. I grabbed it off the hook, nearly knocking over the table lamp.

"*Wei*, Yonghai!"

But it was Auntie Chen.

"Who you think I am?" She sounded amused.

"I was expecting a call from a friend, Auntie."

She chuckled. "You sound very excited for your friend to call. I think maybe this is special friend. You have Chinese girlfriend already, David?"

"No, Auntie. No girlfriend."

"Maybe that's why you looking for different way to go home last week. Take you by girlfriend's house? Huh?"

"Auntie, honestly, there's no girlfriend."

She murmured—I could tell she wasn't convinced—then moved on to the purpose of her call. She was inviting me to dinner a week from Saturday night.

"I make special for you. Okay?"

"Auntie, this is so nice of you! I'd be delighted. Thank you."

"You want to bring girlfriend, too?" she teased.

"Auntie, believe me. No girlfriend."

"Yes, maybe," she said.

To change the subject, I offered to bring something. "I have a hot plate now," I told her. "Maybe I could contribute a dish?"

On the other end of the line, I heard her let out a loud, jolly cackle.

"What, David, already your girlfriend cooking for you?"

———

Monday morning, as she brought a cup of tea to my desk, Auntie shot me a sly, knowing smile. I pretended not to notice, but for the rest of the day I kept feeling her eyes on me, looking for some evidence of the girlfriend she was convinced I had. I suppose she thought it would show: a twinkle in my eye, a lightness of mood. She couldn't have been more off base. What she should have detected was my sadness. But I kept that under wraps. The last thing I wanted was for her to start grilling me again. I could hear it: *Why you so sad, David? Girlfriend no love you anymore?*

On my way home that afternoon, I passed by the park but didn't go in. No sense in torturing myself. I pushed on, an expert now in maneuvering through the rush-hour congestion. When I got to where the Second Ring Road crosses Xinjiekouwai, at the Jishuitan subway station, all traffic had come to a snarled stop. A racket of tooting horns filled the air. From experience, I knew that the light would change at least twice more before I'd get through.

Directly in front of me was a woman on her bicycle. Her young son—he couldn't have been more than five—was riding on the back fender, clutching his arms around her waist. The next thing I knew, the boy had eased himself off the bike and gone over to the curb to take a pee. No one but me paid the slightest bit of attention. When the light changed, we all inched forward. The mother didn't seem concerned that she might lose her son, who was still doing his business at the curb. When the boy finished, he turned around, hustled over to her, and climbed back onto the fender. The light changed again and, with more blowing and honking of horns, we all pushed forward across the intersection.

I kept them in my sight. The boy seemed so young and his balance on that fender so precarious, but I knew he was safe, probably safer than I. No helmet, no safety belt, but he'd be okay. Remarkably so. I'd seen it countless times already: this special relationship between Chinese parents and their children—a kind of mutual, nonverbal cooperation in the midst of utter chaos, like ducks and ducklings moving along a dangerous stretch of marshland. I thought, too, about all the old women I saw every day, dressed in pants and smocks, lovingly babysitting their grandchildren; about mothers deftly wielding a pair of chopsticks to drop morsels of rice into their children's mouths; about grandfathers practicing tai chi with their grandsons. Wherever I went in Beijing, life jostled and jerked and lilted along to the rhythms of family life. Here, in fact, family life *was* life. The only kind of life that seemed to count.

"My lovely boy in the park has disappeared," I e-mailed Owen from work the next day. "Gone. Vanished. I suspect I'll never see him again. In fact, I'm beginning to wonder if I'll ever meet another gay person here. And don't tell me I'm being a drama queen! It's true. I'm living in the Land of Family Values. Everyone, Cupcake, *every-one* seems to be happily going about their Confucian responsibilities. Family is a duty. And now, to top it all off, Auntie Chen thinks

I have a girlfriend. She assumes it, can't see any other possibility! I learned the other day that the Chinese have the same word for *blue* and *green*. They don't make the distinction. That's how I'm feeling right now, like a blue person in a world where there's only the word for green."

For the rest of the day, I kept to myself. I hardly acknowledged Auntie at all. If she was still giving me the cagey, knowing glances, I didn't notice. I left promptly at five. It was October now. The nasty weather and overcast skies had finally cleared. I had the whole evening ahead, though this did not seem like a happy prospect.

When I pulled up to the university, the guard standing duty at the East Gate nodded to me. I recognized him from the few other times I'd come home this early: a handsome young man with high cheek bones and dark, alert eyes.

"Ni hao." I'd never spoken to him before.

A smile lit up on his face. *"Ni hao."* He seemed surprised that I'd bothered to address him.

I smiled back, then I pushed my bike forward toward the bike plaza. *Don't turn around,* I chided myself. When I did, he was still looking at me.

For the rest of the week, I made it a point to get home before six, before the guard went off duty, just to see him. There he'd be, dressed in that regulation baggy blue uniform and policeman's cap, about three sizes too big. He always seemed as pleased to see me as I was to see him. At first we just traded greetings and a smile, but by the end of the week, I was having short conversations with him, awkward, stop-and-go exchanges about the weather or the quality of the steamed dumplings at the street vendor's stand outside the gate.

"Here we go again!" I e-mailed Owen. "I call him my Soldier Boy. It's just a crush, and I know it, but that's what I'm reduced to here. I feel like Gustav von Aschenbach. The only difference is *my* Tadzio keeps looking and smiling and paying attention to me. It's driving me nuts!"

But that Friday, when I got home from work, Tadzio was gone. Another guard was on duty. My heart sank. I'd left work on the late side, and there had been a larger-than-normal tie-up at Jishuitan, but it was still before six o'clock. His not being there seemed as unfair as if all the banks had closed early, leaving me without any means to get through the weekend.

I stopped in front of the guard house, pulled out my guidebook, and began rifling through the pages. I wanted some excuse to wait there. I figured maybe my darling had stepped inside for a few minutes. If I gave him some time, he'd be back.

"Hello, Mr. Davis!"

Startled, I looked up. Winston Chen was hustling towards me. Although we hadn't seen each other since the night he had met me at the airport, I recognized him immediately. He was wearing the same sporty white nylon windbreaker.

"*Ni hao,* Winston!"

His arm was lazily draped around the neck of an attractive Chinese woman. She was wearing tight, black jeans, a frilly top that hugged her ample breasts, and blood-red lipstick over lips sealed in a cold, inconvenienced pout. Her name, Winston told me, was Ling. When I said hello, the expression on Miss Ling's face remained frozen.

"You are looking for somewhere, Mr. Davis?" Winston motioned to my guidebook.

I stammered through an explanation: end of the week, thought I'd check out a new restaurant. Winston turned to his date and translated, but the poker-faced Miss Ling merely stood there, frostily suffering this interruption of their Friday evening together.

"So, it looks like I'll be seeing you tomorrow night," I said. "Your mother invited me for seven o'clock." I turned to the Ice Princess, willing to give her one more chance. "Will you be joining us, Ling?"

The grin on Winston's face collapsed. He shot a quick, anxious look at Ling.

"Okay, thank you, Mr. Davis. Nice to see you, but we have to go now." He grabbed my hand in both of his and shook it nervously. "Very sorry. Too much things to do. We see you later. Goodbye. *Zaijian.*"

He turned to Miss Ling, said something to her in Chinese and hustled her away. I was halfway to the dormitory when Winston came rushing back, panting.

"Hello, Mr. Davis. Excuse me."

"Winston, what's up?"

Fifty yards away, Miss Ling was sulkily waiting.

"Mr. Davis, I think you are my friend?" He looked like a scared little boy.

"Yes, of course, Winston."

"I think, then, maybe it is better if you not say, ah, maybe you don't see me when . . ." He faltered, entangled in the elaborate syntax of his cover up.

"You mean you don't want me to mention to your parents that I saw you with Ling." Winston beamed at me.

"You understanding me, Mr. Davis?"

"No problem, Winston." I gave him the thumbs up. "It'll be our little secret."

———

Auntie's apartment was larger than I'd expected: an entrance foyer big enough to accommodate a small dining table, a living room, an efficiency kitchen, and a hallway, which I guessed led to the bedrooms. Except for a calendar and a cheap scroll painting, the walls, painted a pale, milky green, were bare. It was the same color I'd first seen at the airport the night I arrived. Now that I'd been in Beijing over a month, I recognized it as the interior color of choice in most state-owned buildings.

Auntie introduced me to her husband, Xiaohe. He was a short, sturdy man, perhaps already sixty. Like Winston, he wore his hair in a crewcut, only his was salt-and-pepper, a color that matched the gray cardigan sweater he was wearing. His eyes were bright and lively. He shook my hand for several moments before he motioned for us to sit at the table, where several large bottles of beer had already been set out on the flowery plastic tablecloth. Winston poured.

"Gan bei!" I said, raising my glass for a toast.

Xiaohe chuckled. "David, you learn Chinese quickly."

"No, I'm afraid I'll never learn it well. I'm too old."

"Not old," he objected. "Every day you will learn a little more."

He was the first Chinese I had met who had not directly asked me my age. I liked him immediately.

The beer was delicious, and I quickly downed the entire glass, which earned Xiaohe's merry approval. As he poured me another, Auntie disappeared into the kitchen. Soon she was bringing out platters of food. While we three men ate and drank, Auntie kept going back and forth between the kitchen and the table, delivering courses. At each new arrival, she would stand back, a look of deep satisfaction on her face, watching us dig in. When I insisted she join us, she just giggled.

Winston ate briskly, his head bent low to his rice bowl, shoveling in gobs of food with deft, greedy movements of his chopsticks. He didn't speak a word and interrupted his chowing down only long enough to help himself to more food or to take another swig of beer. He looked in a rush. Whatever the case, Xiaohe took no notice. Instead, he fixed his attention entirely on me, keeping my glass full while asking me question after question about my personal life.

"My wife tells me you are not married."

It was the issue I knew we'd eventually come to.

"Yes, that's right." I guessed what was coming next, so I cut right to the chase. "In fact, I live alone." Winston stopped eating. "In America, most bachelors do. Americans tend to like their privacy."

Xiaohe's face lit up with recognition. "Ah, yes. Privacy." He chuckled. "In China, we have no privacy. We live—I think you have this expression—very cheek to cheek?"

"Yes, very cheek to cheek." I paused to watch Xiaohe pour me another glass of beer and in those few seconds realized I'd probably already had too much. I knew I was going to start saying things I shouldn't, and here came the first one: "In fact, I've noticed how even the guards at the East Gate sleep four or five to a room."

Xiaohe's eyes widened.

"And more than five in the university. In the dormitories, eight students in a room. When I was a student, *twelve!*" He looked around. "A room no bigger than this one." His eyes widened even more. "It's true!" He seemed quite pleased to be awakening me to the facts of cheek-to-cheek living in China. "No privacy," Xiaohe repeated. "Here everything is common knowledge. But not so much a problem, I think."

I didn't dare look at Winston, but out of the corner of my eye I could see him slouching in his chair, staring at the ashtray.

When dinner was over, Auntie brought out a bottle of after-dinner spirits.

"You have tasted before?" Xiaohe asked, pouring me a tumbler full. *"Baijiu."*

I took a cautious sip. The taste reminded me somewhat of grappa.

"Delicious!" I pronounced, much too effusively. I was sure I had betrayed how lightheaded I was.

At that, Xiaohe eased himself up from the table and, without a word, disappeared down the hallway. I looked over at Winston, who was taking a deep, insouciant drag on his cigarette. In my tipsiness, I wondered if he smoked that intensely after sex with Miss Ling. And then I wondered if he ever even had sex with Miss Ling, and if so where they did it. Winston caught me staring at him.

"How's Ling?" I whispered.

He blanched and his eyes darted to a place above my head. I turned around. His father was coming back down the hall carrying a photo album.

"So, now I would like to show you some pictures of my family."

He reached for the bottle of *baijiu* and poured me another tumbler full. Then he sat down, opened the book and pointed to the first photograph, a small black-and-white snapshot of a young man standing stiff and tall in front of an official looking building.

"Do you know this person?" The gleam in his eye gave it away immediately.

"It's you?"

"Me!" Xiaohe squealed with delight. "When I was a student."

"You were very handsome," I told him. "Just like Winston."

Auntie poked her head out of the kitchen. "More handsome!"

I glanced at Winston. He was staring at the ash tray again.

"And this one," Xiaohe continued. "Can you guess?"

"Lili?"

"No!" My wrong guesses seemed to delight him just as much as my right ones. "This is my sister. My youngest sister, Meimei."

As Xiaohe began to expound upon the details of his youngest sister's life, Winston silently offered me a cigarette. I took it, figuring the nicotine might help to keep me awake. Auntie joined us, setting down a pot of tea. I downed three cupfuls before Xiaohe had turned the page.

There were photos of parents, more sisters and brothers, aunts and uncles, cousins, Auntie's family, too, the Chens. Each snapshot had a story, and every story included mention of a marriage, a spouse, children. There were no bachelor uncles, no unmarried cousins. I kept studying the photos, hoping for evidence that even one of the people staring out at me might have a different story to tell—that there might be at least one Uncle Carmine in this family, too—but for as many generations as Xiaohe had photographic proof, his relations seemed an indefatigably straight clan.

For the next half hour, we all continued in this vein: Xiaohe happily lost in his reminiscences, Winston sitting back, morosely smoking his cigarettes, Auntie Chen resting her cheek in her hand, and me tipsily hoping a queer Chen or Zhou might pop up in the family photo album. At last, Xiaohe reverently closed his book.

"As you can see, David, no pictures of grandchildren yet. My son is still looking for the right woman."

I tried focusing on both parents at once. "I'm sure Winston will do his dilial . . . I mean, *filial* duty." Xiaohe reached for the bottle of *baijiu,* but my hand beat him to the glass. I covered the lip. "No more tonight. In fact, I think it's time for me to be going home." Xiaohe nodded sadly.

As soon as I stood up, I felt so dizzy that I thought I would pass out. I was aware of Xiaohe making a speech, something about how much he and his family had been honored to have me as their guest, but all I could do was nod foolishly and pray I didn't collapse on the floor. Then Auntie made her speech—"so happy, so honored"—and again I nodded, adding my own profuse thanks. When all the formalities had been expressed, Winston offered to accompany me back to the dormitory, but I said that it wouldn't be necessary. He insisted and flashed me a covert look.

"Oh, why not?" I gave everyone another foolish grin. As we were about to leave, Xiaohe clasped his hands over mine.

"You are the nicest American we have ever met."

I was so touched, and so tipsy, that I almost leaned over and kissed him.

Outside, the cool night air felt good. Winston pulled me into the shadows.

"Mr. Davis, you can go this way?" For a second I thought he was making a pass at me. "Please, I am going to meet Ling now. I think it's okay you walk alone?"

"Sure, Winston, sure." I touched his arm, partly to steady myself and partly because I wanted to feel the body he had in store for his sweetheart.

"Thank you, Mr. Davis."

"That's two you owe me," I called out as he jogged off into the dark October night.

It was almost one when I got back to the dormitory. When I tried the main door, it was locked. Inside, I could make out the front desk, dark and shut up for the night. I knocked on the plate glass. There was no answer. I knocked again, harder, then pounded with my fist. The only reply was the steady chirping of the crickets in a flower bed nearby.

I thought about returning to Auntie and Xiaohe's. They'd put me up, I was sure. But it would be awkward. They'd want to know where Winston was. I sat down on the steps to consider my options.

The rain that had been threatening all day was starting to come down in a misty drizzle. The possibility of camping out for the night, huddled up against the dormitory, seemed pretty bleak. I banged on the door one more time—still no answer—then headed for the East Gate. I figured one of the guards could help me. When I got there, the night guard was at his post.

I stumbled through the first few words of a sentence I knew I couldn't put together, hoping he'd see the distress on my face and figure out what I wanted. He shook his head.

"*Wo shi . . .*" I began again. I am. *I am what,* I thought. *I am locked out. I am tired. I am totally fucked up.*

The guard stared at me.

"Key," I said. "Key." I reached into my pocket, pulled out my room key and held it out to him. "Key." I pointed in the direction of my dormitory.

"Yaoshi," he said.

"Yaoshi! Of course." I pointed once again toward my dormitory. *"Yaoshi."* The guard shook his head forlornly. Just then, the rain started to come down more heavily. He looked up into the chilly night sky, then motioned for me to follow him.

We went into the guard house office. It was painted the same milky green as Auntie's place, only here the paint was peeling off in large, brittle flakes. From somewhere, the guard produced an aluminum cup, dipped it into a plastic pail of water and offered me a drink. When I declined, he quaffed it down, then said something, which I didn't understand. Putting his hands together, he mimicked resting his head on a pillow.

"Where?" I asked. *"Zai nali?"*

The guard pointed to the room beyond the office and once again motioned for me to follow. It was the barracks. In the darkness, I could vaguely make out the bunks. The air smelled of kerosene, garlic and body odor. The guard spoke, and someone sleepily grunted something in reply. It seemed as if no one was fully asleep. The guard spoke again. I recognized a few words: *student, key.* When he said the word for American, the other guards perked up. A few lifted their heads from the thin pillows. Someone turned up the kerosene lamp. There was a brief conversation among them all, punctuated by some sleepy laughter. Then one of the guards got out of his bunk. We recognized each other immediately. It was my toy soldier.

"Ni hao!"

He turned to his buddies and—this much I could understand—started explaining who I was. I wondered how in Chinese you'd say, "This is the old faggot who flirts with me," and braced myself for some razzing, but the guys merely seemed amused by the whole situation. When he'd finished explaining, my guard turned back to me and patted his mattress, indicating that I should take his bed. I shook my head vigorously.

"No, thank you. This is your bed," I managed to get out in primitive Chinese, but this only triggered more animated discussion among the guards. They seemed confused and upset. My guard began tugging at the sleeve of my jacket, pulling me closer to his bed. Two other guards started arguing with each other. Everyone was talking at once.

"Okay! *Haode! Haode!*" Accepting the offer seemed the easiest way to let everyone save face.

The guards nodded their approval. Again my guard motioned for me to make myself comfortable. His smile was so sweet I wanted to pull him into bed with me. I took off my jacket. It seemed only natural that I should strip down to my underwear—all the guards were in their shorts—but by now I was sporting a boner. I was thankful that I was wearing briefs and a baggy pair of corduroys. I indicated that I was chilly and would prefer not to take off my clothes. This, too, amused everyone.

"Get in, get in," my guard urged me in Chinese.

I looked down at the cot. The sheets were wrinkled and dingy. Gingerly, I lay down and pulled the flimsy blanket over me. The cot smelled like mildew. I took in a few deep breaths, trying to relax. It felt good to be lying down even though I couldn't imagine falling asleep. The animated talking continued—it sounded like another disagreement—and then there was more laughter. I opened my eyes. My guard was making motions for me to scoot over to the far side of the cot. I shot up.

"Together?" I let out a nervous guffaw. "But it's so small. *Xiao xiao.*" I made motions with my hands to indicate how narrow the cot was. It must have come out all wrong, because the guards broke into loud objections. I realized they thought I was unwilling to share. "Okay, okay!"

I eased myself over to the wall side of the cot. With playful impatience, the guard nudged me over even more, then climbed in. More laughter and murmurs of assent rose from the others. The guard settled himself beside me, his body almost spooning around mine. Someone turned down the kerosene lamp. Soon the barracks were silent again.

I lay utterly still, trying to think of anything that would make my erection go away. I was sure that at any minute my body would betray me. The slightest indication on my part that any of this was pleasurable, that I actually *liked* sharing a bed on a dark, rainy Chinese night with a guy half my age—I didn't want to think about how much trouble that would get me into.

My guard stirred, readjusting himself on the cot. I could feel him moving his left arm, first here, then there, trying to find a comfortable position. The next thing I knew, he had wrapped it around my waist, cuddling me in a sleepy embrace. I remained frozen, not even daring to swallow for fear I'd gulp too loudly. Saliva collected in my throat. I thought I might choke. I kept my eyes open, staring at the damp, whitewashed wall two inches from my face. The only sound came from the soft, steady rain shower outside.

Suddenly, a sharp beam of light swept across the room and a voice, loud and angry, detonated in the doorway. Gruff commands. The guards stirring. More commands. Reluctant murmurs. My bedmate got up, grabbed my shoulder, and shook me. Feigning grogginess, I turned over. The beam of light hit me in the eye. I held out my hands to shade my face. More shouting. The flashlight beam moved away, settling just to the side of me.

"What are you doing here?" a voice demanded. Despite the tone of hostility, the sound of someone speaking English reassured me. I moved over and sat at the edge of the cot, better to conceal my erection.

"I'm locked out of my dormitory."

By now an electric light had been turned on. Squinting, I made out that my interrogator was an older guard—a captain, I guessed—with a fat, pasty face.

"Why you lock out?"

"I stayed out too late. I don't have a key to the outer door."

My soldier boy began explaining in Chinese, but the captain yelled at him to be quiet.

"Where you go this late hour?"

I was about to tell him about having dinner with Auntie and Xiaohe—invoking the good name of a university professor might help, I thought—but I decided against involving them.

"Look, I went to a karaoke bar. Is that such a crime?"

"Not such a crime, but you cannot sleep here," the captain growled.

"Fine. I don't want to sleep here." I asked him where he expected me to go.

"I have keys to your building."

"It's the visiting dignitaries' dormitory." I said.

"I know which one," he snapped back. "Please, follow me."

As I got up, I glanced over at my soldier boy. He was standing there, in a sort of half attention, his hands at his side, his eyes slightly downcast. The other guards were standing, too.

"See you later, guys." I spoke in English. It seemed better to try to pass myself off to the captain as someone who understood nothing.

———

It was almost three in the morning before I finally got to bed. I buried my head in the pillow, trying to bring back the smell and feel of my guard, his hand over my waist, his forehead pressed into the nape of my neck, trying to imagine a different way our night together might have played itself out, trying to imagine a different China.

It was so quiet that I could hear the ticking of my battery-powered travel clock, the one I'd bought from a street vendor during my first week here. Even in the dark, I could call to mind the exact color of its plastic case: the same milky green as Auntie and Xiaohe's apartment walls, that color that predominated all over Beijing—on hospital walls, train station waiting rooms, pedestrian crossovers, latrines. More than the deep luscious blue of the Temple of Heaven or the imperial red of the Forbidden City, that homely shade of green was the color I knew I would remember China by. The color of its foreignness. The color, Owen would have said, of a country where homosexuals aren't in charge of anything, even the decor.

Chapter Eight

A week later, Tyson walked into my office and set a fax down in front of me.

"They've finally got an apartment for you. The agency just sent word."

"Yes!" I leaned back in my chair and raised my arms in victory. "No more hot plate! No more cold showers after nine at night! No more being locked out."

"There's just one catch, Mate. I'm afraid it's a bad news/good news situation."

I brought my arms down and looked at the sheet of paper in front of me. Tyson pointed to a sentence halfway down the message.

"Apparently, there's been a mix-up with the flat that we were promised. They say that one's no longer available." He looked at me apologetically. "China, you know."

"So now what? Another month in the dormitory?"

"No, that's the good news." He picked up the fax. "The agency found another place. Nicer one, they say."

"Fine." Tyson waited for me to notice the expression on his face. "But what?"

"It's a two-bedroom. You have to share it."

"Share it? Tyson!"

"I know, but it's the best they can do right now, Mate. From what I understand, you'd have to wait three or four more months for a one bedroom."

"Tyson, this is a huge, international city."

"With too many Westerners wanting to move into not enough quality housing units."

I looked out the window of my office. It was mid-October now and the weather was turning autumnal. I was already sleeping under three blankets and had just learned that the university would not be turning on the heat for another month.

"But I don't know anyone to share an apartment with."

"You don't have to. They already have a fellow in a two-bedroom looking for another person to share." Tyson glanced at the fax. "His name is . . . Stewart Haslip. American research fellow." He looked up. "Another Yank." The look on his face said, *That should please you, Mate.*

"What does he research?"

"Doesn't say."

I shook my head.

"Tyson, I don't know. I was really hoping for a little more privacy."

Although I'd yet to bring anyone back to the dorm, I had begun to visit the park again. Evenings, I discovered, were the best time for cruising. That's when the fishermen, the strolling couples, the percussion ensembles vacated the place, leaving it to those few gay men brave enough to take the chance. In the weeks since I'd met Yonghai, I'd gotten a better idea of the scene. In comparison to what I'd known back home—the ant colony of activity that was the Fens on a hot summer night—the park was pretty tame. The groves of pine trees that I'd noticed on my first visit turned out to be where most of the action took place. It was the usual stuff: furtive, skittish, and quick when it involved sex, though more often than not, a lot of the guys I met just wanted to talk, especially the ones who spoke English. I'd even gone out for coffee with one of them. So far, however, no one had gone back to the dorm with me. That, apparently, was just too risky.

"I'm not asking for a lot here, Tyson. It's just that it would be nice to be able to occasionally entertain a gentleman friend overnight."

"Overnight, eh?" Tyson looked as if he considered the prospect about as likely as a visit to Zhongnanhai, the walled compound where the party bosses now lived. "David, I'm not sure that's an option. This is still a very tightly controlled society, you know. I don't mean to pull rank on you, but I *have* been here three years, and . . ."

Something inside me snapped.

"Then don't pull rank!" I shouted.

We looked at each other, both of us rather startled, I think, not saying a word. Tyson glanced over his shoulder, saw that my office door was still open, and closed it.

"I don't think we need to involve the rest of the office in this, do you?"

I sighed.

"Tyson, I appreciate the perspective you have here, but, tightly controlled or not, this is also a city where gay men are dying to meet each other. They're out there, believe me. I've met a few of them, I've talked to a few of them. They've told me their stories. The loneliness, the secrecy, the anxiety about being found out. The other day, one guy told me that he fully expected to be married by age thirty, because he couldn't imagine displeasing his parents. It's heartbreaking."

"It *is* heartbreaking," Tyson said.

But as we looked at each other, I knew that none of what I had just told him adequately explained why I might want to invite one of these guys home with me. There was a connection, but I wasn't sure that I could explain it, even to myself.

"You know, Tyson, when I first came here, I felt so many things all at once: excitement and confusion and incomprehension and disgust. You went through it, too, I'm sure. Everything you look at is so different, so not like what you know. I felt as if there were a huge proscenium arch between me and all of Beijing, like the best I could hope for was to watch it parade across the stage in all of its bizarre, wonderful, horrendous spectacle. And then I started meeting people—meeting *guys*—talking to guys, and suddenly China, this 'giant mystery of the East'"—I drew quote marks in the air with my fingers—"well, it finally started to become real for me."

Tyson nodded.

"I can't explain it any better, but those guys in the park—the stories they tell me, the way we sometimes just hold each other in the dark—I feel like they're giving me an important part of Beijing, like they're translating China for me into a language I know."

"The language of gay brotherhood, is that it?" Tyson asked.

"Something like that. I don't know. You put a caption on it and it reduces the whole experience to a slogan. But, yeah, I want to connect with these guys, and if that occasionally means sleeping with them, then I'd like to have that option, too."

Tyson glanced down at the fax.

"Well, are you willing to wait until January for the possibility— *possibility,* mind you—of a single?"

I buried my face in my hands. *January,* I thought. November, December, January. Three more months.

"This place they're offering. It does have *two* bedrooms, right?"

"Absolutely. Two bedrooms." Tyson paused. "Only one bath though."

I looked up and shrugged my shoulders. "Okay, that I can handle. What else can you tell me about it?"

Tyson consulted the fax again.

"Eleventh floor of a new building. Twenty-four hour security. Near the Asia Games complex. And . . ." He read directly from the fax: "'Many attractive convenience for Western living style business man.'"

"I don't suppose we could ask them whether this Mr. Haslip has any objections to sharing 'many attractive convenience' with a poofter, could we?"

Tyson took off his glasses.

"This is a Chinese agency we're working with, Davey. I don't think such an inquiry would translate well."

We faxed the agency back to say, yes, I'd take it. The rest of the afternoon was taken up with business about the rent, the lease, a moving date. The agency gave me Stewart Haslip's telephone number. I called him that night.

"Yes, hello there," he said when I identified who I was. "I was informed that you'd be calling. Glad to have a chance to talk to you."

He sounded formal, and old. Older than I.

"I haven't had a roommate in years," I told him, figuring that Johnny and, before Johnny, Erik did not count as *roommates.* "From what the agency tells me, though, it sounds like a big enough place that we won't be getting in each other's way." I wanted to establish boundaries as soon as possible.

"I think you'll find it quite suitable," Mr. Haslip said. "I hear you're a doctor."

I laughed. "My mother would love to hear you say that, but, no, I work at one of the Western clinics here. I'm the office manager."

"Ah, ha."

I couldn't tell whether this was an expression of surprise, disappointment, or just more of Mr. Haslip's clean, efficient way of speaking.

"And you, you're a research fellow?" I prompted.

"In a manner of speaking."

He explained that he was doing research on Chinese music. Back home, in Philadelphia, he was a graduate student in musicology, working on a thesis about Oriental influences on European opera. He'd arrived for the summer, then decided to take a year's leave of absence in order to stay on in Beijing. When his grant money ran out, he'd taken a job with a photocopy and printing business."

"Brochures, pamphlets, name cards. That sort of thing," he explained. "The new entrepreneurial China, you know. It's all about getting a piece of the business pie. Money, money, money. Quite sad, really, what's happening here."

The voice and manner still sounded middle-aged to me, but his biography seemed like that of a younger person. I couldn't quite picture him.

"So, like, *Turandot . . . Madame Butterfly . . .* Are those the kinds of operas you're working on?" I wanted to let him know that I was no philistine when it came to classical music.

"Well, yes," he said, "those are the obvious examples, aren't they? There are several others, of course. Less familiar works for the most part. Stravinsky's *Rossignol. The Pearlfishers* by Bizet. I don't suppose you've heard of an opera called *Lakmé.* It's by Léo Delibes?" I told him I had. "Ah, so you like opera, do you?"

"Moltissimo."

The bit of Italian didn't fetch any reaction. Mr. Haslip went on as if he hadn't heard me.

"My parents have just shipped me a box of my compact discs. Once we're roomies, you're welcome to listen to them, provided, of course, you handle them carefully. People think compact discs are indestructible, but they're wrong."

I had never heard anyone pronounce every single consonant in "compact disc" before.

"You won't have to worry about me," I assured him. "I grew up with vinyl. I'm used to handling records and CDs delicately."

There was a pause at his end of the line, as if Mr. Haslip were mulling something over.

"Excuse me," he said at last. "I realize this is a bit personal, but do you mind telling me how old you are? Your voice sounds fairly young, but you seem more . . . well, quite a bit more experienced than I thought you were."

"Why, how old were you expecting me to be?"

"Somehow I'd gotten it into my mind that you were a young doctor," he said. "Twenty-eight, twenty-nine?"

I laughed. "Add twenty years to that."

"Oh, good," he said. There was a relieved tone in his voice. "I was definitely not looking forward to sharing a flat with some *kid* whose idea of great music is Madonna."

"And how old are you?" I asked.

"Well, you see, I *am* twenty-nine. Thirty in December. But, don't let that dismay you. I loathe the culture of my generation. Yes, let's meet. I think this will work out far better than I expected."

———

The next day, as soon as I met Stewart (he was no longer Mr. Haslip to me), I decided he was gay. You had only to look at the things he furnished the apartment with—the collection of opera recordings, the Qing dynasty tea service, the silk placemats and porcelain candlesticks on the dining table—to see that here was a gay butterfly ready to pop from the chrysalis. I assumed he could pick up that I was gay, too, but he said nothing to that effect as he showed me around the apartment.

"This is quite the view you have," I told him, looking out of the picture windows down to the plaza below.

"*We* have," Stewart corrected. "Yes, I suppose, if you don't mind all the construction going on down there."

I was not physically attracted to him. He was tall and lanky, well over six feet, with pale skin and red hair, my least favorite color, meticulously cut and combed to tame what otherwise would have been, I saw as I studied his face, a mass of unruly curls. Still, I was dying to know if my suspicions about his sexuality were correct.

"I haven't been up this high in a building since I climbed the monument in Provincetown last summer."

Stewart didn't go for the bait. He didn't even seem to register what I'd said.

"Look at that," he continued, pointing beyond the window. "Cranes, cranes, cranes. Everywhere you look. It's shocking what they're doing to this city. Mao knocked down the old walls, and Deng is letting them knock down just about everything else. Anything that's at all attractive or charming seems fair game."

"You like beautiful things?" I walked over to the table and picked up one of the candlesticks.

"Careful," he said. "That's late Ming."

"It's lovely."

"Thank you. Yes, there's a good antique market near the Temple of Heaven. Do you know it?"

I told him I didn't but that I'd love to see it sometime.

"I'll take you there, if you care to go."

Gingerly, I placed the candlestick back on the table.

"My first partner, Erik, loved antiques. We used to go scouting out the antique shops on Beacon Hill."

"Of course, about the only thing you see in the American shops is Canton export porcelain. You'll be amazed at what's available here. Though you have to know what to look for. There's a thriving business in fakes. How about some tea?"

I followed him into the kitchen. While Stewart fixed us a pot, he continued to deliver himself of his opinions about the new China. It boiled down to this: he was aesthetically outraged at what was happening. The destruction of Beijing's cultural heritage, all in the name of progress, was, in his words, "an egregious crime, as barbaric as the bombing of Dresden."

"So why did you decide to stay?" I asked.

He chuckled, the first lighthearted expression I'd heard from him.

"Well you might ask." For a moment, he brought all his attention to pouring the boiling water into the pot. Then he turned to me. "The short answer is that I had more research to do."

He placed the pot on a tray that he had already prepared with cups, milk and sugar, hefted it up, and motioned for me to precede him into the living room. "Take the sofa," he said. "It's quite a bit more comfortable than the easy chair. By the way, I didn't ask you if you had furniture."

"No. Originally I was promised a furnished apartment."

"Well, I guess I'm your man, then. Of course, the furniture is all rented—except for that library table over there, that's mine—but there's even a full bedroom set in the second bedroom."

He poured.

"So, what's the long answer?" I asked as he handed me my cup.

"Long answer?"

"To why you're staying in Beijing." I took a sip. The tea was jasmine.

"Oh." Stewart finished pouring himself a cup. "Well, you know, the desecration notwithstanding, the city does have its beauty. And China is, or at least was, one of the world's great civilizations. There is so much to see here. I haven't even been to the Great Wall yet. Or half the sights in Beijing. I woke up one day and realized I just had to stay a while longer. Maybe for no other reason than to be a witness to the rapid change going on. I'm keeping a rather elaborate journal—perhaps I should say series of journals: I'm working on the third volume already—chronicling my year here. Sometimes I think about dropping the thesis entirely and writing a memoir instead."

I thought of my own abandoned dissertation. It had been over twenty years now since I'd stopped working on it to find myself as a gay man. It occurred to me that my story might be of some use to Stewart, but I decided to hold off until I got to know him better.

"Of course," he continued, "the great time to have been in Beijing would have been at the turn of the century, before the republic was declared. Do you know the works of Victor Segalen?"

I told him I didn't.

"He was a French doctor who was posted here in the final years of the Qing dynasty. Became quite the scholar: fluent in classical Chinese, wrote an important book on the sculpture of ancient China. He also wrote a series of exquisite poems called *Steles,* based on those inscribed stone slabs the Chinese used to set up in the temple courtyards and along the highways as memorial offerings to the ancestors. Segalen wrote *Steles* as his own kind of offering, to China, which he obviously adored. He was here for almost ten years."

"He sounds fascinating."

Stewart put down his cup and began to recite something in French. I was so startled by the shift in language that he was finished before I could refocus my listening.

"It's the first strophe of 'Supplication.' One of the love poems from *Steles.* Do you know French?"

I told him I did, but he paid no attention and immediately launched into an English translation:

"'You will be beseeched with smiles, with looks and a certain languor, with offerings you push away, on principle, you still a young girl."

He stopped, staring out into space. He seemed utterly lost in a dream of another China.

"'You will be beseeched with smiles,'" I repeated. "There's still that about China, isn't there?" I wanted to know if the smiles of Beijing accounted at all for his distraction from his thesis. Stewart came back from his reverie.

"There's a novel, too. *Réné Leys.* Quite autobiographical, in some respects. About his relationship with a young Belgian man, the tutor who worked with him on Chinese."

"They were lovers?"

Stewart's face went sour.

"Good heavens, no!"

"Well, I just assumed . . . you know, the exquisite taste, the rarefied sensibilities."

"Since when is exquisite taste the exclusive province of homosexuals?" he demanded.

"Well, of course not." I hated the meekness that had crept into my voice.

Stewart put down his teacup with the decisive clink of china on china.

"David, I like you, and I think we'll turn out to be a fine pair of apartment mates, but you need to understand that we're not riding in the same rickshaw. I'm not of your persuasion."

"Persuasion? It's not an ideology, you know." I was relieved that at least we'd gotten the issue on the table.

"Fair enough," Stewart said. "But all the more reason why I hope you won't keep bringing up the subject. I know the prevailing stereotype would have it that a heterosexual man cannot love opera and French poetry, but I would think that *you* of all people would understand differently."

I was curious to know what he'd meant by that "you of all people." I had a feeling it had something to do with my age, but I decided to let it rest for now. There would be time enough, I figured, for us to talk about that.

The next day, I moved in.

During our first weeks together, Stewart and I danced an awkward do-si-do around each other. Despite his assertions that he was okay with my sexuality, he managed to find little time to hang out with me. To be fair, Stewart was not a "hang out" sort of guy, but even so, I sensed that he was going out of his way to avoid much interaction. He claimed he preferred to have dinner on his way home from work. He had a favorite restaurant, he told me, a place where he could be alone to write in his journal, a huge leather-bound book— "Volume 3," he called it—that he toted wherever he went. In fact, except for the evening I moved in, when we did share a meal (at which, on Stewart's suggestion, we drew up the "house rules"), we did not eat together at all for the first two weeks I was there. Moreover, once he came home from the restaurant, Stewart would go right to his easy chair, to read or listen to his operas, never to chat with me. Occasionally, I'd sit down to listen with him—*Lakmé* was his current favorite—but he would barely acknowledge my presence. If he did speak, it was more often than not only to remind me about one of the house rules: not to leave personal toiletries on the bathroom sink, not to call him Stew.

Dutifully, sometimes in amusement, occasionally with annoyance, I complied. If Stewart wanted to keep our sharing the apartment strictly on the level of a business arrangement, then so it would be. He was courteous and respectful, and the flat was such an improvement over my grim little dormitory room that I felt I had little to complain about. Still, I kept hoping that he'd let down that screen he had put up between us. His verbal dexterity, his taste in music, his appreciation of Chinese culture—there was so much I liked about him, so much that I felt could lead to a good friendship. What was the point of his holding me at bay? I assumed he was threatened by my homosexuality. But on the few occasions when I dared broach the subject, even just to mention that I was meeting guys, Stewart reminded me that he was not interested in hearing about my "personal escapades," as he summarily dubbed them.

One Saturday morning, a few weeks after I'd moved in, we found ourselves in the kitchen together, a rare occurrence. Stewart was fussing over a pot of tea; I was brewing my weekend coffee. Perhaps he was still half asleep, or maybe he was finally relaxing with the idea of my presence in the household, but in any event he started up a conversation.

"You know," he said, "every once in a while I get homesick for a good scone."

"Raisin," I added. "With lots of butter!"

Stewart turned to me and smiled. He was wearing his brown cardigan sweater, his Saturday dress-down look.

"My parents are sending me a tin of English biscuits, but, oh, a fresh scone . . ." He sounded as dreamy as the Flower Duet from *Lakmé.*

I decided to take one more crack at moving our relationship forward.

"If you're game, I know a pretty good European-style coffee shop on the Sanlitun Road. I think I saw scones there the other day."

The café was called Luna di Pekino, an operatic reference that immediately peeked Stewart's interest.

"You know what that is?" he said, as excited as I'd ever seen him. "It's a line from *Turandot*! Why haven't I heard about this place before?"

Indeed, I got the feeling that it was more out of curiosity about that wonderfully improbable name than because of any abiding interest in being buddies with me that Stewart agreed to go. We decided on an afternoon visit to let the day warm up a bit. It was now the end of October and the mornings were cold.

And so, after lunch, off we went, Stewart with Volume 3 tucked into his briefcase, and I with an aching crush on one of the counter boys, one of the many charms of Luna's that I had not mentioned to Stewart.

With its wide blue umbrellas, Italian coffee and earnest attempts at Western-style pastry, Luna's had been, from the day I discovered it, a favorite retreat. I liked to sit over an espresso or cappuccino and watch the comings and goings on Sanlitun. The street was popular with tourists and the expat community because of all the shops and stalls there that catered to Western tastes. There was even a excellent cheese shop, run by an Italian woman who kept a herd of dairy cows out on a farm in the country. I guessed that Stewart would love her *bel paese,* and I promised I'd take him there after our coffee and scones.

As we sat down at one of the outdoor tables set up on the terrace, a chilly, dry gust of wind blew through, scattering napkins, menus, and the visitor's magazine to Beijing that had been left at each place. I caught the magazine and tucked it under the napkin dispenser.

"What have you heard about the winters here?" I asked Stewart.

"Ever been to Chicago in January?"

"That bad, huh?"

"And extremely dry. The winds blow in off the Gobi Desert."

He reached into his briefcase and pulled out his journal.

"I notice they're selling rabbit-fur hats across the street." I motioned to one of the outdoor stalls along the sidewalk. "Maybe afterwards we should check them out, too."

Stewart turned and looked.

"My parents are sending me a felt-lined knit cap with flaps. It's what I wear back home."

Without another word, he opened his journal and began to write. I waited for him to notice that he'd abandoned me, but Stewart was already lost in his scribbling.

"Well, I think I'll go over and check out those hats after we have coffee. Okay?"

"Sure," he mumbled.

I pulled the visitor's magazine from under the dispenser and started flipping through the pages. Just then, a young Chinese man dressed in an open-collar shirt and sport jacket approached us. He was holding the telltale bulging briefcase.

"CD-ROM?" he whispered.

His pen still to his journal, Stewart shook his head.

"*Bu yao*. Go away!"

Undeterred, the young man looked at me, rested the briefcase on our table and snapped it open. Inside was an enormous batch of CDs in cheap photocopied wrappers.

"Please. Take look," he invited. "Many American musics." He scooped up a handful and thrust them at me. "Twenty kuai."

Ever since I'd arrived in Beijing, I'd been refusing to buy pirated merchandise. But the temptation to look—twenty kuai was under three dollars—was too irresistible. I put down the magazine and began to rifle through the discs. At that, the man walked off the café terrace and leaned against a tree at the curbside: close enough to keep an eye on me, but far enough away to seem divorced from the proceedings lest an officer of the law pass by. I'd witnessed the way it was done on previous visits to Luna's.

Stewart glanced up from his journal and scowled at me.

"David, I wish you wouldn't do that while we're sitting at the same table."

"Here's a Schwarzkopf album." I held it out in front of him.

"I have it," he said frostily, "and I paid the full, legal price."

"Okay, okay." I began stuffing the CDs back into the briefcase and gave the man the signal to approach. His look was so expectant that I hated to deliver the bad news.

"Bu yao." I shook my head.

Without comment, the man gathered up the rest of the CDs and went over to another table, where he began his spiel all over again. I looked back at Stewart; he was scribbling away.

"Writing your impressions of post-Maoist capitalism?"

Stewart put down his pen and shut his journal decisively.

"There are days when I really hate this place." The wind picked up again, ruffling even his tight, fastidious haircut.

"Oh, come on, Stewart."

"The spitting, the pushing, the pollution, the illegal hustling. The *ugliness*."

I glanced back at the pirate merchant. "Oh, I don't know. I'd say that one was rather darling."

Stewart ignored me. "China was one of the world's great civilizations, and now it's been reduced to . . ." He held out his hands, inviting me to consider the size of the reduction. "To this. This crass, in-your-face consumerism."

Stewart rarely used expressions like "in your face." It was a sign that even his meticulous vocabulary could crumble under stress.

The waiter came over and asked if we'd like to order. He was the one I had a crush on.

"Yi bei kafei." I put in a big smile with my order.

"One cup coffee," he repeated, translating my pidgin Mandarin into pidgin English. "Espresso, cappuccino?"

"Cappuccino. And . . . how about it, Stewart, coffee and a scone for you, too?"

"Just coffee, thanks," Stewart said tartly.

The waiter nodded—he seemed confused by Stewart's sulky mood—turned and smiled at me, then went back inside the tiny shop. When I looked back at Stewart, he was slumped in his chair, his lanky arms folded across his chest, glowering at the air. Which suddenly was filled with the sounds of Chinese teenage pop music drifting on silky, sentimental currents from inside the coffee shop.

Stewart picked up a packet of sugar and began irritably flicking it with his finger.

"Lighten up," I told him. "Not everything has to be *bel canto.* Come on, we all have our moments with this place."

Stewart continued to glower. The waiter came back with our cappuccinos and my scone.

"Xiexie," I said as he set everything down.

He gave me another smile and returned to the shop. I leaned back in my chair, cupped the back of my neck with my hands, and, over the teeny-bop music that was still perking away, warbled out, "Hey ho! Hey ding a-ling a-ding!"

"Could you please stop that?" Stewart scolded.

"I thought you liked English madrigals."

"You know what I mean."

"Stewart, if there's beauty in the world, I don't see what's so terribly wrong with showing a little appreciation for it."

I broke my scone in two and offered him half.

"Since when," Stewart said, ignoring my peace offering, "did appreciation and *flirting"*—he twisted the word, wringing it like a wet dish rag—"since when did they become synonymous?" The wind ruffled the umbrella again, and Stewart buttoned up his cardigan sweater. "Why a person of your intelligence and sophistication should feel he has to . . ."

"Stew . . ."

"My name is Stewart."

I paused, giving myself time to sprinkle a packet of sugar onto the foam of my cappuccino.

"Have you ever heard of loneliness?" I wondered if this was the time to tell him the Johnny story.

"And have *you* ever heard of restraint?"

"Restraint!" A woman at the next table looked over at us. I lowered my voice. "What do you think I've been doing for the past two weeks? I have complied with every one of your . . ." I thrust up my hands, ready to parry his objections. "Excuse me, every one of *our* rules. I put the CDs away as soon as I finish with them, as *we* agreed. I don't leave my toiletries lying around the bathroom sink. I let you listen to your operas in peace. And I have refrained from parading my sex life—tame as it is!—in front of you. What have I been if not a paragon of restraintful respectfulness?"

For a few moments neither of us spoke. As I stirred my coffee, Stewart picked up the visitor's guide and sullenly flipped through the pages.

"I'm sorry," he muttered, casting aside the magazine. "You've been a fine roommate. I just think I need a break from all this."

He reached over and picked a tiny morsel of scone from my plate. I nodded toward the magazine.

"Did you see the weekend getaway package they're advertising in there?" I opened to the ad and spread it out in front of him. "'Tour through Hebei province, walk along remote section of the Great Wall, visit to a typical farming village.' You told me you hadn't seen the Great Wall. Here's your chance."

From across the table, Stewart craned his neck toward the ad. The skeptical look on his face reminded me of someone on a diet who has just been presented with a box of chocolates. He pulled the magazine a little closer and read some more.

"Not a bad price either, huh?"

The prospect of having him out of the apartment for a weekend was delicious. Stewart looked up from the magazine.

"So?" I coaxed.

"So what?" he mumbled.

"Why not go? Get out of the city for a weekend."

"What about you?"

"What *about* me?"

"Don't you want to go, too?"

"I thought you wanted to get away from all this. I assumed that included me."

"David, in case you haven't noticed, I actually do enjoy your company. If we're going to be roomies all year, we need to start learning to get along better." He turned the magazine to face me. "Besides, the price of the tour is based on double occupancy."

I shook my head. "Stewart, you sure do confuse me sometimes."

"The feeling is mutual, David." He picked up another piece of the scone. "By the way," he said, studying it carefully before he popped it into his mouth, "I don't think 'restraintful' is a word."

Chapter Nine

Early the next Saturday morning, Stewart and I took a cab to one of the state-run tourist hotels, where we met the rest of our group for the weekend tour to Hebei province. We were nine altogether: six tourists; the minivan driver; our tour guide, a portly, middle-aged fellow named Mr. Chang; and an attractive younger woman, Miss Jiao, who was either Mr. Chang's secretary or his mistress. I noticed that they had arrived with only one overnight bag between them.

Our fellow tourists were a quartet of just-retired Americans, two couples from Indiana, who, almost from the beginning of our outing, pretty much stuck to themselves. I wondered if they'd assumed that Stewart and I were a couple and, if so, whether we weren't being given a homophobic cold shoulder. I looked for some indication that they also disapproved of Mr. Chang's liaison with the heavily made-up Miss Jiao, but apparently those suspicions hadn't entered their minds.

The ride out to the Great Wall took all morning and part of the afternoon. Mr. Chang explained that we were bypassing Badaling, the nearest and most frequently visited section of the Wall.

"My company show you some part that is much more authentic," he promised.

We passed scrubby villages, huge hydroelectric plants, fields and orchards, brown in their late-autumn decay. Mr. Chang kept turning around, feeding us commentary on the passing countryside: statistics about produce, farm yields, the success of Deng's land reforms. At the dot of noon, as if to show off the efficiency of the New China, he announced that it was time for lunch.

We pulled into a bustling, dusty market town, in front of what Mr. Chang called "a typical Hebei province restaurant." In Indiana they would have called it a "homestyle" place. Instead of booths and framed Bible quotations, we had large round tables for ten and a gaudy porcelain guardian spirit high up on a shelf in one corner. No sooner were we seated (under the gaze of every other diner) than the waiters and waitresses, a half dozen of them, began scurrying back and forth, setting dish after dish before us.

One of the Indiana wives asked for a fork, which caused a moment of anxious incomprehension among the wait staff. No, they were very sorry, Mr. Chang translated, but they did not have any Western-style utensils. At which point, one of the waiters leaned into the table to demonstrate the proper use of chopsticks. One by one, he gave each member of the Indiana contingent a short lesson. When he turned to me, I picked up my sticks and, smiling broadly, click-clicked them at him. He smiled back.

"Quit it!" Stewart whispered under his breath.

As we ate, Stewart tried to start up a conversation with the retirees, but he could not win them over. They kept answering his questions in succinct, perfunctory sentences, then returned to their food and their own conversation. In this way we made it through lunch — me flirting with the waiter, Stewart awkwardly throwing out questions that went nowhere, the Indiana folks alternately picking at and dropping their bits of chicken and tofu and green beans, and Mr. Chang, Miss Jiao, and the driver carrying on their own conversation.

"What's wrong with them?" Stewart whispered to me as we waited inside the minivan for the others to come back from the rest rooms.

When I explained my suspicions to him, his jaw dropped.

"What!" he exclaimed. "That's ridiculous." He turned to look out the window, then turned back to me. "Of course, if you hadn't been so obviously flirting with the waiter."

"Stewart, I am not going to bury my sexuality so that other people will feel more comfortable."

"This is China, David."

"What's that supposed to mean?"

"What that's supposed to *mean*," he shot back, "is that we are . . ."

He sighed. "Why is it so important for you always to find the gay underbelly here?"

It was the first time I'd heard him use the word "gay."

"Maybe precisely because China *is* so enormous," I told him. "Maybe finding the gay underbelly is the only way I can fathom getting a handle on any of it."

Just then Mr. Chang and the others began to climb aboard. Stewart turned away from me and sat straight up in his seat.

"Otherwise," I continued, "the whole thing would just feel like one big, thick, brick wall." One of the Indiana ladies squinted at me through her drugstore prescription glasses. I lowered my voice and whispered. "Gay is my entry point, Stewart."

It wasn't until the driver revved up the van that Stewart spoke again. *"Entry point!"* he scoffed.

────────

We drove on, the land becoming ever more rugged and hilly. And then suddenly, as we jostled around a bend in the road, there it was, the Wall: low and sensuous and animal-like as it snaked along the contour of the land, outlining the crest of the hills.

"My, oh my!" one of the Indiana ladies exclaimed.

"Woo dingy!" said her husband.

Mr. Chang turned around again and explained that we were about to visit a section that few Westerners had ever seen.

"Soon we stop," he said. "Must walk now. No tourist facility." The minivan pulled over to the side of the road. "Please, this way," Mr. Chang directed.

We hiked through a grove of trees, bare except for a few glossy, red-orange fruits hanging from their boughs.

"Persimmons," one of the Indiana men said. "Now that's something I know a thing or two about."

I kept my eye on Stewart. As soon as we'd gotten off the minivan, he had moved away from me and joined Mr. Chang and Miss Jiao. They took the lead, followed by the Indiana Quartet, me holding up the rear. Eventually, we all caught up to one another at the base of one of the gray-brick guard stations.

"Stairway over there." Mr. Chang motioned to where we were to climb. "This very old section. From time of Han Dynasty."

He lit up a cigarette and, between heavy drags, told us the story of the building of the Wall, and how the workers, when they collapsed from sickness or exhaustion, were discarded like refuse into pit graves at the base. He pointed, indicating where. Nothing but rubble and weeds and dusty yellow soil.

"Government not restore this part yet. Must be careful where to walk."

While the others took out their cameras, I wandered off, mounting the stairs up to the walkway and along the top to a guard tower at the highest peak. There, in the parapet, overlooking that undulating gray-brick dragon, I sat and watched the others far below. It seemed as if the wives had finally warmed to Stewart.

As Mr. Chang had warned us, the bricks were loose here. I picked one up. A mottled, mousy gray, it was the size of a loaf of bread, but heavier than I'd expected. I thought about what a fantastic souvenir it would make: over two thousand years old, lifted from the very Wall itself. I'd be able to tell some pretty terrific stories with this thing. It felt to be about as heavy as one of those ten-pound weights at the gym, something I could manage in my backpack. Taking it could be justified in lots of ways: after all, the government hadn't cared enough to restore the Wall anyway; and a country that ripped off international recording artists could hardly complain about being ripped off a little in return. I hefted the brick again. Its dusty clay felt good in my hands—ancient, archaeological, full of significance.

Suddenly, Mr. Chang hollered for us to reassemble on the minivan. I looked at the brick one more time, then down at Mr. Chang. He was far enough away that I could hardly make out his features. Quickly, with a sleight of hand that rivaled those of the CD pirates on Sanlitun Road, I slipped the brick into my pack.

The sun was already behind the hills by the time we all reboarded the minivan.

"Next we visit typical Hebei province farm village," Mr. Chang announced.

"A farm," one of the Indiana ladies repeated. She seemed quite pleased.

———

It was dusk by the time we got to the village. We were met by some of the hamlet's officials, who, with official smiles and gestures, motioned for us to follow them. We walked along the outskirts of the settlement, past walls insulated against the coming winter winds with piles of dried corn stalks. Chickens scattered from our path. Crowds of playful, giggling children tagged along. Every other living creature—the dogs, the donkeys, the villagers themselves—stared at us with hushed curiosity.

"Look at those darling children," one of the wives said. "I don't think they've ever seen Americans before."

I checked my irritation with her. We all pay attention to what we can, I reminded myself.

"This way, please," Mr. Chang gestured. We followed his heavy, waddling body through the doorway of one of the village houses.

The room we entered, illuminated by a single, bare light bulb, was the size of a small American studio apartment. It was built entirely of concrete: concrete floor, concrete walls, concrete sleeping platform, under which, Mr. Chang pointed out, was a wood-burning stove.

"This called *kang*," he explained. "You can sleep very warm here." He turned to one of the ladies. "You don't have this on Indiana farm, I think."

"No, we surely don't."

"You want to try?" He patted the sleeping platform.

"Gracious. Not me." She looked at Stewart and me. "Maybe one of you young fellows?"

I wondered what it meant that I was finally being acknowledged. Maybe here in this farming village, on turf they were familiar with, the Indianians finally felt at ease.

When Stewart and I declined, Mr. Chang ushered us into the next room. There, the family of the house was gathered around a new television set, watching the evening news. I couldn't tell whether our intrusion had been expected or not, but they stood when we entered, smiling and nodding awkwardly to us, the mother bouncing a baby in her arms, the father motioning for us to take a seat in the sofa or on another bed platform. One of the Indiana wives sat down; the other stretched her arms out to the mother and infant and asked if she could hold the baby. When the mother handed over the baby, it immediately began to cry.

"The world over," the Indiana wife remarked.

Again Mr. Chang gave us the official spiel about what a model community this was: impressive increases in material prosperity, sanitation, calorie intake. As he spoke, I could feel the brick weighing down my backpack.

"Now I think we go to hotel," he announced. "Already very late."

Outside the house, a crowd had gathered: two hundred or more villagers whose silent, respectful air made them seem almost like mourners at a funeral. One of the officials said something to Mr. Chang and he nodded.

"I think before we go, quickly, for village people you can sing typical American song?"

One of the Indiana farmers said that he thought that would be "just dandy." We ended up muddling our way through "My Country, 'Tis of Thee." The wives had high, warbly, Sunday hymn-sing voices; the husbands sang off key. Stewart's voice was rich and clear, almost operatic.

As we sang, I looked out over the crowd. In the dim light, it was hard to make out faces. Briefly, I made eye contact with one young man and smiled. He hesitated, flashed me a bashful smile, then just as quickly turned to a young woman next to him and whispered something to her. She looked up at me, and I shot her a smile as well. A broad grin blossomed on her face, and she broke into a giggle.

When we finished the anthem, the villagers applauded enthusiastically. Mr. Chang made a brief speech, there was more applause, a few bows between Mr. Chang and one of the village officials, and then we began to move toward the minivan.

All at once, there was a stirring in the crowd and a sudden hush, from which there emerged, floating on the air, a light, clear soprano voice singing in Chinese. Everyone stopped and listened. Someone was returning our gift of song with a song of her own. Gradually, I made out where the singing was coming from. I looked over the heads of the crowd. There, under a bare, dim light bulb was a teenage girl, her hair cut short and wearing the baggy shirt and trousers that were the standard village attire. As she sang, she gestured with her hands and body—a delicately turned wrist, a coy tilting of the head. I looked over at Stewart. He was transfixed.

The villagers had gathered around the singer. Old and young, men and women—on every face expressions of respect and pride. A group of girls, about the same age as the singer, were clustered immediately behind her. I looked at the faces of the girls and then at the singer. The girls, the singer. Back and forth. Something was weird here. I compared their facial features, their skin tone, the cut of their hair. And all at once I realized that the singer was not a girl at all, but a boy, a young teenager whose voice had not yet changed.

The boy's song rose in intensity. His gestures became even more theatrical. It was hard for me not to think of female impersonators I'd seen at certain clubs during my summers in Provincetown. When the song ended, in a diminuendo of almost painfully shy sweetness, we all applauded, and the boy bowed demurely. I looked at Stewart. He was holding his fingers to his lips.

"American friends, must depart now," Mr. Chang sternly announced. He turned to me. "Very too late." Just then, Stewart rushed over.

"Mr. Chang, couldn't we stay a few more minutes? I'd like to thank the singer."

"Not possible" was Mr. Chang's terse, official reply. "Must depart now. Very too late. You spend too much time at Wall."

"Mr. Chang," I intervened, "in America, Stewart is a musicologist. He studies the music of other cultures."

"No time." Mr. Chang poked at his watch. "Hotel planning typical Hebei province banquet. Must go." He barked out something to Miss Jiao, who was already leading the others to the minivan.

I looked at Stewart, ready to give him a when-in-Rome shrug, but he looked so angry that I held off saying anything. All the way to the hotel, as we swayed and lumbered over the rough terrain, he didn't speak a word.

After we had checked into the hotel and had sat down to dinner, Mr. Chang poured us all tea.

"You like Great Wall?" he asked me.

"Hen hao."

Mr. Chang smiled. "You speak very well Chinese." He turned to Miss Jiao to solicit her agreement. She nodded.

"I liked the village better," Stewart announced sullenly.

The smile on Mr. Chang's face disappeared. He leaned his heavy bulk over to the lazy Susan in the center of the table and caught a slice of fried sweet potato with his chopsticks.

"This county grow more sweet potato than all other county in Hebei province. Very much work."

"You don't have to tell me how much work farming is," one of the Indiana husbands said.

Stewart put down his chopsticks. "Mr. Chang, what was that boy singing about?"

Mr. Chang glanced over at Miss Jiao, then back at his food, which he slowly began to stir with his chopsticks.

"Boy sing typical peasant love song." He pointed to the food platters on the lazy Susan. "You not try fried sweet potato?"

"But what were the words the boy was singing?" Stewart insisted.

In a hushed voice, Miss Jiao said something to Mr. Chang in Chinese.

"Boy sing song about young man who leave village." Mr. Chang looked at all of us as he spoke, all except Stewart. "Young man go to city. Girlfriend of young man very sad he go away."

"And the young man is singing about his girlfriend?" Stewart persisted.

"No, no. Young man not singing," Mr. Chang said. "Young girl singing. She say she will miss young man very much."

One of the Indiana wives turned to the other. "You see, it's always the gals who get left behind."

The Indianians began to chuckle. So did Mr. Chang and Miss Jiao, but Stewart pressed on with his questions.

"So the young *girl* is singing," he said. "The words of the song are the words *she* is saying?"

I watched the Indiana folks shift their attention to their plates. Miss Jiao spoke again and Mr. Chang said something back to her.

"Miss Jiao say not very typical for boy to sing this song. This song typical for village girl to sing."

"I see," Stewart said. "But would it be considered . . ." He looked at Miss Jiao, then back at Mr. Chang. "Would the village people think it strange, um, not typical, for a boy to sing that song?"

"Typical for village people," Mr. Chang said, and then he consulted with Miss Jiao again. "In big city like Beijing, not typical."

"I see," said Stewart. "So a city boy would not sing such a song?"

Mr. Chang nodded. "Not such a song."

"What would happen if a city boy sang that song?" Stewart pressed.

"City people laugh," Mr. Chang said.

"I see," Stewart said. "So a country boy might sing such a song, but a city boy would not."

"Not city boy," Mr. Chang repeated. Miss Jiao whispered again. "Miss Jiao say maybe even in village that boy too old to sing like girl."

"How old was that boy?" Stewart asked Miss Jiao.

Under the table, I tapped Stewart's leg.

"Maybe that boy thirteen, fourteen years old," Mr. Chang said.

"Okay, so what if the boy was eleven or twelve?" Stewart looked at Miss Jiao again. "If he were twelve, and he sang like a girl, would city people still laugh at him?"

Mr. Chang looked at Miss Jiao.

"I think maybe yes," she said very softly. It was the first time either of us had heard her speak in English. "Because he sing girl song. This song only for *girl* to sing." She motioned to the lazy Susan. "Now I think you eat some sweet potato, please?"

After dinner, we retired to our rooms. While Stewart used the bathroom, I stripped down to my underwear. It was freezing. The hotel had yet to turn the heat on for the season. I took a sweatshirt out of my travel bag and pulled it on.

Next to the bag was my backpack. Crouching down beside it, I lifted out the brick. I was intensely aware of myself, squatting there like a Chinese peasant, the pack between my legs, hovering over my purloined possession. I imagined generations of Chinese smugglers before me—perhaps centuries of generations of smugglers—cutting just such a figure, hunched over the precious worldly objects they had managed to snatch up, devising schemes to transport their treasure abroad. I eased the brick back to the bottom of the pack and dusted off my hands.

"Mind if I write for a little while?" Stewart asked, emerging from the bathroom in flannel pajamas. His hair was wet and perfectly combed.

I told him it was fine with me. He got into bed, pulling the down comforter up close, propped his back against the thin pillow, pulled his knees up, and, steadying his journal against his thighs, immediately began to write. I got into my own bed, turned my back to the table and table lamp that separated us, and closed my eyes. For a minute, the only sound was the occasional soft scratching of Stewart's fountain pen on the pages of his book. Then I heard him turn to me.

"Why did you try to hush me up when I was talking to Mr. Chang?"

I turned over to face him.

"Come on, Stewart, you should have heard yourself: 'So, if the boy had been eleven and a half and was a city boy, but had walked from the city to the country and sang the song in a medium-high voice only to country people, but had used feminine gestures . . .' Jesus, Stewart. You were, I think it's safe to say, exhibiting a rather inordinate amount of interest in that kid."

Silence. I looked up at him. He was sitting there, his journal abandoned at his side, his hands behind his neck, staring out across the room.

"What's wrong with that?"

"Nothing, but . . ."

"I don't need protecting, you know." He turned and looked me straight in the eye. "I knew exactly what kind of impression I was making down there."

"Sorry," I apologized, but Stewart continued to stare at me.

"Exactly," he repeated.

I let the word die in the chilly air. At first, I thought he was just being his testy old self. But something about the way he kept staring at me made me uncomfortable. I was the first to break our eye contact.

"It was weird, wasn't it?" I said, settling myself on my back now, gazing up at the ceiling.

"What was weird?"

"You know, how feminine that kid was. I mean, he was such a little queen."

"He was beautiful," Stewart said.

I turned over on my side and looked at him. "A real cutie, wasn't he?"

"Goddamn it!" Stewart snapped. "Have you ever considered that there are other kinds of beauty? The kid was brave, David. Brave."

"Sorry," I said. I turned onto my back again. The hotel was only two years old, but already the cheap paint on the ceiling was peeling. "You're right, Stewart. He was brave."

For a few moments, neither of us spoke. Then I heard him stirring.

"Can I ask you something?" he said.

"Sure."

"You wouldn't ever . . . you know, sleep with someone that young, would you?"

"Fourteen? Absolutely not!" I couldn't believe Stewart was grilling me like this, but it sounded as if he was hungry for information. "I know you think I'm a letch, Stewart, but I draw the line there. I don't sleep with teenagers. Just look."

"I wouldn't either." He paused. "I'd just look, too."

I didn't dare respond for fear I had misinterpreted him again. I just kept staring at the ceiling, waiting. I knew that he was feeling the same expectancy.

"What?" I invited.

"We're not going to sleep together, you know." I didn't answer. "Because," he continued, "even if I do have feelings in that direction, I don't think that you and I . . ."

I turned to him. "I agree."

"Good," he said. "I just wanted to make sure you understood."

"I do."

I waited for him to say something more. He was staring at me. There was excitement and terror in his eyes.

"Look, I'm sorry," he said.

"About what?"

"I don't know. I guess about not having been quite ready for all this." I tried sloughing off his apology, but Stewart interrupted. "Because, you know, for a long time it's just felt like . . . like too much for me to deal with." He paused. "My sexuality."

"And now?"

"It still feels like a lot to deal with, but . . ." I waited. "I'm going to be thirty in a few weeks." I waited. "I can't keep running halfway around the world, can I?" I waited again. Stewart chuckled, the kind of chuckle you can sometimes mistake for crying. "David, I'm scared."

"I know."

Suddenly, he let out a whoop. "And excited!"

"Like the man said, it's a big, big country."

"I don't know. Maybe it was those fried sweet potatoes, but right now I'm feeling more than a little dizzy. My head is spinning so fast!"

"I don't think it's the sweet potatoes, Stewart."

He looked me straight in the eye.

"Yeah, I don't think so either." There was a giddiness in his voice. "My, oh my. Woo dingy!"

The two of us burst out laughing. We laughed and laughed. And each time our laughter would begin to subside, one of us would let go again, and we'd laugh some more.

"What happens next?" Stewart asked when we had finally quieted down. "I have no idea what I'm supposed to do now."

"Now as in *now*?" I was panicked that he'd changed his mind and was angling to crawl into bed with me.

"Now as in the rest of my life."

"One day at a time, Cupcake."

"What did you call me?"

"Cupcake. It's just my customary term of endearment. If it's too, you know, swishy for you, I won't call you that anymore.

Stewart toggled his head. "Let me think about it. Is that what you call your . . . I mean, back in Boston, do you have a . . . well, what's the preferred term? a lover? a boyfriend?"

I gave him a quick rundown of my situation—about Erik and Johnny and Owen—and promised I'd tell him the whole story when we got back to Beijing.

"And you and I," he said. "I mean, it's fine with you if we remain just friends?"

"If you mean, am I looking to sleep with you, no, I'm not." I waited. Yes, he should know this, too: "To tell you the truth, Stewart, you're really not my type anyway." I reached across the space between us and gave him a good-buddy punch in the arm. "But I really like being your—what's your word?—*roomie*."

He giggled. "So is that too swishy? Saying 'roomie'?"

"I love it, Stewart. It's one of your many endearing idiosyncrasies."

"Oh, dear."

"What?"

"I thought it was *you* who had all the endearing idiosyncrasies." He pondered this a moment, as if it were news that he could be endearing. "Well, thanks," he said at last. "I like being your roomie, too, David." He took his journal off the blanket and placed it on the night table. "And to tell you the truth, you're not my type either." We chuckled again, like a couple of school girls. "Shall I shut off the light now?" he asked. I told him yes.

In the darkness, I lay there listening, first for sounds from Stewart and then to what André Malraux once called "the great silence of the Chinese night"—maybe Mr. Chang would have called it the "typical silence of the Hebei province night."

Minutes passed. There was something else that needed to be spoken.

"You awake?" I asked. Stewart murmured. "I have something to tell you, too."

"What?"

"I stole a piece of the Wall today." I heard Stewart stir. Then the bedside lamp came on. He squinted at me. "A brick," I told him. "It's in my backpack."

"Why?"

"I don't know. I guess at the time it just seemed worth taking. It didn't feel like such a big deal."

"And now?"

"And now it feels like a big deal. I kind of wish I could put it back. But I can't, can I?"

In the lamplight I could see my breath condensing in the cold air. "Can I have it?"

I looked at Stewart. "What?"

"Can I have it? The brick. I'll take it off your hands."

"Jesus, Stewart, whatever for?"

"I guess I'd like something to remember this day by. It's been a big one for me, you know."

I smiled at him. "What about your journal? I thought that was your memory book."

His eyes went to it, lying there on the night table, and he shook his head. "Too many words, David. Not enough music." He clicked off the lamp. "Not enough music."

In the dark, I heard him humming to himself. It sounded like the Flower Duet from *Lakmé.*

Chapter Ten

After our trip to Hebei province, Stewart and I fell into a more comfortable domestic pattern. We began to have meals together, we listened to music together, and together we went out on weekends to see the sights of Beijing. He seemed perfectly content with this arrangement, but I was frustrated. Like an older brother, I wanted to show him more of the ropes, the gay ropes, but the city offered almost nothing in that regard. It seemed like such lousy luck, that Stewart should have come out as a gay man here, in Beijing, twelve million strong, a city that continued to astound me with its lack of any real gay life. It had to be here. But where? There were the parks, of course, but Stewart absolutely refused to step foot in them.

"Stop worrying about me," he said one evening toward the middle of November as we were coming home from celebrating his thirtieth birthday with a dinner out. "I don't need to meet other"—he dropped his voice—"*gay* people right now. I can wait for all that."

We were in a cab. Stewart was still skittish about saying the "G" word in public, even if that public was only our cabbie, a man who, as we'd learned when we got in, didn't understand a word of English.

"Why is it so important to you anyway?" he asked.

"Because I'd like to see you expand your knowledge of what being gay is all about. It's too important, Stewart. You shouldn't have to put it in the deep freeze for a year. Hell, it's too important a part of *my* life to put it in the deep freeze for a year."

"Well, I am not about to loiter in some seedy park, on the off chance that I may meet . . ."

I put my hand on his arm. "It's not such an off-chance, you know."

"No, David, no! I draw the line there."

"All I'm saying, Stewart, is that you need brothers. *Gay* brothers."

"So, what about you? Aren't you . . . you know, that kind of person to me?"

"Of course I am. But don't you want to meet other gay people? This is your life now, Stewart."

When Stewart didn't respond, I became quiet, too, distracted by the various rattles and clanks of the cab as it sped along the Ring Road. The jostling rhythms and the warmth of the heater lulled me into a reflective mood. What was this life that I'd told him he must prepare to enter? I thought about my neighborhood back home, the South End, Boys' Town, typical middle-class, *fin-de-siècle* gay urban village. I thought about the cavalcade of beautiful people, those new American centurions who strode the sidewalks there everyday—the gym bunnies and muscle boys, the guppies and alpha males, the newly affluent beneficiaries of the economic boom of the nineties. I thought about the clothes they wore, the music they listened to, the books and magazines they read, the kinds of parties and cars, haircuts and decorative accouterments they lavished on themselves. I couldn't imagine Stewart going for any of it. I knew the adjectives he'd lob in that direction: vulgar, crass, trivial, narcissistic. I'd felt those same things myself on occasion, even as I'd let my head be turned, time and again, by the handsome, toned faces of those yum yum boys and their bewildering, beguiling culture. Gay brotherhood, I thought, what's become of it? Was I trying to educate Stewart for entrance into a community that, apart from the pecking-order bonhomie of the bars and discos, no longer existed?

"What are you thinking?" I asked him.

"I was thinking, So *where?* Where am I going to meet"—his eyes went to the cabbie—"you know, other gay men? David, please, I am not about to go merrily traipsing off with you into any parks."

"Okay, you're coming in loud and clear."

"So where?"

"I'm working on it, Cupcake."

Stewart knew this was more of a joke than a reality. Aside from the scrap of paper that Ross had given me with the listings for a few cruising spots and the bar that he'd said was hard to find, I had no other prospects . . . for either of us.

The cab pulled up in front of our building. As we got out, a blast of cold, dust-filled air smacked us in the face. There was no denying that we were entering the deep freeze period of our year in Beijing. We paid the cabbie and ran into the lobby. Near the plate-glass door, a tall, potted plant rustled in the icy blast. The tips of its leaves were brown and crinkly.

In our mailbox, there was a single piece of mail, a postcard for me. A picture of the Golden Gate Bridge. I recognized the handwriting immediately. On the way up in the elevator, I read it:

Ni hao, David. By the time you get this, I'll be back in Boston and e-mailing you again. Still, I wanted to let you know that I was think-ing about you, even on vacation. I went to Golden Gate Park today and looked out over the Pacific Ocean and imagined you somewhere far off across the horizon. As pour moi, SF still enchants. By the way, whatever happened to your Soldier Boy? (How discreet do I need to be here? Do the authorities still read and censor mail?)
Love, Owen

This was, as far as I could remember, the seventh or eighth year in a row that Owen had made his annual fall "pilgrimage" to San Francisco. He adored the city and its environs, more, he claimed, for its bookstores, museums, restaurants, for the views of the Bay, and the churches along the Camino Real than for its gay scene, which he partook of only temperately.

"But every year?" Stewart asked when, back up in the apartment, I read him the card. "Why not some variety?"

Coming from someone who had been listening to *Turandot* every day for a week, this seemed like an odd question.

"Owen loves it there." I moved to the other side of the living room and turned up the thermostat. "He says it's the culture and the climate, but I think he's also happy just to touch down in the middle of a very gay city. He once told me that San Francisco is where he goes to be reminded of why it's so great to be gay."

"He needs to go to San Francisco for that?"

Without waiting for an answer, Stewart began to search through his shelves of CDs for something to play.

"Yes," I insisted, "he does." I could put up with a lot from Stewart but not any criticism, implied or actual, about Owen.

Stewart didn't notice. He was too engrossed in finding a CD. At last, he pulled one out. It was *Turandot* again. As he squatted down to put it into the changer, I fled to my room, shut the door, and threw myself on the bed. *If I had turned thirty today,* I thought to myself. Christ, Stewart was behaving like an old lady.

Suddenly, the sound of those first ominous chords in *Turandot*— Puccini's musical depiction of the cold, harsh brutality of Beijing— blasted through the walls. I grabbed my jacket and went back into the living room.

"I'm going out for a while," I shouted over the music.

"Where?"

"For a walk."

"David, it's freezing outside."

I shot him an angry look. It said, Not as freezing as it is in here! I didn't stick around to see whether Stewart caught it or not.

A short cab ride later, I was in the park off the Second Ring Road. There weren't many guys about, but I met one in a matter of minutes. He was leaning against a tree in a dark grove of pines, a regular spot with many of the guys who came here. The moonlight on the plumes of his breath in the frigid air gave him away. Almost as soon as I approached him, before we'd even spoken, he took my hand in his. A minute later, he had pulled off one of my gloves and was intertwining his fingers within mine.

"Ni xihuan lai wode fangjian ma?" I whispered.

"I can speak English," he said. "I think maybe better than your Chinese." In the shadows, I could see him smiling at me. "Yes, I would like to come back to your apartment."

That night, lying in bed with Eryan at my side, I decided that I had to find the Ta Ta Club, the bar that Ross had told me about.

Meeting guys in the park was okay, and Eryan, the first guy I'd actually taken home with me, was lovely—wonderful to make love to and afterwards to cuddle with—but before he'd drifted off to sleep, he had told me that he wanted to be my boyfriend.

"Maybe I can live here with you?" he said.

I almost asked him to leave right away, but I realized he was more innocent than conniving. It broke my heart, how earnest and hopeful he was, how much trust he put into the passion we had just given to each other. I would have loved to trust that, too, and had, many times before over the years. (Erik and I became lovers practically overnight; or to be more precise, over the course of a glorious October afternoon, when we went on our first date, a bike ride along the Charles River.) But now, twenty years later, I couldn't bring myself to jump at that kind of opportunity so precipitously. Of course, when you're a forty-nine-year old gay man and someone half your age tells you he wants to be boyfriends, the prevailing wisdom says, Go for it. But I just didn't feel right about Eryan's proposal. Maybe I was becoming wiser about the ways of romance. Maybe I just wanted to play the field some more. Maybe he wasn't the one. Whatever the case, as sweet as he was, I couldn't picture myself falling in love with him. Not just then.

Early the next morning, I told Eryan that I was due at work by eight and that he had to leave. When he asked me if he could stay with me again that night, I said that Stewart didn't like my bringing guys around all the time.

"You sleep with other guys?" Eryan asked.

"Sometimes."

"Okay, I understand."

That, too, nearly broke my heart.

All day at work, when I wasn't nodding off in front of my computer, I kept thinking about how I could find the Ta Ta Club. The only person I could think of who might even have heard of the place was Tyson, but when I asked him, he said no.

"But it can't be that hard to find, Mate. Where did this chap say it was located?"

"Off the Sanlitun Road. Tucked away down some alley. Tucked away pretty well, if you ask me. I've been there three or four times and haven't found it yet."

The look on Tyson's face did not encourage me.

"Well, I'd be careful, Davey. You don't want to go wandering down dark alleys you know nothing about. Some shady fellow spots a guy like you poking around where he shouldn't be and . . ."

Tyson left the rest of his sentence to my imagination.

"Man oh man, I might as well have taken a job in Islamabad or Ulan Bator."

By the look on Tyson's face, I saw that he finally understood how miserable I was.

"Okay, let me ask around a bit," he offered. "I'll make some discreet inquiries among my more, ah, worldly friends. Give me a few days."

Two hours later he was back in my office.

"Use this wisely." He placed a fax in front of me. On it were directions to the Ta Ta along with a simple map. "My source was going to write all this out in Chinese, but I told him no. I didn't want you showing this to just any man in the street. You get there *on your own*. In English."

"Tyson, however did you manage this?" The map and directions were clear and easy to follow. All those afternoons at Luna's I'd been within a few blocks of the Ta Ta.

"'Accomplish the hard task by a series of small acts,'" Tyson quoted. "That's Laozi, Mate. You should read him sometime."

"But how?"

Tyson shrugged. "I made a call to a friend. That friend made a call. Et cetera and so forth—a series of small acts—until we got the task done."

"Tyson, you're amazing." I leaned in and kissed him on the cheek.

When I arrived home that night, I couldn't wait to tell Stewart the news. But as soon as I got inside the apartment, I knew something was up with him. He was slumped in his easy chair, reading, but the atmosphere in the room was anything but cozy-literary. "Frosty" would describe it more accurately.

"Hi."

Stewart said nothing. I tried again.

"Guess what I have?"

Still no response. He was staring stonily at his book.

"Tyson found me the address of that bar I was telling you about. The Ta Ta Club."

Nothing.

"Turns out it's really close to Luna's. Isn't that wild?"

Silence.

"Okay, sourpuss, so what's going on?"

Stewart spun around. "What's going on? The guy you brought home last night. *That's* what's going on."

"Eryan? What about him?" My mind raced with the possibilities. Had he come back during the day? Had he stolen something?

"What about him?" Stewart repeated. "Here's what about him: When I went to the bathroom this morning, I discovered a glob of his hair in the shower drain."

I almost laughed in Stewart's face, but I held back and gave him the requisite look of contrition.

"Stewart, I'm sorry. Look, I'm not sure I'll be sleeping with him again—Eryan's a little too eager to get married—but if I do have him over another time, I'll ask him not to leave any evidence of his personal hygiene in our bathroom. Okay?"

Stewart scowled. I gave him plenty of time to say whatever else he needed to, but he went back to reading his book.

"Stewart, excuse me, but what about the Ta Ta?"

"What about it?" he muttered.

"Do you want to go?"

"Not interested."

"Oh, come on. We can go this Saturday. One beer. We'll stay for just one beer."

"No thanks."

"What's wrong now?"

"Nothing."

"Look, Stewart, I'm getting tired of your mixed messages. You didn't want to go to the park. Fine. I found a gay bar. So, what's the deal now? Are you interested in meeting gay men or not?"

He slapped the book down. "Not if I have to meet them the way you're meeting them."

"Whoa!"

"Sorry." His voice backed off.

"Stewart, I am not asking you to approve of my nocturnal activities. I'm not asking you to befriend the men I bring home, or even to acknowledge their presence. But I have my needs—as you, I'm sure, have yours . . ." I paused. There was another way to approach this.

"Cupcake, gay life isn't always neat and pretty, and you might as well learn that right now. It isn't neat, it isn't pretty, and"—I picked up a CD from a pile by the player—"it isn't all bel canto. Frankly, sometimes it's a mess. Clogged shower drains and all."

"Of course, it's a mess," Stewart said. "There are days when I think I understand that better than you do. It's just that I'd rather choose which part of the mess to take on. I mean, why can't I just be"—he sighed—"*gay*, without buying into all this business of . . . of"—he waved his hands in the air, as if trying to conjure up an appropriate imbroglio—"this business of picking up men in seedy places?"

"How do you know the Ta Ta is seedy? And even if it is, what alternative do you have? I mean, it's not like you can find friends by reading the gay personals column of the *China Daily*. Come on, give it a chance."

Stewart sat there, mulling it over.

"Aren't you even a little bit curious? Really, we'll just stay for one beer. Promise. How awful could it be?"

He roused himself from the sofa and went over to the CD player.

"I can just picture it," he scoffed.

"No, you can't! And neither can I." I was talking to the back of his head. "That's the whole point, Stewart. We don't know what it'll be like. Neither of us. It'll be an adventure. *Our* adventure. After all, we're in China to discover new things, right?"

He kept his attention fixed on setting up the CD player.

"You know, Stewart, you remind me so much of myself, when I first came out. So hesitant to put my toe in that water." I paused. "And so dying to try."

I waited. A half a minute passed. He turned around.

"Okay," he said.

"Really?"

"Yes. This Saturday. For *one* beer."

"I promise."

He turned back and pressed the play button. Once again, those loud, ominous chords erupted into the air—the opening of *Turandot*.

"Stewart! What are you doing?" He turned around. I thrust my hand out, pointing to the album. "You have been playing the same goddamn CD for a week now!"

"I'm studying it."

"Well, can't you study something else for a while?"

A sly smile appeared on his face. He looked at the CD, then up at me.

"David, *Turandot* is where I go to get reminded of why opera is so great."

Chapter Eleven

All that Saturday afternoon, Stewart kept asking me questions about what the Ta Ta would be like. How big was it? What kind of guys went there? Was there dancing? Somehow it didn't make sense to him that I wouldn't know the answers to these questions any better than he.

"But you've . . . you know, you've done all this before," he said. We were having dinner at home, a light meal because Stewart protested that his stomach was too jittery for anything substantial.

"Not *this* before, Cupcake."

I was beginning to understand that Stewart saw me as a major player in the gay world. This was flattering, but hardly accurate. If anything, I had lived most of my gay life chagrined at what little experience I did have. My falling in love with Johnny had been, I now knew, kindled in part by the idea that he would take me into territory I'd only heard about, a place where life would be far more exciting, alive, and spontaneous than the quotidian realities of domestic life with Erik.

"Stewart, you have to understand that this is all new to me, too."

"Okay, but at least give me an idea of what I should wear."

"Wear what you'd wear to any bar."

"I don't go to bars, David." He pushed his plate away. "Sorry, I'm not hungry."

"Cupcake, wear anything you feel comfortable in. I'm wearing chinos and a polo shirt."

"I don't have a polo shirt."

"A regular shirt, then. A shirt and sweater. A pullover."

In truth, I had fretted about the costume, too. With a frou-frou name like Ta Ta, I had wondered if the bar's dress code might not be a bit more upscale. I pictured Shanghai nightclubs in the thirties: tuxedos, slicked-back hair, champagne corks popping. I heard boys hooting to each other, "Ta Ta, darling." Opting for chinos instead of jeans was my private concession to this dandified image lingering in my mind.

"My cardigan sweater," Stewart said. "Do you think that'll be all right?"

I tick-tocked my head. "Do you have anything just a little bit more . . . you know, sexy?" Panic appeared in Stewart's eyes. "How about that nice gray vee-neck sweater?" I suggested.

"You think?" He got up to bring his plate to the sink, then halted midway. "But what if someone comes up to me and starts talking?"

"Stewart, you talk back. That's what human beings do."

At nine, we got into a cab and told the driver to take us to the Workers' Stadium. According to Tyson's informant's map, it was from the Workers' Stadium Road that we would best approach the alley to the bar. As we made our way across town, Stewart went dead silent. Only his right knee, bouncing up and down in a frantic vibrato, told me he was still awake.

I, too, was in my own private world, repeating to myself a line I'd memorized earlier that evening: *Duibuqi. Women fan cuowu.* Excuse us, we have made a mistake. I wanted to have it ready, just in case. I could picture us walking into the Ta Ta, taking one look around and realizing—for a dozen reasons I dared not share with Stewart—that we had no business being there.

We got off in front of the stadium. The air smelled of coal—an oily, acrid stench that signaled the official beginning of the heating season. All over the city, furnaces in every public building were being stoked up for the winter. Stewart started coughing.

"Are you all right?" I asked.

"The question is, Are *you* all right?" he replied. "You were a nervous wreck in that taxi."

We made our way, via the map, to the alley. It looked as if it served as a market during the day. Wooden booths lined both sides. The ground was strewn with the discarded remains of rotting fruit and vegetables. A few merchants were still about, hunkered under blankets in the dark recesses of their stalls. Aside from a couple of feeble street lamps, the only light came from the charcoal braziers around which they were catnapping.

"Careful," Stewart said. In the dim light, he motioned toward a puddle that I was about to step in.

A hundred feet down the alley, the ramshackle booths gave way to a small plaza—really just the conjunction of two alleys meeting at right angles—and there, at the corner, stood a small, one-story building. Its white stuccoed walls and red-tile roof gave it the incongruous appearance of a Spanish hacienda. To the left of the heavy paneled door, in letters handsomely shaped and twisted in what looked to be wrought iron, the words *Ta Ta Club* had been mounted on the stucco wall.

Stewart turned to me.

"What do you think?"

"One beer and we'll go."

If it's possible to be amazed and disappointed at the same time, that's how I felt when we walked in. The place was surprisingly American-looking, so much so that we might have been in any of dozens of similar clubs back home. It was about the size of a high school science lab, large enough to accommodate a dozen cocktail tables. A small bar, outfitted with four or five swivel stools, took up one end. Amply stocked with American and European spirits, the bar was illuminated by a neon sign whose cool blue glow hinted at the refreshment to be enjoyed from a popular brand of German beer. The walls were painted in bold swatches of pink, turquoise and silver—abstract designs that vaguely resembled the spry, energetic figures in a painting by Keith Haring. Western pop music, the sugary sweet variety the Chinese loved, drifted through the smoke-heavy air. About the only aspect of the place that was non-Western was the clientele. Of the twenty or so guys who were there—I barely looked, so quickly had my jitters returned—almost all of them were Chinese.

"Where do we go?" Stewart asked.

I motioned toward the bar. Stewart didn't move, frozen like an animal caught by headlights.

"Go!" I whispered and pushed him forward.

There were two empty swivel stools at the bar. We took them and put in our order for beers. As the bartender tapped the keg, I took a second look around. Most of the Chinese guys seemed to be in their twenties. They had the boyish good looks of so many young Chinese, but were far better dressed than most of the people I saw daily on the streets. Some talked quietly with their friends; others flirted and camped it up. Their queeny mannerisms seemed like some of the bravest, most transgressive behavior I'd seen so far in China. I glanced at Stewart. He was hunkered over the counter, his attention entirely fixed on a matchbox that he was turning over and over in his fingers. I bent my head in close.

"Stewart. It's okay to look."

At that moment, our beers arrived. I raised my glass.

"Here's to you, Cupcake. A watershed moment in your life." As Stewart took a big gulp, I twisted around in my stool out toward the room. "So, what do you think?"

"It's nice." His eyes stayed focused on his glass of beer. "What do you think?"

"I don't know. Actually, I'm kind of amazed. I mean, it's only beginning to sink in. Think of it, Stewart: every man in this bar is gay."

He giggled, or hiccoughed. I couldn't tell which.

"Yeah, I know." He still hadn't looked up. "So, what do we do now?"

I cupped his chin in my hand and forced him to look at me.

"What *you* do now is you turn around and look at what's happening here. Miss Manners says it is perfectly acceptable for a gentleman, of whatever persuasion, to sit at a bar and observe the passing scene while leisurely nursing his drink."

"She does?"

"Stewart, turn around!"

Dutifully, Stewart did as he was told. And there we sat, the two of us, as demure and upright as two maiden aunts at a wedding, surveying the crowd. Aside from another Westerner, who was sitting on the stool next to me, we were the only non-Chinese in the place. I was dying to ask Stewart what he thought of some of the guys, especially the ones who were clearly looking in our direction. But I figured it would make him too self-conscious. I wanted to give him time to settle in. So we continued to sit, not saying a word. I watched Stewart take a nervous sip of beer, and another, and then another. In no time, his glass was three-quarters empty.

The man next to me was talking to a young Chinese boy. I tried eavesdropping on what they were saying, but there was too much noise for me to make anything out. When the boy got up and left, the Westerner turned toward me.

"You see it happening all the time now." He talked as if we had been in the middle of a conversation. "Fastest growing GNP in the world, and what's it leading to?" I shook my head. "They're all looking for a piece of the action, that's what."

Hesitantly, I nodded. It was all the invitation he needed to continue.

"Even the money boys. They're getting two hundred *kuai* now, just to blow you."

I held out my hand. "Hi, I'm David Masiello."

"Yeah, hi." He gave me a brief, perfunctory handshake.

"And this is my friend Stewart Haslip."

The man nodded in Stewart's direction. Stewart's leg started up the frantic vibrato again.

"Used to be," the man continued, "these guys would sleep with you just for the affection. And the gifts. Now they want to be your fucking mistress. Full-time on the payroll. Little whores."

"You sound like you've been here a while," I said.

He raised his highball. "It's my third."

"I meant you sounded like you've been in Beijing a while."

"Yeah, that, too." He leaned toward the bartender and whispered something to him. Soon two more beers appeared in front of me and Stewart.

"Thank you," Stewart said.

Our companion gave him a jaded little nod, then turned his attention back to his glass. For a moment, I wondered if that was to be the end of our conversation. I guessed him to be about my age, late forties. His hair, thick and curly, was graying, but it was easy to see that at one time he'd been a sandy blond. He was wearing an expensive silk-blend jacket and an impeccably laundered white shirt. At the hem of the jacket sleeve I could see a heavy gold watch. His skin was wrinkled from too much sun, and I instantly conjured up an image of long summers sailing off exclusive New England beaches.

"This is our first time here," I volunteered. He didn't respond. I tried again. "In fact, I was kind of amazed to learn about this place."

He turned to me. "Why?" I could see that he was having trouble focusing on my face.

"Well, you know. Somehow I'd picked up that there weren't any gay bars in Beijing." I chuckled nervously. "Certainly not one with a queeny name like the Ta Ta."

He frowned with incomprehension. "It's Mandarin. You know that, right? *Ta ta.*" He pronounced it with the proper tones. "It's Mandarin for 'he and he.'"

Stewart leaned in toward me. "David, even I knew that." He giggled. "You didn't know that?"

I shook my head foolishly. "I thought it was, you know, 'ta ta!' as in 'goodbye.'"

Our companion frowned at me again.

"Why would anyone want to name this place the Goodbye Club? Baby, these boys want to say hello, not goodbye."

I glanced quickly at Stewart, giving him a feeble little apology of a smile. When I turned back, our companion had swiveled around in his stool. He was looking out over the room. The boy he'd been talking to had joined some of his buddies at one of the cocktail tables. They were handsomely dressed, in Western-style polo shirts, tailored black jeans and the heavy-soled black shoes that were popular back in the States that year. A couple of them, their heads leaning conspiratorially toward each other, were looking our way and grinning.

"You were talking to that guy when we first came in."

"That's Christopher."

"And he's a . . ." I wanted to get this one right. "A money boy?"

Our new friend looked me straight in the eye.

"Know any Beijing factory workers who dress like that?"

"So, is that who comes here? Money boys?"

"Money boys, yeah sure." He seemed annoyed that I was trying to pigeonhole the crowd. "And guys who work for international companies, and poor kids who nurse a lousy cup of tea all night in hopes that someone'll buy them a drink. Everyone comes here eventually." He looked up, almost as if noticing me for the first time. "How long did you say you've been in Beijing?"

"I didn't." I paused, making sure I still had his attention. "I arrived in August. Stewart's been here since last June."

"You guys together?"

"Yes," Stewart said.

"He means are we a couple, Stewart. Boyfriends." I turned back to our companion. "No, we're just roomie . . . roommates."

"Really?" He studied my face as if he didn't quite believe it. "Let me buy you guys a drink."

I raised the second bottle of beer.

"You already have."

He blinked. "Have I already told you my name, too?" He held out his hand. "Channing Plessey." We all shook hands a second time.

Just then Christopher glided up to us with his trio of friends. The silky haircuts on all four of them billowed and bounced as they moved with studied sissy-boy elegance.

"Nice to meet you, Channing." His soft voice enunciated each syllable of Channing's name, making it sound Chinese. He glanced at Stewart, smiled shyly, then kissed Channing on the cheek. I was about to introduce myself when he wriggled his fingers goodbye and disappeared into the crowd, coyly followed by his cohort of friends.

"I hope our sitting here didn't scare him off," I said. "I mean, maybe he thought . . ." But I had no idea what a boy like Christopher might be thinking.

Channing's gaze floated from my face to the baseball cap I was wearing.

"Oh, he'll be back," he said languidly. Reaching over, he took hold of the bill and tipped it up. I'd just gotten a haircut, a scissors-and-comb job that I hoped would approximate the buzz cut I always got back in Boston. Channing let the cap fall back onto my head. "Besides, Christopher knows I only go for Chinese boys. How about you two? What are you looking for here?"

I readjusted my cap.

"We're just taking in the scene."

Channing guffawed.

"Oh, like you've already done the Forbidden City, so now your 'taking in' the Forbidden Barroom." He clasped me on the shoulder. "Relax."

"Sorry. I guess I'm a little freaked out about being in a gay bar in Communist China."

Channing wagged his finger at me. "No, no, no. Nowadays, we say 'The People's Republic,' my dear. 'Communist China' is very retro. Communist China is what good Catholic boys like you used to pray for, right?"

"And how did you know I used to be a good Catholic boy?"

"With a name like David Masiello?"

I think it was this evidence that he really had been paying attention that finally made me warm up to Channing, and with that we started trading stories. He'd grown up in Manhattan, on Fifth Avenue, gone to prep school in Connecticut, then to Yale, his father's and grandfather's alma mater, where, as he put it, he had "scandalized the family by doing drama for four years while getting by on gentleman's C's." After years as a corporate lawyer in New York, he had come to Beijing to help open a branch of the firm. He'd been in China three years.

"Do you like it here?" Stewart asked him.

"Do I *like* it here?" Channing rattled his glass—there was only ice left—and tried to get the bartender's attention. "Ever done any acting?"

Stewart shook his head.

"I've started a little amateur theatrical company here. We use a mixture of expats and English-speaking Chinese. Twice a year, we mount a show."

Stewart said that he'd never been in a play, that in high school the thought that he'd forget one of his lines used to terrify him.

"Last spring, we did *Streetcar Named Desire*." Channing interrupted himself to grab the bartender's arm and order us all another round. "For the winter production, I think we'll try something by Lorca. *Blood Wedding* maybe."

He slowly turned and looked out over the smoky room, which was filling up with more patrons, both Chinese and now Westerners, too. Suddenly, he turned back.

"Do I *like* Beijing?" The bartender set down his drink, and Channing took a generous sip. "Let me put it this way, baby. Beijing is not home, and for some of us that is a delicious blessing."

Stewart and I left before midnight, after our third beer with Channing, who, as abruptly as he had come into our lives, disappeared, excusing himself to go to the men's room, and never returned. For the entire taxi ride home, Stewart was silent. I let him be alone with his thoughts. I wondered if my suspicions about what had detained Channing in the loo were running through Stewart's mind as well.

On the elevator up to the apartment, I finally broke the silence.

"So, what did you think?"

"We didn't meet anyone."

"What do you mean? We met Channing."

Stewart shook his head.

"Ick, what a creep. I'd just as soon never set eyes on him again."

"Okay, so next time we'll concentrate on meeting some Chinese guys." The fact was that I, too, was disappointed that we had spent all our time with Channing.

"Next time?" Stewart looked at me as if I had just announced that I wanted to spend another evening hauling buckets of night soil. "You want to go back there?"

"Of course. We barely got a feel for the place."

"Enough of a feel for me."

"What do you mean?"

The elevator arrived at our floor. Stewart got off without answering my question. I tailed him into the apartment.

"Stewart, what do you mean you don't want to go back?"

He threw his coat on the sofa and made for the CD player.

"Stewart?"

"What?" he snapped.

"Channing Plessey is not the Ta Ta, Stewart. He's not the gay world."

I hated myself for saying this. Channing was indeed the gay world, just as much as Stewart was, as much as Owen and I were, or Erik or Johnny or my Uncle Carmine. As much as Yonghai, and Eryan, and Christopher and his money-boy sidekicks. We were all — as the Sisters of St. Joseph had taught me back in Catechism class — all part of a mystical body, though I'm sure those good ladies had never envisioned a mystical body like the Ta Ta Club.

"Stewart, one day at a time. Relax. Your life is going to turn out just fine. Whoever you think you are, you are not going to lose that by going back for one more visit to the Ta Ta Club. Trust me on this, little brother." He didn't respond. "Come on, I saw lots of guys there who seemed perfectly lovely. I think a few were even paying quite a bit of attention to you."

Stewart shot around. He was clutching a CD case. His hand was trembling.

"I have to do this my way, David. Do you mind?"

"Of course, I don't mind. Just as long as there *is* a way to your way, Stewart. I just don't want you retreating into your land of operas and never emerging again. That's all, Cupcake."

Stewart slammed down the CD case.

"And stop calling me Cupcake!"

Winter

Chapter Twelve

Winter came early that year. By the beginning of December, the weather was so cold and dry that my lips were constantly chapped and my hands in need of lotion three or four times a day. I stopped riding my bike to work and started taking public transportation. Often I'd stay late at my desk just to avoid the packed busses full of sneezing, sniffling commuters.

The apartment had electric heat, so we stayed warm, but the only place where I managed to get the chill fully out of my bones was at the Ta Ta, where I began spending (sans Stewart) two or three nights a week.

It was on my fourth visit to the club that I ran into Channing Plessey again. He was at the bar, sitting in the same seat he'd occupied when I first met him.

"Where've you been?" he asked.

"I was about to ask you the same thing." I ordered a beer.

"Been trying to scrape a cast together for *Blood Wedding*."

"*Scrape?* Sounds discouraging."

"It is. Everyone in this town is too fucking busy making money to put on a show." He nodded over to the San Miguel that the bartender had placed in front of me. "What's the matter? Don't you like the local brew?"

"Frankly, no. It tastes metallic."

Channing leaned in toward me. "It's the formaldehyde. But you get used to it. If you're hoping to make any real friends here, you should drink Chinese. Guys who come in here and buy imported stuff are seen as rich sugar daddies."

I glanced down at the cocktail he was nursing. It looked like scotch and water.

Just then, a gaggle of Chinese boys squeezed by us. The cold night air was still clinging to their quilted silk jackets.

"Ah, mercy," Channing sighed.

At first I didn't catch on. "You okay?" I asked.

Channing nodded over to where the boys had joined their friends at a table. "The one in the yellow jacket."

I looked. He was short, about five feet five, with a face whose soft prettiness was hardened only by a pair of high, angular cheek bones and a coarse crew cut. When the boy noticed that we were looking at him, he flashed us a broad grin. Dimples appeared at the corners of his mouth. He hunkered closer to his friends and they all started confabbing.

"Hold my place," Channing said. "I need to take a leak."

He began to ease himself off the stool. I grabbed his arm.

"Don't get lost this time."

Channing gave me a puzzled look. He had no idea what I was talking about.

"A little part of me is always lost," he said and moved off into the crowd.

"Your boyfriend?"

I turned to the person on my right. A Chinese guy.

"*Bu shi,*" I told him. "He's just a friend. *Wode pengyou.*"

"Please, can we speak English?" he asked.

He looked to be about thirty, but without the boyish sexiness of many of his compatriots. He had a slightly puffy face. His skin was dull and sallow. I could tell that his haircut was a home-done job. Nor were his clothes as au courant as those worn by many of the Ta Ta crowd. He introduced himself: Guozhen.

"My English name is Edward. With my American friends, I prefer Edward." He had a nice smile, sweetly sincere. "You do not have boyfriend?"

"No," I said. "I'm taking a breather from boyfriends. *Breather,*" I repeated. "It's like a vacation."

"Yes, yes," Edward said. "I know 'breather.'"

"Your English is very good."

"No, not good. Many words I don't know."

We were facing each other on the stools. Over Edward's shoulder, I could see Channing. He'd returned from the men's room and was chatting up the kid in the yellow jacket. Edward turned around to see what I was looking at.

"Money boy," he pronounced.

I looked again. "How can you tell?"

"Can tell," Edward said. "You don't see?"

"I see that he's cute." I gave Edward's face another quick study. I wondered if Chinese guys found him more attractive than I did.

"Your friend, he is sugar daddy?"

I laughed. "Edward, you *do* know a lot of English! No, I don't think he's a sugar daddy."

"Okay," Edward said, "but I think with this boy, he will pay."

I put my hand on Edward's shoulder and toggled him playfully back and forth. "Now how do you know *that*, Edward. Huh?"

"Just a guess." He smiled and folded his hands in his lap. "I think that is how you say? Just a guess?"

———

The next day was Sunday. When the phone rang toward noon, I was on the sofa, reading. Stewart was preparing lunch. It was Channing.

"Masiello, where'd you disappear to last night?"

"Shouldn't I be asking *you* that, Channing? You abandoned me again. I had to find a new friend on my own."

When I looked up, I saw Stewart in the kitchen shaking his head.

"And did you?" There was a suggestive coyness in his voice.

"A *friend*," I emphasized. "A very nice Chinese guy named Edward. We talked for quite a while. In fact, we watched you leave with Yellow Jacket. You seemed terribly engrossed."

"Jesus," Channing exclaimed, "we were hardly out of the bar when he started kissing me, right there in the alleyway."

"Edward thinks he's a money boy."

"Who's Edward?"

"I just told you. The guy I met at the bar last night."

"Tell your Edward he's wrong."

"And does Yellow Jacket have a name?" I asked.

"Mingzhu." Over the phone, I heard Channing taking a long, hard drag on a cigarette. "It means something like Bright Vermilion. You know, one of those patriotic names left over from the Cultural Revolution. He was born the month Mao died."

"Nineteen seventy-six? Channing, he's *twenty?*"

Stewart came into the room carrying two glasses of water. He stood there, waiting to hear what would come next.

"Yeah, he told me he was twenty-one, but he was figuring Chinese style."

"And what does Bright Red do?" I looked up at Stewart and rolled my eyes.

"His name's Bright Vermilion, and he doesn't fuck. They're all terrified of AIDS here."

"For *work,* Channing. What does he do for work?"

Stewart set the glasses down on the dining table and retreated into the kitchen.

"He's a waiter." Channing took another deep drag. "I think. We spent hours just cuddling in bed, watching some historical soap drama on TV. Christ, those things are lame."

"And he didn't ask you for money?"

"Hell, no!"

"So this one's different from Christopher?"

"Who's Christopher?"

I sighed.

Channing continued, "Look, what are you doing today?"

I glanced out my bedroom window. It promised to be another frigid December afternoon.

"I think I'm going to stay in. I'm reading a memoir about growing up during the Cultural Revolution. Do you know that kids denounced their own parents?"

"What about the Ta Ta tonight?" Channing asked. "A couple of Chinese boys are dying to meet you."

"Which couple of Chinese boys?"

"Come and see." I didn't answer. "Good," Channing said. "I knew you'd see it my way."

That night, when the promised Chinese boys didn't show, I spent the evening standing in a corner, drinking beer, a Beijing brand this time, and watching Channing work the tables. At eleven Edward came in. I gave him a little peck on the cheek, which embarrassed him. We spent the next half hour talking, but all the while I was trying to make eye contact with one of the boys at another table. When Bright Vermilion arrived, Channing gleefully abandoned his table hopping and swooped down on the kid. The two of them went off to a corner table. At midnight I went home alone.

———

During the next few weeks, I saw Channing and Bright Vermilion together every time I went to the Ta Ta. Sometimes it would be only the two of them, and sometimes they would be sitting at a table with several of Bright's friends, who, as far as I could tell, all looked like hustlers. They had the fancy, fluffed-up haircuts and expensive Western fashions that could only be bought with more money than any of them must have been making. Channing and I occasionally exchanged a few words of catch-up talk, but generally he was too preoccupied with his entourage.

Occasionally, I'd see Edward there, too, either alone or in the company of a friend of his, a boy he'd known since childhood who was as demure and plain-looking as Edward. The two of them seemed quite ill-suited to the lively, self-conscious flirtatiousness of the place. I always took time to talk with Edward. His English was good—he was a librarian at Beijing University—and his conversation interesting and intelligent. But though Edward seemed like one of the few genuine guys at the Ta Ta, try as I did, I couldn't bring myself to think of him as sexy.

Just before Christmas, as the Ta Ta bedecked itself for the holidays (there was a tree and lights and a little mechanical *Dunche Lao Ren,* Old Man Christmas, who waved and pivoted from his perch among the liquor bottles), I took a break from the bar. It had begun to wear on me, especially the attitude of so many of the Chinese guys. Whether they were money boys or not, they seemed interested in meeting Westerners solely for the perks—the free drinks, the invitations to the discos, perhaps the chance to get a job with an American company. On top of all that, I hadn't managed to pick up anyone there, and I was lonely for a little companionship.

Instead, I went back to cruising the park off the Second Ring Road, where, despite the colder weather, it was still easy to pick up guys. In the space of a week, I hooked up with three: one I took home for the night; with the other two I just fooled around right there in the dark. They excited me in ways the Ta Ta boys could not. The sad, tentative neediness of these fellows, so unlike the studied affectations of the bar crowd, seemed much more trustworthy and real. I gave my phone number to the guy who had stayed over, but he never called back. Just as well, I supposed. With him, with any of these guys, attempting a relationship would have been ludicrous anyway—the language barrier was too great, or they lived in workers' housing with hundreds of other men, or we just didn't have anything in common. Sometimes I worried that I was just taking advantage of the situation. What, I asked myself, was I getting away with here in China? But just as often it seemed that China, in the person of these sweet, lonely, needy boys, was getting away with something over me. In Owen's Daoist book of sayings, which I kept by my night table, I read a passage from Zhuangzi: "Unable to restrain yourself, let yourself go and your spirit won't be irritated." *That,* I told myself, was precisely what I was doing.

Meanwhile, Stewart remained true to his word. Most nights he stayed home, listening to music or writing in his journal, a practice he'd taken up again. We didn't talk about my evening activities, and he never found out about my one overnight guest. I had made certain the bathroom was spotless the next morning before Stewart even woke up.

Then, on Christmas night, after dinner with Stewart, Tyson, and Tyson's girlfriend, I decided to check out the Ta Ta again. The first person I ran into was Edward.

"How about your friend Channing?" he asked after we'd exchanged Christmas greetings and news of our comings and goings, expurgated on my part, since we'd last seen each other. "He still go with money boy?"

"Channing tells me he's *not* a money boy." I was surprised at the anger in my voice. "As far as I know, he hasn't asked Channing for a penny." Edward gave me a quizzical look. "Penny," I insisted. "A one hundredth of a dollar. Like a *fen*."

"David, I think maybe you are upset?"

"Sorry." I looked at Edward—his eyes, his skin, his haircut—trying to imagine him as a boyfriend. "Edward, I guess I just don't understand this money boy stuff."

"They have difficult life, David. Bad job, little money. I think money boys ashamed of what they doing." He looked sad. "They want somebody take care them, so they don't have worries anymore."

"Is that what Mingzhu wants?"

"May be."

"In our culture, people don't respect that kind of relationship."

"Don't respect here, as well. But different. Sometimes necessary."

"For whom?" I asked.

Edward looked confused. "For money boy." Then his face brightened. "Ah, yes, sometimes, I think, necessary for sugar daddy, too."

As I left the bar that night, making my way down the alley of closed up vegetable stalls, I thought about asking Edward out for dinner some time. I figured that if I spent enough time with him, I might learn to see him as a romantic partner. Why, I asked myself, kicking a frozen head of cabbage down the alley, *why* did love always have to start with sex appeal?

It was not until the first week of January that Bright Vermilion made his move.

"He took my portable CD player," Channing told me over the phone one evening. "We left the apartment together this morning, and when I came home from the office this afternoon I discovered it was gone."

"Maybe your *ayi* took it," I offered rather hopelessly.

"She doesn't come until Tuesday," Channing said. "No, no one else could have taken it. Besides, Mingzhu was acting a little funny this morning. He got on the first bus that came by and—Jesus, it's so obvious to me now!—when he waved at me from the window, I got this feeling that he was waving goodbye forever."

"I'm sorry," I said.

"The little shit."

"Are you going to report him to the police?"

"Are you crazy! Do you know what the police would do to him? Besides, I don't know how to get in touch with him." Channing laughed. "I don't even know his last name."

I offered to take Channing out to dinner, but he told me that the Ta Ta was sponsoring a drag party that night and he wanted to be there.

"Chinese boys do drag so well," he said. "That deliciously smooth skin, you know. Plus there's that whole transvestite tradition in Peking opera they can draw on. Masiello, this is such a fabulous culture."

Imagine my surprise, then, when the following Saturday, Channing strolled into the Ta Ta with his Bright Vermilion. At first Channing didn't see me. They breezed over to a table to join some of Bright's friends. Channing treated these guys as if they were buddies, laughing it up with them, paying for drinks, but I could see that the boys preferred to talk and whisper among themselves. When at last even Bright Vermilion stopped paying him attention and lost himself in a conversation with a couple of the other boys, Channing got up from the table and wandered over to the bar.

"Hello, darling. Happy New Year." He grinned. "*Our* kind of New Year."

"Channing, I thought you'd broken up with him."

Channing glanced in Bright's direction. The boy squad nodded to us and started laughing.

"Oh, everything's cool again. We straightened things out."

"Why? So he can rip off more of your stuff?"

Channing took a sip of his drink. "Different culture, different values."

"Channing, that's bullshit. Theft is theft."

"Oh, he returned the CD player."

"What did he say?"

"He said he didn't know he was doing anything wrong. He just wanted to listen to some of his CDs."

"Come on, what's he doing with CDs and no CD player?"

Channing took another long sip of his highball. "Sir Richard Burton—you know? the Victorian English explorer?—when he was in India, he took several mistresses. And you know what he said? He said they helped him get a feeling for 'the syntaxes of native life.'" He chuckled. "I love that! 'The syntaxes of native life.'"

The bartender placed a bottle of San Miguel in front of me.

"Look, I did not order this," I told him in direct, no-nonsense, government-issue English. "No."

———

All through that bitter January, Channing continued to sleep with Bright Vermilion. Whenever I saw him, he'd give me a progress report.

"The way he curls up with me, David, that delicious little body nestling right into mine. I never thought I'd be so happy about the cold weather."

In passing, almost as an afterthought, Channing would occasionally mention that he had discovered something missing—a magazine, a shirt, a hundred kuai note—but he'd quickly dismiss it and slip right back to singing the praises of his Bright Vermilion. I resisted telling Channing he was a fool, partly because it was none of my business how he conducted his love life and partly because I wanted to see how this thing would play itself out.

I thought that day had come one Saturday morning toward the end of January when Channing called to say it was all over between them. He sounded intoxicated.

"The minx hasn't called me in three days."

"He's done that before," I said. "Come on, Channing, I bet you'll hear from him soon enough." I wondered what he would hear in my voice: encouragement or cynicism.

"Can you come for dinner?" he asked. "I need some company."

I told him that I had plans with Edward. Although we weren't dating or sleeping together, Edward and I had started doing things together—dinner, a movie, winter walks around old Beijing. That night, we had plans to go out for Mongolian hot pot.

"Bring him," Channing said.

"Do you want us to bring some food?"

"Sure," he said. "And if you can scare up a decent bottle of wine, bring that, too. French, not that Great Wall shit."

At eight, we showed up at Channing's building. When the door-man rang his apartment, there was no answer.

"I know he's expecting us," I told him. "Can we just take the elevator up?"

The doorman was Chinese. He eyed Edward suspiciously, then waved us on. We had to knock on Channing's door several times before he opened it.

"I was napping," he said. "What time is it?"

"Dinner time." I raised the bag of take-out.

There was no sign of recognition on Channing's face. We entered the apartment, the first time I'd ever been there. It was splendidly appointed. Beautiful carpets covered the floor—some Chinese, some Persian. The furniture, too, was sumptuous and eclectic—leather sofas, Ming dynasty chairs and chests in rosewood, a huge coffee table that looked Middle Eastern, a silver samovar. The walls were covered with paintings, Chinese, Japanese, Western. The place was a testament to a rich life richly lived. Smiling over it all, a two-foot tall Buddha, burnished in gold leaf, stood in one corner, his hand raised in blessing.

"Do you guys want a drink?" Channing asked. He turned and stumbled over the corner of one of the carpets. When I offered to make coffee instead, he acquiesced and plopped himself onto the sofa. "I think the coffee maker is that way." He pointed toward a room off the living room.

The kitchen was a mess of unwashed dishes and glasses—several days' worth. I made the coffee and brought out three mugs into the living room. With his hands folded in his lap, Edward was sitting in one of Channing's easy chairs staring patiently at the blank television screen. Channing had fallen asleep. I woke him up and put the mug in his hand. He took a sip.

"Did I ever tell you about the great Italian coffee at the Swiss Hotel? A shot of grappa in a double espresso with a couple of coffee beans thrown in."

I looked over at Edward, who was demurely staring down at his folded hands. Channing snickered.

"I come halfway around the world and what do I find: fucking Italian coffee."

"Channing."

"Same shit everywhere."

"Channing, he was trade."

Channing looked up at me. "Masiello, I was thirty-nine, *thirty-nine,* when I came out."

"Channing, each of us is on his own timetable."

"Oh, is that right?" A drunken anger filled his voice. "And is that how *you* comfort yourself, Masiello?" He shot a glance at Edward, still sitting so quietly, his eyes downcast like a monk in prayer, then turned back to me. "Timetable, huh? Do you have any idea what it's like to walk into a gay bar for the first time when you're thirty-nine?"

"Channing."

"Do you know what it's like to overhear someone call you a troll?"

"Channing, we're the same age. I've been there. Not everyone is like that."

He looked up at me.

"You're right, Masiello. Not everyone *is* like that. Not here they aren't. They've got Pizza Hut, Baskin and Robbins, Kentucky Fucking Fried Chicken, but they haven't learned 'troll' yet." He looked over at Edward again. "Right, Eddie? No troll. Not yet." He closed his eyes and leaned his head back against the sofa. "Yes, indeed, we should all be eternally grateful for the Confucian virtue of honoring the elderly." He sounded exhausted. In another minute, he was snoring.

As Edward and I started cleaning up the kitchen, there was a soft knock on the door. I went back into the living room and opened it. It was Bright Vermilion. We stared at each other for a second, then I let him in without saying a word. When Bright noticed Edward, he tensed up.

"It's okay," I said. "My friend. *Wode pengyou.*" That seemed to reassure him. He nodded to Edward and they exchanged polite, quiet greetings.

"Channing is sleeping. Channing *shuijiao.*"

Bright walked over to the sofa, squatted down and put his cheek on Channing's forehead. He turned to Edward and said something in Chinese.

"He say Channing drinks too much." They exchanged a few more words. "He think we should put Channing into the bed."

The three of us carried him into the bedroom. With my hands under Channing's back, I felt another hand on mine, whether Edward's or Bright Vermilion's I couldn't tell. It was an innocent enough occurrence—moving a limp body is an awkward business—but when I imagined that it was Bright Vermilion touching me, I got an erection.

We laid Channing down. The hand that was touching mine slid away. Bright Vermilion crouched by his side and began to massage Channing's temples. I noticed how thin and beautiful his fingers were, feminine in their delicacy, though underneath the unpared nails, I could see dirt.

"I think we go now?" Edward said.

I glanced back at Bright Vermilion. It seemed risky to let him have the run of the apartment with Channing practically comatose.

"What do you think?" I asked. Edward nodded that it was okay. When we left, Bright Vermilion was still caressing Channing's forehead.

The elevator was slow in coming. As we stood in the corridor, an awkward silence came over us. I wanted to confess my uneasiness about leaving Channing alone with his paramour, but I was afraid I'd offend Edward. At last the elevator came. We got on. The doors closed and Edward adjusted his scarf. His fingers were as thin and dainty as Bright's.

"So where's this hot-pot place you're taking me to?" Edward ignored my question.

"David, what is 'troll'?"

"Troll?" I forced an amused chuckle out of my mouth. "A troll is a little man who lives in the forest." I paused. "Forest?" I asked him.

"Yes," he said. "I know forest. But why does someone say Channing is a troll?"

"It means something else, too." I hoped this would satisfy him, but Edward waited for me to continue. "Edward, troll is a word some people, some *gay* people, use when they think another man is not good-looking."

"Yes," Edward said. He looked down at his jacket, then back up at me. "I think we have word for that kind of troll in Chinese, too."

At that moment, I wanted to reach over and take him hard in my arms. I wanted to smother him with kisses, tell him he was attractive beyond belief, declare my passion and undying love. I wanted to protect him from the cruelty of the world, its superficialities, its banality, its trite, adolescent notions of what was beautiful. I wanted him to become my boyfriend, my lover, my own best one. But I couldn't. A dozen dinner dates, a hundred walks under frosty, moonlit Chinese skies would not, I knew, make any difference. Edward would be my friend, my *pengyou,* this word that in China rang with such heartbreaking overtones, but he would never—I knew this—never become my bedmate.

I opened my mouth, trusting that something kind and true and generous would come out, but Edward spoke first.

"David, I think maybe Channing is not a troll. Not inside his heart."

"No, he's not, Edward. You're right. He's not a troll inside his heart."

"And I think also maybe he is lucky."

"Lucky." I smiled at him. It seemed like such a Chinese thing to say. "Yes, lucky. He's lucky."

I reached over and rearranged Edward's scarf against the cold.

Chapter Thirteen

That year, the Chinese New Year fell on the seventh of February. In the days leading up to the holiday, I made my resolutions: to see more of the city; to spend less time at the Ta Ta and do more things with Stewart; to join a health club; to finish *Moby Dick;* to call my mother once a week and e-mail Owen more regularly; to buy a larger dictionary and learn more Chinese; to stay out of the park off the Second Ring Road. This last resolve was easy to maintain because the weather had turned excruciatingly cold, but I put it on the list anyway. I wanted to impress upon myself that I was taking a new path. Where exactly that path would lead me—was I really going to give up sex altogether?—remained unclear. All that was certain was that we were in the depths of winter on the North China Plain. Everyday I had to endure the lashing winds and plummeting temperatures. It made me want to lie low, hibernate, retreat into a dark season of introspection. I bought a journal.

And then I met Bosheng.

We met on the Saturday afternoon before the New Year at a café in the Xidan district, one of a chain of French coffee shops that had recently opened in the city. It was not as charming a place as Luna's, but the pastry was better and there were more tables, spread farther apart. That meant more privacy. I had gone there to read and write in my journal.

The café was packed. Western eateries always drew a good crowd in Beijing, but now the holiday season had brought in even more customers than usual. By the time I had gotten my café au lait and croissant, there were no free tables to be had. I spotted Bosheng immediately, sitting by himself, a sketch pad in hand. Casually, I wandered over to his table and, in my best Mandarin, asked if I could join him. He looked up from his drawing, gave me a smile as bright as a New Year lantern, and motioned that I should take a seat.

"Xiexie," I thanked him.

He smiled and nodded again. *"Bu keqi."*

I figured he didn't speak any English, which was both frustrating and a relief. It would have been so tempting to flirt with him if he could have understood my language. But already he had taken up his sketch pad again. I followed suit and pulled the copy of *Moby Dick* from my backpack; yet the words I started reading might as well have been Chinese, so little did they register in my brain. I kept reading the same paragraph over and over again, unable to concentrate, wanting to steal another glimpse of the handsome man sitting across from me. At last, placing the book face down on the table, I made as if to take a break, leaned back in my chair, and picked up my cup of coffee. I took a sip and stared out into space, pretending to let my mind wander over the passage I had just read, while all the while I furtively drank in his features.

He had a long, delicate face accentuated by a head of black hair, cut in shaggy bangs that fell over his forehead, a pair of high, angular cheekbones, and the whisper of dimples at the corners of his mouth. "Feminine" was my first impression, though his bushy eyebrows, full, heavy lips, and prominent Adam's apple added a touch of "butch." He was wearing a long-sleeved striped jersey over which he had put on a pair of American-brand overalls. The denim was soft, not coarse; the pockets in the bib sported an array of pencils and pens. As he sketched, I watched his fingers. They were delicate, too, almost bony, though his grip was strong and resolute.

I figured that it would not be rude to watch him as he went about his drawing. After all, artists out in public were used to that— certainly in America, and why not in China, too? Besides, the Chinese were always staring at me. A little spitefully, I decided that I could turn the tables just this once. He was angled slightly to the right, drawing I couldn't tell what. I tried to follow where his gaze went, and when it seemed that the likeliest possibility was a young woman at a nearby table, my heart sank. I was about to pick up my book again, when he spoke.

"Excuse me," he said. "What does 'Moby Dick' mean?"

I was so startled, not only that he spoke English but also by the fact that somehow he had been paying attention to me, that I became flustered.

"Oh, it doesn't mean anything. I mean, it's just a name. Moby Dick."

He seemed puzzled by this. "But Dick is first name in English, I think. Nickname for Richard. Yes? Why does this person put first name where family name should be? Why not Dick Moby?"

I couldn't help laughing.

"I'm sorry," I apologized. "I'm not laughing at you. It just sounds so funny that way. You see, it's not the name of a person; it's the name of a whale."

"Werhl?"

"Whale." I extended my arms far out. "A very big fish—well, not a fish really, but . . . a big animal that swims in the ocean. Bigger than a car." I made my arms go even wider. "Almost as big as an airplane." He seemed impressed by that, but still confused. I brought one hand to my head and traced imaginary plumes of water from an imaginary blow hole under my baseball cap. "It blows water from the top of its head."

My tablemate shot me a smile of recognition.

"Ah, *jingyu!*" Flipping to a new page in his drawing tablet, he made a lovely quick sketch of a whale, which he proudly showed off to me. "This is?"

"Yes, that's it."

"How do you say again?"

"Whale."

"Wheyrhl." He giggled at his own mispronunciation.

When I complimented him on his drawing, I noticed how embarrassed he looked. He was practically blushing. "May I see some of your other sketches?"

"Not for showing," he said.

"Oh, please?"

"No, not good enough for showing."

I decided not to press the issue.

"Ni shi huajia ma?" I hoped that asking him if he were an artist in his own language might make him feel less on the spot.

Yes, he admitted, he was an artist. I watched as he closed the sketch pad and placed it on his lap.

"And do you show in a gallery?"

He looked up, smiling with amusement.

"No, not showing in gallery."

"Not yet anyway," I encouraged.

He blushed again, but this time did not look down. I took the opportunity to study his eyes. They were deeply, deliciously black. Small puffy bags under his lower lids emphasized their almond shape and made him look a little sad. The French would say *triste*. I held out my hand.

"My name is David."

He shook it. "My name is Bosheng." His fingers were as soft and delicate as I had imagined. The handshake broke the ice. With a little more prompting from me, Bosheng began to tell me about himself.

He was twenty-nine, a graduate student in art at one of the city's painting academies.

"But this is not my city," he said. "I come from Harbin, in the northeast. I have been living in Beijing only one half year."

"Hey, same as me! I came here in August."

I told him about the job and how—I could hear myself babbling now, just wanting to keep the conversation going—how I had lived on a campus myself during my first few months in the city.

"Such a big city," Bosheng said, and again I caught the faint trace of sadness in his eyes and in his voice.

"But I imagine, living in a dormitory you have made some friends."

"No, I don't live in a dormitory," Bosheng corrected. "I have a teaching fellowship, so with my money I can afford a small place to live by myself." He paused. "I think it's better that way."

My mind raced with all the possible ways to interpret that sentence.

We spent another half hour talking and, I was beginning to convince myself, flirting, too, though I could not be sure. Bosheng was alternately shy and funny, evasive and straightforward. Whenever I sensed that he was warming up to me, he would suddenly turn bashful again. I was dying to get him to show me his drawings. I was sure they would be the key to understanding who he was, but I didn't want him to think I was prying. As the winter afternoon faded outside and the café took on the pallid aura of the overhead fluorescent lighting, I hazarded an invitation to Bosheng to join me at a restaurant for dinner. To my delight, he accepted.

"Your choice," I told him as we made our way through the frosty streets of Xidan.

He led us to a quiet little out-of-the-way place. It was cozy and shabby and, to my mind, utterly romantic. We gave the waiter our order and settled in with a couple of beers to wait for our food. In less than two minutes, he had finished off his beer.

"Do all artists drink that fast?" I teased. He was already motioning for the waiter to bring him another.

"Just thirsty," he said. When the waiter brought the second bottle, Bosheng was careful to pour only half into his glass, but this, too, he drank down quickly. I watched him studying at the bottle. I had the feeling he was avoiding my gaze, but suddenly he looked up.

"David, are you married?"

I made sure that I held our eye contact before I told him no.

"I am not married either," he said.

"But you're young," I told him.

He shook his head forlornly. "Not so young." I waited for him to go on, but his attention went back to the bottle of beer.

"Besides," I continued, "right now you have to put all your concentration into your painting, not"—I watched him closely as I said it—"on women."

Before he could react, the waiter brought our food. Bosheng had ordered splendidly: a pork dish, sweet and sour eggplant, a whole steamed fish, and bean curd soup. I couldn't imagine that he could afford to pay for all this, not even with the stipend from his teaching fellowship. I began to suspect that I'd been picked up for a free dinner, but the aromas of the food were so scrumptious and my holiday mood so upbeat that I decided not to care. I took up my chopsticks and tried the fish.

"Bosheng, this is fantastic!"

He seemed simultaneously pleased and embarrassed by the compliment. For a while we ate in silence. I watched him finish his second beer. This time, without his asking, the waiter brought him a third.

"Difficult to put concentration into painting," he said after taking a long quaff.

"Why?"

With his chopsticks, Bosheng began poking at the steamed fish.

"My parents wanting me to come home and get married."

"Ah, yes."

It was his turn to be surprised by my reaction.

"You understand?"

"Well, I've met quite a few guys here in Beijing who feel the pressure to get married."

"Not pressure. Just what I must do."

The distinction was lost on me. I tried another angle.

"But if you are an artist, what you must do is paint, no? Your career is important, too."

"Not important to my mother and father. They wanting me to get married."

"And you?" I waited as Bosheng kept poking at the fish. "What do *you* want, Bosheng?"

"Don't know."

"Why not?" It felt a little ruthless, grilling him like this. But I wanted to push him—and myself—toward more candor. Bosheng seemed like the kind of guy I would never have met at the Ta Ta, which was all the more reason why I was so attracted to him.

"Maybe you are like me," I suggested. "Maybe you prefer not to get married." He looked up at me. I put as much nonchalance into my voice as possible. "I mean, maybe you like guys instead?"

"Guys instead?" At first I thought he hadn't understood. I watched him rearranging strands of carrot and scallion around the steamed fish, as if he were trying to dress the thing up again. Then he laid down the chopsticks and looked up at me.

"Two years ago, when I am still living in Harbin, I understand that I am liking guys instead. Nobody explaining to me what I am feeling, but I know."

I put down my chopsticks, too.

"How did you know?"

"I was living in the dormitory. One night I am in my bed, and I start to cry. I was missing . . . I don't know, something, so much. One of my roommates, he heard me and invited me to sleep with him. Just for comfort. No problem in China. Just sleeping together, like brothers. But for me I know then it's something else."

I nodded. "And now that you're in Beijing . . ."

"This year, I am trying to meet guys like me. Gay people. That's the English word, yes?" I nodded. "But it's very difficult. Don't know where to find."

I chuckled. "Yes, I know."

"Sometimes, I like some guy, but he doesn't like me. Or he likes me only for friend. I meet some American gay man, too." He smiled sadly. "I think it's easier to find American gay man in Beijing. They not so shy."

I wondered if "predatory" was a word he might have used. It made me squirm to think that I could have come across as one of those "not so shy" Americans.

"So it's difficult to concentrate on my painting," Bosheng continued. "I have so many worries."

He described the rigor of his courses, the criticisms he'd endured from his professors, the loneliness of his first year in the capital. I thought back to my own graduate school days and how I'd ultimately abandoned the program to find myself as a gay man. Maybe if I'd been Chinese, I'd have stuck with it. Bosheng's next question threw me:

"You like me, David?"

"Yes," I told him. *"Liliwaiwai."* It was the first new expression I'd learned since my New Year's resolution, an idiom that, literally translated, meant "inside inside–outside outside." The idea was that I liked him *completely*. It made him smile.

We ended up going back to my apartment, where, for the next hour, as we sat on the sofa, Bosheng let me hold his hand while he told me more stories about his life, even sadder ones, about loneliness and long years of waiting and unrequited love. I listened in adoring awe, drinking in the exquisite combination of his good looks, gentle modesty, and stoic resignation to the fate of being homosexual in the P.R.C. He was so much of what I liked in Edward, but with the added good measure of his sex appeal, which I found intoxicating. I wanted to be the man Bosheng had always hoped would come into his life, the man who recognized and loved his simple goodness. When I asked him to stay the night, he asked me why.

"Well, because I like you. I like you a lot." Although we hadn't talked about his sexual history, the thought occurred to me that maybe he didn't sleep around. "Bosheng, I know we've only just met, but"—I squeezed his hand—"I would like to be your special friend."

"Special friend for tonight," he said, slipping his hand out of my hold, "but maybe you not think I am special friend tomorrow."

"But why wouldn't I?"

"With Americans, too much breaking heart."

"I would never break your heart." It seemed like the kind of promise I could already make to him.

He looked up at me.

"Chinese guy, David, we fall in love too easy. Not experienced in love like you American guys. You go to bed one night with Chinese boy, the next day, he mistaking it for love and wanting you to be his lover and begin a marriage. This happen to me two times already since I am in Beijing. I fall in love with two American guys. One is Peter. I sleep with him one night, then I never see him again. Other is Richard. That's how I know that Dick is nickname. Richard and I sleep together for one month, then he not wanting to see me anymore." Bosheng shook his head. "Too much breaking heart, David."

I held him out at arm's length.

"Bosheng, listen to me. I am not like that."

He slowly shook his head. He didn't want to hear all this again.

"I am twenty-nine, David. I tell you already: my family wanting me to come home and getting married with some girl."

"But you wouldn't do that, would you?"

"Don't know. But I think I cannot disappointment my parents."

"Can't you explain to them . . ." I cut myself short. Even I knew what a ridiculous question this was. I took his hand again.

"Bosheng, you have to be true to yourself." It seemed like such an American Boy Scout thing to be telling him, such a whale of a platitude.

"Sorry, David, I think I must go now."

When I kissed him good night (he turned his lips away and gave me his cheek), I felt as if I were layering bandages on a tender wound. I took one more chance and asked if we could see each other again.

"Yes, I like to see you again, David." I must have looked surprised, because he added, "Want to be your friend, David. Just cannot be special friend, okay?"

"Okay."

I suggested we spend New Year's Eve together, but Bosheng said that he had plans with his colleagues from the painting academy. He promised he'd call me after the holiday. When he left, I watched him as he walked all the way down the corridor to the elevator. He did not turn around when he got on.

The next day, I invited Stewart out for New Year's Eve dinner, just the two of us. If one of my resolutions was to spend more time with him, ringing in the new year together seemed the obvious first step.

"But what about your new friend?" he asked. "The one you brought home last night?" Stewart had met Bosheng when we first came in, then had discreetly retired to his room. "Wouldn't you rather be with him?"

I feigned surprise. "Bosheng? Oh, come on, I've only just met him. Don't you think that would be rushing things a bit?"

"I don't know. You seemed pretty smitten last night."

"Smitten? All we did was walk in and say hello to you."

"Smitten," Stewart repeated. He ambled over to the CD player. "Look, if you like him, then you should ask him out for New Year's Eve. What have you got to lose?"

I stared at the back of Stewart's head.

"Well, *like* him, yes, but . . ."

Stewart turned around.

"David, your face was glowing like a Christmas tree last night."

"It was?"

"It was."

"Bosheng says he just wants to be friends, not special friends."

"Friends can lead to special friends, no?"

I laughed.

"Stewart, since when have you become the love expert around here?"

Stewart grinned.

"See what happens after three months of living with you?"

"Well, as a matter of fact . . ." I started laughing, like a kid who's been caught doing something he shouldn't. "I did ask him. But he can't. He already has plans."

Stewart shook his head in amused wonder.

"David, you are so predictable."

I leaned in and kissed him with exaggerated slurpiness on the side of his neck. It was the first time I'd ever shown Stewart that much physical affection.

"Happy New Year, Cupcake."

Playfully, he wriggled out of my hold.

"Excuse me, but weren't you going to go buy a new dictionary today?"

The Jianguomen was packed with holiday shoppers. A festive spirit danced in the blisteringly cold Sunday afternoon air. As crowded and cold as the city was, it felt good to get out of the apartment for a few hours.

I spent a half hour browsing in one of the avenue's bookshops, leafing through one dictionary after another, but none of them satisfied me. One had faint ink and paper as thin as tissue; another was full of typographical errors, two on the title page alone; in a third, some of the plates were printed askew.

I was about to move on to another shop when I spotted a dictionary that I thought might do. It wasn't perfect, but it seemed the best of the lot: a reassuring feel to the paper; crisp, readable print; illustrative phrases accompanying most of the definitions. As a final test, I looked up a word that had been bothersomely missing from my little tourist dictionary. There it was, nestled between "gauze" and "gaze."

Gay: *tóngxìngliànde*. I studied the four characters that followed the pinyin transcription. *Tong* I knew; that meant "same." And the third character, *lian,* contained the radical for heart. I guessed the whole thing added up to something like "same heartedness." I liked that. It was how I already felt about Bosheng. Same-heartedness.

Just then, I noticed a Chinese man standing next to me, staring at my face.

"Excuse me," he said, "but may I suggest that you do not buy that dictionary?"

By Chinese standards, he was tall, a few inches under six feet, with a plain, fleshed-out face. I guessed him to be in his early forties.

"Why not?"

"I think the scholarship is not good." He cupped his hands in front of his belly. "Maybe you can find another one that is more accurate. With definitions that give you more . . ." He paused. "I have forgotten the word. Delicacy, maybe?"

"Nuance?" I suggested. "Shades of meaning?"

"Yes. That's it. Shade of meaning."

I grinned at him.

"But what if I'm just a silly American tourist who only wants a simple phrase book so that he can find the nearest McDonald's?"

"Oh, but I think you are not in Beijing to buy hamburgers."

I looked at him more closely. His lips were thin and pale, a scholar's lips perhaps. His hair fell in an unflattering bowl cut. The shapeless parka he was wearing, a dull beige in color, underscored his sallow complexion; and his sweater, a Chinese machine-knit thing, in more neutral tones of gray, dull brown, and beige, hung baggily on his torso.

"You're right, I'm not in Beijing to eat hamburgers." I put a slight formality back into my voice. He was not someone I wanted to flirt with.

"And what *is* your business here?" he asked.

I told him.

"Office manager." He nodded as if considering the Confucian virtue of such a line of work. "But I think you are also a student of human behavior. You are here, perhaps, not only to manage an office but also to . . . hmm, check out the Beijing scene?"

I complimented him on the idiomatic quality of his English.

"I read many American books. Especially modern American novels." He paused. "Love stories."

The whole time we spoke, he never took his eyes off me. I had a feeling he was still trying to figure me out, as if a year's stint as an office manager couldn't possibly be reason enough to keep me, or any American, in Beijing during the dead of winter.

I was about to ask him what his favorite books were, when he excused himself again and asked how old I was.

"Forty-nine."

"And are you married?" I smiled. "Yes," he agreed, "I know that Americans consider to ask such questions impolite, but I think in English you have an expression: When you are visiting in Rome, you must conduct yourself like a Roman."

"Yes, we have that expression." He waited. "No," I conceded, "I'm not married."

He nodded. It seemed as if he had expected that answer.

"But I am detaining you from making your purchase." He pointed to the dictionary. I invited him to suggest another. Without hesitation, he pulled a dictionary from a display shelf. "This one, I think. Many more words, more . . ." He hesitated. "This word that you told me? New . . .?"

"Nuance."

"Many more nuances. Try it."

As the cashier rang up my purchase, Jiantao—by now we had introduced ourselves—told me that he was meeting a friend for coffee and asked if I would like to join them.

"Coffee? In Beijing?" I smiled. "But, Jiantao, what happened to 'When in Rome'?"

"Ah, but once a week, on Saturday afternoons, I have coffee. A little extravagance." He pronounced it as if it were two words, each accented on the first syllable: *éxtra vágance.*" Without thinking, I corrected him, and he apologized.

"No, please," I counterapologized. "I think your way of pronouncing it is charming. It hints at the original meaning. It comes from Latin, you know: *extra vagari,* 'to wander outside.'"

"You see, I think you *are* a scholar."

"I don't think so. I just like languages."

He looked me straight in the eye. "Well, then, my friend who likes languages, will you join me for a bit of wandering outside?"

Out on the street, the wind had picked up. Despite the intense, dusty cold, the bustle along the Jianguomen was brisk. Hundreds of shoppers, bundled up in parkas and quilted jackets, their heads wrapped in baggy knit caps, pushed and jostled along, toting cheap plastic bags full of goods. As we moved through this river of humanity, Jiantao huddled close beside me.

"David, do you like Beijing?"

"Yes, I do."

"And what is it that you like about the city?" He threaded his arm through mine.

"Well, I like the people. I think the Chinese are very . . . kind."

We came to an intersection. Across the street, a new business complex was going up. Billboards in Chinese and English announced, "Joint Venture for a New Year of Friendship! Happy Partnership for a New Millennium of Cooperation!" I stared at the big, bold lettering, bright yellow over a fire-engine red background and thought about Bosheng—sweet, decent, honest Bosheng—maintaining his integrity even in the face of a world of hollow slogans and broken promises. As we waited to cross, Jiantao grabbed my arm more tightly.

"Yes," he said, "many Chinese will show you kindness, but that is only because you are a guest in our country. Excuse me, David, if I tell you that not all Chinese are so kind. You must be careful."

"Oh, I'm careful." The light changed and we began to cross the street. I used the opportunity to remove my arm from Jiantao's hold. "So now it's my turn to ask how old you are."

"Guess," he said.

To me he looked over forty, but I guessed thirty-five. He smiled. "Thirty-eight."

"And you are married?"

"No, like yourself, I am not married."

"Thirty-eight and not married! But, Jiantao, I think in many ways you are not doing as the Romans do."

He chuckled.

"Yes, I am a bad Chinese."

"But maybe a good American?" I teased.

The smile on his face dissolved into a frown.

"No, I have no wish to be an American. I am very proud to be Chinese." We had reached the other side of the street, and he took my arm again. "We will have some coffee now?" He pointed to a café. "Please," he said, opening the door and bowing slightly.

Once we were inside, Jiantao immediately spotted his friend.

"David, will you please wait here? My friend is sometimes uncomfortable with foreigners. I will first go and explain who you are." He hurried over to the table, leaving me at the entrance.

The café was identical to the one where I had met Bosheng: espresso and cappuccino machines from Italy, posters of the Arc de Triomphe and the Côte d'Azur, glass display cases with neat arrangements of croissants, French bread and Chinese versions of French fruit tarts.

Soon Jiantao was back, inviting me to come join him and his friend. The friend, whose name was Guoyang, was younger—still in his twenties, I guessed—and considerably more attractive than Jiantao. Where Jiantao's lips were thin and pale, Guoyang's were full and rosy. Thick black hair fell over his forehead in a profusion of rakish bangs. His eyes were dark and bright. Over a handsome, light gray pullover, he wore a silk scarf in shades of deep purple and blue, tied like an ascot.

"You have new dictionary?" he asked shyly in English that was not nearly as accomplished as Jiantao's. The pitch of his voice, soft and high, was rather feminine. It suddenly occurred to me that the two of them might be gay. They might, in fact, be lovers.

"Yes." I pulled out the dictionary and showed him. "What do you think?"

Guoyang looked at Jiantao, and they exchanged some words in Chinese.

"Guoyang says it is not for him to have an opinion about your new dictionary," Jiantao said.

"And why's that?"

Once again, they conferred in Chinese. I was beginning to gather that Guoyang could understand English better than he could speak it.

"Guoyang says that it is typically American to have an opinion about everything," Jiantao translated.

"And the Chinese?" I looked at Guoyang again. He was blushing. "You don't have opinions?"

"Have," Guoyang said, "but not so important to speak opinion every time."

Jiantao interrupted. "I think you have been here long enough, David, to understand that we Chinese are not so self-expressed as you Americans."

"Do you think so? I don't know, I've met some pretty self-expressed Chinese."

"Yes?" Jiantao seemed both amused and curious. He turned back to Guoyang and the two of them conferred again.

"Guoyang and I would like to buy you a cup of coffee."

"No, please, my treat," I insisted. "As a thank you for helping me to select a new dictionary."

"Okay, we accept with pleasure," Jiantao said.

While I waited at the counter for our order to be filled, I glanced over at my new friends. They were animatedly talking. If they were lovers—and I was now convinced they were—then they'd be the first gay couple I'd met in China. I wished Bosheng could meet them. He needed some encouragement that a relationship between two men was possible.

When I returned with the coffees, Guoyang and Jiantao quickly broke off their conversation.

"I have been explaining to Guoyang where you come from," Jiantao said. "Boston, Massachusetts."

"Yes, my friends back home say I'm very gutsy to come halfway around the world for a year." I turned to Guoyang. "Gutsy? Do you understand?" He looked at Jiantao to translate, but Jiantao shook his head. "Guts are your internal organs." I slapped my stomach. "Gutsy means, coming directly from your gut, from the innermost core of yourself."

Jiantao said something in Chinese and Guoyang nodded.

"Yes," he said. "Not afraid. Full of virtue."

"So, David, do you consider yourself a person of virtue?" Jiantao asked.

"Well, I'd like to think of myself as a good person."

Jiantao smiled impishly. "Do you know Kong Fuzi?"

"Confucius."

"Yes. He said he never saw a man who loved virtue as much as sex. What do you think of that?" He was chuckling.

It was the first time that I'd heard a Chinese person say the word "sex."

"That's quite an opinion for a Chinese!"

"Not opinion," Guoyang interjected. "It's fact." He was blushing again.

When I got home that evening, I had a surprise for Stewart.

"How would you feel about not going out New Year's Eve?"

"Why? Bosheng change his mind?" He was lying on the sofa reading.

"No." I paused. Stewart looked up from his book. "I've invited some guys here for dinner instead."

Stewart slowly laid the book face down on his chest.

"What guys?"

I explained about Jiantao and Guoyang and how I'd met them.

"They're a couple. They actually live together. Not in state housing, of course. Jiantao works for a joint venture. He makes enough to afford his own place." I went on and on, filling him in on all the details that I'd learned that afternoon. I could hear myself gushing with excitement. Stewart slowly eased himself up from the sofa.

"We're cooking for *them*?"

"It doesn't have to be Chinese."

"You want us to cook *American* for them?"

"Well, Chinese then. Anything."

"On four days' notice?" As he got up from the sofa, Stewart shook his head. "All my special cook books are back home in Philadelphia."

———

It was Stewart's and my first dinner party together, and we fussed and argued like an old married couple about how to pull it off.

There were decisions of all kinds to be made: what to cook (we settled on chicken), how to prepare it (stir-frying seemed safest), what to drink (beer and wine, we decided) and then again which nationality to buy. Every choice entailed another round of negotiation. In the two and a half years since Johnny had died, I hadn't had to deal with anyone else when I prepared to entertain guests. Wrangling with Stewart brought back all the aggravations, and pleasures, of married life.

For Stewart, there was a different set of challenges to face. Not only was it to be the first time he would entertain a gay couple, but it was also the first time he would entertain *as* a gay man. By the afternoon of the party, he was a wreck, scurrying about our apartment, setting the table, arranging the flowers, selecting CDs to play throughout the evening: Chopin for openers, a Haydn string quartet with dinner, some Dvořák volin and piano duos at dessert, and Italian opera arias in reserve.

"In reserve?" I asked.

"I don't know," he said, and shook his head in such bewilderment that I decided not to press it further.

At seven-thirty, when the doorman rang us up to announce our guests, Stewart sprang from the sofa where he had been trying to relax and pressed the button on the stereo, launching Artur Rubinstein on a journey through the Chopin B-flat-minor nocturne. Then he rushed to the door, looked down the hall, closed the door, returned to the sofa, and two seconds later, sprang up again when he thought he heard someone outside the apartment. It was two more minutes before the elevator actually brought Guoyang and Jiantao to our floor, during which time Stewart had managed to straighten the candles, fluff the flower arrangement and refold all four dinner napkins.

They were dressed in much the same way as when I'd first met them. Jiantao had on another dowdy sweater; Guoyang wore a beautiful pullover, this one a deep, luscious plum color, and his characteristic silk scarf. Stewart started to greet them in Chinese—it sounded like a little speech he'd prepared—but halfway through he got flustered and switched to English.

"But your Chinese is excellent," Jiantao said. He flashed me a broad smile. "Better than David's, I think."

That broke the ice and we proceeded into the living room, where Stewart choreographed the seating: our guests on the sofa, he and I in the easy chairs. As soon as we all sat down, Stewart leapt up again. I noticed Guoyang trying to suppress a giggle.

"Drinks!" Stewart announced. "What would you all like to drink?"

When Jiantao asked for scotch, Stewart shot me a pleading look.

"Jiantao, I'm afraid Stewart and I thought that since we are, as it were, in Rome, we would do as the Romans. So tonight we can offer only Tsingtao beer and white wine: Great Wall brand."

"Very thoughtful and entirely appropriate," Jiantao said. "I'll have a glass of beer, please." He turned to Guoyang. *Ni xiang he shenme?*"

"Yes, I can understand," Guoyang said softly. "Beer for me also, please."

Stewart rushed off to the kitchen without asking me what I wanted.

"You know, you guys never did tell me how you met," I said.

Guoyang blushed and looked at Jiantao. For a moment, neither of them spoke.

"We met in a park," Jiantao finally volunteered. He reached over and took Guoyang's hand. "Two years ago."

"A park?" Stewart called from the kitchen. "That is *so* romantic!"

"Well, I think maybe not so romantic." Jiantao looked knowingly at me. "I think you can understand, David, in this country the places for men like us to look for a boyfriend are very few. If you are a straight guy, sure, you can flirt with girls at school, at work, in the street. Even in the middle of Tiananmen Square. No problem. But gay guys?" He looked at Guoyang, who lowered his eyes. "So you pick up someone at the gay night scene—maybe you know about some of these places, David?—someone you think you like, and you don't let go. Because if you let go this one, you worry that it may take a very long time to find the next one."

Stewart returned from the kitchen, gingerly balancing a tray with four Pilsner glasses, their rims sporting four perfect heads of beer. I had never noticed the Pilsners before and wondered if Stewart's party preparations had included a shopping expedition for new glassware.

After we toasted to the New Year, Jiantao related how he and Guoyang, after they first met, had spent several months getting to know one another: dinner, movies, conversation. They had been dating close to a year when Jiantao introduced Guoyang to his parents.

"I told them, this is the person I love." He smiled. "You see the result of foreign cultural influence?" Glancing lovingly at Guoyang, he continued. "My hope was always to find someone I love and who loves me and, if possible, to have a life together that is more than just sex. To have . . . hmm, can you say 'feelings exchange'?"

Stewart gushed again. "Feelings exchange. That is so romantic!"

Jiantao shook his head. He looked annoyed. "Not romantic. Re-alistic. In America, you have too many romantic dreams, and you expect all those dreams to become real. You want them all." There was an abrasive edge to his voice. "That's why you Americans are always changing your partners."

I was about to challenge him on that, but he continued.

"We Chinese can't afford so many dreams, so many romantic freedoms. The atmosphere here is more challenging than in your country. We meet more difficulties than you do in America. We cannot be so romantic."

The Chopin nocturne had reached a particularly lyric passage. For a few seconds, no one spoke. We listened to the music, each of us, I guessed, following those sensuous lines toward some definition of romance that made sense to him. I knew Jiantao had a point. The Chinese, maybe especially gay Chinese, did not have the luxury of dropping in and out of love affairs. In his own way, Bosheng had told me the same thing. And though I wanted to believe that I would behave differently if only Bosheng would give me a chance, it pained me to recall my own skittish reaction to Eryan, the guy I'd taken home from the park back in November, the one who had wanted to be my lover after we'd spent that one night together. I had never even called him back.

It was Guoyang who broke our silence. "We Chinese have a lot of dreams, too." His thin, shy voice was barely audible above the music.

Jiantao immediately interrupted.

"But in China we make the dreams real together. Not alone. Whatever the dream is, Guoyang and I are in it together."

"What do you think will happen as China becomes more Western?" Stewart asked. "I mean, do you think you'll . . ."

Jiantao didn't let him finish.

"Of course, we will learn from the West, but we will try to protect those aspects of the Chinese tradition that are good." When he stopped to take a sip of beer, Guoyang spoke up.

"Maybe, too, we will learn from you Americans to have our own sauna and to have our own bars." The shy smile reappeared on his face.

Jiantao hastily put down his Pilsner.

"But that's not enough! We should also stand on the traditional Chinese concept of love. Chinese people understand love is a commitment to each other. Not a pleasant diversion that you abandon when you are tired of the other person. When a problem comes, we will try our best to help each other. And whenever happiness comes, we will try to share it, too."

"Sauna?" Stewart asked.

For a second no one answered him. Chopin continued to flutter in the air like a butterfly on a carefree summer afternoon.

"A sauna's a bathhouse," I explained.

Stewart frowned. "Wait. I'm confused. I thought there already were bathhouses in China."

"Stewart, Guoyang means a *gay* bathhouse."

Stewart looked at me as if I'd just told him that the Great Wall was made of rice cakes.

In spite of the awkwardness of the evening, Stewart decided that he liked Jiantao and Guoyang enough to want to see them again. The very next day, the first of the new year, he called them up to arrange another get together, a concert of traditional Chinese music that he had read about in one of the English-language newspapers. From then on, the three of them began to spend a lot of time together—dinners, concerts, museums, nighttime strolls into the hutong neighborhoods of old Beijing. I was sometimes invited to join them, but usually I begged off. I thought it would be important for Stewart to be branching out on his own, without me.

Stewart enjoyed these outings immensely, returning from each one with an enthusiastic recap of the evening—what they had seen, what they did, what they talked about. He loved to repeat for me the ancient tales and legends that Jiantao and Guoyang were teaching him, especially the ones with homosexual themes. There were poems about "blossom boys" and "half-eaten peaches," stories about the emperors and their boy lovers, the sacrifices they made for each other and the tears they shed. Stewart would fall into such effuse rhapsodies recounting all this that I started referring to his dates with the guys as his "Misty Moon and Sweetmeats Evenings." It was a sarcastic dig on my part. I should have been happy that he was finally increasing his familiarity with the culture of homosexuality, even if all of his experience was still only chaste and literary. But some little perversity inside me would not let me be glad for him. He was all too green and agog. I wished I could fast-forward him ahead three years.

Meanwhile, Bosheng and I were seeing more of each other. I was quite smitten by him, but Bosheng—whom I had started calling Bo—kept making it clear that he only wanted to be friends, a situation I reluctantly accepted.

One frigid night toward the end of February, as we were finishing dinner at a restaurant, I asked him if it was the difference in our ages that stood in the way of his considering me for a boyfriend.

"Not difference in ages," he said. "Age is not important, David."

"So why won't you give me a chance, Bo?" Under the restaurant table, I began to caress his leg with my foot.

"I already explain."

"But you know I'm not like those other guys. Like Peter, like Richard." I had heard the stories so many times now that I felt I knew his faithless lovers intimately. "Bo, I want you to understand . . ." I stopped, partially because I didn't know what else to say, and partially because his beauty—those intense black eyes and heavy black eye-brows, his high cheekbones, the delicate contour of his neck—all that loveliness always caught me up short. "You *know* me, Bo. I wouldn't do that to you."

Bo lowered his eyes. "David, when I was with those other guys, I thinking I know them, too."

"But . . ."

He didn't let me finish. "And even if I have boyfriend, I think I must not disappoint my parents. They still wanting me to get married."

Delicately, I moved my foot away.

Toward the end of the month, Stewart's company gave him a week's vacation. He surprised me by announcing that he was going to Hong Kong for a few days. When I remarked that Hong Kong might prove to be expensive, Stewart said he'd be staying at the YMCA. I shook my head. Only a few months before, the idea of Stewart's staying at a Y would have been perfectly ludicrous. Privately, I wondered if he was planning some Village People activity, his maiden voyage, as it were, into the world of gay sex. It seemed unlikely, but I wished him well and reminded him to play safe.

I decided to celebrate the free apartment by throwing a small dinner party. Guoyang and Jiantao immediately came to mind. I'd hardly seen them since our New Year's Eve dinner together. To make it a foursome, I added Edward. I thought Guoyang and Jiantao would also enjoy him. At the last minute, I asked Bo as well.

"I accept with pleasure," Jiantao told me when I called to invite them, "but Guoyang won't be able to attend. He has gone to Hong Kong for a few days. A sudden business trip."

I spent the next half hour sitting on the sofa, staring at Stewart's CD player and arguing with myself about whether my suspicions could be true. A coincidence, I told myself. Hong Kong was a big, popular place. Lots of people from Beijing must go there every day. But the unusual suddenness of Stewart's decision and his avowed hatred of the glitzy consumer culture that the city stood for worked against my best hopes until finally I had to admit the strong possibility that Stewart and Guoyang were having an affair. Wretchedly, I wondered if my own bed-hopping, as modest as it had been that winter, had somehow given Stewart a signal that anything was okay, even sleeping with the lover of your friend.

The dinner party was a success. Bo, Jiantao, and Edward, all of whom had never met, turned out to be quite companionable and were kind enough to speak English to each other, a gesture of such courtesy to me that I became even more despondent at the thought of Stewart's treachery. When, at one point, Jiantao asked where Stewart was, I tossed off something about his "going south" for a vacation and steered the conversation to another topic. Still, I couldn't keep my curiosity in check for long.

"Hong Kong's so expensive," I ventured casually as we were moving from the table to the living room to have our coffee. "Is Guoyang's company paying for the whole trip?"

"Yes," Jiantao said, "but they economize. They have put him up at the YMCA. Young Men's Christian Association." He smiled. "You see, David, how Western we are becoming?"

Around eleven, the party broke up. Jiantao and Edward left together. They had discovered that they lived near each other and decided to share a cab. Bo stayed behind to help me clean up.

"Did you have a nice time?" I asked as we were washing the dishes.

"Yes," he said. "Very nice time, David. I like your friends. And you? Did you have a nice time?"

I rinsed a plate and handed it to Bo, who swaddled it in his dish towel.

"Bo, I always have a nice time when I'm with you."

From the living room, *Turandot* filled the air. Earlier that evening, Jiantao had discovered the CD among Stewart's collection and asked if we could play it, adding that Guoyang had been looking for a copy to give to Stewart ever since they'd learned that it was one of Stewart's favorite operas. I had left it playing after the others had gone, not because I expected Puccini to work his romantic magic on Bo—Western classical music meant nothing to him—but because the opera brought Stewart back into the room for me, the Stewart I thought I'd known all these months and the new Stewart, the one I didn't know, the one who was beginning to grope his way through the unfamiliar territory of love, or whatever it was exactly that he and Guoyang thought they had going. I turned back to the soapy dishpan.

"Bo, do you think Jiantao and Edward will sleep together tonight?" He didn't answer. "Bo?"

"Jiantao has boyfriend."

"I'm well aware that he has a boyfriend, but the boyfriend is in Hong Kong right now."

"I think he should be faithful to his boyfriend."

"Damn it, Bo, I know what he *should* be! That's not what I'm asking you."

Bo looked up. "Why you worry, David?"

"It's not a question of worry. It's a question of information, Bo. You're Chinese. The two guys who left together are Chinese. I want to know what's going on, and I assume that you, far better than I, can figure it out."

"Nothing to figure out," Bo said. "They just taking taxi together."

"Ah, yes, I forgot. Only American boys break hearts, not Chinese boys. Chinese boys aren't cunning, are they, Bo? No, they're just naive, sentimental, romantic kids without a conniving, duplicitous bone in their bodies!"

I knew that Bo wouldn't understand half the words I was using, but I didn't care. I had to get this off my chest, in words that made sense to me.

"David, why you so angry?"

"Why?" I stood there, trying to grab hold of a piece of that question. "Why?" As if touching him would bring me an answer, I cupped his shoulders in my hands. "Damn it, how I wish I could convince you . . ."

I broke off. What precisely was it I wanted to convince him of? That there *was* someone out there for him? That the pattern of things could be different? That with *me* they would be different? There were no words left, either in Bo's language or mine, that would ever convince him of that. I let go of the dish I was washing and clasped him tightly.

Bo rested his head on my shoulder. I felt all the weariness that was draining his body. I felt it in mine, too. Weariness and sadness and loss. Maybe if we just held each other, didn't let go for a long time, all this distress would go away. As I continued to hold him, I became aware of our breathing, how it had relaxed into a deep, slow rhythm. I wanted it to stay that way forever. But time did not dissolve. In another minute, as if we could read each other's minds, we quit our embrace. When I tried to make eye contact, Bo avoided my look. For a second, I wondered if Bo had been lying to me all along. Maybe a guy like me was not his cup of tea; or maybe there was someone else he was seeing. Here in Beijing, who knew how to read anything anymore? But he had a different surprise in store for me.

"I going home next week. My parents have found girl for me to marry."

"What!"

"I know for a week now, David, but I am afraid to tell you."

"Bo, I don't know what to say."

"Don't have to say anything."

I wanted to tell him about the guys I'd met that winter, guys who had told me even sadder stories than his, stories about being gay and married and miserable. One had even confessed to his wife that he was gay, but she had only laughed in his face, so preposterous was the notion; another had deliberately chosen the homeliest girl in their village in order to have an excuse to be away from home as often as possible. *Don't do this,* I wanted to yell at him, but I could see in Bo's eyes that he was resolved to go through with it, if for no other reason than to please his parents. They had been the subject of so many of the stories he had told me.

"I'm going to miss you, Bo. Miss you terribly."

"Miss you, too, David. Never forget you." There were tears in his eyes.

I had half a notion to ask if I could come to the wedding, but I knew whatever life we'd had together had to come to an end.

"I'll never forget you, either, Bo." The last person I'd said that to was Johnny.

We said good night—we embraced but did not kiss—and Bo left. This time I could not bear to watch him walk down the hall toward the elevator. I closed the door to the apartment and just stood there, stunned. *Wow* was the only word I could summon up—whispered now into the sudden awful silence of the room— the only sound that could begin to capture what I was feeling.

I began to turn off the lamps, but too much was swirling around in my head. I wasn't ready for bed. I needed something else. Another drink? To sit down with my journal? To e-mail Owen? To talk to Stewart? The little red power light on the stereo caught my eye.

I cued up the beginning of *Turandot* again, lay down on the sofa and took up the libretto. In all the times that Stewart had played this opera, I had never once followed along with the words.

The music crashed and soared in tumults of anger and agony, viciousness and lyric suffering. It was a nightmarish vision of Peking, a nightmarish vision of humanity, cruel, pitiless and cold.

"Muoia!" came the bloodthirsty shrieks of the crowd as they shouted at the Prince of Persia. "Die! We want the executioner!"

For a few cynical moments, I wanted to put Stewart and Guoyang into the hands of that executioner, too.

But there was pity in that music as well. I heard it, the fleeting tenderness that Puccini had managed to work into that ghastly opening scene. As the executioner leads the Prince to the gallows, the sight of his sweet, pallid face momentarily converts the fury of the crowd.

"O giovinetto!" they cry out. "So young! Mercy, pardon!"

I closed my eyes. Yes, I thought, so young. When all else fails, it's youth—that most unearned of virtues—youth that wins forgiveness, that escapes unharmed, that gets the reprieve. What marvelous luck. At least while it lasts.

I bundled up in my coat and left for a nightcap at the Ta Ta.

Chapter Fourteen

It took Stewart only three days after he returned from Hong Kong to announce that he was moving back to Philadelphia. The official reason—the reason he gave to his parents when he called to tell them—was that he had decided to resume his graduate studies. In truth, he wanted to get as far away from Beijing as possible.

The thing with Guoyang had been a disaster. The boy liked Stewart well enough, but had made it clear as soon as they had checked into the YMCA together that he was only interested in a sexual relationship, nothing more. As soon as they had made love (Stewart confessed to me that he came within five minutes of Guoyang's touching him), Guoyang announced that he wanted to visit a sauna. He invited Stewart to come along, but Stewart refused and spent the rest of his vacation moping around museums and eating alone in European-style restaurants. Guoyang would come back to the Y only to shower and change. During the day, he was going to business meetings for his company; at night he sampled the many delights that gay Hong Kong had to offer. On the plane back to Beijing, he had slept the whole way.

I don't think Jiantao ever found out about his lover's escapade, but Stewart said he could never see the two of them again. By the beginning of March, he had quit his job and packed up all his things. The morning of his departure, he gave me one of his teapots, his copy of *Turandot,* and the address of his parents on the Main Line outside Philadelphia. Lastly, he handed back the brick from the Great Wall. I didn't dare ask what he meant by that. Was he telling me this talisman of his coming out had lost its charm?

"Stewart, try not to punish yourself too much. You were taking a chance on love. That's okay." My mind flashed to Bo. Was he married by now? Was he happy? Miserable? Was he thinking of me? "Cupcake, we don't have much control over who we'll fall in love with."

"A chance on love," Stewart echoed. "A ridiculous, absurd, dangerous chance. Jesus, David, what was I thinking?"

"You were thinking you didn't want to be alone anymore. You were thinking he could have been your soul mate. Those aren't absurd thoughts at all. They happen in opera; why shouldn't they happen in your life?"

Stewart sighed. "They're prettier in opera."

The doorman rang us up to say that the taxi to the airport had arrived. Stewart gave me a well-this-is-it look. We hugged each other, perfunctorily at first, then long and close.

"Addio, caro," he whispered into my ear.

As much as I didn't want to see Stewart go, at first I thought I'd love having our place all to myself. The lease was only for a few more months, short enough that I could afford to swing both the apartment and the remaining payments on the rented furniture. I thought about the freedom to come and go as I pleased. I thought about the guys I could bring back and how I wouldn't have to worry about disturbing Stewart or making sure the bathroom was spotless the next morning. But then, suddenly, there was no one to make dinner for anymore, no one to teach me about opera or to debate gay politics with, no one to complain to about the weather, or to shock with my tales of nights out in gay Beijing. There was nothing but an apartment, clean and white and efficient, with a good view and electric heat and no feeling whatsoever that it was anything I wanted to share with any one else.

I started staying home more. I made flash cards of new Chinese words I wanted to learn. I wrote desultory entries in my journal. One night, I took up *Moby Dick* again. I had to go back and reread the early chapters. I got to the place where Ismael wakes to find Queequeg hugging him in bed, "in the most loving and affectionate manner."

"At length," I read, "by dint of much wriggling, and loud and incessant expostulations upon the unbecomingness of his hugging a fellow male in that matrimonial sort of style . . ."

I flung the book across the room.

"Damn you!" I shouted. "Damn you!"

Five minutes later, I was on my way to the Ta Ta. The place was feeling more and more like home.

As soon as I walked in, I ran into Channing Plessey. We hadn't seen each other since the evening back in January when Edward and I had left him in his apartment with Bright Vermilion. He was alone at the bar, a bottle of club soda in front of him.

"Where've you been?"

It seemed to be his standard opening line with me. I had no idea how to begin to account for the past two months of my life.

"Working," I told him.

He chuckled suggestively.

"You mean, working it, don't you?"

I gave him a look that said, Don't push it.

"Oh, get off it, Masiello, lighten up." He patted the stool next to himself. "Come on, let me buy you a drink. Is it still San Miguel?"

"Thanks."

I hiked myself up onto the stool, happy to drop my sour attitude. I was curious to know about Bright Vermilion, but it seemed uncouth to start up the conversation this way. On the other hand, Channing had no such qualms.

"Where's your friend?" he asked.

"Who?"

"The tall red head. You know, the one I thought was your boyfriend. He looked like a scared bunny rabbit the first time I met him. What's his name? Sebastian?"

"Stewart."

"Yeah, Stewart."

"He's back in the U.S."

"Yeah? All winter, I kept thinking I could have used him in *Blood Wedding*. That long, El Greco-like face . . ." Channing sculpted it in the air. "Perfect." He broke his reverie and turned to me. "Why'd he go back?"

"I think he'd had enough of Beijing."

Channing studied my eyes. He could see I wasn't coming clean.

"Masiello, what is it exactly that you don't like about me? That I'm a rich WASP? That I'm a lush? That I consort with money boys? What?"

"Channing, I have nothing against you."

"Then take that stiff iron poker out of your ass."

"Sorry. It's been a rough couple of months."

My beer arrived. I clinked it against Channing's bottle of club soda.

"*Gan bei.*"

"*Gan bei.*"

"So how did it go, *Blood Wedding*?"

Channing shrugged. "It went. Next time, I think we'll do *Flower Drum Song*. Something light and fluffy and full of parts for pretty Chinese boys. What do you think?"

I smiled.

"I'm sure it will have a certain appeal."

Channing let out a belly laugh.

"Ah, Masiello, always the perfectly measured response." He shook his head in amusement. "Are you sure you're Italian?"

"If you met my mother, you'd have no doubts."

I took another sip of my beer. When I put the bottle back down, I realized that Channing had been watching me intently.

"So how's it going?" he asked. "Really."

"I don't know. It's going." I slowly pushed my bottle across the counter until it touched Channing's. "Like I said, it's been kind of rough the past few months."

I gave him a quick digest of my life since we'd last seen each other: my frustrated affair with Bo; meeting Jiantao and Guoyang; Stewart's secret fling in Hong Kong and subsequent flight back to Philadelphia.

"Ouch!" Channing said.

"Yeah."

"So what about that guy, what's his name? The Chinese guy I used to see you with here occasionally? You brought him up to the apartment that night."

"Guozhen. Edward."

"Yeah, Edward. What about him? Any boyfriend potential there?" I shook my head. "He's not interested, huh?"

"No, *I'm* not interested. I mean, he's a sweet guy, and we do stuff together sometimes, but . . ."

"Meiyou huaxue."

"What?"

"No chemistry."

I nodded. Just then a Chinese boy came up behind Channing and put his arms around him. It was Bright Vermilion.

"Hello, darling," Channing arched his neck up and kissed Bright on the lips. "Do you remember David?"

Bright said hello to me. His English had improved since the last time we had spoken.

"It's nice to see you two together," I said.

"Nice be together," Bright said. He whispered something in Channing's ear and they began to confer quietly together in Chinese. "Okay, I see you later, David," Bright announced when they had finished. "Bye bye." He gave Channing another peck and left. I noticed that the usual entourage of pretty boys was not in his wake.

Channing looked at me, contentment written all over his face.

"He's in school now. Preparing for entrance exams for the university. It's going to be tricky, but I think we'll pull it off."

"Are you two living together now?"

Channing shook his head.

"Pretty impossible to pull that one off. No, he's still living with his parents."

"And the money boys? His friends?"

"Oh, they're around." Channing swiveled out toward the room. "He doesn't see them much anymore." He chuckled to himself. "The little minx knows I'd break his arm if he did. No, actually, this has all been his doing: the decision to go back to school, dropping those hustlers"—he raised his bottle of club soda—"my easing up on the booze. All of it. Most nights, after work, he just comes right over to my place and studies." Channing leaned in toward me. "The doorman is horribly jealous."

"*I'm* horribly jealous!"

Channing studied my face again.

"Why?"

His question caught me off guard.

"Well, because . . . I mean, isn't it obvious? You have a boyfriend."

"And what does that mean?"

"You don't think having a boyfriend helps?"

"Of course it helps, but you can't put your life on hold while . . ."

"Channing, I know all that."

"Then stop walking around as if you *have* put your life on hold."
He paused. "Why'd you come here tonight, huh?"

I snickered.

"I was tired of reading *Moby Dick.*"

"Hungry for Mo Bi's dick, is more like it."

"Come on, Channing, don't be crude."

He stared at me hard.

"Masiello, why don't you give that good Italian Catholic boy act
a rest? You sit around petting your disappointments like they were a
pair of Chinese lap dogs. I've got news for you, David: it's not the
Qing dynasty anymore. Put down those puppies and get out into the
world."

Gazing into a mirror had never been something I enjoyed. From
the time I was a teenager, I didn't much care for the way I looked: the
Roman nose, the ears that stuck out. In time, the disenchantments
only multiplied: my hair got thinner, lines showed up in my face.
Johnny—blond, blue-eyed, Irish American Johnny—thought I was
sexy. For the eight years we were together, I had lived as if that were
true. And when he passed away, I had tried holding on to it, that sexy
way of seeing myself. There were days when I could pull it off, and
days when I couldn't. I had learned to live with the equivocation, too.

But now Channing was holding up another mirror, one that only
a few other people—Johnny, of course, and Erik before him, and
Owen—had ever dared to put in front of me. If we're lucky, we all
have at least one good friend in our lives who shows us the self we've
carefully hidden, even from ourselves. Right then and there, sitting
at that bar in the tiny, smoke-filled Ta Ta Club, with the pink and

turquoise faux–Keith Haring murals on the walls, I faced a choice: I could get angry at Channing for presuming to know me better than I knew myself, or I could laugh at the aptness of that silly, embarrassing, disagreeable image: David cultivating his disappointments like a pair of Chinese Shi-tzus.

I laughed.

"Okay, so I'm ready to join the world again."

"Welcome back."

"I don't know: why am I such an asshole sometimes?"

"Easier to let the shit out that way." Channing kept staring at me. "Masiello, you ever been to the baths?"

"Once in California. I didn't much go for it. Not enough romance for me."

"No, I mean here."

"Here?"

"Yeah. Here. Nobody's told you about the gay bathhouse?"

"Here?"

Channing let out a hearty laugh. "Yes, baby, *here*." He explained that there were still many old bathhouses in Beijing and that one— he'd been there a few times himself—had a sizable gay clientele.

"Not exclusively," he emphasized, "but . . . Well, you'll see."

"Is it safe?"

"What? Are you afraid you'll drown in the pool?"

He gave me a general overview of the place and told me how to find it: which subway station to get off at, which road to follow, where to turn.

"Look for a white sign with these words painted in black." On the back of his calling card, he scribbled down four Chinese characters and handed it over.

"Tell them Channing sent you."

"Really?"

"No! Not really!"

I studied the four characters on the card.

"You sure about this, Channing?"

"Sure about what?"

"That I should go there?"

"It's not a question of *should,* Masiello. It's a question of *would* you like to?"

I glanced at the card again. I could read a couple of the characters.

"You know, I think this good Italian Catholic boy is about to . . ." I didn't quite know how to finish the sentence, but Channing seemed to understand.

"Yeah," he said, nodding in agreement. "It happens, David. It happens."

When I left that night, it was snowing outside: the middle of March and it was snowing, the first real snow we'd had all winter.

In the morning, when I looked out my bedroom window, eleven stories down to the plaza below, the world was glistening under a beautiful, white blanket, cleaner than anything I'd yet seen in Beijing. The wind was howling, rattling the plate glass window until I thought it would shatter. My building was only a year old, but for a few seconds I thought those North China gusts might blow it down. It was the kind of blast that makes you feel very small, aware of all the bluff you bring into the world.

I glanced down at my gym bag, a crumpled heap of nylon abandoned on the floor. One of my New Year's resolutions had been to join a health club. It hadn't happened.

I got down on the carpet, crossed my hands over my chest, took a deep breath, and hauled myself up. *"Yi."* And then again: *"Er."* And again: *"San!"* By the fourth sit-up, already aching, I was yelling like a kung fu master. *"Si . . . wu . . .* Aargh!" At the sixth, the telephone rang. When I answered it, a familiar voice asked, "How much snow did you get?"

"Stewart! Where *are* you?"

"Where do you think I am? Look, I just heard you had a bad storm there last night, so I thought I'd call."

"Stewart, you are halfway around the world! How the heck did you . . ."

"Don't you remember, David, we've got television over here. We have newspapers. We even have the Internet."

"So how are you, Stewart? What's going on?"

"Not much. It turns out I can't reenroll at the university until next fall. So I'm just hanging out."

Hanging out was an expression I'd never heard him say before, and I kidded him about it.

"Well, that's what it's called, right?" He sounded defensive. And sad.

"You okay?"

"Yeah, I'm all right." It didn't sound that way, but I let it pass. "So, what's going on with you?" he asked. "How's things at the Ta Ta?"

"The Ta Ta?" I laughed. "Cupcake, you're the last person I would ever have expected to ask about the Ta Ta. The Ta Ta's fine. Why?"

"No reason. It's just that whenever I picture you, David, I see you at the Ta Ta."

"Well, picture this: I ran into Channing Plessey there last night. Remember him? He and Bright Vermilion are quite the item. They're really making a go of it." As soon as it was out of my mouth, I winced, realizing how painful it must be for Stewart to hear happy news of an American-Chinese couple. I changed the topic as quickly as possible. "Channing told me there's a gay bathhouse here in the city. Can you believe it?"

"Well, that should please Guoyang, shouldn't it?"

I winced again.

"Actually, I was thinking of checking it out today."

"What! Are you crazy! Jesus, David, you're going to end up in jail!"

"Stewart, I have no intention of ending up in jail. I mean, for what? Taking a shower?" Stewart laughed. It was good to hear some cheer in his voice. "Hey, Stewart, I miss you."

Twelve thousand miles away, he began to cry.

"Oh, God, I'm sorry, David. I promised myself I wasn't going to do this, but . . ." He let out another sob. "I am so lonely here. I miss you. I miss Beijing. I miss . . ." Another fit of tears.

"I know, Cupcake, I know" is all I could say.

"I hate this place, David. And my parents, they're driving me crazy. All they want to do is take me out to dinner and introduce me to their friends as their graduate student son who's just returned from China." He sniffled. "They don't understand anything. And it's so bland here. So sterile. Everything's wrapped in plastic. I look at people walking around, and they seem so . . . so *oblivious*."

I sat down on the bed. On and on he went about how skewed American culture was: the self-satisfaction, the pace, the obsession with material wealth. I was going home myself in a few months. I wondered if this was a preview of what I would feel. Stewart had more to tell me.

"David, it is so goddamned *straight* here! I've come back to this place that I used to be so much a part of, and now it feels so . . . so foreign to me. I mean, I just want to scream. I've been here a week, and already I'm walking around in a daze."

The advice that Channing had given me the night before was ready on my lips:

"Stewart, you need to get out, have some fun, make new friends. You shouldn't wallow in sadness. Look, you must know some gay people back there, right?"

"Not that I know of." His voice was meek, almost apologetic.

"Well, what about taking yourself to a bar? A club? Cupcake, you've got to put yourself in a position to help things along. Moping over Guoyang isn't going to accomplish a thing."

"Okay, okay." He sounded impatient with me. "So give me the name of a bar here."

I'd never been to Philadelphia, I told him. I suggested he look in the local gay paper.

"Where do I find one?"

"Anywhere. Where's the gay neighborhood in Philadelphia? Go there." I laughed. "You can always find gay newspapers in gay bars."

"Very helpful, thanks."

"Okay, so call the gay hot line.

"No way!"

"Oh, for heaven's sake, Stewart. You're in *America*. No one's going to arrest you for making a phone call." As a last resort, I suggested he call Owen in Boston. "Owen Wiszniewski. I've told you about him. He went to seminary in Philly. He still has friends there. I think he knows the city pretty well."

"He's a *priest*?"

"No. It was a failed calling. Look, he's a wonderful guy, Stewart. You'll enjoy talking to him and he'll send you to a nice place. Nothing too kinky, I'm sure. If you're too shy about calling him, you can send him an e-mail."

"I can't believe I'm doing this," Stewart said as I dictated Owen's telephone number and e-mail address to him. "Calling halfway around the world to get the name of someone who can give me the name of a gay bar in Philadelphia."

"Yeah, it happens, Cupcake. It happens."

Chapter Fifteen

The bathhouse wasn't as hard to find as I'd thought. And the attendant, a hunched-over old man as wrinkled and merry as any of those benevolent fishermen you see in antique Chinese scroll paintings, was quite pleased to sell me a five-kuai ticket, for which I got a pair of plastic sandals, a small piece of soap, and a numbered key to a locker. He gestured toward a door behind him and I went in.

The changing room was a maze of small wooden lockers, like bread boxes, stacked one on top of another. Slowly, I made my way along the first row. Halfway down, a huddle of men, all in various states of undress, were lost in conversation. When they caught sight of me, the talking immediately stopped and they parted to let me pass.

"*Xiexie,*" I thanked them. The words caught in my throat. No one responded.

At the end of the aisle, I came to an open area where a half dozen cots has been set up. Draped in towels, men were napping or getting a massage. Here, too, all activity stopped as soon as they spotted me. I made a show of examining my key. It was stamped "87."

"*Bashiqi?*" I asked.

One old guy raised himself up from the cot and pointed to the next aisle. I hurried on, conscious of being followed by a dozen pairs of eyes.

At last I found my locker and tried the key. To my relief, it worked. I sat down on a nearby bench and began to untie my boots. Just then, I noticed a middle-aged man sitting on another bench a few feet away. He was glaring at me.

"Why do you come here?" he hissed. He was wearing nothing but a towel and a pair of thin beige socks. "How you know about this place?"

"A friend told me."

He pursed his lips. "Yes, but do you understand where you are?"

"I think so." I held out my hand. "*Wo shi* David."

The man considered my hand suspiciously, then cast his eyes down the row of lockers before he shook back.

"My name is Xinlu." His hostility had yielded some.

"*Hen gaoxing . . .*"

"Please, speak English."

"Really, I'm just here to relax. I mean no harm." I began to unbutton my shirt.

"Mean no harm," he said, watching me undress, "but maybe do harm anyway."

I guessed he was in his forties. His chest was hairless and very pale; his legs spindly. He was wearing glasses—heavy, black-rimmed things—over dark, bulging eyes, so big that they reminded me of the eyes of the mollies my father used to keep in his fish tank.

"I'm not a tourist," I told him. "I live in Beijing. I work here." I slipped out of my pants. "The man who told me about this place is a friend of mine." I paused. "A friend from the Ta Ta Club."

Xinlu nodded. "Yes. Okay." For a brief moment, his gaze went down to my crotch. "But still, you must be careful here. Not everyone in this place is so sympathetic."

By now, two or three guys had congregated nearby. Xinlu didn't seem to mind.

"Your first time here?"

"Yes."

"All right. I'll show you around."

I pulled off my undershirt and slipped out of my briefs, wrapping the towel around myself as fast as I could. I overheard one of the eavesdropping lads say, "*maode.*" Hairy. The night back in November, when I'd slept with Eryan, he had taught me the word. He had told me he liked hairy chests.

In our plastic sandals, Xinlu and I flip-flopped over to the shower area. It was a huge place, longer than a basketball court and two stories tall with a dingy skylight overhead. Most of the room was taken up by a shallow pool, about as large as three or four American hot tubs, where men, neck-high in water, were relaxing on submerged tile banquettes. At either end were a dozen or so ancient shower heads, all being used. The air was thick with humidity; the light a gloomy grayish-green.

As we waited for showers to become available, Xinlu told me a little more about himself. He was forty-two. He worked for the state television system. He was still living at home.

I tried to pay attention, but kept being distracted by the men under the showers. Some were in their twenties and thirties—their bodies lithe and willowy; others were older. A few of the younger guys were helping each other to wash, playfully lathering up each other's backs and chests. Though one or two were sporting erections, the overall feel of the place was innocent, with an easy, almost presexual camaraderie. I was intensely aware that I was the only Westerner, the only circumcised person, the only one with hair on his chest.

At last, two men moved away from the shower heads and Xinlu and I took their places. He kept his glasses on. I soaped up, trying to appear nonchalant, but I was shaking. I hoped it didn't show. When Xinlu offered to scrub my back, I declined.

We finished up our showers and walked over to the central tub. Its murky water was crowded with bathers, two dozen guys or more. Again, the crowd was mixed: half in their twenties and thirties; the rest older men, upwards of sixty. Some must have been married, because they had brought their young sons along, kids around five or six, who were splashing about, the only ones oblivious to my presence.

"Are you sure there's room in there for us?" I asked Xinlu. "It looks awfully cozy."

"David, all of China is *awfully* cozy." The word seemed to amuse him. He pronounced it as three distinct syllables. Aw-ful-ly cozy. "Sometimes, aw-ful-ly lonely, too."

He motioned for me to sit down on one of the banquettes. When I did so, the water came up almost to my neck. Most conversation in the pool stopped.

"So, just how many of these guys are, you know . . ." I lowered my voice. "The 'G' word?" Xinlu gave me a quizzical look. "G—A—Y," I spelled out.

"Okay to talk, David. No problem. These guys do not understand English."

"But they're all . . . gay?"

"Can't be sure," Xinlu said. "You must look . . . hmm, I don't know how to say it: not only with your eyes."

Opposite us, on the other side of the tub, I noticed three young men, twentysomethings, who were whispering and giggling like a trio of silly American queens.

"Those three?" I asked.

"Yes, of course." Xinlu seemed annoyed to have to answer such a obvious question.

"But the others," I said. "I mean, the straight ones. Do they know what's going on here?"

Xinlu furrowed his brow. "'What's going on?'" he asked.

"Do they understand that there are gay people here?"

"David, most people in China don't know what's going on. Even if you are gay, you do not always know what's going on."

Seeing Xinlu talking to me seemed to reassure the others in the tub that I was okay. Gradually the curiosity I'd generated waned and people resumed their own conversations.

"What about you, Xinlu? Have you ever had a boyfriend?"

"Once." His eyes drifted away for a few seconds before returning to me. "About ten years ago. I was thirty-two." He paused again. I waited, hoping I had not pried too much. But then a faint smile appeared on Xinlu's face.

"We met here. He was businessman from Shanghai. Married, of course." He smiled again. "We have a very ancient expression in Chinese: 'He was like a wild crane in a flock of chickens.' That was my friend, David. Very handsome, very . . . I don't know how to say it. Just 'like a wild crane in a flock of chickens.' Do you understand?" I nodded my head. "Afterwards, whenever my friend came to Beijing, every two or three months, we stayed together. I loved him very much."

"What happened?"

"After about a year, he found another guy, younger than I am, and moved him into his house in Shanghai."

"But he was married, you said. What about the wife?"

"She was there, too. Of course!"

"The three of them were all living in the same flat?"

Xinlu laughed. "More than three, David. My friend's son and his son's wife, too. But in different rooms. My friend and his boyfriend slept together. His wife was in another room. The son and daughter-in-law in another room." He nodded his head. "It's true."

"So what happened?"

Xinlu smiled. "I think you will not believe this either. My friend had the opportunity to move to Australia. For his job. When he left China, he asked me to take care of the boyfriend."

"The guy he dumped you for?"

"David, I think you need so much time to understand Chinese people."

Suddenly, a peel of delighted shrieking burst from the mouth of one of the children at the opposite end of the pool. To hush him up, the boy's father pulled him in close, enfolding the child in his arms. It was then that I noticed that several people in the pool were still staring at me.

"You know, I've been here over half a year, and I still can't get used to the way people stare at me."

Xinlu smiled again.

"You staring, too, David."

"But I don't."

"Yes, I think so, just in a different way. Coming here, for example. That is a kind of staring, too, I think, no?"

"But . . ."

Xinlu held up his hand.

"No problem, David. I know you are a sympathetic person. Only want to understand my country."

"I hope so, Xinlu."

"Yes," he assured me.

"So what about your friend's boyfriend? Did you take care of him?"

"Yes, of course—he was all alone—but I was not in love with

him. He was factory worker." Xinlu shook his head. "But lazy. He preferred not to work. Instead of going to work, he was often coming to visit me at the television station. Almost every day. He was calling me 'brother,' asking me to buy him lunch. I was so embarrassed. He had no education. And so very dirty. But kind, too. A good person. After a few weeks, I was beginning to see that he was not so bad. He was just having a difficult life. No chance for a better situation."

"What did you do?"

"One night, I invited him to have dinner in a restaurant. We talked a lot. I started to understand him better." His eyes avoided mine, focusing instead on the empty space in front of him. "We became boyfriends."

Xinlu looked sad. As I tried to think of something to say, his foot glanced mine under the water. And then, tentatively, but with unmistakable deliberateness, he began to caress my ankle with his toes.

"And then?" I asked. "What happened next?" Slowly, I moved my foot away.

"I took the boy to live at my house." Xinlu looked up at me. He didn't seem the least bit upset that I'd rebuffed his advances. "I was living with my mother and my married brother." He stopped to cough. Covering his mouth, he turned away from me, but his toes — *someone's toes* — started caressing mine again. "Yes, I was very happy that year," he continued. "My boyfriend and I were living together. I couldn't believe."

As he spoke, I looked around the pool, wondering who else might be playing footsie with me. The queens were on the opposite side. Then I noticed a young man, a few feet away, hunkered down up to his lips in the water, as if he were hiding. He kept is eyes lowered, but I could tell he was watching me.

"But my boyfriend was not so happy," Xinlu said. "He was missing his friend in Australia. And drinking too much."

I tried not to be obvious, but my attention kept going to the young man who was running his toes up and down my leg. I had a boner now, but the water was so dirty that no one could tell as long as I stayed low in the pool. The young man's hair was cut in a short crewcut, but his eyebrows were thick and bushy, like . . . My God, it was Bosheng! He'd cut his hair, but those eyebrows and high cheek-bones gave him away. I must have done a double take, because Bo made a tiny motion with his head for me not to say anything. Mean-while, Xinlu, oblivious to what had just transpired, was continuing with his story about the boyfriend.

"He lost his job. Couldn't find any work. I spent a lot of money trying to help him." Xinlu coughed again. "Getting cold, David. Maybe we should leave now?"

Under the water, Bo continued to run his toes up and down my leg.

"If you don't mind, Xinlu, I think I'll stay in the tub a few more minutes. You go ahead. I'll catch up with you in the shower."

"No, I think it's better you have Chinese friend stay with you."

"But you're cold. Go ahead if you want. I'll catch up."

Xinlu shook his head. "No, I stay with you."

As if to reassure me, Bo's foot patted my leg. Meanwhile, Xinlu had picked up his story again.

"After we were living together six months, my brother said to me, 'Xinlu, you are a professional person; you have a university educa-tion. This boy is a factory worker. Explain to me why you are friends.'"

"How did you explain?" I shifted, as if trying to get more com-fortable, all the while stretching my leg out even farther, offering it to Bo.

"I told him it does not matter my friend is a factory worker. I re-minded my brother that in China we are all *tongzhi*. You know? Comrades."

"*Tongzhi.*" For a split second, my eyes met Bo's, but he looked away.

"After some time, my family started to understand who my new friend is. My mother began to talk to him like he is another son."

"That's beautiful, Xinlu. *Meihao.*" I let my face open up: Bo low-ered his eyes again.

"Please, just speak English," Xinlu reminded me.

"So then what?" I asked.

"We lived together another two years," Xinlu continued, "but my boyfriend never was happy. He always was thinking about his other friend in Australia. Some days he was coming home very drunk; some days he was not coming home at all. Always very sad. Then he told me he could not live with me anymore. 'Xinlu,' he said, 'you cannot give me what I want.'"

"What did he mean?"

Xinlu looked straight at me with a sad, brave smile, inviting me, I think, to consider his looks, his age, his status as one of the world's workaday chickens among its few magnificent cranes. Then he patted me on the shoulder. "I think now, David, we should get out of the water."

As we were easing ourselves from the pool—funny how you can will an erection away when you absolutely have to—I stole a glance back at Bo, who remained hunkered down in the water. The queens started giggling. Xinlu slipped into his flip flops and headed for the showers. I deliberately left mine behind, setting up a pretext to go back alone and fetch them, a way to buy another minute with Bosheng. I hoped Bo would figure it out. As we showered—and here, again, Xinlu offered to scrub my back, which I again declined—I kept looking over at the pool, trying to get Bo's attention, but he wouldn't look at me.

Back at our lockers, Xinlu and I began to towel off. I dried myself languorously, trying to figure out what to do next. I wasn't about to leave the bathhouse without seeing Bo again. What was he doing here? Was he married? Had he told his parents the truth? Had he been lying to me all along? My mind was running wild.

Meanwhile, Xinlu kept asking me questions about my life back in America: did I live alone, and was I married, and did I have a boyfriend? When I told him no, that my lover had died almost three years ago, a look of deep sympathy came over his face.

"I am sorry," he said quietly.

Just then I caught a glimpse of Bo peeking around the end of the aisle. When he saw that I'd noticed him, he pulled back behind the lockers.

"Oops, my sandals! Xinlu, I left my sandals back at the pool. I'll be right back." Before Xinlu had a chance to say anything, I wrapped the towel around my waist and hustled off. When I rounded the corner, there was Bo, a towel around his waist, waiting for me. I had never seen him with his shirt off. His torso was perfection: lanky upper arms, a hairless chest, just a trace of pectoral definition.

"Bo! What are you doing here?" Already my erection was coming back. I motioned for him to follow me. Although I had no idea what I was doing, I managed to lead us to a secluded corner at the back of the locker room where an overhead light had burned out. When I turned around, he approached cautiously. "I'm not going to bite you," I joked.

"I miss you, David."

"I miss you, too." I wanted to embrace him then and there, but it seemed much too risky. "So what are you doing here, Bo?"

"What you doing here?" His tone was neither hostile nor playful.

"Bo, maybe we should go somewhere. Do you want to have coffee? dinner?"

"What about your friend?"

"Xinlu? I just met him here today. We're not together, if that's what you mean. Come on, I'll introduce you."

"No!" For a second I thought he was going to run away. "Can you meet me outside? Just you?"

"Where outside?"

"At the Xizhimen station?" He smiled. "I saw you there when you got off the subway. I followed you to this place."

"You did?"

"I will see you there in twenty minutes, okay?" He turned and disappeared down the row of lockers.

Xinlu wanted to have dinner with me, but I told him I had already made plans with another friend.

"*Another* friend?" His eyes brightened. "Then that means, I think, you consider me your friend as well."

"Yes, of course." I was dressing so rapidly that my feet got tangled up in my underpants.

"So, another time?" When I looked up, Xinlu was staring affectionately at me.

"Of course, Xinlu." I pulled on my pants and shirt, then sat down to lace up my boots. All the while, Xinlu just stood there, in nothing but his thin, ugly beige socks and a pair of long winter underwear. When I got up to put on my jacket, he was holding out a scrap of paper.

"I think we can exchange telephone numbers, David? I would like to be your friend."

———

Bo was waiting for me at the station. Despite the fact that he was bundled up against the cold—a gray quilted jacket and a padded cloth cap, the flaps pulled down over his ears—I recognized him immediately.

"Why did you cut your hair?" I asked him, looking at the cap. I had half a mind to pull it off his head and rub my hands all over the bristles of his new crew cut.

Bo gave me a sheepish look. "Wanted to look different."

"For the wedding?" I ventured.

"What wedding?"

"Three weeks ago, you were going home to get married and give your parents a grandson. Wasn't that the plan?"

"The plan," he said. I waited for him to explain, but he didn't volunteer any more information.

"Bo, did you go home?"

"Yes."

"And did you get married?"

A pained look came over his face, as if he were about to admit that he had committed a crime. I waited.

"Not married, David. I tell my parents I cannot marry this girl."

"But another one? Did you tell them you would marry another girl?"

"David, I think they are understanding I will not get married."

I grabbed his arm. "Come on, Bo, we need to talk."

In the dying, late-winter light, we walked the snowy back streets toward Fuchengmen, our heads bent to the wind. Neither of us spoke, but in my mind I was conducting a conversation with myself. I sensed that I could probably sleep with Bo if I wanted to—to think he had followed *me* into the bathhouse—but then what? Where would this go? Where *could* it go? In the three weeks that he'd been gone, I had very neatly convinced myself that Bo had been right all along. We hardly knew each other. I was American, he Chinese. *Too much breaking heart,* he'd said. I prayed to all the powers in both our heavens that he hadn't halted the wedding solely on account of me.

At the next block, Bo stopped at a small nighttime market. Under the harsh, bare light bulbs strung across the stalls, we watched as a woman fetched a chicken out of a cage of squawking fowl. She turned it upside down and stroked its feathery breast, cooing and whispering seductively to the bird. Then, in one swift, deft motion, she ran a knife across its throat. As the blood dripped out, filling her plastic pan and spattering the snow on the ground, the bird continued to allow itself to be caressed until it drooped its head, falling into an irreversible slumber. We moved on down the alley, back into the darkness.

"Where are we going?" I asked. "I'm getting awfully cold."

"Maybe we can go to have some tea?" Bo suggested. He motioned toward a snack shop.

I'd gotten my bearings now. I could see the crown of the White Dagoba Temple peeping up over the rooftops a few streets over. I considered begging off and making my way home on my own. As if he had read my mind, Bo took my hand.

"Please, David?"

Inside, crouched around a small table on low plastic stools, we ordered tea.

"Bo, how long have you been back in Beijing?"

"One week."

I tried calculating whether that was sufficient time that I should have heard from him. I would have liked to ask him if he had tried to call me, but I didn't want to make him uncomfortable, nor did I want to seem too eager about resuming our friendship.

"So you're painting again?" His professional life seemed like a neutral course to steer.

"Yes. I lose my teaching fellowship, but the academy still takes me back, just as a regular student."

I wondered if he were still living in the small hutong studio he had told me about, but I skirted that subject, too.

"David, I think you are angry with me."

"No, Bo, not at all. I'm happy you've figured out what you really want." I meant about the painting, but he seemed to take it another way: embarrassment appeared on his face. I decided not to clarify the matter.

"I never knew about this place," Bo said. "The bathhouse. I'm just following you from the subway station and you go there."

I laughed. "It took an American to introduce you to one of the secrets of the city, huh?"

"You know about this place a long time, David?"

I shook my head. "No, somebody told me about it just a few days ago."

"A Chinese person tell you about it?"

I sensed what Bo was angling for here, and it made me smile.

"No, not a Chinese person."

"We have bathhouse in Harbin, too," Bo said, "but I think not like this bathhouse."

I studied his face. Besides the new haircut, he looked—I couldn't quite pin it down—a little older? more tired? a bit wiser? There was something, maybe just the look of three weeks' more experience, in his eyes. I wondered how I looked to him. More jaded? More resigned? Less ready to throw myself into impossible romances?

"So do you think you'll go again, to the bathhouse?" I asked.

"I don't know. Depends."

"Depends?"

"Maybe I'm not staying in Beijing, David."

"But you just told me the academy wants you back. And your parents seem to understand what your . . . your situation is. So why wouldn't you stay? You have such a wonderful opportunity here, Bo. Your studies, maybe another fellowship. Don't give that up." I told him that Harbin could not possibly offer all the advantages that Beijing could. Certainly not for a gay man, I added. As meager as it was, gay life in the capital was still *something* to be reckoned with.

"This is a good city to be a painter in, isn't it?"

He conceded that it was.

"Bo, you have to keep your soul alive. Do you understand? This is a city that will help you do that." It was presumptuous of me to say it, but I added, "There's nothing in Harbin for a person like you."

"Person like you," he quietly echoed. He seemed to be studying that idea. "Yes, Harbin is my home, but all the time I am there I am missing Beijing."

"So, Beijing has become your home now, too. Maybe more of a home than Harbin?" Bo considered this and nodded. "I understand, Bo. You know, I'm supposed to go back to Boston in a few months, but there are days when I wish I could stay here. At least a few more months."

I had no idea whether this was the truth or not. It just came out. A conversational tic, or a deep secret I hadn't known before that moment—I couldn't tell.

"Why do you want to stay?" Bo asked.

"Well, for one thing, there are so many things I still want to get to know in this city."

A silence fell between the two of us. Bo looked down at his teacup. He picked it up and swirled it around. We both watched as the tea leaves whirlpooled in the cup, then settled. When at last Bo put the cup down, he looked up at me.

"David, you want to come see my studio?"

It was close to midnight by the time Bo and I reached his hutong. After tea, we had walked across town to his neighborhood near the Bell Tower. The dimly lit streets were silent in the brittle, icy air. And though there was no one else about, for the last several blocks, Bo made me stop talking so as not to call attention to ourselves. When we got to the gate of his compound, I felt as if we were breaking into a bank, so furtively did he insist we walk through the maze of narrow, gray-brick passageways to get to his room. About the only thing I could see were the plumes of my breath, caught in the frosty moonlight. At one point, I nearly toppled over a stack of charcoal bricks that had been piled up in the alley. When we reached his door, Bo put his fingers to his lips.

His studio was no bigger than my bedroom, a cramped little cell that contained everything he needed for washing, cooking, sleeping and painting. A single, low-watt bulb hung from a cord above us. There was a hot plate and a plastic pail for washing; another for pissing. Aside from his easel and painting table, the only other piece of furniture was his bed, which occupied a good third of the room.

Over the crumbling, whitewashed walls hung his artwork, the first I'd seen: handsome studies and finished paintings, mainly still lifes, in bright, cheerful poster colors.

"Bo, these are beauti . . ."

He slapped his hand over my mouth.

"Wait." Switching on a small radio near his bed, he tuned it until he found a station that came in clearly. Soft, easy-listening Chinese music filled the air. "Will cover our talking," he whispered. "My neighbors are listening all the time."

We kept on our jackets as he showed me more of his artwork—sketch pads full of drawings and watercolors. These were mostly portraits, including several self-portraits. He had an artist's way of bringing out the beauty in himself without making it seem egotistical or self-aggrandizing. We were holding the sketch pad together. When he turned the page, I moved my hand over his, cupping his fingers in mine.

We made love—tender and unrushed—under a mound of thin down comforters that Bo had piled onto his bed. The room was so cold that we practically suffocated ourselves to keep from exposing any part of our bodies to the frigid air. Afterwards, Bo wrapped himself around me, his legs and arms entwined in mine, and dozed off.

For a while, I lay awake, cupping his head in my hands, my fingers softly exploring his crew cut, and thought about what I had gotten myself into. I did not want to be the third American in less than a year to break his heart, but suddenly it was so obvious to me that all my promises could not erase the fact that I would be leaving Beijing in a few months. Why hadn't that struck me earlier when I was so desperately trying to woo him? I could only hope that Bo had returned to Beijing a sufficiently changed person that he was now less vulnerable to the hard knocks of gay life. We would, both of us, get over this.

An hour before dawn, Bo shook me awake.

"You must go now," he whispered, turning up the radio again.

As we quickly dressed, I stole another glance at his paintings. They still seemed lovely to me, but now perhaps too pretty—the equivalent in paint of the easy-listening music still wafting from the radio. *Sentimental* is the niche I put them in. He's got to toughen up, I told myself.

"Quickly, please!" Bo whispered.

We hurried out. The sky was just beginning to lighten. Once we'd negotiated the labyrinth back to the road, Bo escorted me to a main thoroughfare, one I didn't recognize but along which ran a bus route that would take me back to a subway stop, Bo assured me. The first traffic of the day, mostly men and women on bicycles, was gliding sleepily along.

"Bus stops there," Bo said, pointing across the street.

I looked into his eyes. Neither of us had mentioned getting together again.

"This was a beautiful night," I told him.

Bo blushed again. When I went to kiss him goodbye, he pulled away.

"David, you crazy!"

When I got home that morning, there were three messages on my answering machine. The first was from Stewart:

You were right, David. Owen is very nice. We had a wonderful talk. He gave me the names of a few bars here. A nervous little giggle interrupted his message. *Actually, I'm thinking about going up to Boston to meet him. We kind of flirted over the phone.* Stewart giggled again. *Call me, David. I need more information!*

The second was from Xinlu:

Very nice to meet you, David. I am sorry you cannot have dinner with me, but I like very much to see you again. You are sincere person. You can understand me, I think. I like to introduce you to my family. I hope you will give me a call.

The third was from my mother:

Honey, I thought you'd be home at this hour. Maybe I still don't understand this time-change business. Call me when you can. Sono speruta di parlare. Sai? *I'm dying to talk to you.*

Whenever my mother switched into Italian dialect, it was a sign that she was trying to reach the deepest part of me. I knew she missed me a lot. I looked at my watch: a little after seven. Which meant it was Saturday night, her time. I felt a pang of longing: if only it could still be Saturday night here.

In the kitchen I made a pot of tea, then took it to the living room. Standing in front of the picture window, letting the mug cool, I looked out over the vast expanse of high-rise complexes that constituted my neighborhood: nothing but tall, bland buildings, as far as the eye could see, an architecture of stupefying mediocrity. And more were coming. I counted the outlines of five or six foundations, blanketed now under the recent snowfall. Cranes, pillars of reinforced concrete, heaps of steel—the new China, wide open to the West. A wonder, a disaster.

When the phone rang, I dashed for it.

"*Wei?*"

"Honey, where have you been?"

"Ma."

"Did you get my message?"

"Of course, Ma."

"You didn't call back."

"I was out late, that's all."

"Yeah?"

"It's a big city, Ma. There's lots to do."

"I dreamt about you last night," she said, already off on another tack. "You were back in the United States."

"Hang in there, Ma. A few more months and I'll be home."

"You were working in a hospital. You were a brain surgeon. I think you had won some big honor. I remember sitting in the audience and everyone was applauding . . ."

"Ma! Quit it!"

"What? I'm just telling you my dream, David."

"Well, it's enough, Ma. *Enough!*"

"Eh, *io sono la mamma. Che vuoi fa'?* What do you want from me, David? I can't help my dreams. I dream about your father, too." She sighed. "Whenever I need help, I still talk to him. Like the other day: I got stuck in a huge traffic jam on Route 128. Bumper to bumper. We crawled. At the next exit, I got off, but do you think I knew where I was? *Neanche per un minuto.* It was getting dark. I was going along these roads I'd never seen before, *scuro, scuro*. You know? That's when I asked your father to help me. 'Joseph,' I said, 'help me find the way.' And, what do you know, in two minutes I was back on streets I recognized. You see, David? *Vidi?*"

"Ma, I wish you wouldn't drive at night."

"I don't. Honestly. Just once in a while nearby. Sometimes I have to go shopping late. Not too far, honey." She put on her teasing voice. "Eh, what do you want me to do? Stay shut up and never leave the house? *Uffà!*" She chuckled. "Listen, I heard you had a lot of snow over there."

"Not a lot: maybe three or four inches."

"I bet it's beautiful. Is it beautiful, David?"

"Yeah, it's beautiful."

"The Forbidden City in the snow!" she said. "Imagine! David, I'm so happy for you. You're having the time of your life over there, aren't you? Seeing wonderful things. Meeting new people. I wish, oh, I *wish* . . ." She didn't finish. "Honey, I'm sorry if I upset you, just now. I hope you know that I'm proud of everything you've ever done."

"I know, Ma. It's just . . ." She cut me off.

"Everything, David. *Tutto.*"

After we had said goodbye, I lay down on the sofa. I could still smell the scent of Bosheng's blankets on my skin—a musty, pungent aroma, something like dried root vegetables. I brought my hand up to my nose and inhaled deeply. This was Bosheng's smell. *His.* I closed my eyes and tried to memorize it.

What would I tell Stewart? I had to call him back. He'd want to know all about the bathhouse. Had it been any different from the Ta Ta Club? What kind of people went there? Did I *meet* anyone? The answers to these questions did not seem easy.

And Xinlu. I had to call him back, too. Of course we would have dinner together. We might even become friends. But I could not see anything more developing between us. I would never say it—*You cannot give me what I want*—but that's what I would tell him, in my own way. Every disappointment runs its course. It would be the same with Bosheng. I raised my hand to my nostrils and breathed in his scent once more.

The telephone did not ring again the rest of the morning. I kept dozing off and waking up. By midmorning, the apartment was flooded in clean, bright late-winter light. In those slow, silent hours, as the sun's rays traced a path across the walls, I kept thinking I heard someone in the next room, so eerily quiet was the Sunday stillness in my building. So eerily quiet, in fact, that it did not spook me in the least when, toward noon, I heard myself whispering, *Help me, Johnny. Help me. Show me the way, honey.*

Spring

Chapter Sixteen

During the first week of April, the talk around the office was all about the peach blossoms, how they would be late that year. Auntie Chen started it, telling us that the trees needed more time to wake up from the long, hard winter. Why, just the other day friends who lived up in the Fragrant Hills had told her that the buds still hadn't shown the slightest signs of opening.

"Like your hand all close up tight," she said, brandishing a clenched fist in front of my face.

A lifelong resident of Beijing, Auntie had been taking an annual spring excursion to the Botanical Gardens at the foot of the Fragrant Hills ever since she was a high school student. Back in February, she had promised to take me with her. We had even set a date, but as the day approached, she announced that she was postponing the outing.

"No sense to make visit now," she told me. "Nothing there to see."

As disappointed as I was not to be making the trip, I was secretly glad that spring was late. It let me pretend that I had a lot more time in Beijing before I had to return home. In the eight months that I'd been working in China, there was still so much I hadn't seen and done. I'd been putting things off, thinking I had all the time in the world. Now, suddenly, time was precious.

That evening, back at the apartment, I flipped through my guidebook to the city. When I first arrived, I had drawn little red circles in the margins, one next to each museum or temple or historical site that I wanted to see, intending to fill in the circles as I completed each visit. Now, as I ran my finger down row after row of those open red rings—so many of them, like mean, angry zeros in a grade book—I felt like a school kid who had been caught not doing his homework.

From the living room, I could see the last of an April sunset lingering in thin, watery brushstrokes of gray and peachy orange off to the West. I watched as the last of the light faded, then died. To my surprise, I'd come to love this city. Despite the preponderance of ugly construction and the gray, sooty air, there was so much about Beijing that made me happy. And a big part of that, I knew, was Bo-sheng. Again.

A few days after we had slept together, he had phoned me to ask if I wanted to do something with him. Off the cuff, I'd suggested the Temple of Heaven. (I figured, a little callously, that whether our getting together again actually led to anything or not, at least I might start ticking off some of those landmarks I hadn't yet seen.) As it turned out, our second date was wonderful. Bo and I rode to the temple on our bikes, an hour-long trip, during which, whenever we could, we pedaled side by side, talking, laughing, commenting on the passing scene. Every once in a while, we had to stop to consult a map. As we stood there, getting our bearings again, we'd take the opportunity to touch each other surreptitiously, letting our fingers brush, or playfully stepping on one another's foot, anything as long as it conveyed one message: *standing here, talking to you is not enough.*

Once we got to the temple, we roamed around, giving some of our time to sightseeing, the rest to finding secluded spots that were not overridden by sightseers. Once or twice, we even managed to hold hands for a few seconds. At the Echo Wall—Bo standing at one end, I at the other, just as my guidebook directed—he whispered something to me. The sound was supposed to ricochet off the stone walls and be amplified in my direction.

"Did you hear?" he asked when we rejoined each other.

I shook my head. "Too many people around. What did you say?"

Bo smiled. "A secret. Can't tell you now."

We strolled on toward the Hall of Prayer, the crowning glory of the temple, where we discovered that cobalt blue, the color of the roof tiles, was for both of us our favorite color.

"What does that say about us, Bo, that we each love the same color?"

Bo didn't say anything. We walked on, each with our own thoughts, down the long avenue toward the West Heavenly Gate. Along the way, I snapped lots of pictures, mostly of Bo, and thought about the clerk at the film store where I always went to get my shots developed. She would always check out my pictures before she gave them back to me, and always had a comment or two to make, mainly questions about the Chinese people in the photographs. What would she think about a whole roll dedicated to one handsome young man?

"One of us together," Bo suggested when we came again to the Round Altar.

He took my camera and approached a young woman, who gladly complied. As we waited for her to compose the shot, Bo put his arm around my shoulder.

"We are *tongzhi*," he reminded me.

At the end of the afternoon, we raced back to my place, where we spent the whole night making love.

The next time we got together, it was to visit a couple of art galleries Bo knew, little out-of-the-way places where his classmates and professors at the art academy were exhibiting new work. They greeted me warmly, as if I were a long-time friend of his, and this, too, made me feel closer to him than I had expected, or had hoped to expect. That evening, we ended up having dinner, just the two of us, and as I later came to think of it back in America, had "the talk." About Johnny and his death, about being an AIDS widower, about not having the virus myself, and what about *him*, Bosheng?

No, Bo said, he wasn't infected; but when I asked him how he knew—had he been tested?—he shook his head.

"Just know," he said, looking down at his half eaten plate of food. "I think, David, I cannot have."

"Because . . .?" I prompted.

He looked up at me, his face blushing. I nodded. That night, after we'd left the restaurant, Bo took my hand. We were in a dark alleyway that led back out onto the main road.

"I want you to fuck me," he said. "First time."

235

By the end of April, as the weather improved, the office talk about late peach blossoms gave way to a new subject. It seemed that our cleaning girl—her name was Pingguo, but everyone called her Apple—had taken a fancy to Tyson. Five or six times a day, Apple would show up in Tyson's office to do unnecessary chores: emptying wastebaskets that didn't need emptying, mopping floors that didn't need mopping, straightening out his meticulously organized jars of gauze, cotton balls, and tongue depressors. She always appeared just when Tyson had stepped out for a minute, usually to escort a patient back to the front desk. When he returned, there Apple would be, demure and unobtrusive, her eyes lowered, her small body taking up no room at all, but definitely "hovering"—that's how Tyson described it to me—finding any pretext she could just to be near him.

When Auntie Chen learned of the situation, she said we should fire Pingguo straightaway, but Tyson insisted that we keep her on. Apple was a good worker, he told Auntie, and never interfered with patients. Privately, just to me one afternoon, he also said that he felt sorry for her.

"We know nothing about her prospects for another job, do we, Mate?" He made eye contact with me. "Not to mention the fact that she would lose face—with her family, her neighbors, everyone—if we let her go. She's a kid: what? eighteen, nineteen? This must be her first experience with"—he threw out his hands in a gesture of ironic grandeur—"with the glory of Western manhood. I think we can weather this one without a lot of hoopla." He smiled at me. "Maybe when she finds out I'm going to a poofter bar with you, she'll back off."

I hoped it didn't show on my face, but I'd completely forgotten about our plans for that night. Weeks before, I had promised to show Tyson the Ta Ta Club, and we'd set the date. But in all the intervening thrill and anxiety about dating Bo, I'd let it slip my mind.

Fortunately, I didn't have plans with Bo that night. In fact, it wasn't clear if I'd ever have plans with him again. I hadn't seen him since our previous time together, almost a week before, when he'd asked me to fuck him. It had been something of a disaster. Stupidly, we'd gone to his place. I had condoms and lubricant in my backpack, but Bo couldn't relax for fear of his neighbors. We had to negotiate the thing via skittish whispers, and, even when I did manage to enter him, it ended up feeling more like rape than love making. Bo had been sweet about the whole ordeal, but fell asleep as soon as it was over. It was the first time he hadn't held me all night. I went home feeling like a brute. Since then, he hadn't called. And since he had no telephone, I couldn't call him. I supposed I could find my way back to his place, but I couldn't decide if I should. I wasn't sure I could trust anymore what it was I wanted from him.

Although it was a Saturday, the most popular night at the Ta Ta, Tyson and I arrived early enough that we found the place relatively empty, almost sleepy.

"It picks up after a while," I assured him.

Tyson didn't comment, but followed me to the bar, where he offered to buy the first round. In impeccable Chinese, he ordered two beers, then proceeded to engage the bartender in a jovial bit of conversation.

"By the way," I whispered when the bartender had turned away, "all the bartenders here are straight."

Tyson chuckled.

"What?"

"You." He shook his head in amusement. "Stop trying so hard, Davey. Whatever is is fine. I like this place." Leaning on the bar and twisting around, he surveyed the room. "Reminds me of a pub back home. Frankly, I was expecting something a little more . . . you know, outré. I thought you gay chaps went in for more offbeat entertainment."

We got our beers and carried them to a table toward the back of the room. Tyson took a long draught, then set down his glass. I watched him as he checked out the scene around us. At this hour, the crowd was still almost exclusively Chinese guys. The usual assortment of queens, money boys, and regular guys jammed the room.

"So, this is where gay Beijing happens," I told him. "Twelve million people and one gay bar."

Tyson shrugged jovially. "By my reckoning, it only takes one bar to make friends, and these fellows seem like nice chaps."

"It's kind of been my salvation this year."

"How's that?"

"Oh, you know. Don't you occasionally miss the company of other Aussies? That's how I feel about gay companionship. Sometimes nothing else will do." I patted him on the shoulder. "I'm afraid you straight chaps just can't provide everything a gay chap needs."

Tyson took up the playful mood.

"Well, you've never asked this straight chap. Had I known, Davey." He winked playfully at me.

The ice had been broken. Over our beers, we settled into a long, breezy chat. We talked a lot about life in Beijing. Tyson had been living in the city for three years and was seriously dating a Chinese woman, who was also a doctor. They were planning on getting married. This would eventually give Suling Australian citizenship and a ticket out of the country, but Tyson said they were both planning on staying on in China, at least for the near future. He said there was plenty of China he still wanted to experience. I told him I understood completely.

"My year here's almost over, and I feel like it's just begun."

Tyson nodded his head. "Would you like to stay on another year?"

I laughed.

"First, I'd just like to understand what this year was all about."

"Understand?"

"Well, you know . . . figure out what all this has meant to me."

"That might take longer than you think." He was staring at me with that worn, prematurely wrinkled face of his.

"And maybe that's a good thing, huh?" I suggested. "Not having it all figured out so neat and clean?"

"It's one of the things I like about Buddhism," Tyson said. "How it keeps reminding me of how little I really understand."

I took a sip of beer.

"You know, lately, I've been thinking about something Johnny used to say to me."

"Johnny? Your mate who died of AIDS?"

"Yes. He used to worry about the strangest things. I mean, you're a doctor. You must know what dying people are concerned about: *Will it be painful? Will I lose control? Is there a heaven?* Johnny didn't care about any of that stuff. What he worried about were things like the fact that his dying would leave me a middle-aged widower. But his greatest fear was that as soon as he'd figured out his life, you know, understood the reasons why everything that had happened to him had happened, that that would be the end. It was almost superstitious: as if what was keeping him alive was his unsatisfied curiosity about the meaning of it all."

"And how about you, Davey? What unsatisfied curiosity are you carrying around?"

"God!" I laughed. "What unsatisfied curiosity am I *not* carrying around? Tyson, I'm almost fifty years old—my birthday's in June—and there are days when I feel I still haven't a clue. There are days when I astound myself with my lack of certainty about everything. You would think that at my age I would have gotten a little closer to figuring out who I am."

"Maybe there's nothing to figure out." Tyson raised his eyebrows playfully. "You know, someone very wise once told me that the road to enlightenment is always just as long as it was when we first started."

I started to laugh. "Dear, dear Tyson. If I convert to Buddhism and go straight, will you marry me? You are such a good man."

"Was Johnny a good man?"

"Johnny *was* a good man. He had a heart of gold. I know that sounds corny, but in his case it was true. He'd drop anything to help out a friend. He'd just up and leave work in the middle of the day if someone needed him." I let my attention drift over to my glass of beer, wondering how much more I wanted to tell Tyson. "Sometimes that drove me crazy, how scattered he could be." Tyson nodded.

"Johnny wasn't the most disciplined person. He spent money wildly. He drank too much. He was really sloppy about taking his medications. Early on, I tried to find a way to get out of it, our relationship. I wasn't sure I wanted to take it on, you know, what it would come to in the end."

"But you didn't," Tyson said. "You didn't get out of it."

"No."

"Why?"

"Well, because I loved him. And because . . ." The only other person I'd ever said this to was Owen. "Because I thought that, well, what it comes down to in the end is never the point of why you enter a relationship anyway. Being *in* the relationship is the point."

Tyson smiled.

"And you say you're not a Buddhist?"

"Well, I do adore the shaved heads and the saffron robes."

By now the room was filling up. A loud, lively buzz circulated through the Ta Ta, wafting about on heavy currents of cigarette smoke and treacly Chinese pop music.

"Look," Tyson said, "don't feel as if you have to stick close by me all evening discussing nirvana. If there's someone here you fancy, by all means, be my guest."

"Actually, there *is* someone I fancy."

"Yes?" Tyson's eyes did a quick survey of the room.

"Not here. I've been seeing someone. A Chinese guy."

"Good for you, Mate."

"He's a graduate student." I studied Tyson's face. He seemed unfazed. "At one of the art academies here."

I told him all about Bosheng, about how we had first met, his departure to get married, and how we had reconnected at the bathhouse and fallen in love. Tyson listened, occasionally nodding his head, as if he were doing nothing more than taking a medical history from a patient. What I didn't tell him was anything of the recent events: the disastrous night a week ago or my not having heard from Bo since.

"He sounds scrumptious," Tyson said. At that moment, it was the wrong word to hit me with.

"Sometimes I think too scrumptious. Lately, I've been worrying that I'm only interested in Bo because he's . . . you know, young and pretty and, well . . ."

Tyson smiled. "It's a turn-on, isn't it? An old codger like you. Who would have thought?" He slapped my upper arm. "Come on,

Mate, you make yourself sound like you've got one foot in the grave. Exactly how much younger is Bosheng?"

"Twenty years."

Tyson puckered out his lips. "Well, yes, I suspect some folks would construe that as a significant difference. Your Johnny. Was he younger, too?"

"By ten years."

"So you like them younger?" Tyson asked.

"I guess."

"I like them older. Women. A woman in her late thirties, early forties." He shook his head in appreciation. "I used to be ashamed about that. Thought it said something about my relationship with my mother."

"And now?"

"Now? Now it's not *about* anything. It's just what I like. What makes me come most alive, be most myself. Older women."

"I remember when I first went out with Johnny, I used to worry that I was only attracted to him because he was so different. He was younger, hadn't gone to college, came from an Irish Catholic family. He was a house cleaner. Sometimes I worried that my attraction to him was just about . . . I don't know: snooping. That's a crass way of putting it, but do you know what I mean? I thought that maybe what I felt for him just boiled down to a curious fascination with how different he was. That's what I'm worried about now with Bosheng. Only more so. I mean, what if it's just the fact that he's *Chinese* that makes me like him?"

"'*Just* the fact'?" Tyson said. "And how many more 'facts' would it take to truly justify your attraction to him? Is there a minimum daily requirement of politically correct qualities he has to have before you'll stop castigating yourself for falling in love with him? Davey, you *like* Bosheng. That's all the justification you need. You said the same thing about Johnny not ten minutes ago. How about switching off that nonstop, analytical brain of yours for a while? Stay in the present for this one, Davey. Try that on and see where it takes you."

"Yeah. What have I got to lose, huh?" I shrugged my shoulders, wondering if I'd already lost Bo anyway.

Tyson reached out, gently squeezed my cheeks between his hand and tipped up my face, forcing me to make eye contact with him.

"Look, you, there are two ways of making light of things: one way gets at the truth, and the other way, what you showed me just now, trivializes." He shook my jaw and let go.

"Thank you," I said.

"You're welcome."

By the time we had finished our third round of beers, it was close to midnight. Tyson announced that he had to get going. I said that in that case I thought I'd be going to. We got up and began to make our way through the densely packed crowd. Just as we were about to leave, I spotted a familiar face.

"Edward!"

"David."

"But where have you been, Edward? I haven't seen you in months."

His face, still pale and doughy, seemed tired. Springtime had not yet arrived for him.

"I had some problems at home," he told me. "Had to spend part of this winter with my family."

I introduced Edward to Tyson, and Edward in turn introduced us to the guy he was with, an American named Buzz. Apparently, they'd just met that evening. Buzz was from Los Angeles. He had a lively face and a smile as broad as the San Andreas Fault. As we talked, Buzz stood behind Edward, his face pressed into Edward's cheek, his arms draped about his neck, caressing his sternum. I had never seen Edward in such a sexual situation before. It made me happy.

I asked Buzz what he was doing in Beijing. He told me he was working for an auto import company.

"Our clients are mostly Americans and Canadians. Businessmen and their families." He shrugged — "It's a job" — then pressed his cheek up closer to Edward's. "And it keeps me in Beijing with all these adorable Chinese boys. How about you? What are you doing here?"

As I began to run through a quick explanation, Tyson caught my eye and waved good-bye.

"Sorry, mates. Got to be getting home. I'll see you on Monday, Davey."

We watched Tyson elbow his way out of the bar.

"He your boyfriend?" Buzz asked.

"No. He's not even gay."

Buzz shook his head skeptically. "Yeah, right."

I was about to explain my connection to Tyson when Edward excused himself as well. He told us he was going to say hello to some other friends.

"Thank you for the beer, Buzz," Edward said.

It was so unlike Edward to accept a beer and then not drink it with his host that I figured something was up. It didn't take me long to see what that was. As Buzz and I continued our conversation, I realized that he had only one thing on his mind: sex with Chinese guys. In the next twenty minutes, he told me story after story about his recent escapades. He was currently "dating" three guys, all at once.

"Hey, what can I say?" he told me. "I'm just a total slave to the yellow man." He grinned that bright, glaring L.A. grin. "My ultimate fantasy is to go to bed with a Chinese boy who doesn't speak a word of English. I'd love to spend the whole night having sex and not exchange a single word."

I took a sip of my beer.

"So, what about you?" Buzz asked. "I haven't seen you around here before." I had a feeling he'd already forgotten my name.

I explained that I used to come to the Ta Ta fairly regularly, but that for the past month I hadn't been by at all.

"I'm seeing someone now." It was no longer true, I guessed, but I wanted to establish a clear distinction between his kind of dating and mine. Suddenly I felt such a pang of longing for Bosheng.

"So you a rice queen, too?" Buzz leered at me. "Where is he?"

"No, he's not here. I just stopped by with Tyson tonight."

"Oh, right. And tell me again that one's straight." Buzz laughed, then nodded over to the entrance to the club. "He's probably out in that alley right now, getting his dick sucked by some cutie."

I looked down at my empty beer bottle.

"Excuse me," I told him and held the bottle up to explain my departure.

"Hey, get me another, too," Buzz called out. "I'll pay for it." I pretended not to hear him.

For the next ten minutes, I disappeared into the crowd, scouting the room for Edward, but I couldn't find him. Every time I caught sight of Buzz, he was chatting up someone else. He didn't seem to mind that I hadn't brought him his beer.

It was close to one by the time I left the club. The air outside was mild, one of the first nice evenings we'd had that spring. It felt good, a welcome change from the packed, smoky bar. I made my way down the alley and out to the Worker's Stadium Road. It was dead quiet. Not even a taxi on the streets. I started walking in the direction of the subway station at Dongsishitiao. There would be taxis there.

I made my way along the deserted boulevard. As I passed the darkened businesses, I replayed the events of the evening in my mind: my long heart-to-heart with Tyson, bumping into Edward again, meeting Buzz. I thought about first impressions, about how wrong they can be. I'd been so delighted to see Edward in the arms of such a cute, new friend until Buzz had opened his mouth. It made me proud of Edward that he had seen through Buzz's come-ons. Since I'd known him, Edward had not gotten a lot of attention at the Ta Ta. A guy like Buzz could really throw you off kilter, but Edward hadn't fallen for it, not in the least.

What would I have done in Edward's shoes: if Buzz had come onto me, Buzz of the comely face and seductive smile? (Fat chance, but what if he had?) Would I have been able to muster the same presence of mind that Edward had shown? How many times this year—how many times in all my years as a gay man—had I let myself be swept up by a passing smile from someone who proved to be nothing but bad news, bad news I should have seen coming from the start? What was I doing even now? Falling for Bo, twenty years my junior? *A turn-on, isn't it?* Tyson had said. *An old codger like you. Who would have thought?* He'd meant to josh me, show me my own foolish anxieties, but there was other information there as well, and I needed to hear it. This thing with Bo was impossible. A fantasy. An attraction that could never amount to anything. But why was I worrying anyway? Bo hadn't called me in a week. In his own way, he had already let me know that he wanted it to be over. He'd woken up from the dream. I needed to as well.

At Dongsishitiao, I found a taxi and got in. When the driver asked me where I wanted to go, I thought about telling him to drop me off near the park on Second Ring Road. I'd never been there so late before, but I guessed that there would still be plenty of action, especially on such a mild spring evening. If it was really over with Bo—if it *had* to be over with Bo—then why not? *This is the way things are,* I reminded myself. The nearest landmark to the park was Gulou subway station.

"*Gulou,*" I told the driver.

He turned on the meter and headed off.

I once told Owen that every man I'd ever slept with had taught me something about myself: my fears and inhibitions, my capacity for tenderness or lust, devotion or cruelty, the things I didn't know about myself that turned guys on or off. I told him that I didn't think any trick had ever left me untouched. At the time, it had been important for me to say this. Owen had needed to hear it. *I* had needed to hear it. I had needed to explain myself to myself.

Leaning back against the cab, my eyes closed, I thought now about all the guys I'd met in China—the guys I'd slept with and the guys I'd not slept with—the friends, the tricks, the would-be lovers. I thought about Yonghai and Eryan and Edward, about Jiantao and Guoyang, about Xinlu and his magnificent crane, and about the crazy drunken night I'd landed in bed with my toy soldier at the guard house. Memories now. Stories. Stories I had e-mailed to Owen. Stories I had told Stewart. Stories I would tell myself in the coming years. Yes, no matter how hard I had tried to make it otherwise, China had ended up becoming a gay story for me. And, really, was that so bad? Every experience teaches you something. Even the fleeting sexual ones. Yes, there was truth in that.

But there was also truth in this: I missed Bo. Just plain missed him. With an ache that had nothing to teach me. Or everything to teach me.

I leaned forward and told the driver to turn north instead. I gave him the name of my apartment complex. He seemed to understand my change of heart perfectly.

Chapter Seventeen

The rest of that week, I was miserable, trying to decide whether to contact Bo again or not. And if so, then how? I thought about biking over to his hutong, or hanging out in front of the painting academy where he was studying. I even considered another trip to the bathhouse. Maybe he was going there again. It was driving me crazy imagining him pursuing his life without me. I knew I had to let that go, but I couldn't. Not yet.

Meanwhile, Apple still had it bad for Tyson. She had taken to lingering outside his office all the time now. No one knew what to do about it. It was really quite sad. More than once, I winced at the thought that pining after Bo was reducing me to a similarly pathetic state.

The week came and went. By the standards of the clinic, it was a dull one—no emergencies, no hospitalizations. The worst we had were a few respiratory ailments. It was spring now. Although there wasn't as much coal soot in the air, the pollen count was high. This pleased Auntie enormously. On the last Friday afternoon in April, as if she were a Daoist priest who had read the propitious signs, she announced that it was finally time to make our trip to the Fragrant Hills.

The next morning, I biked over to the clinic where I had agreed to meet Auntie, Winston, and Tyson for the excursion. Just as I arrived, Tyson called to say he was running about a half hour late, so Auntie brewed us a pot of tea while we waited for Tyson to arrive. The place was quiet. On the weekends, the clinic was on a skeleton crew, only one nurse on duty for emergencies. The three of us—Auntie, Winston, and I—sat in the staff room, drinking our tea and chatting. I was eager to ask Winston about Ling, but dared not in front of Auntie.

After a few minutes, we were interrupted by the sound of someone out in the hall. It was Apple. As she wasn't scheduled to come in on Saturdays, I guessed immediately what was up. She must have heard about our outing and had found an excuse—she was making a pretense of sweeping the floors—to be around when Tyson came in.

Auntie shot out of her chair and hustled into the corridor, where she gave the poor girl a good dressing down. Although I couldn't see what was happening, I felt sorry for Apple, imagining her standing there meekly suffering Auntie's tirade. I looked at Winston to gauge his reaction.

"It's called a crush," I told him.

"Crush," he repeated. "What is 'crush'?"

"It's when you think you're in love with someone and you can't stop thinking about them. But usually the other person doesn't feel the same way, and then after a while the feeling is over."

Winston considered this a moment.

"My mother tell Apple such feelings must be over not after a while. Must be over now."

"Well, yes, but we can't always choose how we feel, can we, Winston?"

"Have to choose."

The scolding ended as abruptly as it began. In the ensuing silence, I heard Apple crying softly out in the hall. Auntie came back into the staff room, muttering to herself in Chinese.

"Is she okay?" I asked.

Auntie gave me a stern, startled look. "Who okay?"

"Apple."

Auntie grunted.

"Auntie, people do foolish things when they're in love."

"She not in love!"

"Well, she thinks she is."

"I tell her, 'Impossible for you to love this man.'"

"Do you think she understands that?"

"Have to understand that," Auntie insisted. She began to gather up the tea things.

Impossible for you to love this man. Auntie's words thundered in my ears. I flinched at the thought of what she might have said to me about Bo.

Presently Tyson arrived. Each of us greeted him like a cat with a bird in its mouth. No one mentioned the episode with Apple.

With our cameras and backpacks and the picnic hamper that Auntie had packed, the four of us loaded into Winston's Volga. The car hadn't lost any of its shabby charm since the night Winston had picked me up at the airport. A bouquet of cardboard air fresheners still dangled from the rearview mirror above the plastic Buddha on the dash. The speedometer still registered zero. And those loose, metallic sounds still rattled ominously from all parts of the vehicle every time we hit a bump. The day was so beautiful and the ride so noisy that our conversation took on a happy, jocular tone. There were jokes and good cheer all around. It almost made me forget how much I missed Bo. In no time, we had arrived at the Fragrant Hills.

The park was crowded. All about there were strolling couples, picnicking families, groups of school children, their brightly colored knapsacks bouncing on their backs as they hiked along. Everyone seemed to be in a festive, breathe-free-again mood.

Auntie led the way. She was eager to show us the flowering trees. She hustled us by a large stand of forsythia, which had already bloomed and gone by. Tender green leaves now sprouted where the yellow blossoms had been. Back home, Johnny's grave was near a stand of forsythia. I wondered if they had already bloomed, too.

"Hua kaile!" Auntie suddenly exclaimed, putting her fingers up to her lips. "Look! *Lizi.* Plum blossom!" She was so excited she could hardly keep track of which language to use.

There in front of us was a grove of flowering trees, billowing sumptuously in massive cascades of pink and white. With Tyson's help, Auntie bent a branch down to her nose and inhaled deeply. She whispered to herself in Chinese. For a second I wondered if she were praying, but it seemed more likely that she was just savoring a private moment, as if the experience was too personal and too intimate to be shared. She let go of the branch and took in the full splendor of the grove.

"Never, since I am a girl, so many, so beautiful!" Her eyes were moist. "You see, David? It was good to wait. Yes?"

"Yes, Auntie."

We moved on. There were peonies, clumps of lilacs, cherry blossoms. Auntie pointed out how, through a process of whimsical grafting, the state gardeners had created tricolored peach trees. They were in full bloom, an imbroglio of red, white and pink branches all sprouting from the same trunk. It was both wonderfully gaudy and sweetly sentimental. I thought about Bo's paintings back in his cramped little studio.

"Ah, look up," Auntie shouted. "High, high!" she yelled, directing my attention beyond the trees.

There, soaring and dipping in the bright blue sky, was a kite in the shape of a large, elegant dragon. The long streamers of its tail fluttered majestically in the stiff breeze. I craned my neck to get a better view of this colorful creature as it hovered and danced above us. I could even make out the taut string that held him aloft, glinting in the bright sunlight. I followed the tether down to the ground, to where two young boys were controlling the kite. They stood next to each other, one arm around each other's neck, as they jointly manipulated the skein of string with their free hands.

Winston drew up next to me. He pulled out his pack of cigarettes and tried to light one, but the breeze kept blowing out the lighter.

"We go this way," Auntie called out, indicating that she and Tyson were moving on to examine another stand of trees.

I waved at them. "Go ahead. We'll catch up."

I cupped my hands around Winston's lighter and he tried again. This time the cigarette caught and he nodded his thanks.

"How's your lady friend?" I asked.

"Lady friend?"

"Ling."

Winston made a face. "Don't mention."

"Did something happen?"

He shook his head in disgust and exhaled a dragon-like cloud of smoke from his nostrils.

"No good. She always spending money. Always wanting, wanting. Now already she find someone else. Drop me."

"I'm sorry."

Winston took another hard drag on the cigarette and tossed it away.

"No. Don't be sorry," he declared. "I am not sorry."

We started moving in the direction that Auntie and Tyson had taken, but Winston grabbed my arm and forced me to stop.

"Mr. Davis, you understand why I don't go with Ling anymore?"

"Of course I do. Winston, I think it was a very sensible decision. She wasn't your type."

"Why not?" He sounded as if he were challenging me.

"Well, I think you said yourself, you two had nothing in common."

"So why do I stay with her so long?"

"You're asking *me*?"

"You're American guy. You have experience with woman. Did you ever go with someone who is not right for you but you can't do anything about it?"

I thought about Erik. Nine years we were together.

"Sure," I told him, happy to be the American guy Winston took me for.

"So why you stay with her?"

It was a question I'd been trying to answer ever since Erik and I broke up.

"I don't know. Habit, I guess."

"Habit?"

"You get used to things the way they are. Sometimes it's easier to stay with someone than to break away." Winston made a face. He looked almost disdainful.

"No," he said gruffly. "If some woman not the right person, you must leave."

"Well, yes. But did *you*, Winston? You told me Ling dropped *you*."

He shook his head, bewildered—maybe for the first time in his life—by his own behavior.

"I very crazy, I think, Mr. Davis."

"No, Winston, you're not crazy. Just human."

Suddenly, my eye was caught by a familiar figure lurking behind a nearby tree. It was Apple again. Winston's back was turned to her, so he didn't notice, but she and I recognized each other immediately. My surprise must have shown on my face because Winston turned around and looked, but Apple pulled back behind the tree just in time.

"What you looking at?" Winston asked.

Quickly, I turned away from the tree, letting my eyes roam over another area of the park.

"I'm worried that we'll lose your mother and Tyson. Do you know where they went?"

"Can't lose," Winston pronounced. His characteristic certainty had returned.

"Well, let's go find them." Without waiting for him, I headed off in a direction that would take us away from Apple. Winston ran up behind me. Soon we found Tyson and Auntie admiring another stand of peach trees.

"Okay," Auntie said, "now I think we can have picnic. We go this way." She pointed to a grassy area at the bottom of a gentle slope.

As we began to follow her, I surreptitiously tapped Tyson's arm and whispered for him to fall behind.

"Apple's here."

"What?"

"I saw her. Lurking behind a tree. She came to the clinic this morning and Auntie nearly fired her. We thought she'd gone home, but she must have followed us here. God knows how."

Tyson stood there, considering what to do.

"Where is she now?"

"Up there." I pointed to the crest of the slope. "By those peach trees."

Tyson looked down to where Auntie and Winston were spreading out our picnic blanket.

"Tell them I had to go to the loo. I'm going to go find Apple and have a talk. I should have done this long before now."

He was back in less than fifteen minutes. Auntie, Winston and I had laid everything out and were sipping bottled water, waiting for him. I managed to catch Tyson's eye. He gave me a thumbs-up nod.

All through lunch, I tried to imagine what Tyson could possibly have said to Apple to make her give him up. His Chinese was excellent, practically fluent, but how did anyone find the words, in any language, to convince someone to stop feeling what they were feeling? How did you even find words to convince yourself to stop feeling what you were feeling? I needed to do that with Bo, but how . . .

"Maybe I can read you a poem?" Auntie suggested when we had finished eating. She pulled a little volume out of her purse and held it up to us.

"Li Qingzhao. The most famous woman poet of China. My favorite."

"Ah, yes," Tyson said, nodding his head in recognition. He turned to me. "This is Suling's favorite poet, too."

"Please, who is Suling?" Winston asked as Auntie flipped through the pages, searching for a poem.

"My lady friend," Tyson told him.

"You have Chinese girlfriend?" Winston asked.

"Yes, I do."

"How long you two have been together?"

"A few years now."

Winston puckered his lips.

"So, Tyson, you know these poems?" Auntie asked.

"Actually, Suling has only read me a couple. I don't know them well at all."

"Very old," Winston said, gloomily tapping his pack of cigarettes against the picnic basket. "We have to read in school." He made a face.

Auntie looked up, grunted at him, then turned back to searching in her book.

"This book print both Chinese and English. Maybe I will read in Chinese and then, Tyson, you can read in English?" She glanced at Winston, who was lighting up another cigarette. "Just a few." She chuckled. "So he does not fall asleep like in school."

As she began to read the first poem, I closed my eyes, letting the music of the words play in my ears. I'd grown to love the sound of Mandarin, even though most of it was still unintelligible to me. When I returned to the States, I knew I would miss it as much as I would the country. Right then and there, I vowed to keep studying Chinese. If Bo and I were an impossible match—if in six weeks I'd never see him again—at least I could hold on to something of him inside his language.

Auntie finished and passed the book to Tyson. He read the translation on the facing page. It was called "Plum Blossoms"—a lovely poem about another late spring, centuries ago, and the poet's longing for her husband, who was far away in the South, where the trees were already in bloom. The images were simple but vibrant. When Tyson finished, we all murmured our approval. He handed the little volume to Auntie again and she read another, then passed it back to Tyson. Again it was on the theme of spring: a small garden, a jade zither, puffs of rain coming in on the light breeze.

"One more," Auntie said, checking out Winston's reaction. "This one my favorite."

As she began, I recognized that word—*chun*—that had been so prominent in the other poems as well. Spring. It kept appearing at regular intervals, like drops of rainwater slipping from a thatched roof. *Chun . . . chun . . . chun.* Auntie seemed to have this poem memorized, because she rarely consulted the text. As she recited, a look of quiet pleasure came over her face. This time, when she had finished, she handed the book to me.

"David, you like to have a try?"

"Sure, but it's almost too beautiful to read in translation," I said. "Just the sound of it alone is exquisite. Like music."

Auntie smiled.

"Yes, I hope some day you can understand without translation, but now have to make compromise. Chinese music, English understanding."

I began to read:

> Spring has come to the women's quarters.
> The grass turns green.
> The red buds of the plum trees have cracked

But are not yet fully open.
Blue green clouds carve jade dragons.
The jade powder becomes fine dust,
I try to hold on to my morning dream,
But I am startled by the breaking cup of Spring.
Flower shadows lie heavy on the garden gate.
A pale moon is spread on the translucent curtain
In the beautiful orange twilight,
For two years, three times, I have missed
The Lord of Spring.
Now he is coming home,
And I will thoroughly enjoy this Spring.

I looked up when I had finished. All seemed lost in their own thoughts. Even Winston had abandoned his cigarette long enough to listen. Auntie nodded.

"I think it's good translation."

"Lovely," I told her. "'The breaking cup of spring.' That's what it feels like, doesn't it?" I leaned back and looked up into the blue sky. The dragon kite was still aloft. "Everything spilling over in tumultuous profusion." I breathed in deeply. "What a crazy, gorgeous day it's been." For a split second, Tyson and I made eye contact. Only we knew just how crazy.

On the way back to Beijing, everyone was quiet with the dreamy contentment of a day happily spent. I sat in the back seat, my head resting on the Volga's worn upholstery, fighting a notion that was trying to insinuate itself into my drifting thoughts: that the day could only have been more splendid if Bo had been with us. How lovely it would have been if he and I could have shared it together. No, I chastised myself. The day was perfect just as it was. I needed to keep reminding myself of that. Bo was out of the picture. Again.

It was evening when we arrived at the clinic. Winston offered to drive Tyson and me home. He suggested that we leave our bicycles and pick them up in the morning. Before Tyson had a chance to answer, I said we were perfectly happy to bike home. It was a pleasant evening; we could ride most of the way together. All the time I was speaking, I looked Tyson straight in the eye. He got the message.

As I watched the Volga pull away, Tyson turned to me.

"When I caught up with her, she was trembling, the poor kid. I don't think she had ever worked it through in her own mind what she would say or do if she actually had a chance to speak to me."

"What *did* she say?"

"Not much. She hardly even looked at me. In fact, at one point, she tried running away, but I asked her to stay and finish listening to what I had to say."

I didn't want to pry into Tyson's personal conversation with Apple, so I didn't push him to tell me any more, but he went on anyway.

"I told her I was flattered by her attention, but that I could not be her boyfriend." He chuckled. "I was dredging up words I didn't think I knew. I told her about Suling, and how happy I was with her. I told her that I hoped one day she would also find someone who would make her happy but that that person could not be me."

I listened carefully, hoping to pick up words I could tell myself about Bo.

"I told her what Buddha had said," Tyson continued. "That it is foolish to seek comfort in someone else's pain. I told her that when she followed me the way she did, it only brought me pain because I could not concentrate on my work and because I knew that she would continue to be frustrated in her desires."

I nodded.

"That's really about the only time she spoke," Tyson continued. "She said that for a long time she had understood how uncomfortable she was making me, but that she had been unable to stop herself from wanting to be near me all the time. She was speaking so softly I had to strain to listen. She said that Auntie had scolded her several times, and that she was ashamed of her behavior, and then she started crying and I gave her my handkerchief and she cried a little more, and then all of a sudden she just stopped and thanked me and said that really all she had needed was to hear from me directly that I could not be her lover." Tyson paused. "And that was it, Mate." He pulled the handkerchief out of his pocket. "She insisted I keep this. Said she didn't want any remembrance of me, that it would just prolong her sorrow. She's an amazing young woman. Very brave, I think."

"What do you suppose Monday is going to be like?" I asked him.

"Well, I'll call Auntie tonight and ask her to be especially considerate for the next few days. I don't think she needs to know everything, but I'll tell her that I've spoken to Apple and that everyone just needs to be sensitive to her feelings right now. I suspect Auntie's mothering instincts will come out."

"I've got to hand it to you, Tyson. I don't think I could have pulled this off."

"Of course you could have. My philosophy is you just speak the truth, plain and simple, and everything falls into place."

I played that over and over in my mind as we rode our bikes into the center of the city: the truth, plain and simple. The truth, plain and simple, was this: Bo was no longer interested in me. The truth, plain and simple, was this: it would never have worked out with him anyway. The truth, plain and simple, was this: it had been a lovely day without him. And one day at a time, in the months and years ahead, it would continue to be a string of lovely days, plain and simple, without him.

When Tyson and I reached Yonghegong, we said goodbye and turned our separate ways home. I rode on, making plans for Sunday. I hadn't been to the Confucius Temple yet. That would be a nice outing. Maybe Edward would like to go with me. Friends, I reminded myself. Friends were just as important as lovers—maybe more important. Yes, the truth plain and simple. You could find a lot of wisdom in that. *Friends.* I listen to the ring of it. Problem was, I just couldn't find Bo there.

When I got to Andingmen, I turned south, toward Bo's place.

———

Because I'd been there only twice before, I got lost a few times trying to locate Bo's hutong. The streets in his neighborhood were poorly lit. I had to ride slowly, stopping now and then to get my bearings.

As unusual as it was for a Westerner to be in this part of town during the day, it was even more uncommon to be here at night. The dim light was not enough to disguise me. People kept staring.

Happily, when I finally found Bo's street, there was almost no one about. By keeping to the shadows, I was able to make my way to his house without calling any attention to myself. I got off the bike, leaned it against a wall, and then didn't know what to do next. If he were home, then he might be in for the rest of the evening. Unless I actually went in and knocked on his door, I could be standing out on the street all night and he'd never know it.

I decided to try his door. If someone stopped me and asked what I was doing, I'd say I was looking for the art student, that I wanted to buy a painting. I tried composing the sentence in Chinese. I figured I had all the vocabulary to put it together. But could I pull it off? Bo had been so skittish about his neighbors. Would they know I was lying? Would I be putting him in jeopardy? I stood there, weighing the risk. There was a dilapidated brick entranceway into Bo's compound. Even in the dim light, I could see down the passageway into the cramped little courtyard. *A picture,* I told myself. *You're here to buy a picture.* I stepped off the curb and crossed the street.

There was no one in the courtyard. Two more passageways, one at either side, led off into the deeper recesses of the compound. I recognized the one I should take. The corridor's twists and turns came back to me, and I began to remember the clutter—the piles of charcoal, the lines of laundry, the buckets, pails and pots—that were strewn about. Amazingly, I got to Bo's door without running into anyone. The single dingy window to the left was dark. I knocked, tentatively at first, then a little louder. There was no answer. Next door, a woman poked her head out.

"*Wo xiang mai . . .*" I began. She pulled her head back in and slammed her door. I knocked once more, waited. When the woman stuck her head out again, I turned around and went back out to the street.

I squatted down next to my bike and thought about what to do next. It was wait or go. There were no other choices. I decided to wait. At least for a little while. Whenever anyone passed, I hugged my knees close to my chest, lowered my head and tried to look as small, and as Chinese, as possible.

Time passed. How much, I had no way of telling. Perhaps an hour. At one point, I thought of the act 2 Intermezzo from *Madame Butterfly,* where Cio Cio San spends the whole night waiting for Pinkerton to return. It had been one of Stewart's favorite moments in the opera. He'd spent many afternoons playing it. I wondered if I had the stamina to stay out all night. I wondered if I had Butterfly's purity of faith. I kept imagining all the reasons why Bo wasn't at home on a Saturday evening. None of them pleased me.

One month, I whispered to myself. *In a month you'll be home. Drop this.* In my mind, I rehearsed once more the catalog of reasons why I should now, right now, get back on my bike and ride home. I told myself a lot of things that made perfect sense. I decided to give it five more minutes.

Just then, under the light of a street lamp, a few hundred feet away, I caught sight of him, coming down the lane. He was carrying an enormous artist's portfolio. I waited until he came closer, just to make sure.

"Bo!"

He stopped and stared at me, then came closer.

"David, what are you doing here?"

"I . . ." *The truth, plain and simple.* "I wanted to see you again." I nodded toward the portfolio he was carrying. "Have you been painting up a storm?"

He looked down, then up at me, a confused expression on his face. "A storm?"

"Have you been painting a lot?"

"Yes, of course. Two weeks. No break." He seemed confused by my question. "David, I have my painting review on Monday. Remember, I tell you?"

"Your review! Oh, Jesus! No, I forgot. Is that why you haven't called me?"

"I'm staying in the dormitory these weeks, David. I explain you all this. Only three, four hours for sleep every night. Rest of the time, I'm painting, painting, painting. Painting a storm." He seemed amused that I'd let all this slip my mind.

The portfolio began to slide from his grip. I lurched forward to help him catch it. Our bodies touched.

"Bo, when I didn't hear from you . . ." I let him take the portfolio. "I thought maybe . . ." I could feel myself blushing.

"What you think, David?"

The truth, plain and simple.

"I was worried that you didn't like me anymore."

"Why I didn't like you anymore?"

"Well, because . . . you know, because . . ."

Bo shook his head. "David, you really crazy guy. Why you think that? Because I am not relaxed to get fucked? Next time, we can go to your place. I be more relaxed. No problem." He grinned at me. "And then I want to try fuck you, too. Okay?"

"Darling, anything you want!"

The portfolio began to slip from his hands again.

Bo glanced toward his house. "I just take this inside."

I stood there, showing him I was ready to be taken inside, too, if he wanted to risk it. He noticed, hesitated, then looked back at the house.

"You remember how to come to this place, David?"

"Yes, I did."

Again, we both stood there, no one speaking. Bo peeked down the passageway. I wanted to tell him the coast was clear, but didn't dare. He turned back to me.

"Quick," he said.

It was strange to be back in his room. I took it all in again: the radio, the pile of stale-smelling quilts on this bed, the sketch pads, the piss bucket. But during those two times I'd come here before, the place had been little more than a world of strange, alien objects, a backdrop for our lovemaking. Now, suddenly, this shabby little studio struck me as Bo's *home*. Everything I looked at—his red plastic wash basin, the street map of Beijing he'd pinned to the wall, even the little rush broom in the corner next to a pile of trash (he seemed not to have a wastebasket)—spoke of a life as complex and nuanced as my own, a life full of its own routines and pleasures, preoccupations and mundanities. It frightened me a little bit: how much there still was between us.

"I've missed you," I told him.

At first, Bo didn't answer. He just stood there, staring at me. I got the feeling he was looking for something in my face.

"Missed you, too," he said. "Every day."

Chapter Eighteen

That Monday, Bo had his painting review. When I met him later in the afternoon, he didn't tell me much of what his professors had said, just that he had passed. But I could see by the faint smile on his face that his work had been well received. How well, I didn't learn until we went out to dinner that night. In the restaurant, he told me he had been awarded a second-year teaching fellowship.

"Bo, that's wonderful! Congratulations." He lowered his head in modesty. "Hey!" I called out. He looked up. "Congratulations." I blew him a kiss. He shook his head in disbelief.

"David, you crazy."

As we ate, Bo described his week of nonstop work in the studio, trying to finish his paintings for the review. He had slept only a few hours every night, eaten little, left the academy only twice, briefly to wash up at his local bathhouse.

"Not like bathhouse where we meet," he assured me with a mischievous grin.

When I told him again how worried I had been that I hadn't heard from him, he teased me for forgetting about the review.

"You *mentioned* it, Bo. Just briefly. But I certainly didn't think you meant you'd disappear for an entire two weeks." We were sitting across from each other at a booth. I slid my hand under the table and rubbed his leg. "I guess I was too busy noticing how beautiful you were to concentrate on the conversation."

Bo shot me another embarrassed look.

"So, I think you should not pay so much attention to how I am looking."

"But I love looking at you, Bo. The way you look, what you say—I enjoy everything about you."

"You really crazy."

He changed the subject by asking me what I had been doing since we'd last seen each other. I described the trip to the Fragrant Hills, the profusion of flowers, the kites, our picnic. I told him about Auntie and Winston and Tyson. I felt a lover's eagerness to share with him all the particulars about my life. Every detail I gave him was another possible connection he could find with me. I wanted to forge those links. Still, I left out all the business about Apple. I didn't want a story of frustrated love to hover over our evening together.

"You're right," I told him that night in bed. We were curled up in each other's arms. "I am crazy. Crazy about you. So crazy I sometimes forget myself."

"Not forget condoms, I hope," he teased, raising his head from my chest.

In the weeks that followed, Bo and I spent a lot of time together. Every afternoon after work, I would drop by his studio and have a jar of lukewarm tea while I watched him finish his painting for the day. He was working on another still life, a crockery vase with spring flowers. It was, like so many of his pieces, a bright, sunny painting— this one, all pink and cherry red and yellow—executed in relaxed splotches of color that he might have learned from van Gogh or Monet. I knew enough about painting to recognize that Bo had talent. He was not afraid of the paint, was not fussy or timid with it, but laid it on in clean, confident daubs, each one a small, quiet enactment of something, *something*, I loved in him. Trying to pinpoint what that something was—Bo's gentleness, his sense of humor, his attention to detail—was part of the fascination I felt every time I was with him.

We began to sleep together almost every night. After lovemaking, Bo would always nod off before me. In the darkness of my bedroom, I would lie awake, thinking about us, about what we had done that evening, what we had talked about, about every little mannerism of his that I adored: the way he hummed those sad, sweet Chinese tunes to himself as he painted; the way he took off his shoes and lined them up inside my door whenever he came over; the way he always left his rice bowl spotless, not one grain remaining, at the end of every meal.

Sometimes, when we would go shopping at an outdoor market, I'd catch sight of the smooth, hairless nape of his neck as he bent over a display of fruit. The top two vertebrae of his spine would be showing, smooth and round and so astoundingly beautiful that I would have to hold myself back from throwing my arms around him and taking those delicious morsels of backbone into my mouth.

Yes, crazy, I'd think to myself. *Crazy.*

I thought about a lot of other things, too, on those mild spring nights when I couldn't get to sleep. I thought about Erik, our nearly ten-year marriage, the life we had put together, the house we had tried to make into a home.

A "fixer-upper," the realtors had called it. "This neighborhood's going to be Boston's new gay mecca," one had whispered to us. We had a big country kitchen, a backyard garden, a wrap-around porch; we had tattered canvas awnings in the summer and a leaky slate roof in the winter; we had drafty windows and enormous oil bills, squirrels in the attic and two inches of water in the cellar every time it rained. We gave elegant dinner parties for our friends; we kept the lawn mowed and the sidewalk shoveled; we joined the Society for the Preservation of New England Antiquities. Every Christmas we set up a tall tree in the living room and decorated it with Italian and Swedish ornaments—half from my heritage, half from Erik's. We called ourselves "the old married couple," and like an old married couple, we also bickered, and argued, and fought: about what color to paint the walls, and how long to stay at a party, and why we didn't go dancing anymore.

And then along came Johnny. We met at a discussion group for gay men, all of us there to learn how to have, as the advertisement put it, "an extraordinary relationship" with the people we loved. "To release the buddha nature at the core of our interpersonal life." That had sounded good to me, though Erik wanted nothing to do with it, saying the whole thing sounded like New Age claptrap. I went anyway. I wanted to see for myself. When I liked what I heard, I went back the next week. I figured that doing my half of this couple's program was better than nothing.

After a few weeks, the discussions didn't matter any more: I was going just to keep seeing Johnny. I loved it every time he spoke in our group: so spontaneous and playful and happy to be gay, already *being* the extraordinary person we were all there to learn how to be—*Why does he even come here?* I kept asking myself—until one night, as he and I were walking out to the parking lot together, reviewing what had been said in the discussion, he took my hand and invited me into it with him: all the extraordinariness I thought I could ever want.

Six months and a lot of tears later, I left Erik and moved in with Johnny. For a while I was giddy with happiness, so thrilled not to be half of an old married couple anymore. Everything Erik and I hadn't done in years—go to the discos, fly off for a vacation at a moment's notice, have sex—suddenly it was all back in my life again: spontaneity, unbuttonedness, youth. Of course, it wasn't perfect, not by any means. Johnny moved through life too spontaneously. It scared me sometimes, his extravagant, impulsive, capricious nature: the way he blithely spent money, the way the didn't watch what he ate, the sloppy habit he'd developed of forgetting to take his medications . . . and couldn't he just slow down a little, Jesus, did he *want* to die?

"Doll," I could still hear him saying, "that AZT is *nasty!* Let's have another margarita."

In his final months, our lives came to be about hour-by-hour living—coping with another bout of vomiting, diarrhea, chills, sweats. There were days, God forgive me, when I wondered why I'd done it: given up all that homey security with Erik for a roller-coaster ride with Johnny. There was nothing wonderful about it at all, unless you counted the laughter, the silliness, the joy, infrequent but still there, which Johnny managed to bring forth in spite of everything.

All these things came back to me, lying there with Bo by my side. *I am as nuts about this guy as I was about Johnny,* I'd tell myself. And when I was brutally honest, I would even admit that I had once been exactly this in love with Erik, too. *What does that mean,* I asked myself; *what am I supposed to learn from all this?*

These were questions that, under normal circumstances, I would have posed to Owen. I could picture us over beers at the Eagle or

Sunday-morning coffee: "Cupcake," I would have asked him, "am I so crazy about the guy that I'm not seeing straight?"

But Owen was halfway around the world and suddenly, and quite mysteriously, incommunicado. Early on, a few days after I had reconnected with Bo, I sent him an e-mail to tell him the story. Owen shot back a short, hasty note.

"Cupcake, it's so *you*. Reconnecting in a bathhouse! How wonderfully romantic, sentimental, operatic, and trashy all in one. Very Madam Butterfly. Send me act 2 as soon as it develops."

That had been weeks ago. Since then, the e-mails from Owen had stopped coming. Being so out of touch was unlike him, but I was too busy creating "act 2" with Bo to worry.

Every chance we got, we explored more of old Beijing together. At first, I opted for places that I thought Bo, with his painter's eye, would enjoy—the Lama Temple, Beihai Park, the picturesque neighborhood around Shisha Houhai Lake with its arching stone bridges over the narrow waterways that reminded me a little of Venice—but it soon became clear that Bo really only cared to make sure that I got to see what I wanted. Whatever I suggested was fine with him, he said. No matter how much I insisted that he have some say in the matter—after all, I reminded him, he wasn't a native of Beijing either—Bo never took up the offer. In fact, the only time he took charge was to grab the backpack and camera bag out of my hands whenever I was trying to compose a shot. He seemed to have an uncanny sense of exactly when I'd want to snap a picture, because by the time I would stop to raise my camera, there he'd be unburdening me of all those bags I thought I needed on our daily jaunts. Then he'd stand by, waiting patiently as I adjusted the lens, checked the light meter, reframed the composition, snapped the shutter. There was something so gentle and relaxed about him, so patient with me, with the world, with himself.

"Okay, sidekick," I told him one afternoon after I'd just taken a shot of the wonderful bronze globe at the Ancient Observatory, "I want one of you now. Over there." I pointed to another one of the celestial instruments.

"What's sidekick?" he asked, compliantly moving into position.

"Buddy, friend, comrade," I explained. *"Tongzhi."*

"*Tongzhi* don't have to take so many pictures of each other," Bo said with affable sourness.

I looked through the viewfinder. "Over to the left a little, Bo." Mischievously, he moved to the right. "Hey!"

"Hey, you!" he shouted back.

"Just this one and no more. Okay?"

"But why you need so many?" He moved into place.

I pretended not to hear him as I readjusted the lens. What could I say? That I wanted to capture him as many times as possible, in as many situations as possible, because in a few weeks I might never see him again?

One Saturday afternoon, Bo and I rode our bikes to the Temple of Confucius. I was in a great mood. The weather was glorious, so blue and clear that you could see the Fragrant Hills off in the distance. At that moment, I couldn't imagine being any happier.

"Hey, sidekick," I called out to him. "Hey, *tongzhi.*"

Bo looked over at me. "Get real."

"Where'd you learn that expression."

He gave me a look as if I were joking.

"From you."

I laughed. "It's a good thing we're on bikes," I told him. "Otherwise I'd grab you and give you a giant kiss."

He motioned with his head for me to keep my eyes on the road, but I could see that he was blushing.

"Need to turn here," he said.

"Whatever you want, Bo!" I called after him.

Thank you, I whispered as we made the turn. *Thank you, God. Thank you, Buddha. Thank you, Universe.*

We parked our bikes outside the Temple, paid our fee, and walked in. Bo directed me over to a courtyard planted with rows of tall stone slabs. As we drew closer, I could see that the face of each stele was carved with characters.

"This is telling who pass the imperial examination." He traced his fingers over the words. "Every year, they carve on these stones the names of the successful candidates. You must be a scholar, memorize all of Confucius, to get a good job in the government. Was a big honor."

"And once you get your master's degree in painting, will your name be placed here, too?"

For a second, Bo thought I was serious. Then he caught the teasing look in my face and shook his head. He pulled the baseball cap off my head.

"Hey you, show some respect."

Bo started laughing. He put the cap on his head and we wandered on down another row of the scholar's tablets.

"So, I've never asked you, Bo. What's your religion? Are you a Buddhist?"

"Not a Buddhist."

"Anything?" He shook his head, almost as if he'd never considered it before. "It doesn't matter to me," I went on, "but you always seem so . . . I don't know, so calm, so relaxed. How did you get that way?"

He closed his eyes for a moment. When he opened them again, I saw tears.

"Bo, what's the matter?"

"Have to be relaxed," he said. "Don't have a choice. Otherwise, I am so sad."

"Why? What do you mean?" He shook his head. "Come on, Bo, what's going on?"

"You going home."

I nodded. "Yes, I am."

"I wish you can stay."

"So do I, darling. I hope you know how unhappy I am that I'm going home." I wondered if these or similar words were what Richard, the earlier American boyfriend, had told him.

"Maybe not so unhappy like me."

"Why? What do you mean?"

"In Boston, maybe, you can find some other boyfriends, I think."

"Bo."

He cut me off.

"Can find one boyfriend for special."

It was almost unbearable, seeing myself as Bo saw me: as someone who could have his pick of lovers.

"Bo, let's sit."

We were in the middle of the grove of steles. No other tourists were about. I sat down on the ground, my back against one of the stone slabs. Bo squatted next to me, his eyes fixed on the space between his feet.

"Bo, I hope you know how I feel about you." I wanted to reach over and hold his hand, but I knew it would make him uncomfortable. "I can't imagine having a boyfriend who would be any more special than you are to me right now."

He kept his eyes on the ground.

"But . . ." I paused. I hadn't wanted to have this conversation yet. I hadn't even begun to figure out how to say it all, yet here it was: the rest-of-our-lives talk. "You're right, Bo, we have to get real. We both want to be together, but we can't. At least not right now." I didn't dare look at him. The words Bo had spoken to me after we'd first met in the French café at the New Year rang in my ears.

Special friend for tonight, he had said, *but maybe you not think I am special friend tomorrow.*

My eyes fixed on the trees at the edges of the courtyard. I was never so conscious of the care I needed to take with words. "You understand that I have to go home in three weeks." I glanced over at him. He was staring out at the same clump of trees. "But once I settle some things, I can come back. Maybe this fall."

Inwardly, I cringed at that *maybe.* It seemed so wretchedly timid for the hope that I had wanted to hold out to him, to *us.* The logistics of that feeble hope cascaded through my mind, possibilities I'd already considered, on those nights when I couldn't sleep: could I take another year's leave from my job in Boston? It seemed unlikely. And what about my friends, my family? Was I ready to leave them behind for another year . . . another . . . well, how long *would* I be willing to stay in China? Channing Plessey had made a life in Beijing, why not I? But Channing had money, a lawyer's salary. He could afford two or three trips a year back to the States. And Channing didn't have a mother to worry about. My mother. It had been hard for her this year, having me so far away. All the telephone calls and cheerful cards she'd sent me were, I knew, as much for herself as for me. My brother was already planning a big eightieth birthday celebration for her next October. And then there was Owen. Could I bear to be without Owen in my life? And damn it, where was he anyway? Why hadn't he e-mailed me?

As if he had been reading my mind, Bo said, "I don't think you will come back, David. You have very good life in U.S. Why do you want to come back to Beijing?"

I turned to him, my face so close to his anyone would have known we were lovers.

"But how good do you think my life can be without you?"

Neither of us spoke. I looked beyond the trees to the Confucian temple on the other side. Long and low and perfectly aligned along a north-south axis, it was one more example of an architecture I had come to admire this year, an architecture that spoke so eloquently of those ancient Chinese virtues: humanity and courtesy, respect and uprightness in all dealings.

"Bo, we need to take this one day at a time." I listened to myself saying these words. Were they the wisdom of the ancients or one more piece of New Age claptrap?

"Next day same as this day," Bo mumbled.

"Maybe yes; maybe no. That depends on a lot of things, but in the meantime, I don't want to let the next three weeks to go by without you, Bo. Sure, we don't know what's going to happen after I go home, but that doesn't mean we shouldn't enjoy each other now, enjoy every moment together now. Do you understand? This beautiful day, this magnificent temple"—I looked over my shoulder—"even this goddamned hard stele poking me in the back."

A soft smile bloomed on Bo's face.

"If you want," he said, wiping his eyes, "we can make a rubbing of the inscriptions. With a piece of paper and a black crayon."

We were back to being a couple of happy-go-lucky sightseers.

"They let you do that?"

"I think if you pay some money." He lifted himself up, turning to inspect the stele more closely. "This one have beautiful calligraphy." He traced the carving with his finger. "See, here is the scholar's name." He paused. "And this, the name of his native town. Did I tell you that? They always include the name of the hometown of each successful candidate. When a scholar pass the examination, it bring honor to the hometown, too. Native place is very important to the Chinese people."

Our eyes met. There was something very serious in Bo's face. He let me see it for just a second. Then he smiled.

"Okay, sidekick," he said, "so what you wanting to see now?"

Chapter Nineteen

During those final weeks, I wanted to spend all of my time with Bo. Evenings, weekends, nights—it didn't matter what we did or when we did it, as long as we did it together. Reluctantly, however, we made an agreement to sleep apart two nights a week. Bo hadn't been getting much painting done. Because he was scheduled to have a show at the end of the summer (a show, neither of us dared to acknowledge, that I was going to miss), he needed to make more time to work. I had some evening obligations as well. Friends from the clinic and the Ta Ta had started inviting me out for farewell get-togethers. Some of them knew about Bo and me and had invited him along, but Bo always declined.

"But they *want* you there," I tried explaining one evening. "They want to meet you. They want to . . ." I hesitated, trying to come up with words that would be the least threatening. "They want to celebrate our being together."

None of this convinced him.

"But why not, Bo? Are you embarrassed that they know we sleep together?"

He shook his head.

"Are you worried about your English? Your English is better than most of my friends' Chinese."

Again he shook his head.

"Are you afraid you'll have nothing to talk about?"

He looked away.

In the end, I gave in. Bo had his reasons, which only in time I would come to understand. I guessed that maybe he wasn't comfortable publicly proclaiming our relationship. It was all so new to him—not sex with a man, but the idea of being coupled with a man, seen with the man you were sleeping with, known as sleeping with him. I'd gone through all of that once, too.

So I went alone to the farewell parties. But all the time, I thought of Bo. This was, I saw, a microcosm of the way our relationship would have to proceed—apart, thinking of each other, waiting for each other—if ever there was to be a future for us at all. What future, I couldn't imagine, but I was still unwilling to let go of the idea that somehow, eventually, Bo and I might find a way to be together.

"I am waiting for you," he told me the next afternoon, as we got on our bikes after a visit to the zoo. Bo was heading back to his studio for an evening of painting; I was returning to the apartment to dress for a farewell dinner at Auntie and Xiaohe's.

"Wonderful, Bo, but I thought this was one of our nights apart."

"Of course, but I am still waiting for you," he said. "In my heart. When I am painting tonight, I will think about you."

"Bo, *wo ai ni.*"

I had never said these words to him before. I love you. I had never said them to anyone in China before. But at that moment, it felt as if I had been preparing the whole year to speak them. Bo lowered his eyes.

"*Wo ai ni,* David," he whispered.

———

Auntie had arranged for Winston to meet me at the East Gate. I got there early and waited for him to show up. Not much had changed since I had moved off campus. The guard house was as dilapidated as ever. Outside the gate, the dumpling sellers were still at their stalls. And beyond them, out on Xinjiekouwai, the rush-hour bicycle traffic was still rolling by with the same remarkably steady, ever flowing coordination. *Remember this,* I told myself. In a few weeks, it will be gone.

Just then, a cyclist pulled up in front of the main gate. It was my toy soldier, all dressed up in his oversize blue uniform and cap, ready for the evening shift. I watched him get off his bike and push it up the drive toward the guard house. Our eyes met and he flashed me a big smile of recognition.

"*Ni hao!*"

He rushed up, slapped me on the shoulder, and started speaking in rapid-fire Chinese. In the time since we'd last seen each other, my Mandarin had gotten better, but he was talking so fast that I couldn't understand most of what he was saying. I tried to respond as best I could. I used deliberately simple sentences.

Six months months before, when my heart was all aflutter for him, I would have worked this opportunity for all it was worth. I would have stood there indulgently, listening as hard as I could, asking him to repeat phrases, looking up words in my dictionary—anything just to be able to keep the conversation going. How things had changed. Now, I just felt awkward and guilty: awkward to be standing there, nodding my head idiotically, hardly understanding a word; guilty that earlier that year I'd led him on so with all that smiling, attentive geniality, letting him think I wanted to be friends. Well, I *had* wanted to be friends. But things were different now.

I think you are not in Beijing to buy hamburgers, Jiantao had teased me back in the winter.

Just then, Winston arrived.

"What's up, Mr. Davis?"

He shot the guard a quick, suspicious glance.

"Hey, Winston. Good to see you again."

"I hope you are very hungry," Winston said, taking his attention away from the guard. "Tonight my mother cooking many special foods for you." He began to deliver a description of the banquet Auntie had prepared. For several of the dishes, Winston used the Chinese names, which made little sense to me but which the guard, who was following Winston's description with enthusiastic nods of his head and exclamations of delight, clearly found tantalizing. I gathered I was in for quite a feast.

All at once, Winston interrupted himself and whipped around toward the boy, blasting him with what I could only guess was a barrage of vulgar rebukes for eavesdropping. At first, my soldier cowered under Winston's tongue lashing, but soon he found his courage and began to fire back his own salvo of denunciation. When Winston made a move to slap him, the guard pulled away, swore once more at Winston, then turned and pushed his bike into the gate house, chased by more of Winston's invective.

"Jesus, Winston, what *is* your problem?"

"No problem," he said, calmly lighting up a cigarette.

"Then why . . ."

"I having private conversation with you. That guy listening to everything we say." He blew out a complacent puff of smoke.

"But before you came, I was talking to him. He's a friend of mine." Winston shot me a skeptical look. "Yes!" I insisted. "Yes. A friend."

"No, I don't think, Mr. Davis. That guy not good for friend. You can see that, I think."

"I *cannot* see that! Why shouldn't I be friends with that guy? Tell me, Winston."

Taking another drag on his cigarette, Winston looked at me as if I were insane.

"You are a professional, Mr. Davis, have a good job, make a lot of money. That guy not even policeman. Just a guard. Stand there all night, watching nothing. Why you want to be friends with guy like that?"

I was furious at Winston's bullying arrogance; at his class prejudice; at the way he presumed to know better than I who my friends should be. And for the fact that he was right. I had no more business declaring that the guard was a friend than I did to claim that I spoke Mandarin. I still didn't even know the guard's name.

"You know, Winston, it doesn't hurt to try to be friendly to people."

"You be friendly, okay. Say, Hello. *Ni hao.* No problem. But some people, you be a little bit friendly to them, they thinking, Okay, now we can be like two brothers. They not understanding what is possible, what is not possible. You understand?"

I looked over toward the guard house. My soldier was standing at the door, watching us. I shook my head: no, I did not understand. I hoped the guard would see how exasperated I was with Winston.

Winston took a final drag on his cigarette and tossed it away. I got the feeling he thought it was pointless to argue with me anymore.

"Okay, Mr. Davis, we go now. My mother waiting for you."

Silently, we headed off across campus toward his parents' apartment. The sun was lingering in the sky, an orange glow through the trees. We were walking between rows of willows and poplars, the leaves newborn and green. A glorious spring evening filled the air. But I was too busy stewing over what Winston had said to enjoy any of it. I began rehearsing a list of Bo's qualities that I thought would be acceptable to Winston: Bo was educated, Bo spoke English, Bo had a promising career ahead of him. Winston couldn't possibly find any objection in a friendship with someone like that.

Suddenly, I found myself wishing that I had not been invited for dinner. All I wanted was to see Bo, to hold him in my arms, to feel the things he made me feel, to assure him, Darling, my love you for you *is* real. This is not a shallow, fleeting thing. Believe me, I am not a Lieutenant Pinkerton!

Winston had been right about one thing. His mother had gone all out with the preparations, a true Chinese banquet. Course after course of mouthwatering dishes—chicken, shrimp, tofu, beef, a whole steamed fish—kept appearing at the table. They had even hired a girl from the university, who stayed in the kitchen and did the last-minute assembly. This allowed Auntie to join us at the table: an extravagance, I realized, all done in my honor.

Tyson and Suling, whose English name was Janet, had also been invited. Janet's presence seemed to rouse Winston's spirits, even though she was a far cry from the painted-doll look he had gone for in his ex, the Ice Princess Ling. Janet wore little make-up. Her hair was cut short. Her dress, in celery-colored silk, was attractive but nothing that called attention to itself. Still, Winston lavished almost all of his attention on her. His love of gab, his joking nature, his sense of his own manly importance—he brought them all out for Janet's amusement. I got the impression that he was trying to show Tyson that a Chinese man had just as much talent for wooing a Chinese lady as a Westerner did.

As we ate, Xiaohe made sure the alcohol continued to flow. As he'd done during my previous visit to their home, he exercised a heavy hand on the plentiful supply of beer, wine, and liqueurs that cluttered the table. This time, however, I monitored my intake. When Xiaohe insisted I drink up, I explained why I was holding back, regaling them all with an elaborate, comic description of the state of my head on the occasion of the previous dinner party, though I expurgated the part about ending up in bed with one of the university guards.

"Before you go back to America," Winston said, "you should try, um . . ." He turned and said something in Chinese to his father.

Janet groaned merrily. Auntie shook her head.

"Gall bladder of snake in wine," Xiaohe translated. "But I think this only for Chinese people."

"Only for a *few* Chinese people," Janet corrected.

"No, very, very good," Winston assured me. "Makes you strong. And sexy." He clenched his fists for Janet.

"There you go, Davey," Tyson said. "Just the medicine you've been looking for all year." He winked at me. I glanced over at Janet. She was studying my face intently.

Both Tyson and Janet knew about Bo. Tyson had been one of the first people I'd told. In his own hearty, jolly, any-matey-of-yours-is-a-matey-of-mine kind of way, he'd shown his support. I was less sure about Janet. In the past few days, whenever I'd been with them and the subject of Bo had come up, Janet had always gone silent. I'd tried to guess what her objection to our relationship might be. Presumably it wasn't the Chinese factor—a Westerner going with a Chinese—because that described her relationship with Tyson as well. I doubted, too, that she would balk at the discrepancy in our ages. Janet, after all, was in her late thirties, several years older than Tyson, though not, I had to admit, by as many years as separated Bo and me. Then there was the gay factor. I wanted to believe that Janet's medical training in Hong Kong had given her a liberal perspective on such matters, but maybe not.

Why do you care what she thinks? I had argued with myself, but now, as we sat around the table, I had the uncomfortable feeling of being studied by her. *So this,* I imagined her thinking to herself, *this is what a middle-aged American homosexual is all about.*

"Have you ever tried it?" I asked her. "Gall bladder of snake in wine?"

Janet snapped out of her reverie. "Lord, no!" she protested. "It's definitely a guy thing." Her command of idiomatic English was superb.

"Guy thing." I'd had just enough to drink that I was feeling playfully contrary. "What *is* a 'guy thing' anyway?" I looked at Tyson. Apparently, he'd had a bit too much *baijiu* himself. He shot me a baffled look.

"A guy thing," he managed to get out. "Well, there are no generalizations, really, are there? I mean, each one of us lovely specimens of the male sex is unique." He grinned at me, then turned to Janet, then back to me again. "Wouldn't you say, old chum?" Playfully, I shrugged my shoulders. "Sure," Tyson continued, "every man's guts work about the same, but tastes . . . you know, which of us likes football and which of us goes in for"—he pursed his lips again—"well, classical music, that's another matter, isn't it?"

"Snake wine very, very good," Winston assured us again. He lit up another cigarette.

Xiaohe cleared his throat and moved his plate away, resting the palms of his hands on the table.

"Perhaps," he said, like the professor that he was, beginning a seminar, "perhaps all men do share some feelings in common. Feelings which perhaps women do not have." He raised his palms off the table, as if to stave off objections. "For example, a nostalgia for boyhood. For something in boyhood . . ." He cocked his head affectionately in my direction. "What do you say, David? For the freedom in boyhood? Always some happy memories, some deep feelings that do not leave you."

"I think women feel those things, too," Janet offered.

Bowing is head slightly, Xiaohe considered the idea. I could see he was reluctant to agree.

"Different, I think, for the woman." He twisted his glass of *baijiu.* "For the woman, she thinks of childhood, but not her own. Her deepest feelings are always for her children."

I could see Janet ready to bring up another challenge, but Xiaohe continued.

"I have been reading a biography of Mao Zedong. Very interesting. Do you know that when Chairman Mao was very old, in his seventies, he told his comrades that his wish"—Xiaohe paused to emphasize the point—"his wish was to continue to be a schoolboy." He nodded his head, savoring the delight of it. "Yes, to be a schoolboy. You see?" His eyes were twinkling, and a little moist, I thought. "The Chairman himself, a political and military genius, you must agree"—he looked at me—"whatever your politics. After everything he had accomplished. He just wanted to continue to be a schoolboy."

Janet shook her head in disbelief.

"I saw some American tourists today," she said. "On the street. Near Tiananmen Square." She spoke tentatively, as if she were not sure she should be telling this story. "Two guys." She cleared her throat. "I knew they were Americans immediately. Older guys, in their late forties. And they were dressed . . ." She shook her head again, then looked at me as if to apologize. "Well, they looked as if they had just come out of the circus. Baggy shorts with the pockets on the sides, flashy Hawaiian shirts, gold rings in their ears. One had tried to dye his hair blond, but it had turned out bright carrot orange. The other had bracelets tattooed all around his wrists." She turned to Xiaohe. "They were trying to look . . . I don't know, like they were in their twenties." Then she turned to me. "Like club kids."

"You see?" Xiaohe said. To my relief, Janet's description had amused him. "To continue to be schoolboy!"

I brought my glass of *baijiu* to my lips and took a long, slow sip. I understood now what Janet had been searching for in my face: some evidence that I, too, was a ridiculous American clown.

Xiaohe looked at his wife and said something to her in Chinese.

"Ah, yes!" Auntie exclaimed. She pushed herself up from the table and disappeared down the hall.

"We have a little gift for you," Xiaohe explained. "Something from my family so that you will remember China."

"I can't imagine that I'll ever forget China," I told him.

"Yes, we hope," Xiaohe agreed.

Auntie came back and placed a small wrapped package in front of me. I could see it was a book.

"Gosh, thank you. This is so kind of you all."

"Open, open," Xiaohe invited.

I ripped off the paper. It was a copy of the book of poems by Li Qingzhao that Auntie had brought to the picnic. I quickly flipped through the pages. It was a splendid edition, expensively printed on high-grade paper. I hadn't seen books of this quality all year. It made me realize how little of Beijing I had really gotten to know.

"Thank you so much. All of you."

We passed the book around. When it got to Janet, she took it carefully in her hands and slowly leafed through the pages, occasionally stopping to read one of the poems. Her quiet, studious regard for the volume—almost as if she were reading a sacred text—made us all pause and watch her. For a minute or two, a silent, reverential space cleared around the table. Then Janet looked up.

"So much sadness," she said. "So much loss." Her eyes briefly went to mine.

Around nine-thirty, Tyson and Janet announced that they had to be going. When they offered me a lift back to my place, I decided to take it. Auntie and Xiaohe did not seem to mind that their party was breaking up. I noticed that the girl in the kitchen was already busy washing up the dishes. Our early departure probably meant that our hosts would save a few yuan. Considering all the expense that the evening must have cost them, I imagined they welcomed this prospect.

Tyson, Janet, and I set off toward the East Gate. The paths through the campus, never well lit, seemed darker than usual, but comfortingly so, as if with the arrival of spring there was no longer any need for caution or wariness. The only sounds I heard came from the occasional chirping of a night bird, hidden somewhere in the dark leaves of the trees. Even the cyclists who passed by rode along quietly, like benign, indifferent creatures on a nighttime savanna.

"I'm going to miss them," I said. "Even Winston, I think."

Janet turned to me. "So, you must come back."

I didn't respond.

279

"You will come back to see your friend," Tyson said. "Won't you?"

It was an amiable, gracious question, so typical of Tyson's geniality, but something in the way he'd phrased it—that hint, maybe, that my relationship with Bosheng could only be about the occasional friendly return visit—left me feeling sad, aware that no matter how I answered, *yes* or *no,* I would betray the hopelessness of any real future for Bo and me.

"I don't know," I told him. "It's not as if I can jump on a shuttle and come visit him any weekend I want."

"You could stay in China," Janet offered. "Continue to work here."

"I've actually considered that, but . . ."

"Well, why not?" Her voice was suddenly full of brightness. The brightness of Hong Kong, I thought, that city of towering, twenty-first century possibility.

I shook my head. "Because I have too many obligations back home right now. My family, my job, my mother."

"So your mother can move to Beijing, too. I think she will like China."

I laughed. Janet's suggestions were getting more and more preposterous.

"Janet, my mother's going to be eighty years old this year."

"Yes," she said. "I understand." She glanced at Tyson.

We walked on, the night enveloping us in its hushed embrace. When we arrived at the East Gate, I saw that Tyson and Janet had been holding hands. Tyson nodded toward the avenue.

"The car is parked up the street."

"You know," I said, "it's such a lovely night that I think I'll stay out a while longer. I can grab a cab later."

"You sure?" Tyson gave me a concerned look.

"Absolutely. I just need to be alone for a while."

As I kissed Janet goodbye, I noticed my guard, standing outside the gate house, watching us with deep fascination.

"Fortunately, this isn't the big goodbye," I told her. "I'll see you next week at the office party, right?"

Janet nodded. I was aware, once again, of how deeply she was studying my face. I turned toward Tyson.

"And I'll see you on Monday, Dr. McClennen." I gave him a kiss, too, a quick peck on the cheek.

"I'm sorry we didn't get to meet Bosheng tonight," Tyson said. "Tell him we'd love to meet him before you leave."

"I don't know. He's pretty shy about meeting my friends."

"Tell him," Janet said, "nothing to be shy about. We are sympathetic people."

Tyson looked at Janet, then at me. "It's probably not the right time to say this, but if you want"—he checked Janet's reaction again—"we could look after him a bit after you've gone home. You know, take him out to dinner occasionally, call him to be in touch, make sure he's all right. I don't know . . . you tell us, Davey. What can we do to be helpful?"

"Thank you. *Both* of you. I appreciate your concern. At the moment, I'm not sure what you can do. Although one thing I know you *can't* do is call him. He doesn't even have a telephone."

"But if there's anything we can do," Janet said.

"Really," Tyson said.

I took in a deep breath. All this helpfulness: it felt like so many gifts to pack and take home with me. Even more so now, I needed to be somewhere by myself for a little while. "Thanks," I told them. "But you know, sometimes I think that the bravest thing would be to admit that it isn't going to work out."

Tyson shook his head.

"No, Davey, the bravest thing is to go with your heart."

I snickered amiably.

"Do you know how many times in my life I've done just that? Go with my heart? It's getting to be a cliché with me." Tyson didn't answer. "Do you know how many times I've ended up feeling like a fool for going with my heart? I just don't want to feel like a fool anymore."

"Were you a fool when you chose Johnny?"

I craned my neck up toward the sky. The moon was out, but there were no stars.

"Was I a fool to choose Johnny? Tyson, there are days when I honestly don't know."

"And that's okay, too," he said. "You know that, right?"

"Yeah, so I've heard."

Tyson patted me on the shoulder.

"Don't stay out too late, Davey. Sometimes a good night's sleep is the best medicine."

"Believe me, I'm wiped out. I just want to have a bit of a stroll through the campus once more. To say goodbye to the old place." I looked at Janet and smiled. "You know, the nostalgia of boys."

She chuckled.

"Goodness, we all said a lot of silly things tonight, didn't we?"

The three of us kissed goodbye again, but as soon as they left, I could only stand there, lonely and disoriented, not knowing what to do next. I glanced over at the guard. He was still watching me. It made me feel self-conscious. I wondered what he thought of me now, this guy who kissed other men goodbye, this Westerner who used to say hello to him every afternoon, barely a friend, but probably already the central character in a funny old story they told in the guard house: "The Guy Who Forgot His Key." What was he thinking as he watched me standing here, alone and hangdog?

I held up my hand, *hello*. He smiled and nodded. I approached. In my best Mandarin, I apologized for Winston's rude behavior earlier that evening. He said something that I took to mean he had not taken offense with me.

"I'm going home next week," I told him.

He nodded and smiled: his pleasure in my pleasure. *Zaijian,* we wished each other and shook hands. I would have loved to embrace him, give him a quick peck on the cheek, too, but all those impulses now seemed so awkward and mistaken, the will-of-the-wisp intimacy of strangers. As I walked away, into the darkness of the campus, I wondered if that was what I had let all of China become for me this year: nothing but a passing infatuation. From that first silly flirtation with the steward on the plane—what was it all if not just more of the same silly, adolescent muddleheadedness that I had been aswirl in for years?

"Tyson, you're wrong," I muttered into the night air. "You're wrong."

He was just too in love with Janet to imagine anything other than the triumph of love, the glorious excess of it, that breaking cup of spring. No, the bravest thing was not always to listen to one's heart. Who even knew what the "heart" was? A bird chirping in the darkness. A kite tossing about in the fickle wind. A boy forgetting he had to be a man.

I figured there were two ways to end it with Bo. One was outright—truthful and above board, no *maybes,* no *once I settle some things.* If I could be strong and face the facts squarely, he would be, too. I only had to speak the words, as Tyson had spoken them to Apple, and Bo, dear, sweet Bo, would accept them the way he had accepted everything in our relationship.

The other way was the way Bo probably suspected I would end it, the way his other American boyfriends had. I would return home, write a few times, then let things take their natural course, the whole affair just lapsing into a bittersweet memory. Lots of people ended affairs that way. An *affair,* that's what this had been all along. So good to have found the word to lock it into place.

The year I lived in Beijing, I had an affair with a lovely man named Bosheng.

That's how the story would go in the years ahead. Erik had become a story; Johnny had become a story. So, too, in time, would Bo. When I got back to the apartment, I'd look up "affair" in my dictionary. I was interested to know what the Chinese called it.

By now I had come to the small study plaza that I had haplessly cruised back in the fall. The picnic tables, the vine-covered pergola— I remembered it all—a stage set for a week's worth of fantasies and anticipations that had never materialized.

I sat down at one of the tables, recalling how often I had taken myself here—days, nights, weekends—incredulous that no one seemed to use this spot for cruising. I could hardly entertain the memories, they seemed so juvenile now. All that hunger, all that loneliness.

Just then, a little way off in the distance, I heard a commotion. It sounded like a crowd of protesters. I could see lights, too, flashlights and lanterns, strafing the black night, and suddenly, with a racket of shouting and cheers, a crowd of students spilled into the plaza. There were about twenty of them, all dressed in smart blue and white workout uniforms. I edged back in my seat, farther into the dark shadows at the back of the pergola.

The students formed a circle and began to stomp their feet to the rhythm of some sort of slogan, which they repeated over and over. A few were waving large red flags emblazoned with gold characters. It looked like a rally of some sort, and I wondered what was going on back home—an invasion? a caustic political remark? something Clinton had said or done? What might have triggered this late-night demonstration? It occurred to me that I could get into trouble if I stayed, but it was already too late to get out of there without calling attention to myself. I hunkered down and waited.

When the students had completed forming the circle, they let out a whoop and a cheer. It seemed more playful than menacing. The light from the flashlights and kerosene lanterns they were carrying bounced festively about. In the intermittent illumination, I could make out their faces. They seemed as young as American high school students.

Then a young man stepped into the middle of the circle and addressed his comrades. He was slightly taller than the rest, with a lithe, trim body and long black bangs, a little too elegantly coiffed. As he spoke, he kept turning to face various parts of the circle. I couldn't make out what he was saying, but it was impossible not to notice how he kept absentmindedly pushing those silky bangs away from his forehead and eyes. Occasionally, his speech was interrupted by an outburst of laughter from his schoolmates. I began to relax a little, but stayed hidden in the shadows. The leader finished his address with a shout and a clap-clap of his hands. More cheers and laughter. Then the students who were carrying the kerosene lanterns put them down at the margins of the plaza and everyone formed three lines facing the leader, who began to call out numbers—"*Yi! Er! San!*"—each one corresponding to a different position of his hands and feet.

"*Zai!*" he shouted. This time, the students took up the starting position and, to the count of eight, mimicked his movements as he ran through the steps again. It was a folk dance. I guessed they'd been practicing for some time. They swung their arms, turning and bending, turning and swinging, in perfect synchronization. The ones still holding flashlights traced huge arcs of light across the nighttime sky.

Their dancing was graceful, athletic and confident, but it was the leader I was most drawn to. His movements, far more fluid and precise than any of the other students', were wonderfully accomplished, balletic in fact. Where the students turned, he swept; where they hopped, he pranced; where they haphazardly wielded their flashlights, his arms described sumptuous arabesques. Only one small detail of his performance lacked professional polish. He kept pushing back those long, black bangs that cascaded over his brow. I suspected that his classmates had no idea they were being led by a queen. I wondered if he even knew it himself. Once or twice, I imagined that he was looking directly at me, but I kept myself hidden in the shadows.

After half an hour or so, the rehearsal ended. The students let their bodies relax, slumping over and panting hard, catching their breaths. Not the leader. He continued to stand, tall and graceful, his shoulders held proudly back, crossing his ankles one over the other. I watched him as he gave his jacket two smart tugs and once more flipped his hair out of his eyes. Again, I got the eerie sensation that he was staring at me. Then he moved from classmate to classmate, offering a bit of advice here, or a word of encouragement there. He seemed more tactile with the female students, more sissy-talky. With the boys, he maintained a respectable physical distance.

The students began drifting away, taking their flashlights and lanterns with them. A few invited the leader to come join them, but he declined. He stood in the middle of the plaza, facing the study grove, and did cool-down stretches, his arms akimbo, bending left and right. When the last of his comrades had gone, he was left alone in the darkness. The only light came from the moon, which cast a pale, silvery-blue light down on the plaza. Slowly, he unwound from his stretching and began to walk toward the pergola. It wasn't until he said hello to me—he spoke in English—that I realized he really had been watching me all along.

"Did you like the dancing?" He sat down beside me on the picnic bench.

"Yes. Very much." We introduced ourselves. "You're a very good dancer," I told him.

"Thank you."

His knee touched mine. He did not move it away.

"So what are you doing here?" he asked.

I chuckled.

"Figuring out what I'm doing here."

He smiled—"You are a foreign student?"—then nodded to the book that Auntie and Xiaohe had given me.

I told him no and explained my connection the University. When I said that I no longer lived on campus, he smiled again.

"So maybe you can invite me to your flat for some tea or something?" His knee pressed a little harder into mine.

"Yes, I suppose I could."

It was all coming back: that weird, unrelenting logic of horniness.

"Yes?" he said, encouraged.

I studied his face. It was extraordinarily handsome, a bit cocksure perhaps, but exquisite, a balletomane's face. Under his loose-fitting workout suit, I guessed he had an exquisite body, too.

"What is that book?" He reached over for it, an excuse for clasping my hand. He did not let go. We sat there, our faces brushed by the leafy shadows cast by the moonlight, staring at each other. By now I had an erection.

"It's too late to read now," he said. His fingers began to caress the knuckles of my hand. "Don't you think?"

There is something about fifty staring you in the face. It's a threshold, a border of sorts. On one side, all the delusions of youth. On the other, the unforgiving awareness that everything runs out—time, hope, energy, good looks, confidence—confidence in your ability to rack up the points in your favor, confidence that you can organize your life to suit yourself. You begin to learn how to settle for less. That's called resignation. Or wisdom. It depends. On what it depends was the business of that moment, there on that mild spring evening, under the moon-shadowy pergola, this gorgeous dancer's hand on mine.

"Maybe we can take a taxi to your place?" he asked.

In turn I let my fingers caress his knuckles. It bought me a few more moments to think.

Face the facts, I told myself. Anything more with Bo was an impossibility, a wacky, zany, lunatic notion. I needed to *get real.* Bo himself had said so once. And so, why not take this guy home—Ming, or Bing, or Weilong—I'd already forgotten his name. What difference would it make in the great and shabby scheme of things? The course that Bo and I were running would not be altered one iota. We would be history soon enough. All of this would be history soon enough. Wasn't that one of the things I'd come to admire about the Chinese: their stoic forbearance with the way things passed in time?

"So, what do you say?" the dancer asked. "Huh?" He stopped massaging my hand.

Or I could choose not to face the facts. Life with Bo—an impossibility? Why? What were facts, anyway? Didn't I have some say in what "the facts" were? Perhaps my father would have called that attitude stubborn. *Facts are facts,* he would have said. *Stop being cute, David.* Lots of people would have said so. Life with Bo: an impossibility. I could hear it roaring in my ears, my big, Buddha ears.

I looked up at Longming (his name had suddenly come back to me: I knew I would remember it for the rest of my life). He just might have been the most beautiful man I'd met in China.

"Sorry," I told him. "I have a boyfriend."

The Breaking Cup of Spring

驚破一甌春

Chapter Twenty

In Hong Kong, the rain was coming down in unforgiving torrents. Stalwart to the end, the departing British honor guard remained unflinching, standing at attention, as still, it struck me, as the terra cotta tomb soldiers outside Xi'an. Even their dress uniforms were holding up under the heavy downpour, every crease and pleat as sharp as a sword. Then, to the nasal piping of "Auld Lang Syne," the guard filed out of the military enclave, solemnly shouldering their rifles, their final official duty before returning home.

"It's like a funeral," Owen said, wiping his eyes with the back of his hand. Of the three of us, gathered there in front of my old television set, he seemed the most moved.

The camera cut to a shot of Hong Kong harbor, where, the commentator was saying, the sky would soon erupt in a massive fireworks display: twenty-million dollars' worth. He turned to his partner in that conversational way that news anchormen have and said, "You know, we're told by both the British and the Chinese that this handover is supposed to be a 'nonevent,' but twenty-million dollars in pyrotechnics doesn't seem like a nonevent, does it?" The two of them chuckled amiably with the easy-going joviality of Americans.

I turned from where I was sitting in a chair near the bed.

"Do you guys want to watch any more of this?"

"Don't you want to see the fireworks?" Stewart asked. His head was resting on Owen's shoulder.

"Not really. We can go down to the Esplanade on Friday and watch all the fireworks we want."

Owen looked at Stewart.

"They do a big fireworks display here for the Fourth of July," Owen explained. "The Boston Pops, the 1812 Overture, lots of guns, the whole bit. It's a mob scene, but fun."

"Sounds like it," Stewart said, nuzzling into Owen. "Why don't we go?" He nuzzled closer. Three months ago, the idea of a middle-brow pops concert on a steamy, crowded river bank would have been as appealing to Stewart as a return visit to the Ta Ta Club.

"We'll need to go early to get a good spot," Owen said. "We can bring a nice picnic, and the newspaper, and some books to read."

They had met early in April, when Stewart had taken up Owen's offer to visit Boston and be introduced to the gay scene up here. Owen, always the do-gooder, a true bodhisattva of compassion. The story, as I learned it from him, finally, in a long e-mail he sent me just before I returned home, was that it was love at first sight. For both of them. He apologized for not writing or calling or even whisking off an e-mail sooner, acknowledging that he had put me into a communication blackout for over a month. He said that he had been so totally caught off guard by falling in love with Stewart—they were alternating weekends in Boston and Philadelphia—that all of his time and energy had gone into dealing with "this incredible world I didn't think I would ever inhabit." When I got off the plane in Boston, this time gaining a day, Owen and Stewart were both there to meet me, big smiles on their faces, their arms around each other's waist.

Stewart reached for his cup of tea resting on the night table.

"Owen, how about Scrabble? Do you like Scrabble? We could bring my Scrabble board to the Esplanade, too."

"I adore Scrabble," Owen told him.

"I knew it!" Stewart burst out laughing. "When do you suppose we're finally going to discover something that one of us likes that the other doesn't?"

Owen's e-mail had reached me four days before I left China, four days during which my emotions tumbled and bounced like a troupe of tipsy Peking acrobats. Elated and sad, amazed and angry, jealous and frightened, one minute flying high, the next in the depths of despair—the only constant was my love for Bo and my certainty, despite the overwhelming odds against us, that he was the one I wanted to be with for the rest of my life.

I had walked through those final days in a trance, packing my stuff, making trips to the international post office to mail boxes home, doing all the things necessary to wrap up my year in China. Hour by hour, I ticked off the tasks. Day by day, I met my obligations: the office party, a lunch date with Channing Plessey, another with Xinlu. There was even an out-of-the-blue phone call from Jiantao and Guoyang. They had heard I was leaving and wanted to wish me well. (Neither one asked about Stewart.)

As the rain on the television screen continued to fall in long, silvery curtains, all the leave-taking events of my final days in Beijing rushed by me. The parties, the lunches, the goodbye drinks—I had experienced them only as one experiences things in a dream. I'd been exhausted, physically and emotionally, going through the motions of saying goodbye but not really present to any of it. Only my final get together with Edward, dear, sweet, kindhearted Edward, could I remember with any degree of clarity.

He had invited me for a drink at the Ta Ta, two days before I left. Bo didn't want to join us, so I had arranged with Edward to make it an early evening, just one cocktail before I rendezvoused with Bo later on.

"I'm sorry you never met him," I said when we had settled at one of the tables. It was six o'clock, and the place was nearly empty.

"No problem, David."

"I know, but I just wish Bo were a little less shy about meeting my friends. I think this is all still pretty new to him, you know, the gay world."

"No, not the gay world," Edward said. "I don't think that's why he doesn't come to meet me."

"What then?"

Edward looked down at his drink for a moment, then up at me.

"David, I am wanting to tell you just one thing. You are very lucky."

"Yes, I know."

He let out a skeptical murmur.

"Maybe. But maybe you don't know." He paused. I took it as my cue to say something.

"I'm glad we met this year, Edward."

He shook his head, brushing off my compliment.

"You see, David, you are not only falling in love with a gay man but you are falling in love, I think, with China. That is lucky, too." He looked around the room. "Every time I come here, David, I am seeing two different worlds. One is the Open World: open mind, open talking, open body, open sex. That's your world."

I laughed.

"No, please, David. I think it's true. You can't see because Open World is all you know. That's how you are born; that's how you live your whole life."

"And the other world—the Closed World?"

"Not closed. The other world is . . . mm, can you say Veiled World? Do you understand? In this world you do not say directly what you think or mean. Not necessary to say all the time everything you think. I know this world. It's the world for most Chinese."

"Yes, I've tried to explain all that to Bo. I told him my friends would understand if he kept quiet and didn't participate much in a conversation. I just wish he had met more of them."

Edward shook his head again. He looked a little exasperated with me.

"Bo does not need to meet all of your friends. It's not important for him, David. They are your friends, not his."

"But . . ."

"You two are very different, have different personal natures. But now you have wonderful opportunity." He hesitated. "I don't know how to explain. Opportunity for cooperation, for harmony. Do you understand? So I think it's important you do not try to change that different. You love what is different in him, so you have to take care of that different. Don't worry that Bo is a shy guy, doesn't want to meet your friends." Edward laughed. "Maybe I am sounding like your Chinese mom!"

"No, Edward, you're sounding like a friend." I cupped my hands over his. "A good friend."

He pulled his hands out and cupped mine. "I will always be your friend, David."

———

On the screen a reporter was soliciting opinions from passersby on the street.

"The child has returned to the mother," one patriotic resident of Hong Kong told the interviewer. "We don't be jealous of foreigners any more."

"This is the end of our humiliation," said another.

People were crowding into the view of the camera, trying to be seen, waving, grinning, full of party festivity. I looked at the faces, but there was only one I wanted to see.

"What's the matter?" Owen said.

"Nothing."

He leaned over to where I was sitting in the chair.

"Oh, goodie. We haven't played this game in a year."

"What game?"

"The game called David Makes Owen Guess What's Wrong."

I looked over at Stewart.

"You see? This is what you're in for, you know. Owen has this maddening habit of not letting you alone until . . ."

"Until," Owen interrupted, "you acknowledge that you're part of the race of beings on this planet that have messy, uncontrollable, embarrassing feelings."

Stewart laughed.

"So, how about it, Cupcake?" Owen said. "Are you going to tell us why for the past hour you've been staring at the television like it was a test pattern?"

"It's been three weeks and I haven't heard from Bo yet. Okay? *That's* what's wrong. Big surprise, huh?"

"Not even an e-mail?" Stewart asked. He set his tea cup back down on the night table.

"Stewart, Bo doesn't have e-mail. He doesn't have a telephone. I don't know, maybe he doesn't even have a postage stamp."

"You'll hear," Stewart said consolingly. "The mail is slow from China."

"It took less than a week for my letters to get here. My mother got one of my letters four days after I mailed it."

Owen clicked off the TV.

"Cupcake, your mother could probably get the entire People's Liberation Army to mobilize to Mongolia in four days."

Stewart began to laugh.

"Hey," I scolded him, "you haven't even met my mother."

"No, it's the way Owen calls you Cupcake. Back in Beijing, I thought you made that name up just for me."

"Sorry. Owen was the original Cupcake. You'll have to be Cupcake Junior."

"Or how about Mr. Muffin?" Owen said. "Or Pretty Pancake, or Scrumptious Madeleine!"

"I will *not* be Madeleine!" Stewart announced.

"Brioche then? How about Brioche?" Owen snuggled up to Stewart. "You like that better? Brioche?" He threw himself on top of Stewart and started tickling him. "*Qu'est-ce que tu dis, ma petite Brioche?* Huh?"

Stewart erupted into fits of laughter.

"Aargh, get off of me, Owen!"

"Not until my little Brioche tells me what he wants to be called."

I got up from the chair.

"Guys, I'm going for a walk."

Abruptly, Owen stopped horsing around.

"Oh, don't go. Come on, let's watch some more of the handover." He clicked the television back on. The President of China was delivering a speech. During the two minutes that we watched, the translator used the word "solemn" three times.

"Guys, really. I need to get out of here for a little while."

Owen looked up.

"I guess Stewart and I should take off, too. We can just as easily watch this at my place."

"Stay put. Relax. This is not about kicking you out. I like having you guys here. Just do me a favor. If you're still here, answer the buzzer when it rings. There's a carpenter coming after lunch to take some measurements for shelves I'm putting up in the kitchen. If for some reason I'm not back in time, let him in."

"What shelves?" Owen asked. He sounded miffed, as if I'd not let him in on some important business that affected us both. Before Stewart came on the scene, I'd have double-checked every domestic decision I made with Owen. Now we were in that awkward period when we were trying to reestablish what our relationship was all about.

"I'm finally getting around to making room for Johnny's cookbooks," I told him.

At the mention of cookbooks, Stewart perked up.

"What kind of cookbooks?" he asked.

"Everything but Japanese." I chuckled at the memory. "Johnny couldn't stand the idea of sushi."

"Tons of dessert books," Owen added. "The more chocolate recipes the better."

"And anything with Grand Marnier." There was so much to teach Stewart about Johnny.

"Oh, my God," Owen said. "Remember the time Johnny made that fabulous bitter chocolate and orange mousse?" He turned to Stewart. "To die for! You would have loved Johnny."

"I wish I had met him," Stewart volunteered.

The three of us fell silent for a second.

"Look," I said, bringing us back to something more mundane. The carpenter said he'd be coming around two. Can you be here?"

"We could," Stewart said, "but we kind of have other plans."

Owen furrowed his brow. "We do?"

"Remember? We're going to Tower Records this afternoon?"

"Oops!"

Stewart grinned at me.

"I'm preparing him for the Met this winter. We're taking a five-opera subscription. Did you know they're doing both *Turandot* and *Madam Butterfly* this year? What an amazing season it's going to be!"

Outside, it was daytime and sunny. It was not Hong Kong. It was not China. It wasn't even the first of July yet. On this side of the world, it was still the last day of June, exactly two weeks after my fiftieth birthday, three weeks after my return from Beijing. On this side of the world, people had blond hair, there was thick, lush grass in the parks, the sky was a clear, clean blue.

All of this still startled me. As I walked through the South End, I looked at trees I hadn't thought about in a year: maple, elm, oak, sycamore. Flowers I hadn't seen in a year: petunias, pansies, bearded iris. Building materials I forgotten about: brownstone, granite, red brick, wrought iron, slate. I saw babies in strollers. Black people. Latinos. Muscle boys coming back from the gym. It was a foreign country to me.

On this side of the world, there were no dragon walls, no pagodas, no temples, no bell towers. No one used bicycles to commute to work; you couldn't find hot, steamed *mantou* anywhere. On this side of the world, women in indigo smocks did not sweep the streets with brooms made of rush. (Even the litter in the gutters was different.) Pretty-faced soldiers did not walk along the sidewalks hand in hand. Everything that was sold was sold inside a store. On this side of the world, what was happening in Hong Kong, what was happening in China, the fact that there *was* a China—no one seemed to notice.

On this side of the world, most absent of all, there was no Bosheng.

I continued my walk. I passed the Eagle, passed the community center where I'd taken my first lessons with Mrs. Duan, passed the Chinese apartment building on Oak Street. It seemed so different from the high rises in Beijing, but when I tried to put my finger on what that difference was—the design? the materials? the faces of the residents emerging from the lobby?—it seemed I'd already lost too much of what Beijing was about to pinpoint the distinction.

I made my way into Chinatown and over to Beach Street, which was busy with workaday commerce. People were coming and going, shopping, strolling, hauling things from delivery trucks, hustling about—the amiable, appealing hustle I'd known in Beijing. This was already my third visit to Chinatown since I'd returned home. Something of China lingered in the air here, but even so, it was not China. Not my China. The language I heard was not my China. The young people on the streets—their haircuts, their clothes, the streetwise American faces they'd learned to wear—they weren't my

China. The reactions I got from the shopkeepers when I smiled or said *ni hao*—they weren't my China.

I thought about the way Stewart had felt when he first returned to Philadelphia. Now I had it, too. Disorientation. Homesickness. For China. For Beijing. For Bo. These visits to Chinatown brought a little of him back to me, but only as a hollow sea shell brings back the sea. I'd already booked a flight to Beijing for Christmas, a trip I hadn't even told Owen about. I'd also called a gay immigration lawyer to inquire about our options.

"What if this gay marriage thing passes in Hawaii?" I'd asked him.

"Won't have any bearing at all on federal immigration policy." He suggested that my best bet would be to try to get Bo over here on a student visa. I'd already called several art schools in the area to inquire about graduate programs.

Toward the end of Beach Street, I stopped in front of the display window of a bakery shop full of Chinese cookies and pastries. Most of them I'd never seen in Beijing. I went in. There was a white guy next to me buying a bag of fortune cookies and a tin of ginseng tea.

"How about this?" he asked the cashier, holding the tin in front of her. She was a pretty Chinese woman in her mid-twenties. "This stuff is supposed to be really good for you, right? Keeps you young and healthy." He smiled flirtatiously at her. "Like you." She gave him an uncomprehending look.

I started putting together a translation in my head: This man, *zhege nanren* . . . wants to know, *xiang zhidao* . . .

"What about you?" he asked her, his voice louder now. "Do you drink this?" He pointed to the tin. "This. You drink?" He pantomimed raising a cup to his lips. "Good?"

I abandoned my translation and left the shop. Jesus, is that how I had spoken to people in China? Is that how I had spoken to Bo?

———

When I got back to the apartment, the carpenter was just pulling up in his truck. I went over and introduced myself. Although we had only spoken on the phone, I recognized him immediately: a tall, blond guy I used to see all the time at the Cute Boy Café. One of the Saturday morning regulars. A guy Owen and I had both commented on with pleasure.

"Hey, how's it going?" As we shook hands, I realized that he didn't recognize me. "So, thanks for showing up on time," I told him.

"Can't imagine running a business any other way." We were standing across from my apartment. Andrew looked up at the row of bow fronts. "Great old buildings," he said. "I love working in this neighborhood."

As he studied the block, I looked at Andrew's face more closely. His eyes were a beautiful pale gray, his skin slightly pock-marked, the ghost of teenage acne, I guessed. A whisper of blond stubble covered his chin and upper lip. I had always figured him to be in his early thirties, though the stubble had hints of gray in it. Last summer I would have been trying to flirt with him.

I watched myself watching Andrew, recalling with a twinge of embarrassment the horny, flirtatious David Masiello of the past year, of the past several years, the horny, flirtatious David Masiello of for-as-long-as-I-could-remember: always ready to endear myself to any guy who caught my fancy, a little too eager to flirt, to fall in love, a little too bewildered when love proved elusive. The new bewilderment was this: that I just didn't feel that way anymore. Or rather, I had *decided* not to feel that way anymore. Lying in bed, alone, in the middle of the night, listening to the sounds of nocturnal Boston—a car alarm going off, my neighbors cleaning up from a barbecue on their deck, gay men coming home from the bars—I had been tempted, already several times since I'd been back, to call the sex lines. But I'd resisted. It seemed—but how had this happened?— that I was finally ready to close the door on the rest of the erotic world out there. I wanted only Bo, wanted to save everything for Bo. I was willing to try being a different person to prepare myself for that.

"So, do you want to go up and take a look?" I asked Andrew.

The notion that this could be construed as a double entendre did not escape me. God knows how many times I'd used similar language to invite guys I'd cruised on the streets back to my place.

"Sure," he said, turning to his truck and locking up the toolbox that sat in the back.

We began to walk across the street. He was wearing a faded red tee shirt and baggy denim overalls. They were the kind of overalls you could slip out of in five seconds. Once again, I was aware of myself looking at him, registering his sex appeal, but choosing now to register it, nothing more. I felt like a person who has just had a plaster cast taken off: like someone learning to use muscles that hadn't been exercised in a long time.

"It looks like it's going to be a beautiful summer," I said.

"Yeah, so far, so good."

I let Andrew into the vestibule of my building.

"I'm on the fourth floor. Sorry, but we don't have an elevator in the building."

"Good," Andrew said. "I hate to see it when they mess with these beautiful old Victorians and cram in stuff like elevator shafts and roof decks." He tilted his head up, taking in the height of the parlor floor. "Ruins the integrity of the place."

I went over to the bank of mailboxes next to the stairs.

"Let me just check my mail and I'll show you up."

I opened the box and pulled out a batch of mail: two circulars, a magazine, a bill, and . . . yes! a letter from China. I recognized the stamps immediately. The return address was Bo's. I tucked the letter under the other mail and we began to climb to my apartment.

"This is really nice," Andrew said. He was in front of me going up the staircase. He kept looking around, getting a feel for the building. I guessed he was the kind of carpenter who put a lot of attention into the era of the house he was working on—the style, the materials, the period details. We got to the fourth floor, and I let him in.

"So, as I explained to you on the phone, I've got all these cookbooks and nowhere to put them."

Andrew's eyes were already surveying my living room.

"Beautiful apartment." He seemed in no rush to get on with the job.

"Thanks."

"You do it yourself?"

"The decorating? Yeah."

Andrew nodded his head, quietly approving the look. The guys who had sublet the apartment while I was gone—a couple of gay boys right out of college—had rearranged some furniture, turning my two easy chairs toward each other, changing the angle of the television in the bedroom, changes to accommodate a couple. I'd left this new arrangement alone. It made me feel that I was getting ready to be a couple again, too—like a pioneer homesteader preparing for his bride to arrive on the train.

"Beautiful painting." Andrew nodded over toward the far wall where I had hung one of Bo's still lifes, the crockery vase and bouquet of spring flowers that he'd been working on my final few weeks in Beijing.

"Thanks, my boyfriend painted it."

The word was still so new in my mouth—*boyfriend*. Even with Owen and Stewart, I hadn't used it. For them, Bo was Bo, without a tag. I hadn't told my mother, either, though I knew I'd have to soon. It was going to take a while for her to get used to the idea that I wouldn't be around at Christmas.

Andrew moved closer toward Bo's painting. I watched him admiring it. None of the other art in the apartment was anything like this piece. In the past, I'd always been attracted to more abstract work, dark, brooding things. In the divorce, Erik got one of the best of the pieces we'd owned together: a reprint of one of Piranesi's Prison series; I got the Doré *Dante Astray in the Dusky Wood* that I had bought when I was in graduate school.

As Andrew kept studying Bo's painting, I looked down at the sheaf of mail in my hand and flipped through it once more. There was another letter I hadn't noticed down in the vestibule. It was from the immigration lawyer.

"So now, the kitchen must be . . ." Andrew turned around. "Over here? Right?"

By the standards of the South End, my kitchen was large, with room enough to accommodate a table and two chairs. As Andrew and I stood there, I realized for the first time since I'd been back that it was almost as large as Bo's entire studio.

"I was thinking of putting them here." I pointed to the space between the window and one of the walls. About two-feet wide, it was the kind of ignored space where one might tuck in floor-to-ceiling shelves. Andrew looked it over carefully, then turned and inspected the rest of the kitchen.

"What do you think?" I asked.

He turned back toward the window.

"Yeah, I like it. Makes sense there." He pulled out his tape measure and extended it over the width of the space. "Two feet, three and a half." He looked up toward the ceiling. "What's the height? About nine feet?" He pulled out a kitchen chair and moved it toward the window. I kept my five-gallon jug of pennies on the floor there. He bent down, pushed it aside, and moved the chair closer.

"I need to turn in all those pennies," I told him. "Every time I go to the bank, I read that sign that says there's a penny shortage and I feel guilty."

"Bart and I save change, too." Andrew stood up on the chair and let out his tape all the way to the ceiling. "Every few months, while we're watching some lame show on TV, I bring out the jar and a handful of wrappers and we roll 'em up. You'd be surprised how much money you end up with. Sometimes, it's enough that we take ourselves out for a fancy dinner just on what we have in change. We call it our nickel-and-dime dinner." He turned away from the wall and retracted his measuring tape—"Nine feet exactly"—then jumped down from the chair. "Like, we'll be on the sofa, in front of the tube, and all of a sudden Bart will turn to me and say, 'Isn't it time for another nickel-and-dime dinner?' Let's get out the wrappers."

I guessed that Bart was his boyfriend. I loved the way Andrew assumed that no explanations were necessary. Erik had been my "lover," the preferred term back then; Johnny and I had called each other boyfriends. What would I call Bo?

"How many years have you guys been together?" I asked Andrew.

"Eighteen."

"Eighteen! What, did you get together when you were twelve?" Andrew chuckled.

"Far from it! I was twenty-four when we met."

I told him that I never would have guessed he was in his forties.

"Yup, forty-two."

If it had worked out, Johnny and I would have been together ten years already. Erik and I twenty. Twenty years—hard to believe they had gone by so quickly. In twenty more years I'd be seventy; Bo would be fifty. Suddenly, fifty seemed awfully young. Too young that anyone that age would ever go for someone seventy years old. I knew I wouldn't.

Andrew jotted down the measurements. "So, this looks like a pretty straightforward job." He looked up from his pad. "I can probably do it for you in a couple of weeks."

"Fine," I told him. "I didn't mention it over the phone, but I've got another project in mind." Until that moment, I hadn't, but Andrew's friendly manner and my growing confidence in his skill had planted a new idea in my head.

"What's that?" he asked.

"Do you suppose there's any place in this apartment where you could squeeze in another closet?"

"You need more closet space?" He looked around.

"Well, I might. Down the road."

"Let me take a look. What's the situation in the bedroom?"

For the next fifteen minutes, we considered various possibilities. None of them seemed very satisfactory to either of us.

"I'd love the work," Andrew said when we had finished and had moved back into the living room, "but I really think an armoire might be your best solution. That or move to a bigger place." Something on the mantle caught his attention. "Is that your boyfriend? The painter?"

Johnny's picture was still on the mantle, right where I'd left it when I flew off to China back in August. The sublet boys hadn't touched any of that stuff. Twenty-four, just starting out, and deeply in love—I think they were a little in awe of my place, as if they had been asked to caretake a museum, one dedicated to the Art of Ancient Homosexual Life.

"No, that's Johnny. He died two years ago. *Three* years ago. Three years now." For a few moments, the two of us stared at the picture in silence. "This"—I went over to the telephone desk and picked up a little pocket photo album—"this is my boyfriend now." I handed it to Andrew, who flipped through the two dozen pages, each one holding a picture of Bo.

"He's very cute."

A year ago I would have been thrilled to hear those words; now they scared me. Seeing Bo through another's eyes—Owen and Stewart had said the same thing, *cute,* when they first saw the snapshots—it made me wonder all over again if that was all I'd been attracted to: Bo's looks, his youth, his cuteness.

"You guys don't live together?" Andrew asked.

I chuckled.

"No, he's in Beijing right now." Andrew looked up from the photo album. "We met when I was over there this year."

Andrew handed back the album.

"Now *that* is a long-distance relationship."

"Yup."

"He looks young. How old is he?"

"Thirty-five," I lied.

In the weeks since I'd been back, I still hadn't managed to find time alone with Owen to ask him what he really thought, my falling for a guy so young, so far away, so impossible. I doubted that Owen would bring it up on his own. He'd wait for me to broach the subject, to say that I thought it was a problem. It was what I'd always loved about him, and what had always driven me nuts—how he never presumed to know me better than I knew myself.

"And he's coming over soon?" Andrew asked.

"We hope."

Andrew waited for me to elaborate, but there was nothing more I could say. Maybe the answer lay in the immigration lawyer's letter that was still in my hand.

"Well look," Andrew said, "I'll give you a call next week to set up a time for me to build the shelves."

"That'll be great." I ushered him to the door. "And thanks."

We shook hands.

"Good luck with the boyfriend," Andrew said.

"Thanks, I'll need it. Any tips on how to stay together eighteen years?"

Andrew smiled. "Keep saving those pennies. And once a month, go out on a date, just the two of you."

"It'll take a lot more than a few pennies to pull that one off."

Andrew winced.

"Oops, yeah. Sorry."

"No problem," I told him, but I could tell by the final look he gave me that he thought I had taken on a huge project.

As soon as he left, I started to open my letters, but the phone rang.

"Hey, Mr. Marco Polo. I haven't heard from you in days!"

"Ma, we just had dinner together."

"*Three* nights ago. And I haven't heard from you since. Honey, can you blame me for wanting to talk to you all the time now? You were gone almost a year. It seemed like an eternity!"

Her news was the same as it had been the night we had dinner: my nephew Stephen (three now and "already toilet trained"); my return to the gay health clinic (didn't I think that with all that experience in China I could find something else?); and her eightieth birthday party coming up soon.

"Can you believe it?" she asked. "Eighty. *Ottanta. Mamma mia!* How many more years do you think I'll be around?"

"Ma, you're as healthy as an ox."

"Eh, it can all go in a day. This year alone, when you were in China, two of my friends . . . did I tell you this already?" (She had.) "Two of my friends died. One had a heart attack. You remember Raymond Petrocelli? He and your father used to play golf together. Dropped dead in April, right on the fairway. I'm sure I wrote to you about it. Didn't I? The other one was . . ."

I looked at the two letters in my hand and opened the one from the lawyer. It was short and to the point.

Dear Mr. Masiello:

As we discussed over the phone, I'd be happy to work with you. However, I think it is important that you understand from the outset that the chances are not good that your friend will be granted a student visa. He will not only have to be admitted into a full-time program at an accredited graduate school in the U.S., but his petition for a visa must be reviewed at the U.S. embassy in Beijing by an officer of the

Immigration and Naturalization Service. My experience has been that the INS will deny a request for a visa to anyone from a country like China whom they suspect of intending to immigrate to this country. Moreover, they are not required to furnish an explanation and there is no appeal. The burden of proof is solely on the applicant. In the case of your friend—a single man, without substantial holdings or assets in his home country to suggest that he would return, and studying in a field (art) that is not in the national interest—it will be extremely difficult for him to make a convincing case. I don't mean to suggest that the situation is hopeless, but you should be clear about the chances, which I put at about 1 in 10. If, after considering all this, you still want to work with me, I think we should meet to discuss the procedures your friend needs to follow.

"Did I tell you?" my mother was saying. "The man who does my nails, he's Vietnamese. You know what he told me the other day? 'Miss Adeline,' he said. That's what he calls me. Miss Adeline. 'Miss Adeline, how come you live alone?'" My mother let her voice go high and sing-songy. "'Why one of your sons not live with you? In my country, one son or daughter always live with the parents.' You see, David? You see how the Orientals respect their mothers?"

"Asian, Ma." I put the lawyer's letter on the desk.

"What?"

"Say Asian, not Oriental."

"He's Vietnamese."

There was nothing in the world—not all the tea in China, not all the nail polish in Vietnam—that would have pleased my mother half so much as for me to suggest that we live together. She had started dropping hints shortly after my father died, then again after Johnny passed away. Since I'd returned, she was bringing up the idea, still in her roundabout way, almost every time we talked. In my mother's view of things, it made perfect sense: I was fifty. I was the elder son. I had lost my mate, too. Besides, with a three-year old and a new baby on the way, my brother and sister-in-law had enough on their plate. Apparently, my plate looked empty. As tough as she was, I knew Mom was lonely, and a little scared. Who wouldn't be, with eighty staring them in the face?

"The other day," she continued, "one of my girlfriends said I should consider assisted living. I told her, *No way!* I'm not ready for assisted living. I've been in this house for fifty-one years. I know it backwards and forwards. Why do I need assisted living? What do you think, David? I'm not ready for assisted living yet, am I?"

I told her she was ready for it only if she thought she was ready for it.

"Eh, grazie," she said. "Thanks for nothing." It was not the answer she had been looking for.

I looked at the other letter, the one from Bo. It was an aerogramme. I started slitting it open.

"Ma," I tried again. "As long as you can do it, why not stay in the place that you love?"

"Exactly! That's what I told my girlfriend. Assisted living! Can you imagine? Let *her* go into assisted living."

I unfolded the aerogramme. Bo's letter was only a few lines long. I didn't dare read it.

"Ma, I've got to go."

"Where you going now, Mr. Marco Polo? Back to China? Don't you dare!" She started chuckling, the notion was so absurd.

"Look, Ma, I have things to do."

"Eh, *things*. All right, go, but call me once in a while. And don't forget, your brother's having a Fourth of July cookout at his place. I want to see my whole family there, *sai?* Treat me like one of those Oriental mothers."

"Bye, Ma. I love you."

"I love you, too, honey. You don't know how much."

Owen once asked me if I thought that going to China was going to change my life. He had meant three things. First, did I think that traveling halfway around the world was going to help me get over Johnny's death? And did I really need to change; wasn't I okay just the way I was? And wasn't it a little foolish anyway to think that there could be that kind of magic in just up and moving off to a new place, any new place?

He was right, of course, on all three counts. I knew that before I went. I knew it all through my year in China. I knew it now, as I took Bo's letter into the bedroom and lay down to read it:

My darling David,
  How are you? Thank you for your letter which I receive today. I am missing you very much, but when I read you invite me to come to Boston I am so happy. Yes, I want to be with you. I don't know if this can be possible, but we should try. Please send me some informations what I can do to apply to graduate school. My darling, I know in the future we meet with many difficulties, but I am not afraid. I love you.
  —Bosheng

I closed my eyes, pressing my teeth into my lips, biting down tight: a joy too overflowing to bear. Could I have received a more perfect letter? I looked at it again. I wanted to read it over a hundred times, memorize it, frame it, hang it on the wall over my bed.

I know in the future we meet with many difficulties, but I am not afraid.

I propped another pillow under my head. Owen had left his teacup on the night table. I took a sip of the cold tea and read the letter again, more slowly this time, as if I were parsing a stanza of verse, trying to extract every possible nuance and shade of meaning. I broke the sentences down into phrases: *I am missing you . . . very much . . . I am so happy.* I savored every phrase, each one a touch, a caress, a kiss. *My darling,* he had called me.

I refolded the letter, got up, went to my desk, set the letter down, put my heavy crystal paperweight on top of it. I looked at it, lying there, this lovely, delicate scrap, so precious, the only thing I'd had from Bo in weeks. I picked it up and read it over once more.

This time, I read it too fast. Some of the thrill I'd initially felt was suddenly missing. I could sense it, a twinge of disappointment, like the third bite of a fabulous dessert, even Johnny's bitter chocolate and orange mousse. It just didn't pack the same wallop.

I took the letter back to the bedroom, lay down again, preparing to give it more attention. But when I read it a fourth time now, slowing down, trying to focus more, the letter completely fell apart. It was just words: *receive . . . apply . . . difficulties . . . afraid.* Words, but no guarantees. No certainties. No Bo, here, now, with me.

It was so short, too. Less than half the aerogramme. Bo could have written so much more. Why hadn't he? *I don't know if this can be possible.* What was he getting at? What was he preparing me for?

Did he know something I didn't know? By the time I had read the letter over a fifth time, I was near despair. It was so thin, so bare, so inadequate. Damn it, my letter to him had been four pages long!

The afternoon light was streaming through the window. I covered my eyes with my arm. The aerogramme fall from my hands onto the bedroom floor. I took another sip of cold tea from Owen's cup, trying to think. If it took three more weeks for another round of letters to go back and forth, and if his next one was just as spare, what would I do? How would I make it through until Christmas? And after Christmas? After my ten-day visit there? Then what? Another six months? Another year? Jesus, what had I gotten myself into?

Maybe it was the caffeine in the tea, but suddenly, a bizarre thought came into my head: what if Puccini had written an opera that focused on Pinkerton instead? Poor guy, how long should he have been expected to hold out anyway? No one ever had any sympathy for what he must have gone through. Lord knows what the trans-Pacific mails were like in those days! *Tenente Pinkerton.* Now that might have made an interesting opera. I'd have to bring it up with Stewart sometime.

Thinking about Stewart made me smile. Tall, lanky, goofy, clueless Stewart. Meeting him had been almost as much fun as meeting Bo this year. And *Owen and Stewart*! Who would have ever dreamed it? I started to laugh.

What happened next is difficult to describe, but as I was laughing—and now tears were welling up in my eyes, I was that amused and exhausted and befuddled and scared—I began to ask myself what it had all come down to, this year's leave of absence. In the end, had I gotten anything out of my year in Beijing except a little more sex than I'd expected and a love affair with a guy I was nuts about, a guy who had a one-in-ten chance of coming to Boston, a guy whose letter writing skills left something to be desired, a guy whom I would next sleep with, next *see*, six months from now? The absurdity of all this was dizzying.

My thoughts started to bounce around in my head. I found myself parsing them, too, phrase by phrase, as I had Bo's letter. *Year's leave of absence . . . What did it all come down to? . . . In the end . . .*

What exactly did that mean anyway? *In the end?* Such an absurd English expression.

In the end.

Why all the frenzy about tallying up? Why all the preoccupation with what things came to? What if there were no "in the end"? And what if you could decide to live your life that way—without an "in the end" in mind?

I'd been a lousy student of those Chinese sages. I had barely made my way through half the book of Daoist sayings that Owen had given me, and poor Tyson, always quoting some bit of Chinese wisdom, had never made much sense. Still, some of it must have stuck. Because all of a sudden I saw something that I hadn't seen before, although I think it was always there, waiting for me to wake up to it. And what I saw was this: that I very well *could* live my life that way. There was no "in the end" to reach. No end, and nothing to get. Nothing I needed to have, or acquire, or find. Nothing. All along, the person whom I had assumed to be so incomplete was, in fact— already, and all along—whole, complete, full. Whole without Johnny, whole without my Ph.D., whole even without Bo.

The tears were streaming down my cheeks now, profuse and unstoppable, for the surprise of it was that because I didn't need Bo anymore I was now free to love him all the more. To love him without that treacherous question—*but what happens in the end?*— hissing in my ear. Of course I missed him: there by my side, sharing my bed, wrapping his delicious body tight around mine as he had that first night under his musty quilts. But here I was *now,* and now presented a different opportunity to love him, an opportunity from afar, not a better opportunity, not a worse opportunity— these silly, silly categories!—just a different one. The one that was *now.* Ever since I had returned from China, I'd been sensing it, but now I knew: Bo and I were not lovers in abeyance, not lovers-to-be. *We were lovers.* Today and today and today. And our only job was to find each other, however we could, in each and whatever today we had.

I jumped up off the bed, knocking into the night table and spilling the teacup onto the bedroom floor. It shattered to pieces, but I let it be. So much energy was coursing through me, so much appreciation, so much alertness, more than the collective alertness of ten thousand bicyclists peddling down the Second Ring Road at rush hour. I ran out of the apartment—if the building's fire alarm had gone off just then I couldn't have run any faster—jogged down the four flights of stairs and raced out the door. But what had I expected to find? What was out on the street that wasn't upstairs as well?

Yes, the afternoon was glorious. The trees were in full leaf. (Had I ever seen them like this before?) The sky was cloudless. And over in the Back Bay, the Old Hancock Tower—fifty years old now: imagine it!—was shining steady blue. I laughed out loud.

"Clear blue, clear view!"

We'd have fair weather all day. Today and tomorrow, the forecast had promised. Maybe the next day, too. How wonderful. And how wonderful that it really didn't matter, one way or the other. Not at all.